THE CODE TALKERS

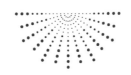

KATHLEEN PARK

The Code Talkers

AUTHOR'S NOTE

You'll notice that I've taken the liberty of inventing a phonetic spelling, *hogahn*, for the English word for the traditional Navajo dwelling, *hogan*. Doing so defeats, in one stroke, both the pushy spell checker, which always wants to capitalize it, and the wrong pronunciation. "Hogahn" is what I heard during my eleven years on the Navajo Reservation. And I'm sticking with it. Thanks for sticking with me, for all of it. — Kathleen Park

ACKNOWLEDGMENTS

My thanks and appreciation to Bill Bernhardt for his books and enthusiastic talks on the craft, and Lara Bernhardt for her expertise in the many steps of production.

Thanks also to my novel critique group, whose insights, comments, humor, faith—and oh, those deadlines—helped more than you know.

To my husband, Norm Park, without whose unfailing love and encouragement, I'd never have finished this book.

CHAPTER ONE

B ack home in Flagstaff, Geneva Granger gathered in one arm the week's mail her daughter Karen had so carefully stacked into two piles. In the other hand, she held a lurid purple construction-paper card: "Welcome Home, Gramma!" Very nice printing, honey, she thought, smiling. But best of all was his self-portrait pasted at the bottom—wide grin shining around the newly missing tooth.

When she dropped the mail on her desk upstairs, a hand-addressed letter slid out. Postmarked Window Rock, AZ. Navajoland. That was familiar, but the handwriting wasn't. No return address. She pushed aside the rest of the mail, opened the envelope, and unfolded the single page from a yellow tablet.

"My name is Margaret Littleben. My father is Harrison Billy I think you know," she read. "He wants me to write for you to come back to the reservation to see him. He can see alright now and he wants to talk about your husband Edward that got killed. He said the newspapers did not say the truth. He said Labor Day weekend would be good."

Geneva dropped the paper and pushed back from her desk

hard but her gaze stayed on the words. "Newspapers did not say the truth? But that's the only truth I have," she whispered.

The image of the huge headline from three years ago rose and pulsed in her memory: SENATOR EDWARD GRANGER KILLED IN CRASH! The photographs of the wind-whipped water and snowy shores of Roosevelt Reservoir loomed again in her mind. No wreckage, no body, neither Edward's nor the pilot's. Nothing but driving sleet and snow for two long days and three nights.

Geneva fought the old wave of sorrow and guilt that rose, curled, and threatened to come crashing down to splinter all rational thought.

She closed her eyes and struggled to push down the memory of the vision—experience—that catapulted her out of bed onto the floor three years before.

No. This makes no sense. No sense that this old Navajo Code Talker, blinded in the war so long ago, and someone she hadn't seen in years, should send her a message about Edward. Harrison Billy couldn't possibly know anything about the plane crash, the investigation, the fruitless dives in the huge reservoir afterwards. Or her endless pain.

Sometimes even now, an unexpected reference, the mere mention of Edward's death, could strike her with the same force as the initial news. Just for an instant, of course. She knew. It was an old fact. This sweep of utter desolation was, after all, uncalled for, she told herself.

Newspapers did not say the truth.

She turned away from the note and went outside to the little balcony that faced northeast toward the beautiful, familiar San Francisco Peaks, the sacred Mountains of the North that bounded the Navajos' traditional homeland.

Grief was one thing, her counselors had told her, and hard enough to deal with, even with knowledge of its stages, even with the dearest supporters. Her grief would not abate until she peeled away the added burden. Her guilt. Her psychic vision of the high, pink mesa spinning away below did not constitute fact. Her failure to reach Edward on the phone the night before the crash did not constitute guilt. You are not guilty, the counselors said. Not guilty. Not. Not.

The early morning light shimmered now among the ponderosa pines below her deck as the distant upper peaks turned pink. Geneva watched but saw nothing, felt only the old hot tears threatening, and the familiar clench of pain behind her sternum.

Sometimes she could laugh at her psychic glimpses, her lifelong curse, as she called it. Sometimes. As a child, it had made her feel different, especially after she ventured to tell a friend in her class. She had thought everyone experienced the same flashes of the future. But the girl became frightened and afterwards avoided Geneva. And the time she'd tried to bridge the distance between herself and her stern father by sharing her secret did not go well either. "Nonsense," he'd said. "Don't speak of it again."

But she did fail to reach Edward the night of the crash, failed to keep trying, failed to call the Navajo police yet again or think of somewhere or someone or something else. Her guilt stood like a boulder in the sea, sometimes apparent, allowing her to steer around it, sometimes submerged. Always there.

She'd finally sought out experts. Experts to explain psychic phenomena. Experts who tried to guide her through the bottomless caves of grief. Too often still, it would come upon her—a choking red surge striking her eyes as she felt herself flung into the sky above an unfamiliar mesa, spinning above the formation that looked like a headless bird with half-folded wings and a shiny wet breast, out of place in the high desert.

After a while she went down to the kitchen, brewed some tea, and took it back up to the balcony, hoping the changing light on the slopes would again soothe her. Mounts Fremont and Humphrey glowed with varied shades of green. The monsoon winds had fulfilled their promises of afternoon showers for weeks this summer, but already the upper slopes were shot through with bright gold as the first aspens proclaimed the coming of fall. September again. Next month Agassiz Peak, sacred to the Hopis, would show its stand of rare reddish aspen. Another October. Better to think of it as an aspen event rather than the anniversary of Edward's death.

But the mountains couldn't work their magic today. She went back in the house to telephone Desbah Chischilly, her Navajo "sister of her heart." Desbah knew the old Code Talker and probably his daughter as well.

Geneva got as far as her desk when she stopped and looked at the little gold clock there. Desbah would just be returning from that big Indigenous Peoples education conference in Hawaii. She was probably somewhere in the air over the Pacific at this moment. Geneva sighed, picked up the empty teapot, and went back down to the kitchen. Waiting for the water to boil, she leaned against the counter and gazed unseeing out the kitchen window.

Come out of it, she told herself and reached for the phone. Call Mason. He'll have some idea about Harrison Billy these days.

Mason Drake, Edward's best friend, "Uncle Mason" to her two daughters and their children, was someone who knew the old Code Talker. She would ask Mason what Harrison Billy might possibly know about Edward's death. And why in the world he would send for her.

"Geneva," came Mason's jovial voice through the phone. "I was about to call you. Just landed in Flagstaff. That committee meeting ended earlier than I thought. I can be at your house in twenty minutes."

"Good. I'll put on some coffee." She tapped the letter, folded tight now in her jeans pocket. Without thought, she switched from tea making to coffee making and put out the plate of Karen's cookies.

Mason, in the second year of his term as senator ten years

ago, suffered a terrible car crash and lay for weeks in a coma. It was Mason, during his year of physical therapy and slow recovery, who'd convinced Edward to run for his seat in the senate. And Mason had been a strong support for her and the girls through those agonizing early days after the crash. Mason had been a family friend for twenty-five years.

But last Christmas he blind-sided her by proposing marriage. Her speechless astonishment was all the answer he needed, and they'd avoided each other for several months after that. Only in May when her daughter Julianna asked Mason to be their baby's godfather, had Geneva and Mason resumed a friendship. Not the old comfortable one, at least not for her, but a friendship.

When Mason arrived, they settled at the kitchen table. "Glad you're back," he said. "Did you enjoy Chicago? Book sales go up again?"

"The conference went well. More than three hundred writers this year."

"Ah," he said, settling back and reaching for a cookie. "I'll bet these are some of Karen's oatmeal-raisin gems. Your girls really take care of their mom, don't they?"

She smiled. "The cookies were waiting for me, with a sweet note from my grandson attached." She pulled out Margaret Littleben's letter. "This was waiting for me, too." She read him the note. "Mason, what could Harrison Billy mean that the newspapers hadn't told the truth about the plane crash?"

"Nothing at all! I think the old fellow is making up a yarn," he said. "Geneva, it's not worth your time. You can't take this thing seriously at all."

"But I have to. Harrison was a friend of Edward's. He wouldn't make light of his death."

"My dear, forget it and come to dinner with me tomorrow night. Then we'll go up to Lowell Observatory and watch the meteor showers. The sky is supposed to be clear well before midnight. That's why I called. Besides, I've got a little surprise for you, something I want to show you before dinner."

When Geneva didn't answer right away, Mason went on. "You hardly know that old geezer, Geneva. And he was a drunk for years—remember that. Promise me you won't go out there now."

Geneva studied her coffee cup, trying not to resent all this pushing.

"I'd take you to the reservation myself—today," he said, leaning closer. "But I have a golf date at Pine Canyon with Senator Clay and a couple of his staff. And then we meet his wife for lunch. You remember, she's from here in Flagstaff— her family owns both banks in Sedona."

He paused then, waiting for her to acknowledge, or more precisely, she thought, to be impressed.

She glanced up and nodded. "Yes, I remember her."

"And then I'm stuck at that banquet with the speaker and his fat wife on Sunday night. That banquet I asked you to accompany me to."

She let another beat go by. "Mmm."

"Oh, Geneva, forget this old Code Talker and his crazy note. Stay home for a while."

"No, Mason. I am going, and I'm going tomorrow. My secretary, Angie, will go with me, I'm sure. And I have a friend who'll meet us, I know."

"Please, my dear. Wait 'til one day next week, and I'll take you. I'll fly us to Gallup and we'll rent a car and drive over to Window Rock, make a little outing of it, and—"

"No, but thank you, Mason." She stood up. "I can surely get a charter on a Saturday. I have to know what Harrison Billy knows."

A few minutes later she watched him trudge down to his car. She could read perfectly well the annoyance—this could scarcely rate as disappointment—in his walk.

She gave a little shrug, closed the door, and turned away.

She paused a moment more, thinking of her twins' enthusiasm for helping decorate "Uncle Mason's bachelor pad," the condo he'd bought in Flagstaff just before Christmas—in addition to his big house in Tempe. Lord, she thought for the first time, did they know of his proposal? They would have approved, she knew that. Would he have actually told them? She made a little face and shook her head.

Back in the kitchen, she absently put their cups in the dishwasher, wishing her crazy psychic flashes would, for once, be useful and convey what the old Navajo had in mind to tell her.

Still, she felt eager to put her plan into motion and called Angie Sanchez. The two women, so different culturally and temperamentally—and a generation apart—had become fast friends in the year since Angie had started working for Geneva.

"What do you think of going with me to the Navajo Reservation, Angie?"

"Sure, I will," Angie said without hesitation. "I've read so much about Window Rock and the other places in your papers, I should finally see them. I'll be ready early. It'll be fun!"

Raised in Albuquerque's South Valley, Angie Sanchez often spoke in the vernacular of its tough Hispanic streets. But she could take a stack of Geneva's manuscript pages bristling with sticky notes and marred with handwritten corrections in two colors of ink, and return them in perfect order, impeccably typed. She lived now in a modern adobe guest house in Flagstaff behind her brother's big home. She kept books for his thriving real estate operation and Geneva's burgeoning career as a writer and speaker. Mostly she took a few courses at Northern Arizona University and played the beloved *tía* to her nieces and nephews.

Geneva, ever the teacher, encouraged Angie's intellectual pursuits. Angie's family culture, however, did not value her education, but only her beauty. Her gorgeous face, luxuriant hair, and perfect figure should attract a rich husband, they said. And high time—she was already twenty-five.

Geneva replaced the receiver with satisfaction. Whatever she might learn from Harrison Billy, the trip would be good. She hadn't been back to the reservation in a while. High time she did.

CHAPTER TWO

As the single-engine charter plane circled the Window Rock airstrip, Geneva felt the dread of what might be an upsetting conversation with Harrison Billy about Edward's death start to lift in favor of a sweeter feeling—almost of homecoming.

The sight of the Window Rock, the high, tilted pink sandstone formation with the enormous elliptical hole through its side, delighted Angie. Geneva smiled, too, remembering good times with Edward and the twins, their picnics in the little park at the foot of the long mesa. Nearby, many of the flagstone tribal offices stood so close to the mesa walls, Edward would always say that someone with a poker could reach out a window and carve his initials in the rock. And the girls, when they were little, always wanted to run behind the offices to see if someone had done just that.

Now on a second pass over the airport, their annoyed pilot mumbled, "Waiting for some big shot's little Lear to get the hell out of my way." A moment later, however, he gave a low whistle of admiration. "That's one sweet craft," he said, watching it take to the air. "Learjet 35, for sure."

"I thought you said Window Rock was a real small town,"

Angie said as they turned for the approach. "How could this place have an airfield that a Learjet could land on?"

Geneva hoped Angie's chatter wouldn't distract the pilot's concentration. She lowered her voice. "Window Rock is the capital of the Navajo Nation, Angie. Tribal officials come and go regularly through this little airport. Even state and federal government people."

Angie continued to stare out the window. "Looks like a lot of folks down there. Do they know you're coming?"

Geneva looked down with pleasure at the colorful crowd milling through the fairgrounds and hodge-podge parking lot next to it and laughed. "They're not here for me. It's the first day of the Navajo Nation fair."

Carnival rides whirled and sparkled in the sunlight. Geneva picked out the jumbled midway alive with booths selling everything from roasted corn in the husk, sausages, the beloved dill pickles children ate like candy bars, to funnel cakes and, of course, Navajo fry-bread. She could almost smell the wonderful fragrance of those plate-sized fried rounds, all bubbled and golden.

"We can be glad we missed the parade, Angie," she said as the plane landed. "They close the highway for hours, as I remember. Let's hope Tucker was able to get through. Otherwise, we'll be standing out there waving our dollar bills at passing cars along with the rest of the hitchhikers."

"*Dios mío,*" Angie murmured, wrinkling her nose.

After they landed, Angie shifted her bags and looked around the tarmac. "This is some big deal," she said, pointing to the two Navajo Police cars, lights flashing, standing at the end of the airport property and two more next to the highway, where officers tried to keep traffic flowing. "There must be a thousand people here."

"Oh, yes, at least." Geneva stood on tiptoe, trying to see past a group near the doorway to the little waiting room. She saw no sign of her old friend's tall black hat or bushy red beard. "I wonder if he's stuck somewhere. Let's go on in, Angie."

"Doc-tor Gen-eee-vah Granger!" boomed a voice that might have come through a PA system. "Hold it right there!"

Angie jumped and looked about. Geneva smiled and shook her head. Tucker Bayless would never change, would he? She put down her bags and opened her arms. A huge man in a worn leather jacket and an old Navajo-style black hat burst out of the building and rushed toward them to sweep Geneva up in a bear hug that lifted her off her feet.

"Oooo-eee!" he cried. "It's been a hundred years, hasn't it?" He set her down and stared into her face. "Hell, girl—you got more gray hair! Who's this pretty thing with you?"

"Thank you for mentioning that, Tucker." Geneva laughed as her breath returned. "This is Angie Sanchez, my indispensable friend and sometimes secretary and bookkeeper."

"Pleased to meet you," he said, shaking her hand.

Despite Tucker's habitual greeting, she'd seen him and Shándiíne only a month earlier in a Phoenix hospital.

As Tucker settled them into his red SUV, Angie said, "I know you used to teach with Geneva, Tucker. Do you still teach math at the high school?"

He maneuvered his vehicle into the barely moving traffic. "Nah, I retired a couple of years ago." Straightening the wheel, he turned to Geneva. "Teaching is not what it used to be when you and Edward were out here, Geneva. Kids here now are just like kids in a city. Drugs, gangs—they'd just as soon flip you off as look at you, some of them. But you know that. You were smart to get out of it when you did. Smart to get that first book done and published—the blockbuster, of course—and now those high-class speeches all over the country. My hat's off to you, girl."

Geneva made a dismissive gesture. "Tell me about Shándiíne. Is she any better since the chemo, Tuck?"

Tucker tugged at his rusty beard. "About the same as I

wrote you in August. After our Millie finished her two years at Diné College up there at Tsaile, she came home. Refuses to leave her mom hardly at all now." He turned eyes full of grief toward Geneva. The docs say it's just a matter of time, Geneva. All they're doing is keeping the pain down. They've given up." He turned his face away, giving a curve in the road more attention than it needed. "But not me."

A moment passed as neither of them spoke. Geneva knew about Tucker's continuing efforts to find a cure, a new treatment, anything that would extend Shándiíne's life—and his hope. Geneva had thought she might go out and see Shándiíne on this trip, but hadn't mentioned it, and wouldn't, uncertain what she might learn from Harrison Billy or where that might take her.

Tucker Bayless had loved his Navajo wife, Shándiíne— meaning "Sunshine"—for more than half his life. Geneva didn't want to think now about his grief.

Neither did he. His usual booming voice returned. "Let's talk about old Harrison Billy, Code Talker extra-ordi-naire, back from the dead, so to speak. I got his daughter to bring him down from Wheatfields. They're waiting for you at her house in Fort Defiance, like I said on the phone last night."

"Harrison Billy," said Angie from the back seat. "I can't get used to that. Seems like his name is backwards—should be Billy Harrison."

Geneva, glad of the change in subject, turned half-around to answer her. "Billy is a fairly common last name out here, Angie. So are Joe, Jim, Sam, Pete, and the like. I think it was the various Bureau of Indian Affairs people and other government or military types who either couldn't understand or find out the Navajo names or didn't care—just slapped something down on paper. You'll see names like Slim, Shorty, Laughing, Curly—"

"Or Jumbo, my personal favorite," Tucker said, chuckling.

"My wife, now, hers was something different. Try Yazzie!" He and Geneva both laughed.

Angie's pretty brow furrowed. "Yazzie? I've seen that one in some of Geneva's papers before."

"It's the Navajo equivalent of Smith or Jones," Tucker said. "It means *small*. Just about everyone out here's a Yazzie or a Tsosie. Me, now, I'm just a plain old Arkansas hillbilly of Scots-Irish descent, come to Navajoland just for a look-see—what—thirty-one years ago!"

They moved slowly through the thick traffic past a supermarket and two gas stations. Everywhere horse trailers, school buses, trucks and cars caked with red mud, and even big, expensive motor homes vied for parking space along the highway. Still blocks from the fairgrounds, they could hear country music blaring from loudspeakers, interrupted occasionally by calls for rodeo participants to start assembling. Navajos, Anglos, and a sprinkling of blacks and Asians milled about or flowed across the highway toward the fairgrounds, oblivious of the crawling cars and trucks.

"Who is this Harrison Billy, anyway, Geneva?" Angie leaned forward with her hand on the back of Geneva's seat. "I still don't know why we're going to see him. Is he an old friend?"

"More a friend of Edward's. I didn't meet him until later. Even though Harrison, along with Mason Drake, was largely responsible for our coming to the reservation," Geneva said. "They met when Edward was taking some graduate courses down at Arizona State one summer. Harrison lived next door to Edward's rooming house and would wake him up at dawn with his chanting." She had to laugh, remembering Edward's goofy rendition of Harrison's dancing and singing. "They became great friends. Harrison was blind, wounded in the war, and Edward got him started on Books for the Blind. He said for Harrison, it was like water to a man dying of thirst. And

Harrison's experience with boarding schools as a boy on—and off—the reservation deeply affected Edward."

"Lord, yes," Tucker said, shaking his head. "How many Indian kids all over the West got jerked up from their families and hauled off to those schools to be 'de-cultur-ated,' whipped for talking their own language, and—worse." He and Geneva exchanged unhappy glances.

Geneva turned back to Angie. "But I met Harrison only once or twice during those early years. He spent most of his time in Phoenix with his sister, especially during the time Edward and I taught here in Fort Defiance."

Tucker nodded. "Harrison was in one of the special Indian units the government called up during World War Two and trained to use their native language to fool the Japanese, Angie. Those Japs were killing us—seemed like they could figure out our messages as fast as we could think up new codes." Tucker ducked to catch Angie's eye in the rear-view mirror. "The Code Talkers used their Navajo words for planes and ships, all kinds of actions, troop movements, and so on. Like *gini*, meaning chicken hawk, for dive-bomber."

Angie applauded. "That's great! Tell me some more."

Geneva smiled at Angie. "And the word for beaver, *cha*, for mine-sweeper. I used to know the one for hummingbird, a fighter plane, but now I forget."

"That was *da-he-tih-hi*, I think," Tucker said. "All that was still classified by the DOD for decades. But I'll tell you this— the Marines could never have taken Iwo Jima without those Navajo and other Indian radiomen. And the Corps finally said so, too."

"So Harrison Billy was one of them? He must be a hundred years old!" Angie said.

Tucker laughed. "Not quite, but lots of those boys were barely grown then. Harrison, I know, lied about his age to get into the Marines. Like a thousand others, his birth in some remote hogahn way out here hadn't been recorded, and he was tall for sixteen. Besides, by 1943, the Code Talkers had already proved their worth, and Uncle Sam wasn't in the mood to quibble."

So young, Geneva mused as Tucker talked. We were young, too, when we came to this place. Edward just finishing his master's, the twins still so small. We believed that education was the best hope of the Navajos. And we never stopped believing.

". . . battles of Guadalcanal, Tarawa, Saipan, Okinawa, and certainly Iwo Jima," Tucker was saying to Angie. "Every year since the Code Talkers finally came to the attention of the world, they gather to be honored at this fair and the two or three others across the reservation. Some of them can still walk in the parade and carry their Marine Corps Reserve flag." He shook his head slowly. "Those Code Talkers were heroes. Still are. Aren't they, Geneva?"

Geneva, lost in memories, barely noticed Tucker looking at her for assent. She nodded vaguely.

"As I got it," he continued, ducking again toward the rear-view mirror and Angie's reflection, "old Harrison hit the bottle off and on for a lot of years after coming home blind from the war. I was glad to hear about the operation on his eyes." He glanced at Geneva. "He must be a whole lot better to go read up about Edward's death and want to talk to you about it. Wonder what he knows."

"If anything," she said. "I'm happy to see him for Edward's sake—they were good friends, but . . ."

"Sure enough, they were friends," Tucker said. "I know Edward tried to look him up at different times after y'all moved to Flagstaff. The last time was when he came out during his campaign for reelection that summer, what—three years ago?" He leaned toward Geneva, his voice softer. "How long's Edward been gone now, hon?"

"Three years next month. October."

"Must've been three years ago in July, then. I had

Shándiíne in the hospital in Phoenix and missed his last speech, the one in October with the tribal bigwigs. But I remember how he looked on that grandstand on the Fourth of July, our senator speaking right here at the Window Rock fairgrounds." He gestured out the window in that direction. "Big and tall he was, with that mane of silver hair, laughing his same old rumbly laugh. Lordy, we were proud!" He slapped the dashboard. "Old Vanderhorst—that superintendent that we all hated so, the one that tried to get Edward fired that time— remember, Geneva? But that day Old Vanderhorst acted like he'd invented Senator Granger single-handed."

Three years, yes, she thought. Three years and two weeks before that November election. And Edward's body never recovered. What could Harrison Billy possibly know about any of it—now able to see or not? *I probably shouldn't have come.*

"Harrison's daughter lives right down here," Tucker said, turning down a lane of mobile homes. "This sure beats driving way up there past Wheatfields where the old man lives."

"What's Margaret Littleben like, Tuck?" Geneva asked. "You said she works in the Economic Development Office."

Tucker's usual loquaciousness seemed to have deserted him. "You'll see."

A stocky woman with an ample bosom and an embattled expression opened the door to her mobile home without a word. She pulled at her blouse and smoothed the sides of her slacks.

"I'm Margaret Littleben," she said at last, in a cold voice. "Harrison's daughter. I wrote that letter to you that he told me to." Without offering her hand or changing her expression, she stood aside for them to enter.

Margaret led them into the dining room while speaking in Navajo to her father, who sat at the dining room table. They seemed to be finishing a conversation. Geneva thought she caught the word *Goldtooth* and then the Navajo word for *boy*. Or was it *son*? She couldn't be sure. Her grasp of the language was no grasp at all—barely a fingertip's touch here and there.

Harrison made a gesture that seemed to mean *wait* or *later* to his daughter. As the three approached, he came to his feet and adjusted the heavy black frames of his thick glasses. Margaret did not invite the guests to sit but went to stand next to her father's chair in what Geneva perceived as a defensive position.

"Come on in," he said in a surprisingly strong, congenial voice. "Sit over here at the table if you don't mind. I can see you better over here."

Harrison Billy had to be well past eighty, but he stood ramrod straight. His full head of thick white hair was cut short, military fashion, and he wore a bright yellow Code Talker tunic. His flat red garrison cap with its Marine pin lay on the coffee table. Geneva guessed he had marched in the parade that morning.

Geneva extended her hand. "I'm Geneva Granger, Mr. Billy. I was happy to get your daughter's message." She didn't say *mystified* but she might have. "This is my friend Angie Sanchez, and you already know Tucker, of course."

Harrison held Geneva's hand for a moment in his dry, warm grasp before shaking hands with both the others. "I remember your voice from a long time ago," he said to her. "It's good to see your face."

Geneva noticed then that his eyes behind the thick glasses were not the opaque brown she'd thought, but a lighter, clearer brown. His brows were flecked with white and a faint stubble of whiskers shone silver on his jaw. He looked into her face for an instant and then away.

When they'd taken places at the table, he nodded toward his daughter. "Maybe you can bring us some of that coffee, Margaret."

Without speaking, Margaret stepped into the kitchen and began noisily assembling things for coffee. Geneva wondered whether Margaret was always that noisy about making coffee or if they'd somehow offended her. But she couldn't think how. Her long experience with Navajos—adults, anyway—hadn't prepared her for rudeness.

"Edward talked about you and your twin girls all the time that summer we met," Harrison said to Geneva. "He had pictures that you sent him in your letters just about every week. I couldn't see them, but he'd tell me just what they looked like. Karen and Julianna on their little bicycles by a magnolia tree at your big house in Memphis. It had four white pillars across the front, I think. Karen had Band-Aids on both knees a lot of times, didn't she?"

Geneva suppressed a gasp. "Oh!" Her voice failed for a moment. "Yes. But how could you possibly remember all that?" She immediately felt that her question sounded almost rude but couldn't seem to go on.

Tucker stepped into the silence. "Damn fine memory you have there, Hosteen. That was a while back, eh?"

Geneva regained her composure and went on to tell Harrison about her daughters, now grown with children, one of them older than they themselves had been in those old photographs. "I'm glad to see that you, too, have your family," she said, smiling in the direction of Margaret's back at the kitchen counter.

Margaret brought the coffee and a plate of graham crackers, nodded wordlessly at their thanks, and withdrew into the living room.

"I know you got to get home to your wife," Harrison said to Tucker. "Margaret's boy Terry will take these ladies up to the Days Inn when he gets back in a few minutes. I thank you for bringing Edward's wife to me, Tucker Bayless." He drew a breath and looked down at his hands. "She's got to know how he died."

CHAPTER THREE

Nobody spoke.

Geneva scarcely breathed. His daughter's note had said that Harrison thought the newspaper accounts were wrong. She worked to suppress her questions, knowing she should observe Navajo courtesy and wait for him to go on. But her mind's eye went again to the newspaper photos three years ago, of ice and snow on the lake shore, the all-too-vivid accounts of the search. A freak autumn storm, they said.

An icy night followed by a horrible winter. Nothing recovered until spring, then only bits of the plane and what they said were remnants of the pilot's clothing. Nothing of Edward.

It was a tragedy. A tragedy she thought at the time she could not live past. But how was it a mystery? She glanced up to see Harrison's face drawn in sorrow, his eyes downcast.

"I believe somebody did something to the airplane before it left," Harrison said. "I've got something to show you later. My grandson, Terry, is going to get it and bring it here." He turned to Tucker. "Or, if you want to, you can take Edward's wife and this lady to their hotel now. Terry will drive me over there tomorrow morning to talk more."

Tucker looked at Geneva. "Is that what you want to do?

You girls are probably pretty tired out after the drive to Phoenix and then the hop over here."

Angie sprang up. "Oh, yes," she said with clear relief. "I'm really worn out. Can't wait for a hot bath, get some of this mud off, and have a good meal." Only after stepping to Tucker's side did she turn and look at Geneva, who seemed unable to move.

"Oh. Tomorrow. I see. All right." Some little mechanical voice in her stunned mind screamed like a distant jay. *Why?* it seemed to say. *Why not tell me now?*

Margaret Littleben's head appeared above the half wall separating the dining area from the living room. "You better do that," she said. "My father is tired now. You better talk tomorrow."

Geneva could only blink. A sound like a swarm of hornets buzzed in her head. This woman had written to her, had invited her—was *invited* really the word? Had at least conveyed Harrison's invitation or whatever it was, to come here. She found herself gaping at the woman and shifted her gaze away.

"That's okay then?" said Harrison, getting to his feet. "Terry's going to take me home tomorrow. We'll stop and talk to you at the Days Inn. Plenty of time." He gave them all a wide smile, but looked, to Geneva at least, embarrassed and apologetic.

Back in the SUV, Tucker seemed preoccupied.

Angie, it seemed, couldn't stop talking. "Tucker, how come you called him Hosteen?"

"Oh, that's just a general term of respect to an elder," he said, glancing at Geneva.

Angie leaned forward. "Why was that *bruja* daughter of his so mad at us?"

"Well now, I don't think Mrs. Littleben is a witch," Tucker said, his voice mild and distracted.

Angie went on. "Did anybody notice how that old man

never quite looked straight at you when he talked? And he acted just as glad as she was to get us out of there?"

Geneva turned in her seat to face Angie. "I can't answer why Mrs. Littleben seemed upset, Angie. But Navajos, especially the older, more traditional ones, don't stare into another person's eyes the way we often do as we talk. I understand that doing so is a sign of either hostility or great intimacy to them. Their glance might meet yours once or twice in a conversation, but that's all."

There, Geneva thought. *Explain something easy you know about. You can wait another day. Breathe. Harrison is really elderly now. Maybe doesn't know what he's talking about anyway.*

The traffic from the fair had thinned, and they arrived at the Days Inn on the Ganado Highway in short order.

Tucker, careful with Geneva's laptop and camera, helped the women into the lobby with their bags. He waited until they had registered and Angie moved toward the elevator before bending down to speak softly to Geneva. "Now listen here, girl —I don't know what that old man meant by what he said, but I don't want you upset by it. Remember, he spent some years in the bottle. And what could he really know about the plane crash anyway?"

Geneva could only shake her head.

"I do have to go on home, but you have my number," he said. "If Harrison Billy has anything to say tomorrow that you don't like, you just send him packing, good old buddy of Edward's or not. I'll come and get you. You hear?" He gave her a long, stern look and then he was gone.

The elevator took the two to their floor, where they threaded through the hallway still lively with fair visitors. "Lucky we had reservations, huh?" said Angie, unlocking the door. "What a day!"

The supper, the shower, and the bed were as good as Geneva's imagination had promised. She tried to relax, hoping for some sign that would tell her whether she was right to stay the course here and learn what Harrison had to say. Or just plan to call Tucker in the morning and go see Shándiíne before going back home.

She wished she could see inside Harrison's mind and pull out what he had withheld at the last moment. As usual, she could not command her psychic ability—if one could call it an ability. More often it was a scary puzzle, scattered clues she had to work against time to assemble into sense. Or a conviction against all reason. More like a curse.

She turned over and willed her eyes to stay shut and her body to relax. Of course, there were the two times those fearful puzzle pieces had flown together to save her family. The unreasonable convictions had kept her from danger more than once. Maybe not a curse, then, but damned unresponsive when she needed an answer. Like now. What did Harrison Billy have to tell her?

The next morning, Geneva noticed Angie gazing out the window, moving in slow motion to pack, and pulling a curl down around her finger again and again. Finally she broke her silence. "Geneva, why didn't that old man ever try to contact you before?" Her almost petulant tone surprised Geneva. "I think he's found out you are a famous person, and he's out to get money from you or something."

"I don't think that at all, Angie. I told you he only recently had the operation that recovered his sight. I gathered that he'd just read the newspaper accounts of Edward's death. He'd have to go to the library in Gallup, New Mexico, across the state line, to do that. I agree that this is all pretty mysterious, though."

"So what time will he be here—with this grandson or whatever?" Angie asked.

Geneva stopped folding a sweater into her bag and looked up. "Is something bothering you, Angie?"

Angie dropped into the armchair next to a window and pulled a lock of hair under her chin. For a few moments she simply gazed out at the distant red cliffs. "I don't know exactly, Geneva. I just feel, well, spooky. I know that doesn't make sense, but—" Just then the telephone at her elbow rang. She jumped out of the chair, then stopped and turned, obviously trying to look as if she had meant to come to her feet in just that way. "Shall I get it?" she asked, not looking at Geneva.

Geneva hid her smile and picked up the phone. "Yes, this is Mrs. Granger." She listened, frowning, for a moment or two. "Of course. We'll come down to the coffee shop. See you there."

"That was Terry Littleben, the grandson," she told Angie. What she didn't tell Angie was how the young man had sounded. She wasn't sure herself. Was it anger in his voice? Why would he be angry? Or something else. Fear? No, of course not.

And why did Angie feel "spooky?" Spooky was Geneva's territory. She brushed her hand across her face and glanced at Angie, who stood looking out the window, twisting a lock of her hair.

A few minutes after the call, they stepped off the hotel elevator immediately in front of Harrison and a tall, sullen-looking young Navajo of about eighteen with spiked hair and several earrings. He stepped aside for them to pass without lifting his eyes. Vivid drawings and inked words that Geneva couldn't make out covered his denim jacket.

"Well! Here you are," she said with a big smile, nodding to him and Harrison. "Glad to see you. Ready for some break-fast?" Angie, she noticed, stood silent.

Harrison somberly introduced Terry, mentioning his parental clans and the fact that he had just graduated from Window Rock High School, where he had been the star basketball player. Angie didn't offer her hand but smiled politely and led the way to the coffee shop.

They settled into a wide corner booth where sunlight flowed through tall windows. Everyone's mood seemed to lift.

Angie took pains to draw the teenager out, and soon he rewarded her with answers that improved past yes and no. Several other diners spoke or waved to Harrison. The waitress seemed to know him well, and they had several brief, friendly conversations in the course of order taking and serving.

Geneva's gaze often rested on the distant piñon and juniper forest rising toward the summit of the Defiance Plateau. Good to be back, she thought. There was much beauty and peace here. And happy memories. It was always good to come back. But when will he tell me what he says he knows?

"We can talk now," Harrison said after the waitress cleared the table and poured him more coffee.

The boy, who had relaxed some and seemed to enjoy his breakfast, shifted uncomfortably and looked about, as if expecting something unpleasant. Angie stared out the window and fiddled with her hair.

"Terry," Geneva said, "will you show Angie around a bit while your grandfather and I visit? There are some interesting paintings in the lobby, and I'm sure she'd like to see the gift shop, too."

To Geneva's surprise, both young people seemed glad to comply and hurried away. A bright gold lightning bolt, whose point ended in a curved knife blade, decorated the back of the boy's jacket. She thought she could make out L-B in ornate letters beneath the lightning bolt. She hoped it wasn't some sort of gang insignia.

"When I got back from the war," Harrison began, gazing into his coffee cup, "my mother's brothers had the Enemy Way ceremony for me right away. But my spirit wouldn't heal. Pretty soon, my wife said she didn't even know me and went off to Gallup. She left my daughter that you met, just a baby then, with her own mother and went off to Gallup. I didn't hear from her anymore."

Geneva nodded. But his gaze remained on his cup.

"Then her mother died and her uncle brought the baby up

there to me in Wheatfields. I didn't know anything to do about a child, and my mother had my two little brothers still at home, so I went looking in Gallup for my wife. People told me my wife had got on a train and left. I went back home and found a woman in Piñon with two girls to take Margaret. But I never married that woman and later found out she wasn't good to Margaret. I was drinking then," he said, but did not bring his eyes up to meet Geneva's.

Geneva knew better than to rush a story told by a Navajo or interrupt with questions. She waited.

"When I found out that Piñon woman wasn't treating Margaret right, I didn't know what to do," Harrison said. "I let her send Margaret to the boarding school at Chinle. Then some Mormons, I think, took her to live with them." Harrison's strong voice dropped to a hoarse whisper. He stared at his hands holding the coffee cup. "I was drinking too much. I was no good."

Geneva still waited, hoping that if Harrison would look up at her, he would see compassion, or at least understanding, in her face.

"About the time I came back here from Phoenix, Edward and you'd already left Fort Defiance and went to teach at the college up at Tsaile," he said. "Edward came out there to the sheep camp to see me. The man at the trading post told me he was coming. But I was ashamed, so I went down in the canyon and hid. But Edward found me and gave me some tobacco and two cans of coffee and some peaches. He was still my friend."

Ah, yes. Geneva remembered Edward's account of that visit. And Harrison's reluctance to meet Edward's wife and family. He was drinking. And he was ashamed.

"He sent money for me sometimes to the trading post," Harrison said.

Geneva remembered and nodded. The sun seemed to dance the length of the pine needles, one by one. And back again.

Edward would have said the breeze was playing a minor fugue on pine needles.

"It was only for food, though," Harrison said. "No liquor."

"Hmm." She nodded again, bringing her attention firmly back to his quiet voice.

"My sister in Phoenix got real sick then, and I went back down there. Two-three years before my sister died, I quit drinking. She wanted me to."

"Yes," Geneva said, "I remember we heard you had left the reservation just before we moved to Flagstaff."

"Last time I saw Edward, Margaret's husband and brother-in-law brought him up to Wheatfields the day before he made that speech to the elders. I wasn't drinking anymore, but I was still blind. That's when he told me."

"Told you? Told you what?"

"About the Phoenix man," Harrison said. "The man that wanted him dead."

CHAPTER FOUR

"What? What man? Who would—?" She realized her voice had risen only as Angie appeared next to the table.

Behind Angie, Terry gestured to his grandfather. "We got to go."

The coffee shop was almost deserted now.

"Check-out time," Angie said. "We've still got to finish packing. Have you called Tucker or that pilot guy yet?"

Both Geneva and Harrison blinked. Geneva held up a hand as if to stop Angie.

Harrison got to his feet. "You come out to my place with us," he said to Geneva. "Edward left his zipper book out there. He said he wrote in his zipper book about that Phoenix man. But you got to open it. You're the one to do that."

Geneva couldn't stop staring at him. Nor form words.

Harrison's voiced dropped almost to a whisper. "I forgot about the zipper book for a long time. I told Terry to get it and bring it here to me yesterday, but he forgot, too."

"We got to go," Terry said again.

Harrison drew his grandson away a few yards. Angie gave Geneva a strange look and walked toward the cash register.

Geneva wasn't sure she could stand. When she did, she fumbled distractedly through her purse, hearing only *man that wanted him dead, wanted him dead* ringing in her ears.

She drew a long breath and moved to the cash register and the waiting Angie. "Angie, will you take care of the bags?"

"I'm on it!" Angie started for the elevator. "Down in a flash. Are you going to call that pilot? How are we getting out of here?"

"We're not leaving yet. We're going to Wheatfields."

Angie stopped and turned around. "You mean today? Now?"

Geneva steadied herself at the edge of the counter next to the cash register. "Yes. Now."

Angie turned back and entered the elevator without a word. Geneva couldn't leave the reservation now. Edward's notebook? How in the world would Harrison Billy have Edward's notebook? Would he have stolen it? She had to learn what else the old Code Talker knew.

Harrison looked at his grandson. "We'll go now."

Terry turned and looked at Geneva for several seconds. "Angie said you're that G. Granger that writes those books about reservation schools and stuff."

When Geneva acknowledged that she was, Terry brightened and gave her a smile that she wouldn't have thought him capable of the second before. He cheerfully carried their bags to his van, helped Geneva and the silent Angie into the back seat, then slid the door shut before seeing his grandfather into the front. The Littlebens, mother and son, Geneva decided, were hard to read.

The noisy van prevented much conversation, but Geneva soothed, or at least delayed, Angie's concerns with a few words. "We'll be back before dark, maybe stay another night at Day's Inn and even take in some of the fair," she said. "No hurry, is there?"

She sat back and closed her eyes. Phoenix man. Zipper

book. It had to be Edward's notebook. But that's crazy. It would have gone to the bottom of the Roosevelt Reservoir with Edward's body. She resolved to calm herself and certainly Angie. She had committed them both to this journey and must make it as pleasant as she could.

They returned to Fort Defiance and connected with Indian Rte. 12. Again the high red sandstone cliffs so close to the highway fascinated Angie as they neared Navajo, New Mexico. "I see an eagle's head in that rock," she cried. "Look, it's a perfect image!"

"Keep looking," Geneva said, now enjoying the occasional flash of gold cottonwoods and the deep pink of the feathery salt cedars. "You'll see a huge black formation they call the Frog, right in the middle of town. Watch for the big green cliff among all this red—out of town a bit, if I remember."

Terry pointed out the blackish volcanic formations here and there among the successive red sandstone ridges. He was making an effort to be congenial, Geneva thought. This teenager almost certainly had better things to do than play chauffeur this afternoon.

At the gas station/convenience store, Terry got out to fill the tank. Harrison went into the store.

"Geneva, what are we doing out here?" Angie whispered, almost fiercely. "You don't really know that old guy, and this Terry kid is really weird—one minute friendly, the next minute he seems all mad. Look at him out there. He acts like he's hoping nobody will see him or something."

Geneva leaned past Angie to see Terry hunched over the gas hose, his chin tucked into his jacket. Just then a car with two young Navajo men pulled up behind the van. One of them got out and started talking to Terry. She couldn't make out what he was saying except that it was in Navajo. Terry looked worried or afraid, and answered sharply, also in Navajo.

"It's a joke, all right?" the handsome one said in English, punching Terry's arm. "You know we're just making a fool out of the old prof. Here, you earned this." He handed Terry some folded bills.

Terry turned his back to the van. If he answered, the wind blew his words away.

"I think I'll get a cup of coffee," Geneva said, reaching for the door. Maybe Angie can either satisfy her curiosity about their conversation or find something interesting in the store, she thought.

Angie sighed and got out as well. Both young men now stood beside Terry as he replaced the gas nozzle. They all moved toward the rear of the van.

When the women came back with their coffee, they noticed the one Terry called Brandon still talking to Terry in a mixture of Navajo and English. Terry stood listening and looking uncomfortable. Geneva heard Brandon say, "But you still owe me, kid."

"Uh, these ladies are friends of my grandfather's." Terry indicated the women with a quick lift of chin and a barely perceptible pointing of his lips. Harrison came out carrying a package, somewhat smaller than a shoebox, wrapped in brown paper. He walked up to the little group and waited, clearly expecting Terry to introduce them all.

"Well, um, this is my grandfather and this is Mrs. Granger and Angie—ah—Sanchez. These guys are the Goldtooth brothers," Terry said, pointing his chin first to Brandon, flashy in black leather jacket and tight jeans, who acknowledged the introduction by cutting his eyes impudently at the women and giving a slight sideways jerk of his head.

"I'm Brandon Goldtooth," he said, as if daring anyone to dispute it, and twirled his designer sunglasses in one hand. "That's Clarence," he said and gave a nod toward his shorter, plainer brother.

"Brandon's a fancy-dancer," Terry said.

"That's right," Brandon said. He looked around, apparently waiting for some response. "The champ."

"How nice." Geneva smiled at them, about to turn back to the open van door.

Brandon, in his mid-twenties, gave Angie an up-and-down appraisal and then narrowed his eyes at Geneva. "Granger? You the one writes those books about teaching on the reservation—all that stuff about Indian education?" His tone was clearly unfriendly.

"I am," she said, feeling a little annoyed. She decided against carrying the conversation further. Why was he looking at her like that? Somebody who didn't like school, she thought. Or Anglo schoolteachers. Or both. "Drive safely," she said pleasantly, her glance taking in both brothers.

They got back into the van with no further talk and resumed their northward climb.

The good-looking Goldtooth brother who had seemed threatening to Terry and insolent to Geneva clearly intrigued Angie. "Who was that guy and what was going on back there?" she asked despite the noise of the van.

Geneva shrugged and tried to beg off conversation, indicating the racket with a wry face. What intrigued her was the package that Harrison had brought out of the store and which he now held with great care on his lap.

They had to stop next to reedy little Red Lake and wait for a flock of sheep to cross.

"Red Lake up some this year," said Harrison, pointing, Navajo fashion, with a quick pucker of his lips. "Wheatfields Lake, too. Good rains."

Geneva peered past Angie. "I thought it seemed wider and longer than I remembered."

A black-and-white border collie moved the muddy sheep along as they followed a big ewe with a bell. The young herder strolled behind them, never glancing at the vehicles waiting in both lanes. Angie went wide eyed at the sight.

The road wandered back into Arizona. Geneva noticed the occasional houses, scattered mobile homes, and small cornfields below the distant mountains as they climbed. Still the old man's words played again and again in her mind: *Edward's zipper book. The man that wanted him dead. The Phoenix man* . . .

Ahead, just past the junction of NM 134 that led to Crystal, an old Navajo woman stood beside the road. She wore a man's shapeless denim jacket over her full, faded green skirt, which ended just above pink socks and muddy white tennis shoes. As the van approached, she held out a hand, not as a hitchhiker might, but almost imperiously.

The sense of expectation that sometimes preceded Geneva's vivid mental images now prickled the skin in front of her ears.

"Go on and stop," Harrison said. "She can ride." When Terry stopped, Harrison opened the sliding door and helped the woman onto the seat beside Geneva. "This is Ooljee Black-goat. Medicine woman." Then he slid the door closed and took his seat without further introduction. Terry pulled the van onto the highway again.

Geneva's and Ooljee Blackgoat's eyes met in instant recognition. Geneva extended her hand and found it enclosed in both of the old woman's for a long moment. Ooljee bent her head slightly, ear toward their hands, as if listening. Then she released Geneva's hand and sat back abruptly, her eyes half closed.

"I know what you want to know." Her voice was low, barely audible over the noise of the van, yet clear. "But there will be trouble."

Geneva opened her mouth but couldn't speak. Angie leaned past her and looked sharply at the woman. "What do you mean? Do you know her, Geneva?" Angie's voice sounded anxious, almost frightened. She put one hand on Geneva's forearm as if to pull her away from the Navajo woman.

"It's all right, Angie," Geneva managed to say. "Never mind, it's all right."

Ooljee Blackgoat smiled and tucked some strands of white hair back into her hourglass-shaped bun. "You're a good woman," she said to Geneva. "You tell the truth with your hands." She lifted her own hands as if over a keyboard. "And you feel the spirit of the land in this place. But you don't know the truth in the water and the airplane. About the man with two airplanes. Maybe you shouldn't find out."

Geneva felt an invisible knock, a light blow, against her chest. And now she wanted mightily to talk. "What do you know about—about airplanes and water? Please tell me."

"A witch killed that man with those little glasses," the old woman said with a sigh. She put one hand up near her eyes, forefinger and thumb making a circle to indicate eyeglasses. "You must be careful."

With that, she reached forward and gave Harrison's shoulder a push. "You remember what I told you," she said to the back of his head.

He didn't turn around but said something in Navajo to Terry and pointed to a faint track intersecting the highway up ahead. Terry slowed and stopped the van. Harrison again got out, opened the sliding door, and helped Ooljee down.

She turned and looked straight into Geneva's eyes. "You must stay away from the death hogahn," she said, and passed Harrison without another look.

"What was that about?" Angie cried as the door closed. "Who is that woman? And where could she be going? There's nothing out here—not a house or a car or anything. Geneva, this is crazy! What was all that stuff she was saying to you?"

Harrison turned in his seat and looked at Angie, smiling a little and nodding. "Don't worry. Ooljee Blackgoat is a crystal-gazer, a kind of seer. Some people call her Listening Woman. She's what you would call a fortune-teller, in a way. I couldn't hear all she was saying to Geneva, but Ooljee is a good woman. Good medicine. Her name means moon."

He turned back to face the road ahead.

Angie stared at the back of his head. Then she turned big eyes on Geneva. "This is crazy!" she whispered. "I know that *hogahn* means house. But what's a death hogahn? And what was all that about airplanes and water?"

"Angie, please. We'll talk later. I need to think," Geneva tried to sound calm. "Don't worry. Please."

"Hey, Angie," said Terry, speaking for the first time since the gas station incident. "Forget about it. It's just crazy Indian stuff. We're almost to my granddad's place. More crazy Indian stuff." He gave a little laugh and moved his head to catch Angie's eye in the rearview mirror. "You'll see."

Angie didn't respond to that, and Geneva felt she should try to soothe her, but instead leaned back against the seat and closed her eyes. A man with little glasses. Death hogahn. Witch. Too much. Way, way too much. But the feeling of rapport, the—what was the right word?—the *bond* she'd felt with the crystal-gazer! She couldn't sort it out. She kept her eyes closed, partly to signal Angie to be calm, partly to make herself relax. Mostly to try to figure out the wonder Ooljee Blackgoat had woken in her.

"Stop here," said Harrison after a few more miles. Terry gave his grandfather a questioning look but pulled over and came to a halt under a pair of leaning piñons. Halfway up a low mesa some distance away and partly hidden behind a hill, stood a low building, probably once a bunkhouse, Geneva guessed. Near that was a corral that looked long abandoned, made of saplings woven in a zigzag pattern, and weathered almost to black. Like many others, this corral used the smooth, vertical sandstone formation for one side of the enclosure. Harrison slid out of the van, told them to wait, tucked the package he'd picked up at the gas station under his arm, and struck off up the mesa.

Geneva got out the van and so did Terry and Angie. Geneva decided that Angie had either resigned herself to the trip and its peculiar happenings or was lulled into drowsiness by the long ride. Soon Angie and Terry fell into desultory conversation. Terry picked up pebbles and threw them, one at a time, toward a boulder in a gully.

Geneva retrieved her camera and walked away from the road, not on the same path Harrison had taken, but one angling away to the left toward another hill. She felt the need to walk. Besides, she might capture a good view of the purple Chuska and Lukachukai Mountains to the north if she could get high enough. She needed to breathe. And think.

The hill Geneva climbed was strewn here and there with sandstone rubble, some slabs as big as flagstones, others no bigger than saucers. Otherwise the sandy earth was so soft that her shoes sank in, making climbing laborious. She rued the last few days of sitting too much and drew in deep draughts of the sweet desert air. Keeping her attention on the now-and-again treacherous earth underfoot, she finally reached the flat top of the hill, and sighed with pleasure.

Layers of subtle shades of rose, cream, gray, and less-subtle rust marked the sandstone hillside below. Geneva made herself stop trying to recall the names of minerals and formations or the geological reasons for their being here, and simply enjoyed them. She brought the camera up to focus and panned right, snapping a shadowed rock hanging in a crevasse and a fan of yucca poised on a point that looked too slight to support it.

Farther to the right, an arroyo cut the earth and fed into a little canyon. The wind shifted, bringing with it a scent of smoke. Descending a few yards, she saw that the canyon grew wider and deeper, with some small trees at the bottom. Just past the trees a plume of dark smoke rose above the round tarpaper roof of a small hogahn.

Within a few more steps Geneva could see little jets of smoke coming from more than half the hogahn's roof. She heard a soft "poof," followed by a series of loud pops, like a string of firecrackers. Or rapid pistol shots. A dirty orange blaze engulfed the roof and blew out a window. On the far side of the hogahn she noticed the back end of a parked vehicle. At that moment a shrill warbling cry went up.

"My God, someone's in there!" she cried aloud and started down the hill. The loose earth and rubble caused her to slide several times before coming down hard on her side. To keep from sliding, she grabbed a small yucca.

"Damn," she said, as its spines cut her hand. But it stopped her and she managed to come to her knees facing back up the hill. She tested the ground before planting her feet again.

She started side-stepping down once more, but this time slid several yards before twisting one ankle and falling to her knees. Pain shot up her calf. Below, the burning hogahn roared and the wind shifted again, pushing dark smoke against the hill.

Unlike most, this hogahn was not made with mud-chinked logs and heavy beams supporting a roof covered with a dome of soil, but of planks and plywood covered with tarpaper. Flames entirely engulfed the structure now. No use trying to rescue anybody. Smoke and ashes rose about her and then blew clear. The heavy camera had swung hard against her inner arms during her descent but now she held it in her lap. As the black skeletons of the uprights held for a last moment against the orange flames, she lifted the camera and took several shots. The silhouette of the woodstove and its leaning pipe stood stark against the fire for an instant before the roof and three sides fell, sending a roiling sheet of sparks out and up. A slender tree nearby burst into flames, and Geneva clicked off more shots, wondering if the rest of the scrubby growth in the canyon would catch as well.

"Geneva, where are you?" Angie yelled. "Geneva!"

Geneva knew she was out of sight, down this side of the hill. Just then a figure ran from behind the truck toward a grove of cottonwoods thirty yards or so beyond the hogahn. She snapped more pictures. He wore a furry-looking, square-ish thing over his head and dark clothes with something around his waist like long strips that flapped as he ran. He stopped running and spun around, arms straight up, holding in each hand what looked like a stick with bulbous ends. The floppy strips streamed out like a dancer's skirt as he twirled.

The smoke thinned again. She kept shooting. The runner disappeared into the trees.

"Geneva!" Angie's voice rose from somewhere above her. "Where are you? Answer me!"

"I'm here, Angie," Geneva called, lowering her camera and squinting through another scrap of smoke toward the little grove where the runner had disappeared. "I'm down here. I've hurt my ankle!"

Angie and Terry helped Geneva back to the van, where Harrison now waited, one hand on the snub hood of the van, the other shading his eyes. When he saw them, he nodded, his expression clearly relieved.

They lowered her into the open van doorway, and Angie lifted Geneva's foot to examine the ankle. Geneva beckoned to Harrison. "There's a hogahn burning in a canyon on the far side of that hill. Somebody might have been inside!"

Harrison glanced in the direction she pointed. "That's the old Peshlakai place. Nobody's lived there for years."

"But there was a truck, I think, next to it. And I saw somebody running away."

The others said nothing to that. Terry looked up the hill and back to her twice, and then moved closer to his grandfather.

Harrison bent toward Geneva. "Was it a rusty red color? The truck?"

"I can't be sure. I could only see a little part of it and there was a lot of smoke."

Angie already had her cell phone out, madly punching numbers and swearing in Spanish. "No signal in this godforsaken place!"

"Harrison, maybe we should flag down a car and have

somebody else call," Geneva said. "I think we ought to wait until help comes so we can show them. You can't even see the place from down here on the road. You can barely see the smoke from here."

Harrison looked thoughtful for a moment. "All right."

Terry walked past the van into the roadway. "Yeah, okay. I'll get someone to stop." Two cars passed before an old couple in a pickup pulled over. Terry returned saying they had agreed to phone the Apache County sheriff from the little store near Crystal.

Geneva looked past Angie in the doorway and tried to see the long bunkhouse and corral Harrison had headed for earlier. She wondered how far that place stood from the burned hogahn and whether Harrison knew anything about the figure running from the hogahn. But she would wait to describe him to the sheriff. Besides, her ankle had begun to throb in earnest. She numbly obeyed Angie's insistence that she stretch her legs out on the seat and accepted the proffered jacket folded between her back and the side of the van.

"I'll move that gear away for you," Terry said to Angie, stepping into the back of the van. "That third seat back there isn't too bad. Besides, we'll be at Grampa's soon."

Angie thanked him, but stayed outside the open door, watching Geneva. "Do you want me to put something under that foot? It's supposed to be elevated, isn't it?"

Terry produced what looked like a rolled-up sweatshirt. "Try this," he said.

Thus ensconced, Geneva smiled at them and closed her eyes, hoping they'd take it as a signal and stop fussing. She touched the camera in her lap and wondered if she had seen a Navajo witch running and dancing through the smoke.

"Here comes the sheriff," Terry yelled. Geneva's eyes flew open and she saw Angie and Terry hurry toward the sheriff's car. A moment later, they and the sheriff started up the hill together. Harrison, she noticed, had not moved from the passenger seat.

"They'll show him, the sheriff," he said. Then, without preamble, "I forgot about Edward's zipper book for a long time. I wish I had remembered."

Geneva couldn't think of an answer. "I see," she said.

After some time, the three returned to the sheriff's car, parked nose to nose with their van. His car radio crackled, and Geneva could hear the sheriff's voice but could make out only a few of his words. "Old Peshlakai place," and, "Burned up, yeah," came out clearly enough, but that's all she could understand.

Geneva expected the sheriff to come to the van and ask her some questions. She made up her mind to describe the running figure and his odd twirling dance. To her surprise, he backed his car, throwing up a spray of gravel, and made a screeching U-turn. He sped off in the direction of Window Rock, siren wailing.

"Oh, no," she said. "There really was somebody in that hogahn."

"Yeah," said Terry, looking greenish-white as if likely to throw up. He sat down in the open van doorway, his back to Geneva, and bent over, head in one hand. He seemed to be mumbling under his breath. Angie leaned with her back against the van. Geneva couldn't see her face.

Harrison got out and bent down to look at his grandson. Terry lifted his head only for an instant, and Harrison patted his shoulder. "It's all right," he said softly. "You didn't go near it, did you?" Terry shook his head.

Geneva knew about the Navajos' strong aversion to dead bodies and the serious threat they believed the *chindíi*, the spirits of evil left behind after death, posed to the living.

"It's all right, then," Harrison said. He beckoned to Angie. "Can you drive this thing?"

"Sure," Angie said and went around to the driver's door.

Harrison helped his grandson to the far rear seat and slid the side door closed. He then returned to the passenger seat. "I'll tell you where to turn, Angie."

Geneva's attention went to Terry, who sat with head bowed and eyes closed. He panted and made odd little sounds. He looked so young and pale. Was he about to cry? No, it seemed more like a whispered litany; maybe he was repeating words of a prayer. She tried to keep watch without staring at him in case he looked up.

It was nearly four o'clock when they finally bumped to a halt in the bare front yard of Harrison's hogahn. A dusty black dog heaved himself to his feet and stood wagging his tail. The hogahn looked fairly new, Geneva noticed, and of good size. The honey-colored, interlaced logs glowed in the slanting sunlight.

"My uncles and some clan brothers built it after Edward got my disability and pension for me," he said, pulling a key from his pocket. "The old hogahn's down the hill there."

Odd, she thought, she never knew Edward had helped Harrison get his pension. Not surprising that he would have, of course.

Both Angie and Terry seemed somewhat recovered and each took one of Geneva's arms. The ankle was now swollen and she could hardly put weight on it. "I have some ice," Harrison said, unlocking and pushing open the door.

Angie eased Geneva into an armchair, her foot on a leather hassock. Terry and Harrison went to the kitchen and returned with a towel and a plastic bag full of ice cubes. Angie took them, wrapped the ice pack in the towel, and arranged it around Geneva's ankle.

"Thank you, all," Geneva said. "This is wonderful."

"You be easy there. I'll be right back," Harrison said, and went into his bedroom. Terry busied himself filling the dog's bowl, and Angie relaxed on one of the couches.

To Geneva's surprise, the hogahn was quite large and filled

with good pine furniture. Above, a loft spanned more than half the round structure, with a wrought-iron, spiral staircase leading up to it at one end. Colorful Pendleton blankets draped over the loft handrail and the backs of the two couches in front of the fireplace. Above the mantle hung a pair of rifles that looked polished and well cared for. On the fireplace mantle stood a row of kachina dolls, carved figures representing spirits or animals or abstract ideas.

Geneva immediately recognized the figures as unusually fine pieces of art. She remembered then that even during his blindness, Harrison always carved. Edward bought many of his early efforts, usually bare wood abstracts—nothing like these dancing gods dressed in fur, down, and leather, wearing fierce masks or animal heads. Nearby a worktable held tools and a powerful-looking attached magnifier.

The kitchen area was separated from the open dining and living room by a carved, four-panel divider in a sun and moon design similar to those Geneva had seen in China. The motifs carved in the dark wood were repeated here and there by bands of lighter wood with painted russet suns and ghostly silver moons. A masterly piece.

Harrison returned, his bright yellow parade tunic replaced by a worn brown velveteen one, faded jeans, and soft deerskin boots.

He noticed Angie and Geneva looking up at the sleeping loft. "My grandson here and a bunch of grand-nephews and nieces come and stay with me from time to time," he said. "I like for them to come." Following Angie's glance, he indicated the rifles above the fireplace with a quick lift of the chin and puckered lips. "They belong to my nephew and grandson. Terry's a good shot."

"I was looking at the kachinas, Harrison," Geneva said. "They're beautiful."

"It's good to be able to see," he said. "Don't whittle my fingers so much anymore."

He took the rocking chair opposite Geneva and sighed. Angie joined Terry in the kitchen. "Terry's going to make us some tea," Harrison said. "Later he can heat up that pot of chili and we'll eat. Maybe then we can talk."

"I need to talk to you now," Geneva said in a low voice. "About that person I saw running from the burning hogahn. I was going to tell the sheriff, but—"

Harrison leaned forward, his hands hanging over the ends of the chair arms. He looked into her face for an instant and then away.

"Tell me," he said.

CHAPTER FIVE

"Well, then," said Harrison, leaning back as she finished telling about the strange figure at the burning hogahn. "You say the man wore something loose around his waist? Might be animal skins or tails, the feet of an animal skin swinging around?"

"Could have been. I really couldn't tell. And he carried a sticklike thing in each hand." She held out her hands about a foot and a half apart.

Harrison rose and went to the row of kachina dolls. "Sticks, you say. Like this?" He brought over a figure nearly two feet tall, with a bat-like mask complete with upright ears. Both its hands closed over leather-wrapped rods that ended in what were clearly heads of clubs, small rounded stones attached with narrow strips of hide. Tiny feathers hung from the shafts and ends.

"Goodness, I certainly couldn't make out all this detail, but they could have been like these." Geneva examined the little open mouth of the gray bat mask, its sharp white teeth and pink tongue. She touched the anklets of the smallest periwinkle shells she'd ever seen. "Harrison, you're an artist! I've seen dolls like this, some not nearly this good, selling for thousands in Phoenix and Flagstaff."

Harrison shrugged. "My niece takes their pictures and sells them for me on eBay. Terry makes things, too," he said, and rose to bring a wide box from a closet. "Toys, I call them. They're gadgets that surprise you."

Angie and Terry returned from the kitchen. "Aw, Grand-dad, they don't want to see my stuff," he said.

But Terry did take out a small wooden contraption and showed how it would strike a bundle of matches and set off a row of firecrackers, he said, when you moved this other thing with the spring, either with your foot or the little chain. "I made some bigger ones that use steel balls for weights. They work better."

"Pretty smart gadgets," Harrison said. "Terry's a good carver. Got good ideas. He makes masks, too. Maybe one of them is like the one that man running away wore." He turned back to the closet near the work table. "Show Mrs. Granger your masks, son."

"I want to see them, too," Angie said.

Terry rolled out what looked to Geneva like a kitchen utility cart, but longer, probably something he'd made. Several masks and headdresses of different sizes lay in a row. One, painted white, resembled a Zuni Shalako mask, with its bird-like features, Geneva thought. Several were undoubtedly similar to real ones, but she knew actual reproduction would be prohibited. As Terry drew the cart closer, she saw one that looked like shaggy fur, reminding her of buffalo pelt.

She pointed. "Oh, that one looks like the one the runner had on his head."

Terry shrugged. "I just made that up," he said. "It doesn't represent anything."

"Looks like something to keep your ears warm," Harrison said. "But Terry made sure a fellow could wear it and move and see out, too. Look how he curved the frame inside just right to hold it away from the face."

Terry ducked his head shyly as he pushed his cart back to the closet, obviously pleased at their attention and his grandfather's praise. His mood again bright, he offered to show Angie the view of the Chuska Mountains from the top of a hill behind Harrison's hogahn.

"You'll be all right?" Angie didn't wait for an answer as she checked Geneva's ice packs. "I want to see this highly advertised sunset." The two went off, talking like old chums.

"What do you think about that person running from the hogahn, Harrison? Don't you think he might have set the blaze?"

"It sure looks like it. He wasn't hollering for help or trying to move that truck away, you said. The police will want to check, but a man dressed up like that—no way to tell who he was." He stood up, went up the spiral staircase, and disappeared for a few minutes.

"Here's Edward's zipper book," he said simply, coming down the stairs. "I didn't ever open it. You should do that." He handed her the notebook in a creased, folded-over paper sack. "Terry was supposed to get it and bring it to me yesterday when you were at Margaret's. But he forgot."

She thought how long the notebook had lain hidden and forgotten and wondered what had stirred the old man finally to remember it. More than that, she wondered why her husband had ever given it to him.

Harrison picked up the empty tea cups and went back to the kitchen.

She drew a breath and slid the black notebook out of the paper. Edward's day-planner, calendar, appointment book, the simple notebook he laughingly called his "three-ringed brain" lay in her hands. She'd assumed that it had gone to the bottom of the lake with him. How sweetly familiar it was, there in her lap.

And yet how strange. Its worn edges seemed to take on an odd magnification, as if a camera were zooming in, but she blinked away the illusion, unzipped the cover and let the book fall open.

The pages bristled with yellow sticky-notes and paper-clipped receipts, pink telephone memos from his office, and here and there a folded flyer announcing such things as a local junior-high basketball game, a Navajo rug auction, his own campaign appearances. All of it familiar and dear. Her hands smoothed the pages, straightening and refolding notes, as she browsed through Edward's scribbled entries. *July 4th, speech — Code Talkers — Window Rock.* The appearance in Window Rock three years ago that Tucker Bayless reminded her of only yesterday afternoon. *September 28th, Josh's science project, 2:30 p.m.* Geneva smiled, remembering their grandson's pride at having his "Senator Grandfather" visit his classroom. Still smiling, she turned more pages.

An envelope bearing her name slid from the pages into her hand. The letter was completely addressed and stamped, but still unsealed. Tears flooded her vision. She drew in a breath and waited for them to clear. Letters. How many hundreds of letters had the two of them written to each other during their marriage? Hardly a week would pass, whether they were together or apart, without a letter or two between them. It was the record of their love, the heartbeat of their marriage. Long or short, the missives might express their deepest hopes for the future, worry over the children, mundane exchanges of mere information, or a day's funny events. Sometimes she would try a poem or a bit of writing for his keen critique.

She never imagined she'd see another of Edward's letters. But here it was. She slid it into her handbag. She would keep it for a private moment.

The next notebook page was filled with irregular "balloons" connected by lines and arrows going in different directions. One of his "thinking pages," Edward called them. He frequently used this webbing device to sort out problems. The balloons all had words scribbled in them, or his own shorthand — odd abbreviations or initials, sometimes a little drawing. The twins called them "Dad's secret code." Geneva had often laughed at his "hieroglyphics," but recognized the value of the process and even taught the "idea network" to her students. Navajo thinking processes were often far from linear, and her students enjoyed what they called "cartoon balloons" as much as Edward did. On several of the last pages, he'd written M^1, which she remembered stood for Mason, G+ in a little heart, his abbreviation for her, question marks, a doodle of big crossed eyes, and a symbol that baffled Geneva: IE^{2-HU}, drawn in an arrowhead. The last page wasn't filled. Only a sprinkling of drawings, several arrows, no, arrowheads, with — what was that? It looked like a bicuspid with little lines radiating from it. And down the page were two more, one larger than the other. And it looked like the pages following had been torn out with some force. Bits of paper were caught in the rings.

"You all right?" came Harrison's soft voice from the kitchen.

Geneva looked up and smiled. "Of course. Thank you."

"I've got more ice if you want. For your ankle. More hot tea, too."

To her surprise, the ice around her ankle had melted, and she wondered how long she'd sat absorbed in Edward's book. "Why, thank you, Harrison. But I need to talk with you now before Angie and Terry come back."

He nodded and resumed his seat. Before she could ask, he said, "Edward gave the zipper book to me the day he met with the elders in Window Rock. I made a joke, said I promised not to read it." He indicated his thick glasses, reminding her of his former blindness.

"But why, Harrison? Why did he give it to you at all?"

After a moment's thought he said, "I don't know why. All Edward said was that he wanted to lose it for a while. Said he'd be back for it." The room was growing dim and Harrison rose and switched on two lamps. "He said he found out something he might have to pay for later. I asked him how much he would have to pay, but he said it would cost him more than money. A lot more. Then I knew he was really worried."

"Your daughter's note said you thought the newspaper accounts were wrong. Why?"

The door flew open and Angie and Terry came in, both breathless. "Navajo police car coming up the hill," Terry said, giving a sideways jerk of his head toward the open door.

"All right," Harrison said to him, glancing at Geneva as if to say *wait a bit*. "Maybe you would get Mrs. Granger some more ice for her ankle."

Terry and Angie moved to replenish Geneva's ice packs. Harrison went to the door.

The last rays of sunlight had abandoned the red cliffs, and the yard beyond the door lay dark. Geneva heard Sarge, the old dog, shuffle toward Harrison. He spoke to it quietly and waited. In a few minutes, headlight beams swung into the yard and a car door opened and slammed shut.

"Harrison Billy?" a male voice called. "I'm Lieutenant Charles Nez, Navajo Police. Are you Harrison Billy?"

Harrison stood in the doorway, illumined by both the lights in the house and the car's headlights. "Right here."

The young Navajo policeman strode to the door holding a long flashlight at his side. "Folks with you in there?"

"My grandson and our guests," Harrison replied.

"Then maybe you should come out here so we can talk," the policeman said.

"Maybe you will come inside so we can talk."

The young man hesitated but stepped inside as Harrison turned and led the way.

"It's about that burned-up hogahn out at the old Peshlakai place," the officer said.

Harrison, however, presented his guests, one at a time, telling where they were from and when they had arrived, and ended with his grandson, the boy's maternal and paternal clans, and the fact that he had recently graduated from high school, where, perhaps Officer Nez had heard, this boy had been one of the best free-throw shooters the Window Rock Scouts had ever had.

The young policeman, clearly trained in Navajo tradition and manners, nodded attentively, went around and shook hands with each one as they were introduced. Finally, he said, "Mr. Billy, I need you to answer some questions. The Apache County sheriff says you and these other folks saw the hogahn burning and later looked inside and found a body." He drew breath and prepared to continue, but Harrison held up his hand.

"My grandson saw the body," he said. "He didn't go inside."

"I saw the hogahn just as it began burning," Geneva said. "But I hurt my ankle and never went down the hill afterwards to look inside. The young people here helped me back to the van and only later, when the sheriff arrived, did they go with him to look at the hogahn." As she said it, she wondered again just where Harrison had gone that day.

Nez made notes in a slim notebook. "And you, Mr. Billy, did you go up to the burned hogahn at all?"

"No, I didn't," Harrison said. "I stayed at the van with Mrs. Granger while the sheriff and these two went."

"But it was you who made the report, or had the folks call the sheriff. It's your name on the sheriff's report."

Harrison nodded but made no reply.

"Will you tell me why you stopped out there in the first place? No one lives on the Peshlakai place anymore. What were you doing there?"

"I expected to find a friend up near there, sketching that old corral," Harrison said.

"Who is this friend, Mr. Billy?"

"Jerome Layton, that professor from Phoenix."

"Dr. Allen Jerome Layton?" the policeman asked, glancing at his notebook for verification. "You know this professor, then?"

"Yes, I know him," Harrison said. "He was here all summer collecting stories from the old people. Out here last summer, too. Stories about how Navajos served in the war, mostly, especially the Code Talkers. That's how come I met him."

"When did you see Dr. Layton last, Mr. Billy? And where?"

Harrison looked down at his hands for a moment and adjusted his heavy glasses. "Four days ago. He came here and we talked some more about Code Talkers."

"I see," the officer said, "and what did you think about that, telling this man about the Code Talkers?"

Harrison frowned and didn't answer for a moment. "Think about it? I thought it was all right. I told him about the training, mostly. That's most of what he asked about. Of course, I didn't serve but a few months before my outfit got shot up pretty bad."

"And that's when you were, ah, wounded?" the officer asked.

"Yes. Head and neck. And blinded." Harrison made a small gesture toward his face.

Geneva wondered where this line of questioning was going and watched with interest.

"But I wonder if it made you angry or upset to be questioned by Dr. Layton," the policeman went on.

Harrison looked faintly amused. He shook his head slowly.

"You didn't run him off the place just a month ago?" Nez asked sharply. "I heard you told him to leave and not come back."

"I ran the skunk off," Harrison said. "Or rather my dog did."

"Skunk? You called him a skunk and sicced your dog on him? Why?"

Harrison's eyes twinkled behind his glasses. Geneva thought she caught a look of mischief as he leaned back in his chair.

"The professor saw something move in the piñon thicket just down there," he said, inclining his head toward the door. "He rattled the bushes with that long walking stick he carries, and bang! That's when the skunk let him have it. And old Sarge—he should have known better—took out after the skunk, and knocked the walking stick away. That's when Jerome fell into the bushes, making it all a whole lot worse. I told him to go back to town and get some tomato juice, enough to bathe in—" At this point Harrison couldn't suppress his laughter another minute. Tears stood in his eyes and he rocked back and forth with the fun of it. Geneva and the youngsters, including finally the young officer, joined in.

Nez stopped laughing and worked up an official countenance again. "All right, Mr. Billy. Are you sure you did not see Professor Layton today?"

Harrison shook his head. "I expected to see him, but he wasn't there."

"We would like to talk with Dr. Layton. We know that he has used the Peshlakai hogahn occasionally. If you see him or hear from him, please let me know. Will you be at home for the next few days, Mr. Billy?"

"I have no plans to go anywhere."

Nez turned to Angie and Terry, who sat at opposite ends of the couch. "So, you two did go up to the burned hogahn," he said, taking up his notebook again. "Suppose you tell me what you saw."

"It was pretty awful." Angie pressed her fingers against her nose as if recalling the smell. "The roof and most of the walls had fallen in on the poor man—I guess it was a man. You could just see the bottoms of boots and one hand sticking out. Everything inside was burned black and collapsed. Except the stove, I guess." She turned to Terry for verification.

"We didn't get close," Terry said, almost as if he'd been accused of it. "It wasn't any use."

Geneva noticed Terry's sudden paleness. He kept rubbing his fingers along the side seam of his jeans.

Officer Nez let a beat pass. "But what did you see? Anything near the hogahn?"

Angie glanced at Geneva. "Like what?"

"The Jeep, or maybe it was a Scout," Terry said at the same time. "It was messed up on the side nearest the hogahn."

Nez wrote in his notebook before looking up. "Did you see evidence of another person? Maybe somebody that might have been nearby?"

"I saw a person running away just as the flames took the roof," Geneva said.

Nez nearly jumped to his feet, spun around to Geneva's chair and bent over her, frowning. "You did? Why didn't you report that sooner?"

"I simply haven't had the opportunity. I thought the sheriff was coming to the van to talk to us before he left, but he didn't."

"Describe this person, please." Nez's expression never changed as he wrote down Geneva's words, flipping over another page in his notebook. When she finished, he kept his pencil poised over the page. "Twirled about? You say the figure twirled? Like dancing?"

"Yes, several times, with his arms raised straight over his head."

"You're Doctor Granger, is that right?"

She nodded, and the policeman recorded her address and telephone number. He kept his gaze on the page, tapping it with his pen. "How long will you and Miss Sanchez be staying with Mr. Billy?"

Angie started to answer, but Geneva replied, "I'm not quite sure," and glanced at Harrison. "We'll likely be leaving tomorrow. Returning to Flagstaff."

Like the policeman's, Harrison's expression didn't change. He gave a small nod but offered nothing further.

Officer Nez looked thoughtful for a minute, drew out some business cards from his notebook, and stood up. "If any of you think of anything else, please contact the Navajo police." He handed his cards around and left.

The minute the door closed behind the policeman, Angie was at Geneva's elbow. "Are you going to be able to walk?" Then in a whisper, "When are we going to leave this place?"

Harrison went into his bedroom, motioning Terry to follow. "We'll fix up this room for you ladies," he called. "I'll bunk with Terry upstairs. Angie, will you stir that pot of chili for me? I set it there on the stove."

Angie gave Geneva a look and disappeared behind the carved screen into the kitchen area.

Terry made a fire in the fireplace and helped Angie lay places at the long plank table.

Harrison produced a heated pottery tortilla container and brought bowls for chili. With what Geneva thought was amazing speed and efficiency, the dinner was ready. Angie seemed to relax at last, and the four ate and talked together as easily as old friends.

The clouds that had added their purple to the flaming sunset "had plans," as Harrison put it. Before the meal was finished, they could hear gusts breaking against the log walls, and soon rain pelted the windows and beat a tattoo on the metal stovepipe above their heads. "Male rain," Harrison said, and began reciting Agnes Tso's poem as if to himself: "'He comes, riding on the wind, kicking up dust, bending the trees, blowing flakes of rain…'"

"'He flees past my window,'" Geneva continued with some surprise. "'To a distant rumble.'"

Harrison looked up, raising his eyebrows above the rims of his eyeglasses. He said nothing, however, only nodded. Terry looked at Angie, whose smile went to Geneva.

Still smiling, Angie said, "Hmm," and rose to collect the empty bowls.

Angie and Terry cleared the table and went into the kitchen. Harrison brought a carved cane for Geneva and helped her back to her chair. "Edward never told me why he was worried that day," he said, reclaiming his rocker. "The only other thing I recall was about the man in Phoenix. I think he was worried about what the man might do."

"Do? You mean do something to Edward? Did he threaten Edward in some way?"

"That's what I think. I think Edward was scared of something the man might do. Maybe it was something about the airplane. When I read in the Phoenix newspaper—I read it on that machine in the Gallup library, you know—said it was the storm blew them down, I didn't believe it. I figured it was on purpose. Something somebody did to the airplane that made it crash. I think something like that was what Edward was worried about."

Harrison hung his head and remained silent for a moment. "I should have made him stay here that night. Or at my daughter's house in Fort Defiance. We both asked him to." He lifted eyes full of remorse to Geneva. "I'm sorry."

At dawn Geneva opened her eyes to the faint light and listened. Hushed male voices came from somewhere above, then some rustling followed by the sound of the front door opening and closing quietly. She knew that Harrison had started his run to meet Father Sun. She recalled her Navajo friend Desbah Chischilly describing the tradition. "You must run toward the rising sun. If the Holy People do not see you running to meet Father Sun at dawn, they will not look out for you all the rest of the day."

As Geneva moved to rise, a vivid stab of pain shot the

entire length of her right leg. She let out an involuntary gasp. Angie came awake immediately. "I'm sorry, Angie," Geneva whispered. "Go back to sleep."

But Angie got out of bed and into her clothes before Geneva could pull herself and the offending limb into a sitting position. "We're getting out of here," Angie said. "You need to see a doctor."

By the time Geneva finished washing up and struggling into her clothes, Angie had packed their suitcases and started coffee and bacon. Harrison and Terry returned, the former rosy-cheeked and in vigorous good humor, the latter looking sleepy and out of sorts. However, after a quick wash, Terry went to help Angie in the kitchen. With the help of Harrison's cane and Angie's strong arm, Geneva joined Harrison at the table. "Terry is going to take you wherever you need to go," Harrison said, pouring steaming coffee into mugs. "You can call your pilot from Navajo, or maybe the little store at the lake will be open. They have a phone."

"She needs to see a doctor," said Angie for the third or fourth time in the last hour. "Look how purple and swollen that ankle and foot are. Where is the closest doctor?"

Geneva lifted a hand. "We'll call the pilot and see if he can come for us at Window Rock this morning. We can be back in Phoenix soon enough, and then we'll get my car and go home. And I will see a doctor." That and a meaningful look quieted Angie for the moment. Terry and Angie set about preparing to leave. Geneva still wanted to satisfy her curiosity about yesterday's events.

"I wonder why Officer Nez was asking you about Professor Layton," Geneva said to Harrison, with her usual directness, remembering too late her Navajo manners. The darned ankle was objecting to her every breath now.

Harrison paused as he bent to retrieve the cane. "I've been thinking about that. Jerome and I were supposed to get together yesterday. We've got to be pretty good friends. I picked up that package for him in Navajo. A new tape recorder and some tapes and batteries he'd ordered that came in the mail. He said he was going to be up there across from the Peshlakai place again, sketching that old bunkhouse and corral."

"But you didn't see him there."

"No, I didn't. I didn't see his Jeep either, but his gear was there, that canvas stool he uses and his folding easel. His plastic cooler, too. I figured he'd be back soon, so I just left the package on top of the cooler. I didn't want to keep you all waiting."

"I see," Geneva said.

Angie returned from the van, bringing with her a whiff of cold, wonderfully sweet mountain air. She tried to help Geneva stand. But after a moment's struggle, Harrison and Terry simply lifted her, chair and all, carried her out, and slid her onto the long back seat of the van, legs straight, foot propped, back cushioned again.

Geneva now felt as eager as Angie to get under way, but for a different reason. They said their good-byes to Harrison and bounced and fish-tailed through the mud to the paved road. She was eager to get home to Flagstaff and call Mason.

He would know how to proceed, might even be able to say who this mysterious Phoenix man could be. He had dozens of connections in Phoenix from his offices there. Connections on both sides of the aisle and at every level of government. Hadn't he, eight years ago, his wheelchair be damned, breezed Edward and her through doorway after open doorway, introducing them, making sure Edward met all the right people before his run for the Senate? And only last year, when she was researching another book on Indian education, Mason steered her through lunches with important committee members, both Anglo and Navajo, smoothing her way, making sure she would get those important interviews with tribal authorities, especially those who had risen to high posts during her absence from the reservation.

Of course he had. And he would help her figure this out sometime soon, she knew.

Terry stopped at the little grocery store near Wheatfields Lake. Angie went in to telephone their charter pilot, who had planned to be in Gallup, minutes away from Window Rock by air, with his cousin for the time Geneva planned to be on the reservation.

She returned to the van, beaming. "Pilot's cousin said he had to go back to Phoenix this morning. So, I called Mason. He's going to fly to Window Rock and pick us up."

"You did?" Geneva tried to adjust her expression to cover a moment's annoyance. She wished Angie had discussed a next step with her before taking it.

Angie admired Mason and "rooted for him," as she put it, trying to promote a romance between Geneva and Mason. Geneva had not spoken of his marriage proposal last Christmas to anyone, not Angie and not even her daughters, who called him "Uncle Mason." For the most part, Geneva simply shushed Angie's more enthusiastic efforts in that direction with quiet tolerance.

But now she just smiled and leaned forward to hear Terry's response.

"That's great," he said. "We'll be there by noon easy."

So again, Geneva adjusted her plans along with her throbbing ankle and sat back to think.

She felt torn between her eagerness to put this puzzle in front of Mason and an equal desire to see Shándiíne and Tucker Bayless. Shándiíne could die at any time. Her last letter to Geneva had been a short, scrawled note that might have been written on a soft or unstable surface, like a pillow. Difficult enough to read for that, but heartbreaking for its content. "Make Tucker and Millie leave this place for a while," she had written. "They must not keep on crying for me."

Geneva resolved to return as soon as her ankle would allow and spend some days with Shándiíne and Tucker. For now, she needed to know what had really happened to Edward. Maybe Mason could find a clue either in what Harrison had said or Edward's notebook.

She and Angie said good-bye to Terry at the Window Rock airport, where she added "burger money" to what she'd already given him for gas and his trouble.

Angie was able to secure a wheelchair for Geneva. She slipped the paper with Terry's and Harrison's mailing addresses into her briefcase as they waited for Mason. Also safe in her briefcase was Edward's notebook. Safe in her purse was Edward's last letter to her.

Her well-wrapped ankle throbbed, and she accepted Angie's offered cell phone and called Tucker Bayless. "I'll phone you from home this evening," she said. "Lots more to tell you. Give my love to Shándiíne." She was glad she hadn't said anything of her hope to visit Tucker's ailing wife this trip. But sorry at the same time.

CHAPTER SIX

"You certainly will not wait, Geneva," Mason said, bending over her an hour later. "I will take you directly to the hospital in Flagstaff. I'll radio ahead and have Dr. Chalmers waiting when we land. Angie, mind that briefcase. Slide Geneva's laptop under your seat." He straightened and surveyed his handiwork. Geneva's legs, covered and secure, rested on the Lear's elegant leather seat, her back was cushioned, belts in place. "All set," he said, flashing his famous smile at both women. It was a statement, not a question.

Mason Drake, at 53, was the darling of TV cameras and women everywhere. Men admired his accomplishments, often repeating the story of his rising first from the trauma of his family's obliteration in a fire somewhere in Mississippi or Louisiana, and his resulting amnesia, and then his boyhood struggle to educate himself. And finally, the long years' climb to the position of Arizona's senior senator. Women of all ages crowded close, all but purring their attraction to him.

"And, then," the interviewer in a recent television special said, pausing dramatically, "during his second term, Senator Mason Drake died in a terrible car wreck. Actually died, the doctors said, but he came back, only to linger in a coma for many weeks. When he came out of that, he had to learn how to speak and walk all over again. What courage, what an example for us all. What a man!" That was how the television interview ended. "What a man!"

"Of course," Mason said, "we'll take Angie back to Phoenix first so she can drive your car home, but that'll only take a few minutes. You know, Angie, I'll try hard to take as good care of your patient as you do." He winked at Angie and grinned at them both. Angie looked at Geneva, pretending to hesitate, but failing to hide her smile.

Angie looked around the sumptuous cabin. "When did you get this airplane, Senator? Did you just rent it or something for today?" She didn't say "Just for Geneva?" but she might have. "It's gorgeous! Where's the Beechcraft?"

Mason stood at the door of the cockpit, one hand above his head on the doorframe. "Well, actually," he said, giving Geneva a soft look, "I got this little Lear some weeks ago. I was waiting for the right time to surprise Geneva with a moonlight flight over Grand Canyon." Here he paused and quirked down the corners of his chiseled lips in theatrical regret. "Ah, well. Another time." Then he ducked into the cockpit, and soon they lifted into the cold, perfect, blue sky.

Mason watched the hospital orderly with the blond goatee wheel Geneva down the hallway. "Radiology is ready for us. I'll have her back in half an hour." He then nodded to Mason, turned the chair smartly, and pulled it backwards into the elevator.

"Hang on to that," Geneva before the doors closed. "Maybe you can figure out what it means."

Yes, he would indeed hang on to it, Mason thought. Geneva had told him about the notebook and pointed out

Edward's "thinking page." *I will certainly hang on to this notebook —never to worry, my dear.*

Mason returned to the waiting room and found a seat by itself in a corner. The notebook fell open to the week of October 20, three years ago. His keen eyes searched the pages until finally he gazed off in the distance, tapping his fingers on Edward Granger's last thinking page.

The image of Geneva's shocked face as Mason's marriage proposal hung in the air between them floated again into his memory. It was as if all the oxygen had suddenly flown out of the room. The old feeling of worthlessness had dropped over him like a collapsing tent in that moment. His father's twisted face, oversized teeth, and dirty mustache pushed the words at him. *You're nothing, you sniveling little bastard, you get that? Worth nothing, and never will be.*

Of course, Geneva had been mute, had said nothing of the sort then or ever. She was silent.

But his father's sneering face blotted out Geneva's heart-shaped countenance and luminous gray eyes. Rollie Smith's oily voice taunted him as it had for all his sixteen years, as it did the night of the small Louisiana town's celebration of its Merit Scholars in the little pavilion in the town square. Mason, whose name then was Leroy, attended the town's lighting of the Christmas tree along with his family. It was his sixteenth birthday, which coincided with the end of semester and the beginning of Christmas vacation.

The mayor took that occasion to praise the high school's honor students by announcing their names over the loud speaker. When Leroy Smith's name was called, Rollie stepped forward from the line of parents seated on the little stage. "And let me tell you," he cried in a falsetto voice, leaning into the microphone, fanning the air with his handkerchief and batting his eyes, "this boy never lets his buddies down, either—not until they're finished, that is."

Leroy jumped off the stage and ran home along the swamp

and frozen fields, gathered his few belongings in a pillowcase, and never looked back. He caught the midnight freight train and rode for two days and nights, jumping off to steal food or join a hobo's camp when the train stopped along the way. He left his boxcar outside a tiny town in western Kansas and wandered toward a big rambling place that turned out to be an obscure church orphanage. He stood reading the sign at the edge of the property for several minutes when a brilliant plan came to him whole, he would remember later. He fell to the ground, smeared mud on his face and into his clothes and hair.

Next, he worked up some tears to flow down his cheeks and rang the bell. He threw himself, crying hysterically, to the ground before the Catholic sister who opened the door. His family had died in a fire in a barn, he thought he remembered, but he couldn't remember where or when. He had been wandering ever since, "so long, such a long, long time." Then he lapsed into feigned semi-consciousness, surrounded by the murmuring nuns. He was too old to be taken in officially, but after caring for him for several days, and beholding his abject gratitude, the kindly matron allowed him to stay. He let the nuns call him Sonny for months before "remembering" Mason Drake.

For five years Mason worked at the orphanage and attended the little college connected to it. He lived in fear that someone at some time might learn of his disappearance, see a photo, or in some other way be able to identify him. He wore his hair as long as the sisters would allow and as soon as whiskers began to grow, he cultivated a beard. By this time, he had reached his full height of six feet, four inches, and was so quiet, hardworking, and unassuming that the sisters and the orphans loved him and never asked too many questions. He lived alone in a tiny apartment in the basement of the library building and worked in the print shop, which proved valuable as he learned to create documents to give himself an identity.

Mason was so intent on working, finishing college, and

planning to get out of Kansas that his social life was almost non-existent. Girls from the town always noticed him, phoned him at the print shop, passed him notes, and during his final year, one of them followed him to his dismal basement apartment. He didn't realize it until the last minute, when he bent to unlock his door.

She came up behind him and pressed her body against his. "Why won't Mason pay attention to Cindy? Cindy just wants to play with Mason," she crooned, running her hands under his shirt. And so, with few words exchanged, Cindy and Mason played the rest of the night. She left, giggling, before dawn. Two nights later, she was back. And so it went, week to week, for the rest of the year. After the first time, he never failed to use a condom, despite her sometimes-desperate urging. She never failed to leave before first light. It suited him well, in spite of some groggy mornings. They never met at any other time or place, and he discouraged questions about family and history, although he was decently attentive otherwise. Cindy's requirement of Mason was the same as his of her. They just played and played. And Mason proved the old man wrong. He liked a woman just fine.

Why memories of his early life, especially of his father, would thrust themselves upon him at such odd times baffled and infuriated Mason. The very fact that they could, loaded with all the old freight of feelings, stir a rage so deep that he felt his hard-won control sometimes slip. He sat up straighter and glanced about. None of the few other people in the waiting room paid him the least attention. With a fierce jerk, he pulled Edward's notebook closer and frowned down at it.

Cartoons, M^1, G+ in a heart, IE^{2-HU}, drawn on an arrow. Stupid code. Why wouldn't Granger just say what he meant in his own damned book, for Pete's sake? Who was going to read his personal day-planner or whatever this tacky thing was? Mason had seen it in Granger's possession a thousand times. So had dozens of other people. Who cared?

But that raised another thought. Drake thumbed back through the loose-leaf notebook. The pages were only haphazardly numbered. He had to read closely and try to remember dates for the events noted there. A laborious fifteen minutes later, he saw there was a gap in time. Pages missing. Most of the pages were two years older than the last twenty or so. There was no mention of SB500 by name. And the silly doodles and arrows and other symbols became more numerous in those last pages. He leaned back and closed his eyes to wonder why.

CHAPTER SEVEN

Geneva's private moment of calm didn't come until the next morning at home. She pushed her coffee cup back and drew in a long breath, feeling both the old knife of grief frozen against her heart and a surge of joy as she opened Edward's last letter.

"My Darling Girl," he began as he always did. "Finished talking with the tribal council and some others a little while ago. Old Samuel John Begay—remember his mother was the famous weaver from out near Ganado in the forties—Mary Denetah, wasn't it?—old Samuel kept me standing out there in the wind for half an hour listening to his complaints about some quarry they want to put in Black Canyon. I still don't know whether it's a done deal or just his suspicions."

She put the page down for a moment, fingering the jade pendant hanging warm between her breasts, the half-heart that Edward had commissioned a Navajo goldsmith to make for their twentieth anniversary. Edward wore the other half. She sipped her coffee, hoping it would melt the tightness in her throat, and picked up the letter again.

"Sweetheart, right now I'm waiting for Harrison Billy to meet me here at the Council Chambers. Then we'll go to lunch if his daughter shows up with the truck. I believe Harrison's drinking days are really over, just as he said. He looks good.

"Funny thing—I think I just saw Mason with some others leaving the side door of the chairman's office and ducking back toward the end of the building. No. Couldn't be. He's in some special meeting in Phoenix. That's why he kept Mickey Barrow there and is sending a different plane and pilot for me tomorrow. Must have been somebody else with a fancy white Stetson, I guess."

Geneva put down the letter, frowning. Their last phone conversation the evening before Edward would have written this letter came back to her. Yes, he mentioned that Mason would be at an important meeting in Phoenix and couldn't attend Edward's re-election speech at Window Rock. She shook her head and continued reading.

"Geneva, I've learned—or think I've learned—something disturbing about SB500. You and Tucker and Desbah and the others worked so hard for it last May and June. But it could be that we trusted the wrong people from the beginning. Maybe you can find out something more about Albert Goldtooth, the older one, not the nephew by the same name that we met in Tuba City. He's to be in Flagstaff Wednesday morning at NAU for a meeting with the nephew and some others —including Mason—in the Havasupai Room. But that's all I know, except that it seemed to be hush-hush for some reason. Will you look into it at the university? Just find out who rented the meeting room, if you can. I should be back home Wednesday evening."

Now Geneva had to stop and wait for her tears to subside. She made no sound, just waited. When she could see his words again, she resumed reading.

"I wasn't supposed to hear this, apparently, but I think it has to do with some land deal on the reservation, a land-use decision Goldtooth wants to go a certain way. Maybe it's the quarry old Samuel is worried about. It looks like <u>Mason</u> could be in on it. I have a bad feeling about this, Gen."

She frowned and went back to the beginning. Twice Edward had underlined Mason's name. She gazed out the window and pondered for a long moment, but she knew nothing more about Mason's political activities now than Edward had that day three years ago. She lifted his letter once more.

Her eyes filled again as she touched his goofy cartoon signature, the one he always ended his letters to her with—a caricature of himself falling backward clasping his heart, from which rose a swirl of little I-love-you-imprinted butterflies. Silly, goofy, wonderful man. God, how she missed him.

Karen arrived the next afternoon with her children, Josh and Emily. "Mom, what did the doctor say?" She swung two-year-old Emily down from her hip saying, "Be careful," to Josh as he flung himself down on the couch next to his grandmother. Geneva laughed and pulled him close.

"I'm fine, Karen," Geneva said, nuzzling Josh's dark hair. "How do you like fourth grade, my beautiful boy? You started last week, didn't you?"

Karen made everyone lunch and Geneva heard all their news. When the children went out to the patio, Karen pulled a chair around to face her mother on the couch.

"All right, Mom. Tell. What made you suddenly take off for the rez? You just got back last Thursday from giving that speech in Seattle. Why the sudden trip to Window Rock?"

She held Geneva's gaze with her own worried hazel eyes, so like Edward's, Geneva thought for the thousandth time. Here was the direct, uncomplicated daughter, so unlike her twin. Better to explain it all to Karen and hope to make it sound reasonable and unimportant than to brave Julianna's rapid-fire questions and lawyerly delving that would leave mother and daughter equally exhausted.

Geneva pulled a sofa pillow under her knee and suppressed

a sigh. "Harrison Billy's daughter wrote me a note on his behalf asking me to come and see him." She raised her hand to stop Karen's questioning look. "Your father's old friend, a Navajo Code Talker—you've heard us talk about him. Anyway, Mr. Billy recently regained his sight and read the newspaper accounts of—the crash. He seemed to think the reports were . . . wrong somehow. And he remembered, after a long time, that Edward had given him his notebook to hold for him."

Karen's eyes grew wider every minute. "Dad's notebook? Why in the world would he do that? He wouldn't do that! Maybe this Harrison guy stole it or something. Anyway, did you get it back?"

A sudden weariness swept over Geneva. "Yes, I did. And, before you ask, I don't really know why he thought the news accounts of the crash were wrong. Not exactly."

She sketched out the rest of the events, the burning hogahn, the evening visit of the Navajo policeman, but skipped Harrison's repeating Edward's cryptic statements about the Phoenix man. Hearing her own words, she thought herself a coward for not telling her daughter all that Harrison had said. Nor did she mention the crystal-gazer, Ooljee Blackgoat, or her warning about the "waters and the airplanes." Or Edward's "thinking page" and its puzzling abbreviations and drawings. Neither did she mention Edward's last letter to her. Or his suspicions, now hers, about Mason Drake.

"Yes, I have Dad's notebook," she said in her end-of-story voice.

"Expecting a call, Mom? You keep looking at the phone. Are you sure you're all right?" Karen went to the patio door and stood watching the children for several minutes as her mother's assurances died away. "So," she said, returning to her seat, "the next morning you and Angie left Window Rock, went off to this Harrison's place way up there at Wheatfields, where he produced the notebook. And on the way, you climbed a mesa, watched a hogahn burn, sprained your ankle, and stayed all night in this old guy's place, where all of you were questioned by the police — about a murder! Is that right?"

"My goodness, you have a gift for making things sound dramatic."

But Karen's usual easygoing humor seemed to have deserted her. She flipped back one side of her chestnut hair in evident annoyance. "The only reasonable thing about all this is that Uncle Mason flew out there and brought you home."

"I'm expecting his call any minute," Geneva said. "Karen, there's no reason for concern. My ankle is not broken. And it's already feeling much better," she lifted her foot gingerly from the hassock and reached for the cane Harrison had given her. "Let me say good-bye to the kids. I think I might take a nap."

Before Karen left, Geneva gave her the film she'd taken and asked her to drop it off to be developed.

CHAPTER EIGHT

"Thank you for meeting me here, Lieutenant Nez." FBI agent Justin Fox extended his hand. Murder on a reservation fell under federal jurisdiction, but he didn't want to offend the local police who began the investigation.

"No problem." Nez shook hands and turned back to reach into the open door of his patrol car. "Here are the shots we took that afternoon. Good thing—it rained hard later that night."

Fox took the envelope but didn't open it. He stood at the edge of the road and looked toward the summit of the hill. "Up this way?"

Nez pointed to the left and they started the climb. At the top, they stopped and looked down on the charred hogahn.

"So, this is where the first witness saw the fire," Fox said. "Mrs. Granger, the senator's widow, wasn't it?"

"Right. She twisted her ankle up here, and the kid, Littleben, and Granger's friend—a woman named Sanchez— came up and helped her down to the van."

"Yes, I remember your notes from that evening. Wonder what she was doing here, anyway. Visiting with the old fellow, you said, but why?"

Nez shrugged. "I found out later she writes books about Indian education. Maybe she was talking to him about educating that grandson of his."

Glancing at Nez, Fox raised his eyebrows, then smiled. "All right. You said Mr. Billy went up a nearby hill. Will you point that out, please?"

Nez turned to the southwest and pointed. "Can't see all of it from here, but behind that little mesa there, is an old corral built right up against the rock. Billy said Professor Layton might have been over there sketching it. He expected to meet Layton out there that day. Had a package for him, he said."

Fox squatted and looked through his binoculars at the low ridge and the little hill beyond it. "But nobody saw either one of them there."

"No. All the witnesses said the old man was back at their vehicle when Mrs. Granger was brought down from here." Nez gestured toward the road below. "That's where he was when the Apache County sheriff got here."

"Mmm." Fox pulled the photos from the envelope, studying them one by one. "Okay. Let's go down and take a look at the hogahn."

They stopped several feet from the burned structure. Only part of one wall remained standing. Fox knelt and studied the ground on the east side, then stood and looked at several of the photographs again. "This is where the tire tracks were, right?"

Nez nodded. "We're still looking for Layton's Jeep."

"Yeah. That could take a while—twenty-seven thousand square miles of reservation." Fox gave a mirthless laugh. "But now we know he was dead before the fire. I want to see where you think the blaze started."

"It was all still pretty hot and smoky when I got here later that day. This is as far as I went before it got too dark—I didn't want to step on any evidence."

Fox looked closely at the place Nez indicated, then glanced again at the photo in his hand.

Just inside what had been the doorway, both men turned on their flashlights and shone them around the ruins.

"The tracks of the M.E.'s gurney where he rolled the body out are still pretty deep," Nez said. His beam played across the rutted dirt floor littered with charred slabs and shattered glass.

Fox turned slowly, scrutinizing the blackened debris on all sides. "I think you're right. Looks like the fire started over here near the door."

Fox squatted and shone his flashlight on a sodden mound of debris and ashes next to a square-ish outline of white ash about a foot in diameter. Four groups of tiny screws marked what might have been corners of a box. "Probably made of a lightweight wood," he said. "But it could have held some kind of trigger for this pile of stuff next to it." He pinched up some of the charred material and sniffed it. "Could've been rags soaked in an accelerant." With the tip of his pocket knife, he carefully dug out two steel balls the size of marbles. Near them, imbedded in the soot and ash, lay three small springs in a line, the last one connected to a bead chain mostly buried in the debris. He leaned aside for Nez to photograph them, then lifted them out and pulled up the chain.

Nez stood and trained his light along the chain rising from the dirt. It rippled up, dripping bits of debris across the doorsill.

"Take it from there," Fox said, indicating the threshold.

Outside, Nez lifted the chain. Nothing covered it now, but he continued to ease it upward, following it with his flashlight beam along the sand. A few yards away, next to a partially burned tree, the chain ended with another spring, this one bigger, lying against the trunk of the tree.

"Well, now," Fox said, crouching and focusing his flashlight on the spring. "Looks like it was tied to the tree with . . . what, Lieutenant, string?"

"What kind of a trap was that supposed to be?" Nez said.

Fox stood up and aimed his light on the other side of the

trunk. "The temporary kind, I think. Whoever rigged this up probably expected everything to be destroyed or covered over by debris, but here's a bit of the cord, a knot, I think. The chain might have been tied just above the ground so that somebody coming from where the vehicle was parked would have walked right into it, activating some sparking device in that box."

Nez pulled out a camera and took more pictures. "Clever in a way, but kind of juvenile, I'd say. A kid trick."

CHAPTER NINE

"Just as I thought," Mason said, helping himself to another slice of cake at Geneva's kitchen table a week later. "That IE$^{2\text{-HU}}$ thing was Edward's abbreviation for a bill that never got out of committee, and deservedly so." He took in Geneva's questioning look and held up a hand. "It was too watered down, Geneva. It would have been worse than nothing, believe me."

Geneva remembered the bitter disappointment they all suffered at the failure of SB500. "The Biggie," as Edward called the bill for Indian education reform, was defeated that summer, after which she and Edward took their long-promised trip to Europe for their thirtieth wedding anniversary. They had a wonderful time, and their efforts to forget that disappointment were mostly successful. Now Geneva thought again of their long fight for the bill's passage, how she and Desbah Chischilly and Tucker Bayless had gathered a group of educators from both the Navajo and Hopi reservations and lobbied for several days in Phoenix before the final vote. Some of them had given TV interviews and gone on radio talk shows trying to raise support. But it had failed.

Of course, for Geneva, Edward's death so soon afterwards had eclipsed everything else. She remembered little of the details of the vote or who had influenced whom at the time. At this moment, however, Edward's letter, his half-formed suspicions—or maybe just worry—came back to her. But Mason was still talking. She nodded and tried to look attentive.

He was saying that efforts after that to put forward similar measures even with all the influence he could muster, had gone nowhere.

So this IE$^{2\text{-HU}}$ wasn't Senate Bill 500. But why would another one have been in committee so soon, she wondered now for the first time. But she didn't ask Mason.

When she'd asked Mason who the Phoenix man Harrison had told her about might be, he had dismissed the question—and Harrison Billy—as utterly foolish.

And now, apparently finished with the subject of Edward's reference to IE$^{2\text{-HU}}$, Mason said, "Have you got another sales report on *The Longer Walk* from your publisher?"

She shook her head and picked up her fork.

The first year or so after Edward's death was like a prolonged drowning to Geneva. After that year, she had struggled, urged by the twins and others, including Mason, to finish her thesis. Her dissertation became, in large part, *The Longer Walk*, the book that gained the attention of not only the world of education, but a wider public as well.

The Longer Walk focused on the historical abuses in Indian education, children taken forcibly from their families and subjected to military-style conformity in the name of education—their hair cut short, their own clothes replaced by uniforms or other non-Indian clothing. And where harsh punishment came down on them for speaking their own languages. She brought to light not only the unwritten policies of stripping children of their "Indian-ness," but also the documented US government practices of "de-culture-ating" them.

But she had not again immersed herself in the uncertain, swirling waters of supporting legislative reform of Indian education. Losing SB500 and losing Edward were too much tied together.

Mason rose to replenish their coffee and frowned at her unfinished lunch he had brought. "You're tired, Geneva. I wish Harrison Billy had never brought any of this up—it's only upset you. Here, let me help you back to the living room. You're not still planning on doing that panel discussion next week with this bad ankle are you?"

Just then the telephone rang. Mason picked up the handset and passed it to Geneva as she settled onto the couch. "Yes," she said into the phone. "Can you hold on just a minute?"

She looked at Mason, who was gathering up his jacket and pantomiming departure.

He bowed and smiled. "I'll call you later. Get some rest!"

After the door closed behind him, Geneva returned to her call. "Desbah, thanks for calling me back. How was your sojourn in D.C.?"

Desbah Chischilly's rich voice bubbled with a laugh. "Too long! But I must be getting younger and prettier, can you believe it? One of those congressmen invited me to a late-night supper, followed by an, 'Ahem, *discussion* of the main points of your proposal, my deah—perhaps in my suite?' Red, white, black, or yellow, they never change, do they?"

Geneva laughed at her friend's mimicry of a male voice. "Certainly *you* change, Desbah, and always for the better. What do you think of the new director of the Minority Progress Office?"

"Ah, yes, Tom Calls His Horse—he's Lakota. And new to the political gamesmanship of Washington but catching on fast. We spent half a day going over my proposal, first at his office with his assistant, a really sharp Anglo-Apache woman, then with Congressman Toledo and two of his staff at a luncheon downtown. He's got some good advisors, I'll tell you that. Anyway, we can talk about it later. How about having an early dinner together? I'll be leaving Flagstaff tomorrow and going back home to Chinle."

After they'd agreed on a restaurant and time, Geneva made her way into her bedroom to rest her ankle, which was healing nicely, she thought. First, she wrote a note to Tucker and Shándíine and propped it next to her handbag to mail. Later she rose and changed clothes. The clumsy fabric "boot" and ankle brace the doctor made her wear slowed everything to a point well past nuisance, but she managed. Her hand was on the kitchen door that led into the garage when the telephone rang again.

"Mom, I picked up those pictures that you took on the reservation," Karen said. "Emily and I are on the way to Josh's soccer game. Shall I drop them off?"

"No, honey, I'm about to leave to meet Desbah at Black Bart's. But that's on your way to the field. How about meeting me there in twenty minutes? And yes," she said, anticipating Karen's next question, "I have the cell phone Julianna gave me. I'll call if I need you. Don't worry."

She was able to deflect Karen's objection to her driving alone by mentioning the advantages of automatic transmissions and beating the rush-hour traffic, and thus made her way to the restaurant, thinking only of dinner with her old friend.

Karen was already waiting for Geneva as she pulled into the parking lot. Karen lowered the window next to Emily in her car seat and came around to Geneva's car, leaned in to kiss her mother, and handed her the packet of photographs. "Gotta go," she said. "Ray is waiting for us at the field. Wave bye to Gramma, Emily!"

Relieved that Karen hadn't insisted on helping her into the restaurant, Geneva waited until her daughter's minivan was out of sight before gathering tote bag, purse, and Harrison

Billy's cane, then maneuvering herself into a reasonable walking position. "Freedom comes on Thursday," she muttered to herself. "Only a few more days of this damned hobbling."

Desbah Chischilly entered the restaurant a moment later and they embraced. "How's the lame and the halt?" she asked, at the same time nodding to the waiter holding up two fingers as a question.

"Just fine, Desbah. And clearly, you're better than ever." Desbah's warmth and enthusiasm always made Geneva grin. "Let's find a table with a lamp so I can show you the photos I took a couple of weeks ago up near Wheatfields."

When they'd ordered, Geneva started her tale of the mysterious note from Margaret Littleben and the trip to Wheatfields with Harrison Billy. She then caught her old friend looking at her oddly, her head slightly tilted to one side. Geneva stopped talking and returned the look, admiring, as always, Desbah's slightly Asian eyes and high cheekbones. Half a decade older than Geneva, Desbah Chischilly always turned heads when she entered a room. And this evening had been no different as they passed through to a secluded table toward the back of the restaurant. Her hair, still unmarked by gray, was no longer braided and coiled as it had been for years, but now cut short except for a long curving swoop that framed one cheek, a style that accentuated her beauty even more.

Tall and slender, Desbah moved with a dancer's grace. And even sitting, relaxed as she was now, she exuded such energy that Geneva wouldn't be surprised if she were to rise and pirouette the entire length of the dining room before Geneva could set her coffee cup down.

"What?" said Geneva, smiling. "Am I dithering? I told you all this on the phone, didn't I?"

"You did, but I don't mind your telling it again. But now I'm hearing something more. Something I haven't heard from you in a long while."

"What's that?"

"You're coming back," Desbah said.

Geneva opened her mouth to speak, and then closed it. "Am I?" she said, more to herself than to Desbah.

"You have something here to sink your teeth into. The fact that it involves Edward could pull you under again, but it isn't. I'm glad."

Geneva could only look at her friend. And wonder if she was right.

Desbah touched Geneva's hand that held the packet. "Let's see those pictures."

"I haven't seen them myself yet. Karen just brought them to me. Oh, here's Tucker meeting us at the airport in Window Rock. He always looks the same, doesn't he? And Angie Sanchez, of course. Now this is the view from the hill above the hogahn that burned. You can see the Chuskas—why doesn't a photograph ever do those mountains justice?" She handed the next one to Desbah without comment.

Desbah peered at the figure running away from the flaming hogahn and took the next photo and the next without lifting her gaze. She laid them side by side in front of her and studied them without speaking for several minutes.

"Here's one more." Geneva brought the last photo close to the lamp. "Look, he's twirling about. You can see those strips— Harrison said they might be animal skins—streaming out as he turned. And he's carrying a pair of sticks—batons, maybe, or rattles. What do you think?"

Just then the waiter appeared with their food, and they gathered the photos and moved them aside. When he'd gone, Desbah moved her plate away and spread the pictures again. "Yes. Probably tails, fox, maybe, or coyote tails. But something is wrong about the whole thing. If he is supposed to be dressed like a Yei dancer, or even like the usual notion of skin-walkers, he's got it all wrong. Look, that stick has feathers, I think, near the end, like an old-time war club. Anyway, do you think he started the fire?"

They speculated some more as they ate, and Geneva told Desbah the rest of the events of her visit to the Navajo Reservation.

"You say Edward's notebook entries went all the way up to the day before he got on that plane?"

Geneva nodded.

Desbah waited until the waiter had removed their plates and refilled their coffee, then pushed a small pad of paper toward Geneva. "Tell me again that abbreviation that he kept referring to. Show me just what it was and how he connected it with the other initials and such."

Geneva had studied those pages so much in the last weeks that she could reproduce Edward's "balloon webs" perfectly. When she finished sketching, she turned the pad around, and Desbah looked at it without speaking for a long time. "And the dates on these?"

"The first ones went back to the summer of that year, but there were several more together in the week before—he died." She lifted her eyes to see Desbah gazing at the pad, frowning.

"It's the big one," Desbah said. "SB500."

"Oh, no," Geneva waved a hand. "It can't be. You remember that it was defeated back in June that year. Mason said it couldn't possibly be that one."

"'Mason said. Mason said.' Geneva, are you in love with Mason Drake?"

Geneva's eyes widened. "No. No, I'm not."

Desbah didn't speak, merely glanced at her and then seemed to study the air somewhere past Geneva's head.

Desbah was the mistress, Geneva thought, of the eloquent silence. But she had learned not to jump into that silence and seem to protest too much. She stirred her coffee and tried to look as contemplative as Desbah did.

It was Desbah who finally spoke. "These sketches of Edward's don't have to reflect the time it was going on, Geneva. What if he was simply working out something that had happened in the past? Ideas he was connecting then to explain events that had happened some time, any time, in the past?"

Geneva felt stunned. Of course. Why hadn't she seen it? Edward was always doing that, mixing thoughts, as we all do, of past, present, and future. It was his own brand of free-flowing notes, not a report for anyone else. Why hadn't she remembered that? Was she losing . . . losing what? Her habit of calling up every detail she could of his face, his laugh, his touch, reliving every memory of him . . . it was what sustained her. Could she be losing her grasp of Edward, letting him slip away? Why hadn't she remembered how he jotted and doodled and scratched unrelated things down in his notebook?

"Come back," Desbah said.

Geneva blinked. "Yes," she said, uncertain of the question.

Desbah smiled. "Stop thinking in a straight line." She pushed the pad back to Geneva. "You must remember how we all fought for that bill. You organized Tucker and four other teachers. I got the BIA director and that Hopi superintendent from Tuba City, and we all lobbied in Phoenix for days before the vote."

Geneva nodded. Edward had orchestrated their meetings with key senators and they'd all been so sure...

"So tell me, Geneva. Where was Mason Drake during that time? He was perfectly recovered by then, practicing law practically next door, and supposedly throwing all his influence behind us, remember?"

"Of course I remember. He'd been in the senate for years before his accident. We saw him almost every day we were there. He still had his powerful friends and he did all he could to get that bill passed."

Desbah was quiet for a time. Finally, she leaned forward, forearms crossed on the table. "No, Geneva, he didn't. He was certainly on hand, but Tucker and I found out later that

Mason's mighty influence was brought to bear against the bill, not for it."

The vivid memory of Mason's look—his terrible look—when Geneva had sat speechless and shocked at his proposal of marriage last Christmas, flashed into her mind. But it was only his disappointment, his shock, she was sure, caused by her rudeness—her absolute incomprehension of the idea—that brought his expression of, of—God, what was it?

"Geneva, what is it?" Desbah leaned forward, her hand on Geneva's arm. "Hey, wake up!"

After a moment, Geneva pulled her purse onto her lap and took out Edward's letter she'd found in his notebook. "Desbah, I need to tell you something."

She unfolded the letter to the second page. "Edward thought there was a kind of secret meeting here in Flagstaff at the university about a land deal, maybe a quarry in Black Canyon. He asked me to find out who rented a meeting room at the NAU student union earlier on the day before he was supposed to return."

"I knew about that Black Canyon quarry deal," Desbah said. "There was a real stink about it for a while, then it died away. But I don't know how it was actually resolved. Or whether, come to think of it."

She gave Desbah the page. "But read the rest of this page."

"Old Goldtooth," Desbah said after a moment's reading. "We thought he was on our side, too. Remember those speeches he used to give about Indian education reform? I don't hear much about him these days. But, Geneva, I haven't heard anything at all lately about the quarry, either. It must be a dead issue." She looked at Geneva and gave a little shrug.

"This thing about Mason ducking behind buildings, now that's interesting," Desbah said. "Edward must have suspected him of having his fingers in it."

Geneva felt a wave of exhaustion. "I think I'd better go home now."

Geneva and Desbah embraced again in Black Bart's parking lot and went their separate ways. Desbah would return to her niece's house for a few hours' sleep before her "miserably early" flight back to Four Corners at Farmington, and then nearly three more hours' drive to Chinle. Geneva would return home to lie waiting for even fewer hours of sleep.

CHAPTER TEN

Police Lieutenant Charles Nez finished his third telephone conversation with his wife that morning, trying to calm her fears that their infant daughter had a cold. As the oldest of seven, he knew a thing or two about babies. But Claudine, herself a surprise baby born two years after her brothers were grown and gone, had never been around babies before. He sighed and crossed the hall near his office door in the Window Rock Police Department in time to hear the fax machine whir into action.

He withdrew the fax as it slid into the tray and began reading as he walked back to his desk. So, it was confirmed. The dental records showed that the body in the burned Peshlakai hogahn was that of Allen Jerome Layton, PhD, chairman of the Anthropology Department at Arizona State University. Until now Nez's inquiries about his being missing had turned up only the confirmation from his department that he was indeed on a trip to the Navajo Reservation. That, and a remark by Layton's brother-in-law: "Something he does all the time — who knows where the hell he goes?"

Nez laid this page next to the autopsy report on his desk. No evidence of fire or smoke in the lungs. So. Layton had died before the fire. But how long before? He'd been stabbed just below the right shoulder blade, probably not the fatal wound. But the right carotid artery had been slashed. Likely a left-handed assailant, the medical examiner said.

As Nez reached for the folder to file the pages, his next steps outlined themselves in his mind.

He would call his friend in the Maricopa County Sheriff's department and ask him to visit Layton's sister and break the news.

Next, he'd send word through Claudine's cousins at Tohatchi for her mother to come tonight with her bundles of medicinal herbs. To placate Claudine and discharge his duties to his mother-in-law. The baby, he was sure, was allergic to the new kitten, just as he was.

He reached for the telephone. Justin Fox would be here in less than an hour, probably with all this information and more. At least Fox was a decent white guy, not like a couple other FBI agents Nez had worked with.

And then they might visit the old Code Talker, Harrison Billy, together.

CHAPTER ELEVEN

"Hello? Is this Dr. Granger?" The young female voice on the phone sounded tremulous, uncertain. "This is Millie Bayless. Maybe you remember me from when you came to my graduation?"

"Of course, I remember you, Millie. But you've always called me Aunt Geneva. Why so formal?" Geneva pushed her breakfast away and leaned forward. "How are you, honey?"

"Aunt Geneva, yes. I'm all right," the girl said, seeming to relax. "We got your letter. My mom wants you to come and see her. My dad has laryngitis and asked me to phone you."

"Well, I'm glad you've called. And I do want to come and see your mom—see all of you. Is your mother feeling better?" The second she asked it, Geneva wished she hadn't. Shándiíne Bayless was not going to feel better. Not ever.

Millie hesitated. "Not much. But she wants to see you. Can you come this weekend? My dad says he sounds like a bear, but he won't bite." Her giggle sounded more nervous than amused.

Geneva agreed to arrive on Friday afternoon and hung up, feeling a slow dread grow in her heart. But no flash of impending disaster for Shándiíne and her family.

She called both her daughters and told them her plans. "You remember that I have that panel discussion at the Chinle chapter house Monday evening. I'll stay with Desbah for a couple more days and be home probably Wednesday. If otherwise, I'll phone."

Early Friday morning Geneva packed her car, making certain to put in the cell phone and its charger that Julianna had given her. What a great gadget to have, she thought. Why she had resisted for so long, she didn't know. At least one good thing had come out of having a bollixed ankle. She stood for a minute beside her desk, and then took Edward's notebook from a drawer and added it to her briefcase. She would go to Desbah's house on Sunday after her visit with the Baylesses. They would talk more about Edward's pages of "thought balloons."

She also put Harrison's carved cane in the car. The aspens would still be splendid in the Chuskas now in early October. She might drive up to Wheatfields and return it to him, particularly if Desbah would go with her.

This time Geneva didn't call Mason to let him know her plan. She was still struggling to believe he had worked against SB500 four years ago, as Desbah said. For the weeks since, she'd tried hard not to think about the significance of that. It would have been a betrayal of Edward, betrayal of all of them. She wondered if Mason could really have done such a thing. And what of the worries about his old friend Edward had expressed in his last letter to her?

She'd avoided Mason since her visit with Desbah in the restaurant. It hadn't been hard to do, since he'd been in Phoenix for most of that time. He was due back tomorrow, however, and she was glad to be driving out of Flagstaff now, watching the last glowing wisps of fog languishing in the tall pines along the Interstate. And she needed to think.

She hadn't seen Millie since June. Nor Shándííne, except briefly in the Phoenix hospital last summer, but they'd exchanged phone calls and a letter or two. She tried to think of the last time she had been to the reservation before the Labor Day visit.

Oh, yes, it was the quick run in July to the tribal offices with Desbah. She'd been researching the history of the Christian schools on and near the reservation beginning in the late 1800s. The two women had been on their way to Mesa for some meeting. She remembered calling but failing to reach anybody at the Bayless home and learning only later that Shándiíne was in the hospital in Phoenix and her family was with her.

"Too many such misses," she muttered. She resolved to make up for neglecting her old friends.

Some hours later, Geneva passed under the wrought-iron arch that bore the Navajo word for "Blue Wind" at the top. Shándiíne had designed it just before Millie was born, and Tucker had found a famous ironworker near Corrales, New Mexico, to make it. Geneva couldn't pronounce the Navajo term, but knew it had something to do with the tiny whorls on the soles of a newborn baby's feet. Maybe she'd ask Shándiíne to tell her the story again. She stopped and got out of the car.

"Come in this house!" Tucker's boisterous greeting came out in a croak. His daughter stood behind him, smiling as shyly as a six-year-old, but looking more like a super model. Millie's elegant face was framed by brown hair that glinted auburn in the slanting sun. Geneva reached out for her, and the girl came into her arms, but withdrew quickly.

Geneva's gaze went past them both to the hospital bed in the living room and Shándiíne's gaunt frame, aslant against the pillows. She was so thin! And her face, a noticeable yellow, looked pinched with pain. Geneva approached, hoping her feelings didn't show in her own face.

A needle in Shándiíne's arm fed a clear liquid from a bag hanging from a metal rack. Behind the bed a monitor of some kind blinked silently. The beautiful Navajo woman didn't speak, but wet her lips and gave Geneva a quick smile. It was her friend's eyes, though, that wrenched Geneva's heart. Those wide-set brown eyes, so lively and inquisitive all the years Geneva had known her, were now flat and dull. A queer flush marked her sculpted cheekbones, contrasting with the yellowish hue of the rest of her face.

"So glad you came," Shándiíne whispered. "Sit down."

Geneva turned away trying to compose her features, fearing that her shock must show. She made much of helping Tucker guide a chair to the bedside and greeting Shándiíne's mother, Bertha Yazzie.

Mrs. Yazzie barely nodded at her and stepped to the other side of the bedside table, hands folded under her apron. She seemed to be guarding her daughter. Tucker seemed unable to find what to do with his hands and hovered at the doorway, straightening things on a low table.

"Mom," Shándiíne said, "maybe you and Tucker can fix us some tea and toast?"

Tucker, clearly relieved to have a task, beckoned to his mother-in-law and Millie. "Right. Come on, Mom Yazzie, help Millie and me make some toast and that good herb tea of yours."

"Tell me about your life," Shándiíne said when they had gone. Her smile seemed to hurt her lips, shining as they were with ointment. "Another book coming out?"

Geneva covered her friend's hand with her own. "Oh, Shándiíne, forgive me for not coming more often."

Shándiíne closed her eyes and shook her head. "No need. But I have something to ask you to do." She glanced toward the kitchen and took a breath. "It's important. Millie must go to college where she planned to, in California. Now she says she won't. I know it's because of me. She —"

At this moment Mrs. Yazzie came to the bedside and set a tray down hard, rattling the teapot and cups. She frowned at Geneva, who looked up into an older, much sterner version of

Shándiíne's elegant face. Accepting a cup and wondering how the woman had accomplished the task so quickly, Geneva stood and moved aside to let her raise Shándiíne's head and place a glass straw into Shándiíne's mug of tea.

"Thanks, Mom," Shándiíne said and smiled a bit, clearly waiting for the older woman to leave. But Bertha Yazzie only stepped toward the head of the bed, out of her daughter's view, and frowned even harder at Geneva, taking her seat again. After about a minute of this, and Shándiíne's continued silence, Geneva stood.

"Maybe I should let you rest a bit," she said, even as Shándiíne's almost desperate eyes begged her to stay.

Mrs. Yazzie nodded. "Yes. My daughter is tired now."

"That's all right," Tucker called from across the room. "I'll just get you settled in the studio." He took Geneva's tea, set it on the table, and scooped up her bags. "Let's go out through the kitchen there, Geneva."

Geneva looked back to see Mrs. Yazzie bringing a wedge of toast up to her daughter's lips, and again turning her frown toward Geneva and Tucker. Millie stood at the far end of the living room, her expression unreadable to Geneva.

Tucker didn't speak until he opened the door of Shándiíne's studio some little distance behind the house.

"I'm sorry as hell, Geneva. Sometimes the old biddy gets like that. I think she's run off two or three of Shándiíne's friends already. Especially the Anglo ones."

Geneva now took a good look at her old friend. They stood under a broad skylight and enough of the late afternoon sun that she could see clearly the shadows and lines under his eyes. The bushy beard hid most of his face, but she could still see the tightness of his forehead and new sprigs of gray in his beard and hair.

"This is terrible for you and Millie, I know. I'm so sorry, Tuck."

They passed into the bedroom area of the studio and he set

down her bags. "Millie and Bertha dusted this all up for you, Geneva. There's the thermostat, you remember. You've got an electric blanket—it'll get pretty chilly tonight."

Then he dropped into an armchair near the window. "The old woman can be a tyrant, sure enough. But I know she's all torn up about Shándiíne. Just like Millie and I are. I try not to cross her—for Shándiíne's sake."

"I understand. Of course. And I'll be glad for a little rest before dinner. Anything I can do to help?"

"No. Just being here is good for us. Ignore the old crow if you can. I'll try to draw her off so you two can talk. She does insist on doing the cooking, so give it an hour and come back in. While she's fixing supper is your best chance."

He left then and Geneva watched through the window as he trudged back to the house. The set of his shoulders told it all, she thought.

She slipped off her shoes and stretched out on the bed. And wondered what it was that Shándiíne seemed so desperate to tell her.

The tidy bedroom was a little appendage at the end of the almost bare, sky-lighted studio, where Shándiíne had painted her exquisite, stylized animals and famous floating dancers for so many years. It held other memories as well for Geneva. Edward had helped Tucker build the studio along with Tucker's friend Chee Hamilton, who became their friend, too, that summer. The Grangers' motor home and Chee's painted teepee appearing in her yard had fascinated five-year-old Millie. The sixteen-year-old Granger twins found their fascination in Chee's successive pairs of brawny nephews come to help. Geneva smiled with the memories. She, Desbah, and Shándiíne cooked endless meals for the workers, ran often to Gallup or Window Rock for supplies, and generally had a wonderful time for two months that summer. It was during those weeks, Geneva and Edward felt sure, that Desbah and Chee fell in love. But that August, Chee went back to his post in Saudi Arabia and, to Geneva's knowledge, had not returned. Desbah often spent her summers in one foreign country or another, where the two would meet, Shándiíne said. Geneva didn't know what tickled her more—that tidbit of gossip or Shándiíne's rare glee in the telling.

Geneva wondered now if she could have looked into Shándiíne's beautiful, laughing eyes on one of those happy days and seen a glimpse of those eyes as they were today, haunted with pain and worry.

No. Thank God we cannot see our future, she thought. Mostly, anyway.

Instead she pictured Edward's tall form above her, framed by bare rafters and blue sky, reaching down for a board, then catching sight of her standing below with a pitcher of lemonade. And smiling down at her with such love. She lifted her eyes now to the ceiling. These very beams, maybe.

She and Edward had slept here during many visits after moving to Flagstaff. She closed her eyes and began to drift toward sleep.

Without thought, she moved her hand to the empty side of the bed. The cold side. A flood of desire made her eyes fly open again. She'd stopped doing that at home. No more half-asleep reaching out for the warm certainty of his body. It had taken months and a variety of efforts. Planting herself firmly in the middle of the bed did no good. Piling up books and magazines, even her laptop, in his place helped some. Finally, she'd let her agent arrange book signings and talks all over the country. Sleeping in hotels and occasional overnights or weekends with friends like the one in Nantucket who now wanted her to come and spend a month—it all helped. Only by replacing their bed at home had she finally cured herself, "de-fanged" this treacherous little sniper of her hard-won emotional recovery. She thought. But here, in this private bedroom where they had always enjoyed a special "sex date" when they visited, she felt desire.

She got up, found the book in her bag and sat down in the overstuffed rocker. But she didn't open the book. Three years, she thought. And she had been here alone several times during that period. She wondered what had really triggered this rush of feeling. It hadn't been swallowed in the pain of missing Edward. Not this time.

A fragment of a line in one of Edna Millay's poems floated up: "...*the poor treason of my stout blood against my staggering brain . . .*"

The chance to talk with Shándíine did come as Tucker said it would an hour later. Seated again at her friend's bedside, Geneva took Shándíine's cold hands in her own and waited. Tucker had hustled Millie into the kitchen with him to help her grandmother, and the room was quiet. Shándíine wet her lips and took a breath.

"I want you to help Tucker get Millie away from here when I die. To California. As quick as you can. They can go on to Laguna Beach and rent a little place we know there until the next semester begins. They can hike and sail and heal." She took another long breath and closed her eyes.

Geneva waited.

"Tucker and I have talked about it, and he promised. But there is going to be trouble. Even though he doesn't believe it."

She had to rest again for several minutes. Tears trickled down the sides of her face. Geneva gently blotted them away. Again, Shándíine drew a ragged breath.

"My mother and aunt mean to fight Tucker for Millie. For Millie and this place."

Now Geneva couldn't keep silent. "What? But Millie is not a minor, and this place is not even on reservation land! It's private land, isn't it?"

"You don't understand. Please. They are very strong.

They've turned against Tucker and mean to get Millie away from him when I die. Please. Help him take our daughter away from here. He can fight the property lawsuit—and there will be a suit, I can tell you, because of some money my aunt says we never paid back, even though we did. Years ago. That's not important. It's—" Here a fit of coughing turned her face to flame and brought Mrs. Yazzie and Tucker on the run.

"For Millie!" Shándiíne gasped, even as her mother pushed both Tucker and Geneva aside and pulled Shándiíne into a sitting position. "Promise me, Geneva!"

Geneva nodded. "I promise," she mouthed, reluctant for Mrs. Yazzie to hear.

"Get away!" the old woman hissed. "Get away!" She pulled the oxygen mask into place and covered Shándiíne's mouth and nose.

By the time Shándiíne had quieted and seemed to slip into sleep, Aunt Nedra Roanhorse and her two daughters-in-law arrived. Both Millie and Tucker were obliged to take their coats and answer their questions. Geneva stood watching Shándiíne for a few more minutes and then prepared to go back to the studio for the night. Without a word, both older women stepped in front of her. Tucker had brought her jacket and stood holding it out to her. The two women bent twin frowns on Geneva. Reaching to take her jacket from him, Geneva stopped, surprised.

"You should go home tomorrow," said Bertha. "You made my daughter cry. She only needs her family now."

Tucker stepped forward. "Oh, no, that's not true, Bertha. You know how easily Shándiíne cries nowadays. It wasn't Geneva's—"

"Tomorrow morning." Without a glance at him, Bertha and her sister turned as one and went to Millie, who was coming toward the little group with a questioning look. They turned her around and went toward the couch in the far end of the living room where the other relatives waited.

Tucker helped Geneva on with her jacket and the two went through the kitchen, where he picked up the covered supper tray Millie had prepared for Geneva. They walked without speaking to the studio.

"To hell with them, Geneva," he said, closing the studio door behind them. "You know you are welcome to stay as long as you like. It's less than two hours to Desbah's place in Chinle. You don't have to go until Sunday afternoon, just like you planned."

"Oh, Tucker. Of course, I know. But they're all upset. And they're right—family is what is important now. They don't need any other reason for wanting that."

He looked at her with fresh misery in his eyes. She wondered if she should bring up Shándiíne's remarkable request but dismissed the thought.

Tucker gestured toward the house. "They'll all be gone Tuesday and Wednesday, Geneva. Even Mama Yazzie, because she's taking Millie to Gallup to get her picture made, something Shándiíne made her promise to do. And before that, there's a dress to buy and a trip to the beauty shop." He opened the bedroom door and turned on a lamp. "Then they're going to go spend the night with some of Millie's cousins and aunties clear out there by Church Rock. Shándiíne wants Millie—and Mom Yazzie—to get out of here and have some relief. Especially Millie. She wants her to have a chance to practice her driving, too. So, promise you'll come back and see us on your way home."

Geneva promised another promise.

CHAPTER TWELVE

B idding good-bye first to Shándiíne, whose eyes seemed less worried and then on the porch to Millie the next morning was brief but pleasant. Millie, too, seemed more relaxed and even talkative. Mrs. Yazzie only hovered on the edge of things, and soon went inside.

And Tucker, after he put her things in the car, gave her his old bear hug. "Don't forget, Geneva. Mama Yazzie and Aunt Nedra will be taking Millie to Gallup and then at least one overnight at Church Rock, so the coast is clear for you and Shándiíne to have a good visit on Tuesday."

Geneva, too, felt more relaxed as she drove, but she had some thinking to do. The pretty scenery and few vehicles on Arizona Highway 264 from Window Rock to Ganado flew past her notice. Any doubt of Shándiíne's lucidity had vanished the night before, when Geneva saw the hostile looks on the faces of Bertha Yazzie and Nedra Roanhorse. The sisters meant her to leave, yes, but more important was their complete disdain of Tucker, who stood only a yard away. They didn't pretend to speak for him or to him in dismissing Geneva. Was it always so? Maybe Shándiíne was right in saying they had turned against Tucker.

Just before the entrance to the little Sage Memorial Hospital at Ganado, Geneva's lane of traffic stopped. Oncoming vehicles moved slowly and only at the signal of a policeman. Two Navajo police cars stood with lights flashing on the side of the road. Behind her, a cattle truck squealed to a stop. Ahead, two men stepped out of their vehicles. "What's going on, Officer?" one of the men called to another policeman hurrying down the driveway of the hospital toward them.

The second man stepped up on the running board of his pickup and leaned over the open door. "We going to be here long?"

The policeman crossed in front of Geneva's car and beckoned to them and the truck driver behind her, who jumped down from his rig. Geneva lowered her window and returned the officer's nod as he came alongside.

"Pretty bad wreck," he said, lifting his arm straight up and waving his hand westward. "Junction with 191. North side. We're letting cars off to go south by Hubbell. You can get off there or wait here. Might be a while."

She could hear the trucker swear as he climbed back into his cab.

Remembering that Hubbell Trading Post had been a favorite Sunday drive destination of her family, she said, "I'll go to Hubbell and wait."

The policeman nodded and signaled to the other officer directing traffic. "Ones going south on 191 can pass through in a few minutes. Taking turns now with east bound." With that, he strode toward the line of new arrivals behind the cattle truck.

The Granger twins, as children, had loved going to Hubbell, where they could always count on others their age to play with in the little park. As teenagers, they would hurry to the jewelry counters, hoping to add to their collection of turquoise and silver. Here Edward bought the splendid Teec Nos Pos rug that hung now in their bedroom in Flagstaff. She thought of another big rug once displayed on the wall here, woven by Navajo women in the 1920s or earlier, who used the label on a can of Del Monte peaches as their pattern. Astonishingly expensive even eighteen years ago. She remembered Edward saying, "Eat your heart out, Andy Warhol, the Navajo ladies at Hubbell beat you to it by half a century."

She came out of her reverie with a start when the trucker behind her sounded his air horn. The cars ahead had already moved on.

When she reached the rambling stone trading post, she was glad to get out of the car and stretch. The old Hubbell homestead looked the same—a long, flat-roofed building with some haphazard appendages trailing out behind, all of it standing in a bare dirt yard. But the several window frames and the broad door frame of the store had been painted white. Progress, she thought, that might have come with the National Historical Site designation. She wandered around a bit, noting how much the trees in the little park across the ditch had grown. Despite the chilly day, the sun drove the fragrance of sage and chamisa into the air.

Geneva turned back to the store and noticed wagon wheels standing against two of the windows. An oxen yoke hung above the doorway, and above it, a bleached skull—probably that of the poor ox, Julianna would always say. As she stepped inside, the sagging wood floor creaked as it always had.

In the dim light of the store, Geneva could make out a tiny Navajo woman about her own age, standing in the aisle facing her. The woman took a step forward. As Geneva's eyes adjusted, she could see the woman was smiling at her. She fairly beamed with glee, excitedly pushing her glasses back in place on her nose several times. Her straight hair, which she wore in a single braid, shone glossy black, Geneva noticed, and resisted touching her own graying mop.

"Geneva? Geneva Granger? Is it you? I saw you get out of your car. What are you doing here?"

"Bessie Jim! My old teaching partner! How are you?"

They came together for a quick hug and Geneva blinked back sudden tears. She noticed Bessie's eyes glistened, too, above her wide smile.

Catching each other up on their lives for the last three years, the two women meandered toward the back, avoiding other shoppers in the narrow, twisting aisles. They found themselves in the rug room, where an elderly white couple looked through a thick pile of rugs draped over a peeled log support.

Geneva explained how she came to be at Hubble this morning. "How about you? Here to sell your beadwork? I still have that gorgeous hatband you made for me . . . when? Sixteen years ago?"

"No, I don't have much time for beading right now. I'm here just waiting for my brother. He's over there at Sage Hospital, getting some tests for his allergies, but I didn't want to wait there. He'll be here soon to pick me up and take me back to Chinle. Our uncle might be finished repairing my new truck. Two nights ago, somebody loosened the oil pan plug and let all the oil drain out."

Before Geneva could ask why anyone would do that, Bessie bowed her head and moved closer.

"Everybody was so sorry about Edward," said Bessie in a soft voice. "And we'd all been together down in Phoenix just that June." She wagged her head slowly. "You know, Edward got my dad's army pension for my mom, after all the years she had tried. Did you know that?"

Geneva shook her head. "Maybe. I must have forgotten."

"Not only that," Bessie said, "but he got her more help for my little sister that has the MS. He got the army people to give her a new wheelchair with special controls. They still live up there in Black Canyon. My mom really cried when she heard about the crash. Especially for my nephew that flew the plane, of course. But for Edward, too."

Geneva blinked. "Your nephew? The plane?"

"Daniel. You know, the pilot. Daniel Ashi was my nephew. I think my brother Andrew —not Harold, the one you know— Andrew will never get over it. He hasn't yet. And Daniel's mother . . . well. It's such a shame."

"Ashi?" Geneva said. "No, that couldn't be. I mean, the newspapers said the pilot was a Daniel Greenshields from somewhere up north. Montana, I think."

Bessie shook her head vigorously. "Oh, no. It was my nephew Daniel from right there in White Cone. He was so proud to have a job flying again." She leaned closer to Geneva. "The poor boy got into some trouble and had been in prison down by Phoenix for two years. But he was still a good pilot. He'd been doing some different jobs for Senator Drake and Mickey Barrow, that other pilot, around the airplanes. Mr. Drake gave Daniel that job just the day before. And Daniel called his dad and mom right away. He was so happy."

Geneva stood still. The words from Edward's notebook came back: "*Different pilot tomorrow. Drake has some other job for Mickey.*"

But the newspapers had said the pilot was Daniel Greenshields. From Montana.

Bessie was off to another subject. She always reminded Geneva of a cricket, so small and lively—and likely to jump in any direction.

Geneva should have kept up with old friends on the reservation better, she thought now. Edward's death had thrown her into such a dark cellar for so long. She and Bessie had been close, not just fellow faculty members. They had spent time in each other's homes, taken trips together. Bessie's daughter— what was her name? Charlene, yes. Charlene was several years younger than the Granger twins, but she always went to Phoenix and Albuquerque shopping with all of them. The twins called her their "little sister."

Geneva felt as if she was just coming up from that dark cellar into the light. She had the urge to hug Bessie again.

But a vision of whiteness and smears of crimson struck her. Snow. Cold, cold, burning snow. She blinked. It was gone. She looked at Bessie, who stood quiet, still smiling a little, waiting.

Bessie cocked her head sideways and raised an eyebrow. "I know you're good friends with Mason Drake."

Geneva suppressed a little start. Bessie was again a jump ahead of her. Had she missed the beginning of this topic?

"Well, yes. Mason was Edward's friend, a good friend—of the family. My girls think the world of him. Yes."

"He's your friend, too? I mean, now is Senator Drake your special friend?"

Again, Bessie was off in another direction.

"Special? What do you mean, Bessie? If you mean something like a romantic connection, then no. He is not my special friend."

Bessie nodded. "Well, then, I want to tell you something. Maybe you remember Albert Goldtooth on the tribal council. He went with us to Phoenix that summer to lobby for SB500. Remember?"

"Yes, of course."

"Well, old Goldtooth and Mason Drake, too, have been working to get a quarry put in Black Canyon where my mom lives. That black rock is something the highway contractors really like because it's so hard. But Goldtooth and Drake have fooled the people in Black Canyon into thinking the quarry won't ruin their year-round creek." She stopped and looked around, then lowered her voice even more.

"There are only about seventy families in the whole canyon, and they run their cattle there because it has grass and water. But the quarry will foul the creek and ruin the canyon. The people just don't know it. I've been going from house to house explaining what this quarry is going to do to them. I've got almost all their signatures, just a few more to go, and I mean to take them to the council next week. And the newspapers."

"Bessie! I had no idea! You're doing something important here."

"Well, I've had some good help." Bessie leaned close again as if to share a confidence. "There's a professor from ASU at Tempe. Jerome Layton." She smiled and lowered her eyes, such a maidenly portrayal of a sweet secret that Geneva almost laughed. "He helps me. He's teaching me about interviewing." Here Bessie glanced away, failing to hide her happy embarrassment.

"So." Geneva tilted her head and tried to make Bessie meet her eyes. "Does that mean, Bessie, that *you* have a special friend?"

At that moment a male version of Bessie stuck his head in and beckoned to her. "Come on, sister. I'll take you to see about your truck now."

Geneva held out her hand. "Hello, Harold. It's been a while."

Harold ducked his head, but shook her hand. "Yah-ta-hey."

"Bessie, I'm going to be at the chapter house for that panel discussion Monday night. Will you be there?"

"I will." Bessie gave Geneva another quick hug. "See you there."

"See you there, Bessie."

"They poisoned my dogs, too," Bessie called over her shoulder as she hurried after her brother. "Came right into the fenced yard to do it. They don't want me to tell on them."

CHAPTER THIRTEEN

"I tell you, Desbah, I can't get it out of my mind," Geneva followed her friend into the guest room and set her suitcase on the floor. "Bessie Jim insisted her nephew was the pilot—and she would know, after all, wouldn't she?"

"Come on into the kitchen, Geneva." Desbah set Geneva's computer on a nearby table.

Geneva laid her brief case on the bed and followed Desbah into the kitchen.

"We heard about Danny Ashi from White Cone, certainly," Desbah said, turning off the burner under the rattling teakettle. "I just thought at the time that the Phoenix paper got his name wrong. And we were all so upset by Edward's death— Tuck and the others who knew him—I didn't think any more about what the newspapers might have said later, about either Ashi or Greenshields. We can find out, of course. But why is that important now, Geneva?"

Why indeed, Geneva thought. "It's not terribly important, I suppose," she said, watching Desbah adding tea to the pot. "But there have been so many little surprises lately. Harrison Billy saying Edward told him that—that somebody wanted him dead, Desbah! Maybe the accident wasn't an accident at all. And Harrison's having Edward's notebook. And what I'd believed about Mason and SB500! Don't you think all this is adding up to something? Something really frightening about Edward's death?"

Desbah poured the tea into mugs. "Could be." She stood, went to the counter and picked up a writing pad near the telephone. "Let's get all this down—what you know, or need to know, anyway." Sitting down again, she flipped to a fresh page. "And let's start with Senate Bill 500. I'm sure that's what Edward's cryptic $IE^{2\text{-}HU}$ means." She wrote SB500 and $IE^{2\text{-}HU}$ with a big equal sign between them.

"The pilot's name." Geneva tapped the page. "Why the wrong name in the media? And why did Edward give Harrison his day planner, his notebook? That one really has me stopped."

Desbah wrote fast, and in a few minutes, they had a list of questions. Then she sat back. "Geneva, Edward had to know something. Something that somebody didn't want him to know."

"Or do," Geneva said. "What might somebody not want Edward to do?"

The two women looked at each other for a moment without speaking.

"Oh, God, Desbah. The election!" Geneva stood up so fast that she bumped the table hard, sloshing their tea. "Is that possible?"

By ten o'clock that night Geneva had answers to two of her questions. Or rather three possible answers for two questions. She had researched the online newspaper archives of both *The Gallup Independent* and *The Navajo Times*. Sure enough, on the screen before her were the obituary and photo of Daniel Ashi of White Cone, a round-faced young Navajo with a tiny mustache, taken, the *Times* article said, at his sister's wedding only two months before his death.

In the airplane crash that also killed Senator Edward Granger.

The Phoenix and Flagstaff newspapers carried the front-page stories of Edward's death that Geneva remembered all too well. They both listed a Daniel Greenshields as the pilot. And a long obituary of Edward, much of it written by her sons-in-law, who had spared their wives and Geneva that job, and—God help me, she thought—by Mason Drake.

Mason. This time she had to think it through. Mason was their friend. She couldn't count the times he'd helped every member of her family. The good times that he had been part of for so many years. Skiing trips, family parties. He'd helped Julianna find an obscure scholarship to finish her law degree and advised her about the clerkship with T. J. Chastain, who now sat on Arizona's Supreme Court. That clerkship had helped her in many ways. Karen's husband, Ray Medina, owed his start in business to Mason's advice about the Small Business Administration. Mason had been Edward's best friend for all these years.

Most of all, she couldn't erase the image of the agony in his face and rain-soaked form nearly collapsing at her door the night he brought the news of Edward's plane crash.

She'd been sorry to hurt him last Christmas when he proposed marriage, but she believed or wanted to believe even now, that his motive was only a desire to help Edward's widow, the twins' mother. There had never been the least hint of romance between the two of them.

But Edward's worry in his letter. Bessie's suspicions. Desbah's flat statement that Mason had worked against SB500. Mason had lied.

The next day, Sunday, passed quickly, the first half lazy and relaxed, the afternoon a happy chaos of Desbah's sisters, nieces, nephews, and a tribe of miscellaneous children come to visit.

By the time Geneva came into the kitchen Monday morning, Desbah was already dressed and ready to leave for her appointment with the Window Rock School superintendent. "I'll be back before lunch. You know where everything is. Coffee's made." She paused and put her briefcase and car keys down on the counter. "You know, I've been thinking about what you said Bessie Jim is doing. I hadn't paid any attention to that quarry question. But she's certainly bringing it back to life. Do you believe she's really in some danger? Some of us Navajos are notorious, you know, for jealousy and its nasty tricks."

"I hope that's all it is—tricks. But doing something that could ruin a new truck and poisoning a person's dogs aren't your run-of-the-mill tricks, are they?"

Desbah shook her head. After a beat, she said, "Oh, almost forgot. Albert Goldtooth will be at the panel discussion. If you still want to talk with him, make an appointment for tomorrow when you get back to Window Rock. He keeps an office over there in the Education building." With that and a quick hug, she left Geneva blinking and pouring coffee into a mug.

An hour and several mugs of coffee later, Geneva sat dressed in slacks and a sweater, her laptop glowing before her. The Internet was down this morning, as Desbah had warned her it might be, and she marveled at her good luck last night in searching online newspaper archives. But she was busy making notes between checking to see if it was working again.

Albert Goldtooth, the elder. If she had first thought to see him to get his opinion of whether Drake had worked for or against SB500 almost four years ago, Bessie's suspicions now put him in a new light. Geneva remembered him as a powerful member of the tribal council in Window Rock. He'd been a well-known silversmith when he was younger, rising to prominence in the art world. Famous for his large bracelets and squash-blossom necklaces, he blended traditional motifs with his own bold designs and unusual use of lapis and opal with gold. His pieces sold at high prices in New York and London.

But it was his work on the council, his fiery speeches about education, that brought him together with Edward, Tucker, Desbah, and the others four years ago. Just how had Goldtooth figured in their work for SB500? She couldn't quite remember. She took Edward's letter out of her briefcase and spread it again beside the computer, this time with a new purpose.

"I wasn't supposed to hear this, apparently," Edward had written, "but I think it has to do with some land deal on the reservation, a land-use decision Goldtooth wants to go a certain way. And it looks like Mason is working with him on it."

She rested her fingers on the page and gazed out the window, where a pair of yellow and black finches fluttered around a bird feeder. She didn't need to re-read Edward's next words. She knew them by heart: "*I have a bad feeling about this, Gen.*"

The telephone rang, jolting her out of her thoughts.

"Chischilly residence."

"Geneva! I found you—and on the very first try! What luck!" Mason's voice fairly boomed over the wire. "I was going to call your cell phone next."

Geneva gave a little start and pulled the receiver away from her ear. For an instant she almost hung up.

"My cell phone?" It took her a moment to remember the new cell phone her daughter had pressed on her the morning she left Flagstaff. She'd yet to use it. And another beat to recall that he'd known all about the panel discussion tonight.

"Yes, indeed. Julianna gave me the number. I thought you'd agreed not to go out there, what with your ankle and all. Didn't we talk about that last week?"

"That was your opinion, Mason. I don't recall agreeing with it."

"Ah, yes. Well, you always were one independent lady. One of your most endearing charms, of course."

Geneva felt her irritation rising. "Why are you calling, Mason?"

"Why? Why, indeed, my girl. I went down to Phoenix for my committee meeting and came back to Flagstaff to find you gone. I'd hoped to take you out for that dinner we missed, remember? And I wanted to take you for a moonlight flight over Grand Canyon in my new airplane. I was disappointed, that's all."

When Geneva didn't say anything immediately, he went on. "What are you and Desbah up to today? I guess you're preparing for the meeting at the chapter house tonight, am I right?"

"Right you are, Mason." Her annoyance mixed with her vague suspicions and their years-long friendship. The memory of him, standing at her door in the rain, his face white, came back vividly. Her tone softened. "Was there anything else?"

"Have I caught you at a bad time, my dear? You sound a bit rushed. Distracted, perhaps. Is your ankle all right?"

"The ankle is fine, Mason. Thank you. But you're right. I am in a bit of a rush. I'll see you later."

"Why, Geneva, if I didn't know better, I'd think you were brushing me off. Tell me what you will talk about tonight. I know the Chinle school board will be represented by Mrs. Davis and George Hardy, but who else will be there? I'm afraid I discarded my own invitation after I had to decline."

"As you know, Mason, it's a panel discussion. No one has a strictly prepared presentation as such. Now I really must go."

Geneva replaced the receiver and held her hand on it for a moment. When had this kind of paternalistic—no, *proprietary*—tone of his begun? She'd thought it only thoughtful friendship until his marriage proposal and her speechless refusal last Christmas. And then, during those weeks of their mutual withdrawal, she had taken onto herself a kind of embarrassed blame for his discomfort. *His* discomfort! And in the months since? Well, it was only their old friendship—the one Edward had valued so much, the one their daughters counted as a beloved given in their lives—that had returned, pretty much intact. Hadn't it? Wasn't it?

But if Mason had, as Desbah—and apparently Tucker—knew, if Mason had actually worked against SB500, then he had betrayed Edward. Betrayed them all. And if it was Edward's seat in the Senate that Mason wanted, he did indeed get it.

"I'm home," Desbah called from the back door. "Temperature is dropping. Snow clouds banking up in the northwest. Did the Internet come back up?"

Geneva's chin slid off her knuckles and her arm thumped to the desk. "Yes! No, I mean. I need to check again. How was your meeting with Superintendent Casey?

Desbah swooped into the living room, drawing a breath of cold air behind her. "Meeting went well. I'll tell you all about it. First let's build a fire in the fireplace, shall we? I want to gather my notes—and my wits—for tonight. And I have some stew to heat up for lunch."

When they'd settled before the fire with their mugs of tea, Desbah watched Geneva take papers out of her briefcase and put them back several times. "Before we get to putting ideas together for tonight, Geneva, why don't we try to calm your mind a little? One minute you're as twitchy as a sparrow, the next you're off in a cloud. We can't really go anywhere right now with this idea about how or whether Drake was involved in anything wrong. Anything past lying to us about his support of SB500 four years ago, that is." She pulled a page from a folder. "But I did get some information about Albert Goldtooth. He lives some distance west of Fort Defiance, and his regular office is in Window Rock, of course. The news is that he'll be right here in Chinle for this panel discussion tonight. His secretary told me so."

Desbah did have Geneva's attention now. "Tonight, you say. But what could I hope to learn about any land deal he—

and maybe Mason—might have had going almost four years ago, anyway? Unlikely that it had to do with the quarry in Black Canyon that Bessie's fighting." She looked out the window again. "You were right about those clouds. I think it's beginning to snow."

By late afternoon, Desbah declared them lucky that the mere dusting seemed to be all the snow they'd get, and there was no need to worry about people getting to the discussion tonight. The electricity went off briefly, and Geneva could hear the wind rising, but now the sun shone on the red and cream mesas and lit glittering swirls of fine snow across the frozen lane. She stood at the living room window to watch.

"The Diné are used to it, even if it is early, not even Halloween," Desbah said as she lined up several kerosene lamps on the kitchen counter. "If they're coming, they'll come anyway. Weather report isn't bad, last I heard. Just cold. And we're only fifteen minutes from the chapter house."

"I know," Geneva said, still at the window, "how October can be."

Desbah didn't say anything for a moment. "Yes, October," she murmured. Then, after another beat, "I saw Bessie and her daughter at the office this morning. Said she was coming, too. Said she has something to tell you."

Geneva turned away from the window. "Something to tell me? More than that bombshell on Saturday?"

CHAPTER FOURTEEN

Geneva guessed some sixty people sat or milled about in the rear of the chapter house near the kitchen and the coffee urns. The fragrance of fry bread and cinnamon funnel cakes lifted and mingled with drafts of cold mountain air, itself laced with cedar smoke. Apparently there had been a meeting of some kind that afternoon, and several people had stayed around for the panel discussion. She heard snippets of conversation about the grazing board's activities and the Tseyi' Shopping Center. She smiled and nodded to a number of people she recognized and who, to her surprise, greeted her by name.

As the last two panel members took their seats to Geneva's left, a young Navajo bounded out of his chair and came to the speakers' table, smiling broadly. "Mrs. Granger? I'm Ned. Remember me? Ned in second-period English. Remember?" His smile dimmed a little with embarrassment as she blinked up at him, clearly at a loss.

"Oh, Ned Claw! Of course, I remember you!" Geneva's smile brightened his again as he pumped her hand.

"I learned present perfect. And Leslie Silko and Momaday and Simon Ortiz. Those poets. You taught me." The young man fairly beamed.

Geneva's eyes filled with sudden tears. "Ned, I certainly remember you. You wrote that wonderful paper on Silko's *Yellow Woman*. What are you doing now?"

Before he could answer, the chapter president behind them tested the microphone, letting go an ear-wounding electronic shriek. "Yá'át'ééh shik'éí dóó shidiné'é. Welcome! Welcome," he boomed.

Reluctantly Geneva let go of Ned's hand, and he ducked away, still smiling, to his seat. The couple next to him she assumed to be his parents, smiled and nodded to her as well.

Desbah nudged her and indicated the door. Geneva followed her gaze. Mason Drake, wearing a grey Stetson and a split-cowhide coat with a shearling lamb collar, paused under the outdoor floodlight. A few brilliant snowflakes swirled against the blue night behind him. A happy commotion rose as people stood and moved toward him.

Geneva nearly gasped. She quickly coughed to cover it and turned her face back to the stage.

"Yá'át'ééh, Senator Drake! What a surprise!" Still holding the thrumming mic, the chapter president and several other officers came down off the dais, hands and smiles extended. Nothing would do then but a little impromptu speech by the loquacious president, abetted by first one and then another of the minor officers left over from the grazing board meeting. "Will you join our speakers at the table up there after all, Senator?"

"Please, please," Drake said, moving toward the kitchen area. "This is a special panel discussion planned by the Chinle Unified School District, and I do not want to interrupt in any way. Please go on. I am merely an interested audience member just like all these fine folks gathered here. But I surely would enjoy a cup of that wonderful-smelling coffee Miz Eloise Bitsilly and Angelina Begay and my old friend Deswood are brewing up back there."

Desbah bent her head and glanced sideways up at Geneva. Her expression said it all: *We've been upstaged*.

Geneva nodded wryly, glancing back as the door opened again. Bessie Jim entered followed by her daughter, Charlene, who was clutching the arm of a young man with a bad complexion. The two carried on a whispered conversation punctuated by giggles.

Bessie smiled and waved to Geneva and Desbah as she and the couple found seats. Before sitting down, Bessie made a curious gesture to Geneva, pointing to her own mouth and then to Geneva.

Geneva wanted to laugh, but only smiled and nodded.

The chapter president had just introduced the panel members and the first topic when the door flew open again and old Albert Goldtooth came in, followed by Brandon Goldtooth. Geneva recognized him as the one who'd confronted Harrison's grandson, Terry, at the gas station the day they went to Wheatfields. The day Geneva witnessed the burning hogahn, met the crystal-gazer Ooljee Blackgoat, and later that evening learned of the murder. What a day that was, she thought, as she watched the elder Goldtooth, festooned with his famous necklaces, rings, and bracelets, squeeze himself into the last vacant seat in the front row, leaving the younger man to find his own. Brandon Goldtooth, again fashionable in black leather and fancy boots, stood near the door and looked directly at Geneva, a sardonic smile on his lips.

"We'll go to the first speaker, Doctor Desbah Chischilly," the president thundered through the mic, which gave yet another short squeal.

Desbah reported on the progress of the district reading tests in the fourth and eighth grades. She then launched into her arguments against the No Child Left Behind Act's shortcomings and requirements, particularly the added burden on teachers. Two other panelists chimed in about what they considered its cultural biases, and the discussion became lively.

"If we'd gotten SB500 passed three and a half years ago, we'd have enough staff to handle all this extra testing and paperwork." This from George Hardy, the Anglo principal from Many Farms whose thick white crew cut contrasted sharply with his unnaturally black mustache. Geneva remembered him as friendly and helpful.

Someone in the audience called out, "Let's ask Senator Drake about that—he's right here. He can tell us."

"Yes, tell us, Senator," cried a thin Anglo, pulling his wife to her feet beside him. "Our youngest boy has autism—and now there's no Special Ed teacher for his level. I know there was a provision for it in SB500. Senator Granger told me so himself. Maybe you'll tell us why it didn't go through."

"Well, now," the president began, making a patting gesture in the air with his free hand. "Let's keep the discussion going up here at the table. The panelists should—"

But his words failed as several others stood up and directed a stream of questions toward Drake.

Geneva and Desbah watched the people gesturing and calling for Drake to stand up. George Hardy barely hid a chuckle as he elbowed Desbah. "This could be fun," he whispered.

Mason rose and bowed slightly to the table and the approaching president, who meekly handed him the mic. "I'd be glad to answer any questions," he said, "but we should wait until the panel has finished its presentation." Smiling, he handed back the mic and sat down.

"Oh, no," Hardy said loudly. "Actually, I think we'd all like to hear from Senator Drake on this subject." He hardly glanced left and right at the other panelists, and ignored Desbah's sharp kick under the table.

Drake stood then and accepted the microphone. Geneva caught his quick expression, an instant's hard flexing of his jaw before he composed his features and stepped forward. "Well, as you know, the late Senator Granger, and Mrs. Granger—

now Doctor Granger—and Doctor Chischilly, Mister Tucker Bayless from Window Rock, and many others, worked hard for that education bill." Drake paused and looked around, nodding again toward the panel. "I was not officially part of the process, as you may remember, as I was still recuperating from my accident, but I did all I could for its passage none-theless."

"Yes, you did all you could—for its defeat," cried Bessie Jim from her seat in the rear.

The murmur of the audience grew louder and she stood up. "We found out what you did, Senator Drake. And everybody here should know it."

Albert Goldtooth brought his bulk upright and turned around, almost purple in the face. "You shut your mouth, Bessie Jim! You don't know anything about it."

"And we know your part, too, Albert," Bessie shouted. "We know how you tried to swindle the Black Canyon folks, forcing them to give up their creek to your dirty quarry. You and the senator here together. The SB500 wasn't the only time you two worked together to fool the people."

Now half the crowd was on its feet. Arguments broke out in several quarters. The chapter president grabbed the mic from Drake, hopped back onto the stage, and brought the squealing microphone to his lips.

"Ladies and gentlemen. Folks . . . Ladies and gentlemen. Please . . . Take your seats, folks. Please." After a few more minutes, the audience did sit down, but not without several more lively exchanges. "Well now," he said, showing a big smile. "It seems we have a pretty good topic going here, about SB500. We all remember how important that bill was to Indian education, how much we all wanted it to go through. Maybe Senator Drake will come up to the dais after all, and tell us what he knows about it. We never heard much at all after it was defeated. Will you do that, Senator?"

Drake could hardly decline at this point. He stepped up on

the dais, took the mic, and stood at the end of the panelists' table, right beside Geneva.

"Thank you, Mister President—Carl—and panel members. I won't take much of your time. I don't wish to interrupt your discussion. But since these good people insist, I'll tell you what happened in Phoenix the day of the vote."

"Tell us what happened before the vote—that's where you played your part." Bessie Jim again.

Albert Goldtooth turned and glowered in her direction.

Drake gave a vigorous nod. "Several days before the vote, as you know, a group of educators lobbied legislators and appeared on talk shows and gave interviews to the newspapers. And I used what influence I still had—remember, I had been recuperating for more than seven months—to convince my former colleagues of the worth of SB500, its value to the reservations of Arizona and its Indian peoples. For days, even weeks, before—"

The lights flickered once and went out. A noise rose, squeals partly of surprise, partly of alarm. Geneva heard Mason swear softly and tap the useless mic. He touched her arm.

"Geneva, dear, I hope this isn't painful for you, recalling all this, I wouldn't have come if I'd thought any of that would be brought up."

Any reply she might have made was cut off by the chapter president's calling for lamps to be lighted in the kitchen. Several cigarette lighters and flashlights were already making spots of light here and there. After the first minute or two, the crowd relaxed, a few people starting conversations with their neighbors. Power failures were nothing new. Women in the kitchen set several glowing kerosene lamps on the pass-through counter, and two men took them to various places, including the stage and speakers' table.

The president was again on his feet. "We'll just wait a little while. The lights might come back on in a few minutes." In the short silence that followed, the wind made a sudden piercing howl at the corner of the building. Someone opened the door, and a spurt of snow blew in. The headlights of a passing pickup lit a thick sideways rush of snow and several inches of accumulation on the street. People stood up, exclaiming, and started gathering their things to leave.

"Well, old What's-His-Name on Channel Four got it wrong again," someone grumbled. "He said just cold, flurries ending by sunset." Laughter and several comments of agreement followed.

Albert Goldtooth beckoned to Drake, who stepped off the stage to join him. Geneva, grateful for the reprieve, hurried behind Desbah to find her coat. Midway through the crowd, they stopped and looked around for Bessie, but couldn't see her.

"She really wanted to talk with you," Desbah said. "There's Charlene."

The daughter and her boyfriend stood buttoning their coats at the door.

Desbah hurried ahead of Geneva. "Where's your mom, Charlene?"

The girl was clearly eager to leave. "I don't know. Probably my uncle is taking her home. He was sitting there in the next row."

Desbah nodded and turned back to Geneva. "I want to talk to her, too, Gen. She shouldn't have got old Goldtooth riled."

Geneva was surprised at the level of Desbah's concern, her own at the moment being to avoid Drake. "Can't we see her tomorrow?" She saw him standing at the front of the room in an intense conversation with Albert Goldtooth. The kerosene lamp on the speakers' table only weakly illuminated their faces, but both seemed agitated.

The hall was emptying, and finally Desbah and Geneva gave up looking for Bessie and started for their car. They had to clear the windshield of several inches of dry snow before they could leave. Geneva glanced up to see Brandon Goldtooth coming from the shadows at the back of the chapter house, tucking something under his arm. She remembered that a deep arroyo cut the land behind the building only yards from the back door. No cars could park there.

He saw her and paused, then lifted his chin in a kind of arrogant salute.

CHAPTER FIFTEEN

The power was still off at Desbah's house the next morning, but her place ran mostly on propane, and warm sunlight streamed in. Geneva watched the wind raise great fans and curling sprays of snow to sparkle in the bright sun. Almost all the sky that Geneva could see from the living room windows shone in what her twins used to call "that wild post-card blue," but the western horizon bore a layer of folded snow clouds.

"No juice at any of the offices in town yet, Geneva. I may just stay in my pajamas, build up the fire, and visit with you all day." Desbah handed her a steaming mug of coffee and settled on the couch. "If this thing blew in from the direction it usually does, you won't want to be on the road to Window Rock this morning. Call Tucker and tell him I'm keeping you for a while longer."

"I'm looking for Tucker's cell phone number now, Desbah. I think I'd rather not ring the house phone in case one of his in-laws answers."

She had to puzzle over her new phone for a time, but finally got Tucker.

"Geneva! Thank God! Are you girls all right? It was just on the news a minute ago."

"We're fine, Tuck. Why? What's wrong?"

"It's Bessie Jim. She's been killed!"

"What? No!" She sat down hard. Her free hand flew to her throat.

"It's true, Geneva. No telling how long the body would have stayed buried in the snow in that ravine, but for those kids that saw a dog pack getting at it this morning."

Geneva handed the phone to Desbah and covered her face with her hands.

The minute Desbah heard Tucker say what happened, she hung up, jumped off the couch, and headed for her bedroom. "Good Lord! Bessie's brother Leon works for me. He'll be devastated. And her poor mother! I've got to go see about them."

The women had barely pulled on jeans and boots when a police car stopped at the bottom of the steep, snowy driveway. A uniformed officer and another man, holding onto his Stetson and bending his lanky frame into the wind, started up toward the house on foot.

Desbah opened the door before they could knock. "Please come in."

"I'm Lieutenant Nez, Miz, I mean, Doctor Chischilly. We met at the chapter house last summer. And this is Agent Justin Fox from the FBI out of Phoenix. Hate to bother you this early in the morning." He nodded to Geneva. "We met before, too, Miz Granger. Doctor, I mean."

Geneva recognized the young officer from the night at Harrison Billy's hogahn.

Desbah nodded, offered to take their coats, and pointed them to seats. "It's about Bessie Jim, isn't it? What can I do?"

Fox took off his hat and turned it slowly in his hands. "Actually, we've come to see Doctor Granger." He leaned past the policeman to look at Geneva standing in the living room.

Geneva gave a little start. "To see me?"

They all sat then. Agent Fox displayed his credentials, gravely folded its case, and slid it back into his breast pocket. Geneva thought he looked downright worried. Then he pulled a notebook from his briefcase and uncapped a silver fountain pen. Just as he did, the power came back on, surprising them with the sudden light.

"Dr. Granger, I've been told that you do not live on the reservation, but in Flagstaff. Is that true?"

"Yes. That's true."

Fox held the pen over the page. "How well did you know Bessie Jim? That is, what was your relationship with the woman whose body was discovered at the chapter house early this morning?"

"I knew her well. Or at least I used to when I lived here several years ago. But why are you interested in that?" Immediately Geneva thought her question might have sounded defensive. She made her expression as bland as she could.

Fox inclined his head and wrote carefully without answering. Geneva had time to study his sandy hair, shot through with gray, and his angular, rather ruddy face. No Native American, this one. She wondered first why she was being questioned. And then why the FBI had sent an agent so quickly.

"Well, ma'am, Mrs. Jim's daughter gave us this envelope. Said her mother wanted you to have it." He drew a fat manila envelope from the briefcase and handed it to her. "If you don't mind, we'd like to know what it's about. We can't require you to tell us—at least not yet—but it would be helpful if you would see whether there's anything here that might shed some light on her death."

Too surprised to speak, Geneva took the heavy envelope and opened it. Papers, clipped together in groups of varying thickness, flowed out into her lap. She saw that each page had some paragraphs in Navajo and some in English. She handed several to Desbah, and they began to read.

"This is an explanation of what the proposed quarry would do to the creek in Black Canyon." Geneva looked up at the agent. "And at the bottom are people's signatures. Bessie told me she was going around letting the Black Canyon residents know what would really happen to their water and grass if the quarry goes in." She turned to Desbah. "Is that what the Navajo paragraphs say, too?"

Desbah nodded. "Certainly not what was said in the press. All this was glossed over. And I remember Councilman Goldtooth answering a question in Navajo on TV, telling somebody that the quarry would not affect the creek the residents depend on."

"That was some time ago," Nez said. "I wonder if the quarry plan is even going to happen. You don't hear anything about it now."

"Easy enough to find out." Fox held out a hand toward Geneva. "May I?"

Geneva gave him the papers she'd been examining and took up another clipped stack. "They seem to be grouped by date, or maybe by area. There aren't many families living in the canyon, Bessie told me. I guess she put the day's pages together after each trip she made there. Hmm, this is odd. Not all of these notes are in Bessie's handwriting."

Fox looked up. "Yes, I see that. And these." He held out two and pointed to the bottom of the pages. "There are initials here, AJL. Does that mean anything to you?" Again, he leveled his intense gaze on Geneva.

"Yes. The day I saw Bessie at Hubbell's, she mentioned that she had a friend who helped her." She returned Fox's steady gaze. "Allen Jerome Layton. I gathered the two were — more than just friends."

The agent bent again over his notebook. Geneva noticed the Navajo policeman writing furiously in his own. She looked at Desbah, who gave a slight, one-shoulder shrug.

Geneva continued to riffle through the papers. One page slid away from the others.

Bessie's handwriting, a single line. *Tell Geneva to make Drake confess.*

Geneva sat far enough from Fox and Nez that she was sure they couldn't read the words. She slipped the sheet under a stack of clipped pages next to the empty envelope, then folded the envelope over it and stood up. "Let me get you gentlemen some coffee."

The men protested, but she left the room, glancing meaningfully at Desbah as she did.

"Good idea," Desbah said, rising. "Going through these papers will take a while, gentlemen. Coffee will be ready in a minute."

Desbah busied herself making a fresh pot of coffee, but watched as Geneva took the single page out and silently showed it to her. Pointing with her lips, Desbah indicated a kitchen drawer. Geneva slipped the paper in and closed the drawer as she drew open another to clink together some spoons. "Sugar's over there," Desbah said, maybe a little louder than necessary.

"Got it. Any more cream?"

As they returned with the coffee tray, Fox took another batch of Bessie's papers from the stack. "Mrs. Granger, Lieutenant Nez here tells me that you were with Harrison Billy the day the Peshlakai hogahn burned. You even saw a figure running from the burning hogahn. Is that right?"

Geneva felt a small shiver. Of what? Fear? No, she thought. She was just on edge. Hiding Bessie's note—any kind of underhanded behavior—set her wrong with herself. "Yes, I did see that man—person—I'm not sure. It could have been a woman, I suppose. I hadn't thought of that before." She made herself look directly into Fox's eyes. "Why do you ask? Have you found out anything about that poor man's death?

"We know now that it was Jerome Layton's body in that hogahn."

Geneva looked at the papers in her lap. Her fingers rested on the initials AJL in black ink next to BJ in blue. She thought of Bessie's words that day at Hubbell's Trading Post: *They don't want me to tell on them.*

She looked up to see Desbah's wide eyes signaling that she, too, made the connection between the two deaths.

Nez glanced at Fox. "We are questioning Mr. Billy again." He went back to his stack of notes.

Geneva waited, but apparently he meant to say no more. "Questioning?" she leaned forward. "You mean today? Are you going up there to Wheatfields?" She couldn't even frame the next question. Surely they weren't going to arrest Harrison. The notion was preposterous.

"The investigation is proceeding." Fox's tone made it clear he was in charge. "Can you describe the person you saw running from the hogahn?"

Geneva told him about the costumed, twirling figure, the sounds like pistol shots or firecrackers, and even mentioned her own photographs of the runner.

"Do you have those photos with you, Mrs. Granger?"

"No, I don't. They're at my home in Flagstaff. Do you need to see them?"

"We'll let you know if we need to talk with you again about Mr. Billy. Or the photos." He bent to take more clipped notes.

Half an hour later, Fox and Nez had finished both the coffee and Bessie's papers and now stood at the door pulling on their coats.

"If we can do anything more, please let us know," Desbah said.

"In fact, there is." The FBI agent turned toward Geneva and took out his notebook. "How may I contact you, Dr. Granger? When are you planning to return to Flagstaff?"

She gave him both her home and cell phone numbers. He

wrote them down and closed his notebook. But Justin Fox's green eyes rested on Geneva just a beat too long, she thought.

Desbah's question of when Bessie's funeral might be brought only, "The body won't be released until an autopsy is done, and that is undetermined at this time."

Geneva and Desbah stood at the window and watched the Navajo police car pull away.

"Do you feel as guilty as you looked just now?" Desbah gathered the cups and moved toward the kitchen. "Remind me never to have you as a partner in a card game. That paper—all those papers—belong to you. Charlene Jim sent them to you. By name."

Geneva picked up the coffee carafe and followed her into the kitchen. "Yes, I know she did, but they aren't mine, really. As for that one page, I didn't know what to do with it at the moment and just wanted some time to think."

"You don't have to justify anything to me, for God's sake," Desbah said. "So, let's see it again."

They settled at the kitchen table with Bessie's note between them.

"That's like Bessie," Desbah said. "'*Tell* Geneva,' not *ask*. What does—did—she think Drake has done, anyway? I mean, I heard what she said at the chapter house, but could she or anybody else know definitely that he was involved in misleading the people about the quarry?" She pulled the note closer and bent over it.

When her questions went unanswered, Desbah lifted puzzled eyes to Geneva.

Geneva tilted her head. "Brandon Goldtooth is Albert's grandson, isn't he?"

"My, you sure are off on another track. Yes, he is. Brandon is a fancy dancer, making a reputation for himself in more ways than one. Calls himself Kachina King . . . or maybe it's King Kachina. He was featured on a PBS special last year doing a solo act both with and without hoops. Old Albert was there, too, on the drum."

Geneva rose to refill their cups. "What do you mean by 'more ways than one'? Do you know Brandon well?"

"No, not well. He's sometimes on the scene in the tribal education department where Albert has an office. Doing what, I don't know. He also attended two seminars on entrepreneurship I gave in Window Rock a couple of months ago, came dressed in a three-piece suit like a banker or something. He came in alone, didn't say much, but gathered all his material, and then left like a shot at the end. Both times. Why he was there at all, I have no idea."

Geneva waited.

Desbah stirred her coffee. "I guess I mean, well, he seems sneaky, somehow. I don't know what I mean. He's just too— too slick! That's what I mean. You know I don't go along with the old Navajo philosophy of never putting yourself above others, always avoiding anything that would distinguish you from your fellows and all that."

She put her spoon down with great care, looking thoughtful, and went on.

"You know I encourage people, young and old, to accomplish everything they can. But, I don't know—Brandon's whole attitude puts me on guard, somehow." She made a fierce face and raised pretend claws. "Lord! How's that for a suspicious, mean old school teacher, eh?"

Geneva laughed and threw up her hands. "Oh, right. Don't forget, I taught beside you for two years before you went to the tribal office. And I got some of your freshmen as sophomores the very next semester. All they could say for the first week was, 'Where's Miz Chischilly? When's she coming back?'"

That was as far as either of them could carry a light-hearted conversation. Their faces grew grave again. Geneva picked up Bessie's note and stared at it, then folded it and tapped it against her palm. "I want to check the Internet."

"I'll be shocked if it's back," Desbah said. "I'm going to pack and then go pick up Leon Ashi."

"Be shocked, then," Geneva called from the dining room a few minutes later as she resumed her search of the *Navajo Times* archives.

In a little while she heard Desbah back in the kitchen and went in to find her filling grocery bags with food.

"Geneva, I'm going to go get Leon and drive him up to their mother's place in Black Canyon. The sun is doing its work—the driveway and most of the streets are clear and will be dry in no time."

"I'll go with you, Desbah. Maybe I can do something."

Desbah set the last bag near the back door. She looked uncomfortable. "Well, ah, best not, Geneva. Not right now."

"Oh, of course," Geneva said. "I do understand." She remembered how Navajo tradition dictated a quick burial and that the family shunned open displays of grief. But she also knew that many now held rather public funerals with eulogies and the like, just as non-Indians did. What struck her most was that she had forgotten, if only for a moment, proper consideration of the culture she'd studied so carefully when she lived here. *What does that say about me?* She smiled at Desbah, hoping she understood that Geneva understood.

Desbah met her gaze and nodded, then shrugged into her jacket and reached for her gloves and keys. "I know that Bessie herself belonged to a church—Episcopalian, I think—but her mother and siblings, especially Harold and Leon, are very traditional. What Charlene might want, I have no idea." She put her hand on the door knob. "In any event, the burial will surely be tomorrow. I'll find out if, when, you may come."

"But Agent Fox said there'd be an autopsy. That will delay things, won't it?"

Desbah grimaced. "Oh, yes, I forgot. Well, all the more need. I might be running some other family members back and forth. Bessie's old aunts and uncles are scattered over half the reservation. I don't know when I'll be back, Gen. Stay here as long as you like."

"Thanks. I just need to do some more work on the Web. If you see anything I can do, please call. Did your cell phone charge enough this morning?"

Desbah patted her purse and lifted a pair of grocery bags. "Yes, it did. I'll call you."

Geneva picked up the other bags and followed her to the car. "Please express my condolences, Desbah. I'm going back to *The Navajo Times* archives and see what I can find about the quarry or the council's decisions or something—I don't know what—that might shed light on who did what about that quarry."

Another hour on the computer passed with little to show. She'd searched a full three years' worth of both the tribal newspaper and the *Gallup Independent* for mention of the quarry and found only the initial arguments when the project went before the council. It wasn't clear whether the bill had passed or failed. She sighed and rubbed the back of her neck, ready to give up. But an item on page two caught her eye.

"Arizona Senator Edward Granger met late yesterday with the Navajo Nation's Tribal Council. Later, Granger made a speech for reelection on the steps of the chairman's offices, introduced by Council Vice-Chairman Albert Goldtooth. A large crowd gathered to hear . . ."

The reporter would have mentioned it if Mason, their popular former senator then, was there at either the council meeting or later at the speech. Could Edward have been mistaken? Not likely. But why would Mason avoid Edward? He said Mason ducked between the buildings. *Ducked.*

She frowned and scrolled back to the top of the page. October 27. Yes, that day. The day before Edward would fly away, with Bessie Jim's nephew Daniel Ashi at the controls. And never come home.

Finally, Geneva closed her laptop and put it away. She tidied the kitchen, then prepared to go on to Window Rock and see Shándííne and Tuck, remembering what he'd said about his in-laws being gone. She tried Desbah's cell phone, but without luck. She guessed that the reservation's spotty cell phone service might not include the reaches of Black Canyon. Instead, she wrote her friend a note and propped it against the coffee maker. Then she sat down and dialed the Bayless home.

"Tucker? It's Geneva. No word on when the autopsy will be, let alone the funeral, and I'm clearly not needed here. I'd best not barge in at Bessie's mom's house right now, Desbah said. She's already out there, so I'm on my way to see you and Shándííne before I go home."

"That's great, Geneva. Yes, I know the feeling. I've spent half my life not knowing when to step into Navajo doings and when not to. Of course, Shándííne usually steered me in or out, whatever the case was. You say you're about to leave Desbah's?"

Fifteen minutes later, Geneva pulled onto the highway, its wet surface steaming under the mid-day sun. Only in the shadows and north sides of the pink mesas did any of last night's snow cling in ragged ribbons.

Highway 191, leading to 264 and the turn for Ganado, played out straight as a yardstick ahead of her. She saw almost no traffic and little of interest save a few purple cloud-shadows on the wide plain and the distant Balahkai mesa to her right. Overhead the brilliant blue was studded with only a few fast-moving clouds. A good road for thinking. Could Mason truly have betrayed Edward? If so, and if he'd been in Window Rock that day three years ago and actually ducked behind a building to avoid Edward, why?

Her cell phone rang, causing her to start so violently that she swerved the car slightly. She glanced into the rear-view mirror. Only a small silver car a good distance behind her. Nothing else. "Hello?"

"Mom, it's Julianna. Where are you?"

Even as startled as she was, Geneva noticed a note of — what? Disapproval? Worry? — in her daughter's voice. "On my way to Window Rock, honey, headed toward the Ganado turn-off now. I'm going to see Shándiíne and Tucker again and spend the night there. Why? What's up?"

"Well, when are you coming home?"

"Julianna, I told you — Wednesday probably, that's tomorrow. Or maybe Thursday. Things are a bit up in the air right now. Did you hear about Bessie Jim?"

"I did, Mom. And it happened right there in Chinle where you were! It's dangerous out there!"

Geneva made a face. It was time to stop all this over-protectiveness the girls had adopted toward her since their father's death. Why hadn't she done it sooner? "Darling, I traveled all over this reservation when we lived here, and so did you and Karen. You know I don't take foolish chances. Please don't worry. How are Thom and little Teddy?"

"They're fine, Mom. Don't change the subject. I wish you'd skip Window Rock and just drop down to I-40 and come home. I went over to water your plants today and ran into Angie. She came to leave off some work she'd finished. We had a good talk. And we agree."

"That's nice, dear. Thanks for watering. Agree about what?" She glanced again in the mirror and saw the little car speed up. It was close enough that she could see a peculiar decal or painted figure, like a kachina, on the bottom of the passenger-side windshield. "Never mind, Julianna. Look, I'm violating my own rule against talking on the phone while driving. I'll call you when I get to Blue Wind. Bye, sweetheart."

She dropped her phone into her purse and checked her

speedometer. Same speed. *Well, he's got all the room in the world to pass. Why doesn't he?*

Her phone rang again. Keeping her eye on the car behind her, she glanced at the little panel. She expected Julianna again.

"Oh, Desbah! I tried to call you before I left. I'm on my way back to Window Rock. What news?"

"The autopsy has been delayed for some reason, Geneva. I'm going to stay out here for a few more days. Since you'll be in Window Rock, and not far away from here, will you do me a favor?"

Geneva glanced in the mirror again. The little car had dropped well back again. "Of course, Desbah. What can I do?"

"Well, Bessie's brother Leon said the storm messed up our office computers and our whole phone system. Worse, the service company we have a contract with won't be able to send anyone until Friday, if then, so it's just as well that I stay here and help. But what we really need is—"

Silence.

"Desbah? Hey, Desbah?"

Geneva listened for a few more seconds. She'd need to pull off somewhere to fiddle with the darned thing to call her back. The shoulders of the road were narrow here and looked muddy. Dropping the phone in her lap, she glanced at the mirror again. There he was, practically on her bumper.

CHAPTER SIXTEEN

Tucker hung up his phone and turned to Shándiíne. "That was Geneva, honey. She's leaving Chinle pretty soon, on her way here." He glanced at the clock and moved to stand beside her again, smoothing her blanket.

Shándiíne lifted the hand that didn't have the IV attached and touched his. She gazed at him with love, and what he knew was an effort to hide her pain. He bent and kissed her.

"Lord, it's peaceful in here for a change, isn't it?" he said. "I thought your Aunt Nedra and her eternally trailing daughters-in-law would never leave. She'd like to think I can't take care of you. Or like you to think so, eh?"

Shándiíne smiled and nodded. "She was that way when Millie was a baby, remember? She was sure I'd drop her or forget to feed her or something. Lots worse than my mother, even. She and my mom will be so taken with the new baby out there at Church Rock, they might want to stay longer. But I don't want to talk about them right now." She shifted and reached for his hand again. "Tucker, you won't forget your promise, will you?"

Tears rose in his eyes. He dropped into the chair and laid his face against her side.

"Tucker? You'll do it, won't you?"

He barely moved his head against her, his voice muffled with tears. "Yes, I'll do it. I will, darlin'. You know I will."

"Tuck, I've asked Geneva to help you get Millie away. I know you don't believe it, but Aunt Nedra and Mom are going to fight you. If you have to come back from California to handle things, Geneva will go and stay with Millie, get her enrolled, and prop her up. Geneva and Desbah will even help you here. Desbah's brother is a McKinley County judge, remember, right there in Gallup."

He raised his head and looked at her. "You've thought this through pretty thoroughly, haven't you?" He mopped his eyes and cheeks and stood up. "Honey, I don't want you worrying about any of this. And I don't want you lining up the troops, either. I can handle it."

Her eyes closed. "I know, Tuck. But just in case." She let a moment pass. "Will you make me some tea?" After half a cup of tea and a few nibbles of toast at Tucker's insistence, Shándiíne sighed deeply. "I think I'll nap a little. Geneva should be here in—what—less than two hours, right? I want to be wide awake so we can have a good talk. I'm glad my mom and Millie will be staying at Aunt Hattie's place."

"Me, too. Millie always likes hanging out with Hattie's girls. They make her laugh. I think they could even make old Nedra Roanhorse laugh. I heard it happened once, about ten-twelve years ago."

"Oh, Tucker." Shándiíne smiled, shaking her head. "Wake me the minute Geneva gets here."

An hour and a half later, Julianna called. "Tuck, is my mom there? I can't get her on the cell phone."

"No, Julianna, she isn't yet. I expect her to roll in here any time now. How's the lawyering coming these days?"

Julianna gave a brief laugh. "The lawyering's coming along fine, Tuck, but I'm worried about my mom. When I spoke with her, she said she was close to the Ganado turnoff. That was more than an hour ago. She should be there by now—well before now. If I haven't heard from her or you in fifteen minutes, I'm calling Uncle Mason. He's been phoning about every half hour, worrying about her. He couldn't reach her cell, either."

"Now, Julianna, no need to haul Mason out here. If she isn't here in the next few minutes, I'll go out and look for her myself. Much more efficient, wouldn't you say?"

A quarter-hour later, Tucker made his fourth or fifth trip from front window to Shándiíne's bedside, trying to step softly. He picked up the phone and went into the kitchen. He tried Desbah's cell phone again. And for the third time, Geneva's cell. Both rang. Neither answered. He couldn't remember Bessie's mom's name, and he knew all the brothers would be there with her, anyway. He even phoned Bessie's house in Chinle. Of course, the daughter wasn't there.

He checked to see that Shándiíne was still sleeping, and went back to the living room window, tugging on his beard. Something was definitely wrong, he knew it.

Millie had their new SUV, but he could take his old truck and go out looking for Geneva. Hell, he thought, where were his multitudinous in-laws when he needed one?

He snapped his fingers. "Jim Sutton's wife. She knows Shándiíne and she's an RN." He flipped open his phone book.

Geneva opened her eyes. Stars. Stars shone directly above in a deep mauve sky. A tinkling melody played somewhere nearby. What was that? Cold. God, she was cold. She tried to move. Pain shot through her neck and shoulder. Her left hand didn't work right. She squeezed her eyes shut.

Upside down. I think I'm upside down. How?

When she opened her eyes again, there was no soft mauve behind the stars at all. Black sky, bright stars. Far, far away.

Her head throbbed. She lifted one hand and touched . . . what? Fabric of some kind? The sharp smell of gasoline permeated the air around her. Car. She was in her car, but slung sideways, head down on the seat and looking up through the windshield.

At five-two-and-nothing, Geneva always swore that shoulder belts were designed to choke her. She retaliated by stopping the rewind with a small, powerful clamp to create some slack. Now that slack had let her twist and slip forward and down to her right. The strap cut painfully across her neck and breast. She squinted to focus on a glow of something white. The air bag, she thought. I've been in an accident. She tried again and again to release the seat belt latch. When she finally did, she slid and banged into the opposite door, which creaked open several inches. But something stopped it. She was on her back and right side at such an angle that she couldn't sit up. There was that tinkling song again. *Für Elise" on a harpsichord? How awful.*

"The cell phone," she said aloud. "Where is it?" She felt around, found her purse strap, but the rest of it was caught somewhere under the seat. The tune stopped at last.

She struggled to right herself. "Damn. Everything hurts." After twisting and pushing against the dashboard and the door, over and over, she succeeded each time only in ramming her right shoulder against the arm rest of the partly open door. The smell of gasoline mingled with that of damp sand and chamisa.

She stopped and rested. "All right," she whispered, "stop shaking. Got to stop shaking. Maybe I can turn over, grab the back of the seat, and try to pull myself up on my knees." She took a deep breath.

Something was out there. A rustle and a scraping noise close by. Trying to let her deep breath out silently, she struggled to push herself up and turn her head far enough to see out the window of the barely open door. No good. The noise came from behind her line of vision, toward the rear of the car. She lay quiet and listened. As she did, her head cleared and she became aware of a regular ticking noise. Cooling metal? Oh, God, the ignition must still be on. She remembered reading somewhere how the electrical system could ignite spilled gasoline or fumes in a situation like this. The car could explode any second. Pushing hard, she reached with her painful left hand and seized the steering wheel, wrenching her body over the console far enough to bring her right hand to the ignition and turn the key off. She held onto the wheel and fumbled for the headlight switch.

"EEEEEE-YAHHHHH!" In the flare of the headlights, a figure stood at the top of the ridge above her. "EEEEEE-YAAHH-YAHHH!" he screamed again, flinging his white-painted arms out. He wore a tall white mask with tufts of feathers, a great red beak, and round yellow eyes. From his shoulders hung something like a cape or shawl, which he spread and lifted rhythmically like slowly beating wings. He held a stick in each hand, which made the cape-wings even longer. Geneva could see a breastplate of white bone hairpipe and a ruff of something fluffy around his waist and hips. Shells circled his ankles, clacking and rattling with every move.

"EEEEEE-YAHHHHH! YAHHHH-YAH-YAH! EEEE-YAH-YAH-YAH!" He began to turn and dance, bending forward, straightening, bending again as he turned, slowly, then faster and faster.

After the first jolt of fear, Geneva simply watched, amazed. With the lights, she could see her car was in an arroyo. Enough light reflected from the bank ahead that she could see the car was tipped up at probably a forty-degree angle. The passenger side must be jammed into the soft dirt.

The figure danced and leaped, lunging from side to side now and brandishing not sticks, but what looked like ancient war clubs, complete with feathers. Or maybe not clubs, but rattles, she couldn't tell. The eerie cries seemed to come from everywhere. Maybe from inside her head. She touched her temple. Wet. Sticky.

Then he was gone. The night fell silent.

Something heavy thudded just outside her partly open door. She froze, scarcely breathing. For what seemed like ten minutes, no other sound or movement except for her pounding heart.

"CH-CH-CHH . . .UNH-UNH-UNH."

A hunched figure in what looked like a buffalo hide and black, furry leggings rose on the ridge, turning and turning, its massive head wagging from side to side, yellow horns gleaming in the slanting light.

More grunting and pawing the earth. Then it disappeared.

Some minutes later, a sleek coyote crept into the light. It threw back its head and howled like a woman in agony.

Now Geneva's amazement gave way to fury. Enough of this shape-shifting show, she thought. She blasted the horn. The coyote figure disappeared.

But she didn't dare turn off the headlights. The arm hooked in the steering wheel hurt. She let go and slid again, head down toward the passenger side.

Cold, cold night. She closed her eyes.

Jim Sutton's wife arrived within fifteen minutes of Tucker's call. She stood now near the door watching him pull on his jacket and gather flashlight and lantern. "You go on, Tuck. Don't worry about a thing. I'll make her some of that soup she likes, and when she wakes up, we'll have a nice visit. You just go do what you need to do. I'm sorry Jim's not here to help you."

"Thanks, Evvie." Tucker gave her a one-arm hug, and glanced back toward Shándííne. "She'll probably wake up soon." He picked up his gear and a rolled blanket. "You've got my cell phone number, right?"

Evvie Sutton made a shooing motion with both hands. "I've

got everything, you know that. Go on now, before you wake her up."

The old truck started without hesitating, and Tucker bounced out to the highway, glad he'd thought of the blanket and thermos of coffee. It would be solid dark within an hour. If he couldn't find Geneva right away, he'd call the Navajo Police.

The hour passed. He'd traveled slowly, checking the sides of the road, stopping at a couple of gas stations to describe her car and ask if anybody had seen her.

Dusk gave way to blue-black night. He knew Shándííne would be awake by now and worried, despite Evvie Sutton's reassurances. At the next gas station, he stopped under the lights and pulled out his phone. "Evvie, has Geneva arrived?"

"No, Tuck, she hasn't. Hasn't phoned, either. Shándííne thinks you should call the police."

"Tell her I'm about to do that right now. First I'll call Julianna again." He hung up, thinking he'd damn sure try to head Julianna off. He could do without Mason Drake dropping out of the sky for the rescue, no doubt having arranged a press conference first.

Tucker looked up to see a Navajo police car nosing into a parking space at the convenience store not twenty feet away. He followed the officer inside and explained the situation.

"That teacher woman? One that writes those books about Indian education?" The big Navajo paid for his coffee and candy bar, screwed down the cap on his travel cup, and led the way back outside.

"That's the one," Tucker said. "Driving a blue Camry about a year old. Any accident reports?"

"Not as of about ten minutes ago," the policeman said. "Say she left Chinle headed this way a little after twelve, one o'clock?"

Tucker nodded. "Something's happened, sure as the world. Can you set up a search?"

The officer opened his patrol car door, dropped into the seat, and secured his coffee cup. "It's dark," he said, frowning up at Tucker. "Gets real dark out here at night." He reached for his mic.

After a conversation with what Tucker assumed was headquarters, the policeman stood up and leaned over his open door. "We're real short-handed this far out, you know, but maybe they can get some men out looking first thing tomorrow."

Tucker kept himself from swearing. "Man, she could be hurt somewhere. And it'll be well below freezing tonight, you know that. Can't you do something now?"

"'Fraid not. But I'll take the report and pass it along. There'll be another cop patrolling down from Chinle in an hour or so. We'll pass the word along."

Tucker had lived on the reservation a long, long time. He knew how thin police manpower was on these thousands of square miles. He shook his head, climbed back into his truck, and watched the policeman roll off into the night. Back toward Window Rock and the end of his shift, no doubt.

In the last three, almost four years, Tucker had kept his watch at Shándííne's side and slowly lost touch with his old colleagues and friends. With the exception of Jim Sutton and two or three other friends—most had now retired and moved to Flagstaff or Phoenix or back to wherever they'd started—there was no one he could think of to call on. Sure as hell not Drake, but he wouldn't risk Geneva's safety over his personal dislike of the man. Another ten minutes.

He wished again for his best friend, Chee Hamilton, who, like Tucker's own Millie, was of mixed parentage, but of an earlier generation. At a time, and in a clan, where it had mattered a great deal more. Chee's embattled youth and too many years of tough military service had left him scarred in profound ways, but he'd finally found his redemption in a new religion. He was serving the Bahá'í Faith now in Switzerland.

Tucker felt real gratitude for Chee's peace and new purpose, but he still missed his old friend mightily.

All this flashed through his mind as he swung his truck back onto 264 toward the junction of 191 towards Chinle. He thought of waiting here until Evvie called him back, but decided to take the chance of running out of cell-tower range and get on with his search.

Leaving the lights of the gas station, he headed down toward the junction and its fewer lights, then into the darkness that would lead to Chinle.

Little traffic now. He slowed again, peering up the slight incline on his right and down toward the plain on his left, only faintly illumined by starlight and a scant moon. He knew the plain was cut here and there with arroyos that would be hard to spot.

Ahead a figure dressed in white or light colors lifted a long white cylinder of a thing up and over in an arching motion. As Tucker grew closer, he saw a man put what looked like a Zuni Shalako mask into the trunk of a small car. The man himself was partly covered in a furry wrap of some kind, but his white arms caught Tucker's headlights. As Tucker approached, he ducked into his car and sped away.

The instant he did, Tucker saw lights slanting up from somewhere below the road. Headlights. He executed a swift U-turn and parked, leaving his own lights on and dragging the big flashlight from the seat as he jumped out.

Within a few yards of the pavement, the land dropped off sharply into an arroyo. Low growth, thick with hundreds of dry tumbleweeds all but hid the drop-off, except where they lay flattened and crushed in a car-sized swath. The left side of the narrow arroyo below was fairly high. At the bottom, Geneva's car rested at an angle, the front and driver's side tilted up. Tucker made his way across the high bank and scrambled and slid down to the car. "Geneva! Good God, Geneva, are you in there?"

The angle of the vehicle made pulling the driver's side door open impossible, so Tucker clambered around to the other side. No good. The door was partly open, but wedged firmly into the ground. He could see her slumped against the passenger door head down, knees drawn up. Was that blood on her head? Was she unconscious? Dead? He banged on the window and tried rocking the car. "Geneva! Can you hear me?"

The sandy bottom of the arroyo, damp from the earlier snow, seemed to Tucker both an advantage and a disadvantage. The car wasn't much damaged that he could see, but the left front wheel was a good distance off the ground. He made his way back toward the hood, nosed partway up the high side of the arroyo.

Moving downhill, he shone his light along the base of the bank, found an eroded place, and crawled back up the ridge. Once even with the car, he took a breath and jumped down to land hard on the hood. The soft earth gave way and the car came down the three feet he needed. He tried the door. Locked. "Geneva! Geneva, wake up!" Lord, was she dead? Frozen? It must be twenty degrees down here. He found a good-sized rock and smashed the window, yanked open the door, and gave her arm a couple of hard pats.

She opened her eyes and looked at him for a long moment. "Tucker, it's damned chilly out here."

It took them a while to make their way out of the arroyo and into his truck, but the heater, blanket, hot coffee, and movement revived her. He finally got a signal and phoned the police. Geneva insisted on waiting. "My purse and computer are in that car!"

"Damn it, Geneva, I'll go back for them. I'm afraid you're going into shock."

"No, please, let's wait in the truck for the police. Just call Shándiíne, let her know all's well, and we'll be along soon."

To Tucker's surprise, the very officer he'd seen at the gas

station appeared within a short time. He pulled his patrol car nose to nose with the truck and left his bright headlights and the flashing blue lights on full force. Geneva bowed her head and shielded her eyes. Tucker got out to meet the policeman, who stepped forward, drawing out a clipboard. "I see you found her. How did this happen?"

"I don't know how," Tucker said, "but she's pretty shaken up and mighty cold. I think she may be going into shock. Can we just get her things out of the car and let her make the report tomorrow?"

The big Navajo came around to Geneva's window, which she managed, to roll down. He bent close to examine her bloodied temple. "I'm Officer Timothy Tsosie. You need to see a doctor." Turning to Tucker, he said, "You taking her to a doctor? I can get an ambulance out of Window Rock."

Geneva shook her head. "I'm fine. Just cold." She couldn't keep her teeth from chattering. Only when she'd finally convinced him she'd come to the police station tomorrow and make a full report, did he turn to make his way down to her car. Tucker led the way and then returned with her purse, jacket, suitcase, and even her laptop.

"Since you say somebody ran you off the road," Tsosie said, "a detective has to come out and look, take pictures. Tomorrow." He peered in at Geneva again. "Are you refusing to go the emergency room? I'm supposed to call the ambulance."

Tucker glanced at Geneva, who shook her head again.

"There's a nurse waiting for us at my house, Officer," he said. "An RN. If she says Mrs. Granger needs a doctor, we'll get her there—hospital's not far from where I live. That'll be better than waiting out here, don't you agree?"

The policeman nodded, raised a hand in dismissal, and Tucker pulled back onto the highway and sped toward Window Rock.

Evvie Sutton pulled open the front door before they reached it. "I'm so glad you're back!"

"Right. Thanks." Tucker put Geneva's bags and computer down and steered her to the couch. "Evvie, will you see to our friend Geneva? I think she's cracked the side of her head. I'm going to make her a hot toddy." He went to Shándiíne and kissed her on his way to the kitchen.

Evvie took Geneva's hand. "I'll take care of you, honey. Keep that blanket around you. Here's another one and I'll get the heating pad. We'll warm you up."

Shándiíne looked alarmed. "What happened to you, Geneva?"

The room was blessedly warm, but Geneva still couldn't stop shaking. "Thank you, Evvie. That sounds lovely. Oh, Shándiíne, I'm sorry to have worried you." She accepted the heating pad and allowed Evvie to ease her back into the cushions and turn her cheek more to the light.

"There was a car—" She drew in a quick breath as Evvie wiped her temple with alcohol. "A small car, silver colored. It kept zooming close behind me and then falling back. Then he flew past, swerved in front of me, and hit the brakes! I had the strangest sense of . . . of flying, soaring."

Shándiíne and Tucker cried out together, "Somebody ran you off the road?"

Geneva blinked. "Yes, I guess he did." She glanced up to see Tucker, struck immobile in the act of handing her a hot drink. She took it from him and managed a smile of thanks.

"And the maniac didn't stop?" Shándiíne's voice was full of indignation. "Nobody stopped to help?"

"Only Tucker," Geneva said. "And I haven't even thanked you, my friend. I think I'd have frozen to death this night without you."

Tucker blinked and reached down to give her shoulder a pat.

Evvie stood up. "Do you have any other cuts or scrapes you want me to look at?"

"I don't think so, Evvie. Thank you. I'm feeling much

better. You must excuse me. I have to call my daughters. They'll be worried."

"Evvie," Tucker said, "I know your daughter and grandkids are at your place by now and waiting for you. I can't thank you enough. We'll be fine."

By the time Geneva had called and soothed Karen and Julianna, and both sons-in-law to boot, her head had set up a pounding she thought might be audible to all present.

She said goodnight to Shándiíne and made her way to her room in the studio on Tucker's steady arm. After a hot shower and a couple of aspirins, she sank into bed. The faint rhythmic clack-clatter of cowry shells and a distant *EEEE-YAH-YAH, EEE-YAH-YAH-YAH* descended with her into sleep.

CHAPTER SEVENTEEN

Wednesday morning Ooljee Blackgoat frowned at her guest, stirred the coals of her little fire in the bare yard next to her hogahn, and sat back down in her lawn chair. The wind lifted the fragrant smoke toward Harrison Billy's knees before veering it into the space between their chairs. "I told you," she said, not looking his way, "that man wouldn't do you any good. You didn't have to help him."

"I want to know where he is," Harrison said, for the third time this morning. "Here's one of his audio tapes that he left at my hogahn. Take it. Find out where he is."

In the forty-three years he had known this Blackgoat, she always was stubborn, but why she had taken a dislike to Jerome Layton, he couldn't guess. She liked lots of other white people, everybody knew that. He drew out a pouch of her favorite tobacco and a new twenty-dollar bill and weighed them down on the chopping log with a polished pink quartz the size of a goose egg that he'd bought for her in Gallup. Then he stood up and indicated her hogahn. "Come on," he said, and started for the door. "It's cold sitting out here. I'll carry in some stove wood and build up your fire inside."

By the time Harrison got her pot-belly stove going and put on a fresh pot of coffee, the old medicine woman had moved her great-grandson's Big Wheel and fire engine back against the log wall and seated herself in a rocking chair. She spread a small gray and red rug across her lap and laid the pink quartz and her own clear quartz, the size of her fist, on it. Holding her hands close above them as if to warm or hide the crystals, she seemed to listen, her head tilted slightly to one side. Harrison poured himself a cup of coffee and stood quiet near the stove. She then placed the audiotape between the quartz pieces and stroked its edge lightly for some minutes, looking intently into the quartz crystals. "He's burned up," she said, lifting her head. "The witch killed him and burned him up. I told that teacher woman not to go there. And I told you not to help him. Long time ago I told you that."

Harrison set his coffee cup down with a clang on the iron stove and bent toward the woman. "It was him, then," he said softly. "I was afraid it was him in that hogahn."

"That police officer with the new baby will come for you after while," she said. "I told you not to help that man with the stories."

Harrison hardly heard this last as he put on his hat, shoved the tape back into his pocket, and started for the door. Grandson Terry was supposed to pick him up at eleven on his way back from his girlfriend's house. Maybe this time the boy would be on time.

Terry Littleben ended up changing the flat on his girlfriend's mom's old car there in the snowy mud at the bottom of their hill. The morning had held no time alone with Francine, no hot chocolate, not even a promise of lunch. And certainly no romance. His jeans, clotted with orange mud and half frozen to his knees and butt, wouldn't even straighten out and meet his sockless tennis shoes when he stood. The small woman still sat behind the steering wheel, holding onto it as if she were going somewhere any minute. He looked back up toward the house. Francine stood on the gravel near the door, huddled in her too-thin satin basketball jacket, bouncing on her toes. He'd called to her twice to go in, but she just waved every time he looked up the hill toward her.

The sun was getting stronger now. Terry welcomed its warmth on his back as he banged the hub cap into place. He tossed the old tire, jack, and tire iron into the trunk and slammed it shut.

"It's ten thirty," said Francine's mother. "The commodity truck will already be at Lukachukai School. They won't have nothing left."

Terry went to the driver's side and ducked down to talk to her. "Well, there you go. You can roll now."

She barely glanced at him. "You got to go pick up your grandfather. You know that. You go on now."

Without looking back, she gunned the engine and bounced off, tires flinging mud as high as his shoulder. He trotted back to the house where Francine motioned for him to follow her inside.

"I made you some coffee," she said, peeling off her jacket. "You want a sandwich?"

He looked at his mud-caked hands. "I got to go on to Fort and get my grandpa. He's going to give me hell as it is. Just let me wash up."

She took both his arms and held them away from her as she pressed her body against his and kissed him. "Okay. I guess he bought your gas again, huh?"

Terry shifted his weight to the other foot and looked out the window.

"Well? Are you going to tell me what Brandon Goldtooth said when you told him you wouldn't do any of his crap for him anymore? Or not?" Francine narrowed her eyes and stepped back from him. "Terry?"

"I got to wash up, Francine."

"You didn't tell him, did you? You promised!" Her voice rose in an exasperated squeal. "Ter-reeeee!"

So there he was, forty-five minutes late. And there his grandfather stood at the edge of Old Woman Blackgoat's yard, his hands in his pockets and a deep frown on his face.

Terry got out and pulled open the passenger door. "Sorry, Grandpa. I got stuck fixing Francine's mom's flat tire."

Harrison climbed into the seat and nodded. "Let's get on to Window Rock. You stop at your mother's work and tell her you'll be driving me places today. Back this evening."

As he swung the van back on the road, Terry glanced over at his grandfather's face. The expected ass-chewing hadn't come. Instead the old man stared ahead without speaking. After some several more miles of silence, Terry couldn't take it anymore. "Aw, *Acheii*, I know you're mad. I couldn't help it. Francine's mom —"

"After you talk to your mother, take me on down to the police station."

Geneva rose stiff and sore Wednesday morning. Her left temple, with its scrape and bit of blood she'd dismissed as minor last night, now shone bluish-purple all the way to her left eye. The mark of the shoulder belt on her neck glowed magenta. She dabbed a bit of make-up on both and shrugged. Everything could have been so much worse.

Geneva had learned from Shándíine the night before that Millie, her grandmother, and grand-aunt Nedra were all still visiting in Church Rock. Nedra's new grandchild had a serious case of croup, and they'd all stay another day. Just in case,

Tucker said, they could cure the baby of his cough by their sheer numbers.

She found Tucker asleep in the chair next to Shándiíne's bed. Shándiíne, too, seemed to doze, her thin chest rising and falling evenly. Geneva closed the kitchen door and started coffee and bacon.

Evvie Sutton, true to her word, came in again after breakfast and insisted on staying while Tucker drove Geneva to the Window Rock police station.

"If they can't get my car out, or if it can't be driven, I'll call Angie and she'll come and fetch me, Tucker. I told my girls not to expect me until tomorrow, and I'd phone them again when I find out more."

In the police station, Geneva handed back the clipboard to the young female officer. "No, I didn't get a license number. And I can't be sure of the make or model. But it was small, a fancy little silver car." As the clerk turned to her computer to enter that information, Geneva remembered the decal in the lower windshield. A kachina, wasn't it? A fancy-dancer? No, maybe not. Not important to mention if she couldn't be sure. "That's all I can report. Any word about my car?"

The officer would check again. Please wait.

Geneva turned back to the bench in the hall. Tucker had gone in search of a coffee pot, she knew, so she pantomimed "Be right back" to the clerk and started walking. The short ride from Blue Wind to the police station had convinced her of the wisdom of keeping moving to ward off the painful stiffness threatening to overtake her whole body.

"Mrs. Granger?" Justin Fox stepped out of an office a few feet ahead of her.

"Oh. Agent Fox. Good morning." She shouldn't be surprised to see him here, of course, but she was.

Fox extended his hand, smiling a little, but looking mostly puzzled. "Are you looking for me?"

"No, no, I'm not. I'm here on a different matter. But now that I see you, can you tell me anything about the autopsy, when Bessie Jim's funeral might be, or—" She stopped. Harrison Billy and Lieutenant Charles Nez were coming through the back entrance.

Fox followed her gaze, nodded, and indicated to the approaching pair the doorway he'd just come from.

She tried to catch Harrison's eye, but he kept his head down, his gaze on the heels of the policeman.

"Please excuse me, Mrs. Granger." Fox bent and looked closely at her. "But I see bruises on your temple and neck. You've been hurt. What happened to you?" He stepped aside to let Nez and Harrison go into the room, and with a slight nod to Nez, closed the door behind them and waited for Geneva's answer.

"Yes, I was in an automobile accident, but I'm all right. Why do you have Harrison Billy here?"

Fox frowned as they moved along the hallway. "We need to question him again about the murder at the Peshlakai hogahn. But I'm not at liberty to discuss anything more." He stopped walking and looked into her face. "Please tell me why you are here today."

Geneva wasn't sure how to read his expression. Did he want her to repeat what she saw that day last month? Surely Nez's report of his interview with her at Harrison's hogahn was available to Fox. To her surprise, he took her elbow and steered her through another doorway into an empty office.

"Please sit down," he said, indicating a comfortable-looking chair. "Tell me about your accident. When did it happen?"

They sat. She noticed that he did not take out his notebook, nor did he have the same air of interrogation he'd used at Desbah's house only yesterday.

"Agent Fox, my friend Tucker Bayless brought me here to make the accident report and find out about my car. He's probably wondering where I am at this moment and why I left the clerk's desk. And he's most anxious to get back to his sick wife."

He rose and went to the phone on the desk. "Liz? Mrs. Granger is here with me. Is Mr. Bayless around there? Good. Will you send him down to the judge's office? And Liz? Do you have information about her car?" After a moment, he said, "Thanks, Liz," and hung up. "Your friend will be right down. But we have no word about your car."

Tucker appeared, carrying two Styrofoam cups of coffee. Fox rose and extended his hand.

"I'm Justin Fox, Mr. Bayless. Mrs. Granger and I met yesterday morning in Chinle. She was about to tell me how she got hurt."

Tucker glanced at Geneva and handed her a cup, then shook Fox's hand. "It's a wonder she wasn't hurt worse."

"The wonder is that Tucker found me and saved me from freezing to death," Geneva said. "But we really need to get back, Mr. Fox. Tucker's wife —"

"Mr. Bayless, I'll return Mrs. Granger to your house. Please don't let me delay you in getting back to your wife." Fox and Tucker exchanged a look.

Tucker let another beat go by, then his gaze fastened on Geneva. "Are you all right with that?"

Geneva agreed immediately. She wanted time to find out why Harrison was here. "That's fine, Tuck. Thanks. I'll be all right."

When Tucker had gone, Fox again turned his attention to Geneva's temple and the long bruise across her throat. "Please tell me," he said.

So she did. About the small silver car swerving in front of her. Her sense of soaring. About the cold. And this time, she told about the figure in the tall mask who danced above her on the ridge and those animal figures that followed. Her own words surprised her. Here she was, for the second time telling an officer of the law that she—and she alone—had seen a costumed, twirling man at the scene of a suspicious accident.

"He danced, you say. And chanted." Fox's expression conveyed only interest. "Describe the mask again, please." Fox took out his notebook. "Can you recall what he looked like well enough to sketch him for me? Especially the mask. I can guess about the other costumes."

Geneva wanted to bite her tongue. She sighed and took the pen, wondering if it was too late to say it might have been a hallucination.

When she finished, she handed the pad and pen back to him. She dreaded to look up and see disbelief, maybe even suspicion, in his eyes. When she did look, she saw only that he was studying the drawing.

"Mrs. Granger, will you come with me and show me where this man was exactly? There may be evidence." He didn't wait for an answer, but reached for his jacket draped over the chair at the desk. "Please call your friends and tell them where you'll be. I want to see the scene of your accident. I'm going to speak with Lieutenant Nez for a moment. Meet you in the lobby."

She still didn't know what he thought of her story, nor was she any closer to finding out about Harrison, but she pulled her cell phone out and called Tucker.

"Glad you rang, Geneva. Your daughters—both and each—have called in the last few minutes."

"Oh, Tuck, sorry if they've bothered you. I told them I'd call when I really know something."

"Well, they're both at Karen's house. You'll catch them there. By the way, Desbah called, too, and I've let her know what's happened. She's glad you're okay. But she can't yet say when Bessie's funeral will be."

Geneva told him about Fox's plan to see the scene of the accident, but still didn't mention the masked dancer. She'd been too tired and shaken last night, nor did she want to open the subject as Tucker delivered her here to the police station this morning. He and Shándiíne would think it odd that she hadn't. Well, the whole thing was odd, wasn't it? She thanked him and hung up.

Yes, I'll catch both daughters, she thought, punching in Karen's number. And I'll catch hell for not calling first thing, even though I told them it would be a while before I learned anything.

"Karen? It's Mom, honey."

"Mom! Julianna is frantic. Are you all right? Did you see a doctor? Are you on your way home?"

Geneva explained again about having to find out about the car, assuring Karen she wasn't seriously hurt. The whole thing again.

"Mom, Julianna has already called Uncle Mason to go and get you. You might be hurt worse than you think."

"No, Karen. There's absolutely no reason for that. Call Mason back and tell him not to come. I've just now filed the police report here this morning, and next I'll see about my car. If I need to, I can easily get a ride into Gallup to rent a car and be home this afternoon, or early evening. If there's any big delay, I'll stay here with the Baylesses again tonight. And I'll call you back when I know something. Please don't make such a fuss."

She closed her phone and went into the corridor. Agent Fox stood at the far end, looking her way. Her hope of seeing Harrison, and the brief wild notion of listening at the door where he was being questioned evaporated under Justin Fox's steady gaze.

He gave her a quick smile. "Seems there was no detective available, so I've sent a patrolman to secure the site," he said, as they pulled away from the police station. "Maybe there will be tracks or other evidence of the man on the ridge you mentioned."

Geneva, fresh from her triumph in deflecting the onslaught of her twins' over-protectiveness, settled back in the agent's car and drew a long breath. She felt comfortable with this man. And maybe she needn't know right now why Harrison Billy was in the Navajo police station this morning.

Fox seemed deep in thought for the first few miles out of Window Rock. Geneva didn't mind. She watched how the Ponderosa pines and juniper grew taller and thicker with the increasing elevation as they rose toward the crest of the Defiance Plateau.

"Mrs. Granger, this is in no way an official question," he said, glancing her way. "And you may certainly tell me it is none of my business, but I wonder why you have returned to the reservation twice now, in two months' time after what I understand has been a fairly long absence."

Surprised, Geneva turned to him.

When she didn't immediately reply, Fox smiled, looking a bit embarrassed. "Sorry. I hope you're not offended. But I also wonder about your interest in . . . or connection to Mr. Billy."

"No. Not offended at all, Mr. Fox. "Harrison Billy was a long-time friend of my husband, Edward Granger."

"Oh. Yes, I remember Senator Granger's accident." Fox didn't go on, but looked puzzled.

Geneva told him of Margaret Littleben's letter and of the visit when Harrison said he believed Edward's death was not an accident.

He looked at her, eyebrows raised.

"Our visit to Mrs. Littleben's home that day was brief, but Harrison, his grandson, and my secretary and I met the next morning for breakfast." Now she waited for him to meet her eyes again. "And that's when Harrison told me about a threat someone—'a Phoenix man,' he said—had made against Edward just before his death."

The little campground at the crest, deserted now in winter, lay just ahead and Fox held up a hand to signal for her to pause. He pulled off into a sandy clearing, stopped the car, and half turned in his seat to face her. "Please. Tell me exactly what Mr. Billy said about this threat."

She did. She also related the odd meeting with Ooljee Blackgoat, even the old crystal-gazer's warning about the death hogahn and the man with two airplanes.

To this last, Fox shook his head. "A crystal-gazer. Yes, I know about those." His expression told Geneva much more. It was clear to her that the FBI agent had little use for psychic phenomena.

"So, you went with the old Code Talker and his grandson on to Wheatfields to retrieve your husband's notebook."

She nodded.

"And that's when you witnessed the fire at the abandoned Peshlakai hogahn."

"Yes."

"But, Mrs. Granger, has there been any clue—any other hint, even—that Harrison Billy's statement about your husband's . . . ah, worries . . . was accurate? If I remember it right, almost no remains of the airplane ever surfaced after the storm. But there was never any reason to suspect foul play."

"You're right, of course." She looked down at her hands. She could feel his gaze but didn't look up. A long moment passed.

"But you don't buy that now, do you?"

When she did raise her eyes, she was startled to see the compassion in his.

He said nothing more but pulled the car back onto Highway 264 and headed down the other side of the high plateau.

Rollie Smith remembered the day, not a week before his release five months ago, when the newspaper came to his hand. He'd never been one for reading newspapers much, but there it was in the warden's waiting room. And without him even thinking about it, the newspaper with his son's picture opened up in his very hand.

"*Senator Mason Drake, R. AZ, Announces Candidacy for Governor.*" Rollie knew that face, never mind the little beard, never mind the years. It was Leroy, sure as rain. Them eyes, same as his mother's, always looking at him like he'd expected something better. Well, it was all the damned kid's fault. Him running off like that, making his mother bitch and moan, crying ever' day and night, looking at Rollie with them same eyes, expecting him to go and find her child, bring him back. What for? The boy hated life on the bayous, said everything smelled bad. Was feared of the water, feared of gators, feared even of a damned crawdad.

But no, his mother would turn them big eyes on Rollie day and night. *Find my boy, get out and find my boy.* Like she had call to order him to do anything, her with that twisted polio leg. Her just as useless on a boat as the boy. Well, she asked for what she got. Wonder if them gators broke a tooth on that steel brace.

He shifted a little now in his seat, flipped his cigarette out the window. And thought of it all again.

A man ain't a man if he'll put up with a woman nagging him like that, week in, month out. Her, and then that school principal, slogging his way up to the house. *Where's Leroy, where's Leroy?* She shouldn't of let out a peep, should of said the boy was at his granny's in Maine like he told her. Her own damn fault. No, it was the boy's fault. All of it. Every stinking day of Rollie's thirty-six years behind bars.

I call your name, Leroy Smith. You want to be Mason Drake? No sir. I call your name, Leroy Rollie Smith. Your daddy calls your name.

And now, only five months after walking through them prison gates, here sits Rollie Smith, in the cab of a brand-new tow truck in Holbrook, damn Arizona. What a laugh. A damn fine truck, a fine paycheck made out to one R. Smith, stamped with the signature of A. Goldtooth, Leroy's partner in this fine trucking company. Leroy was paying his daddy's fine wage, not even knowing it. And he'll soon be paying a damn sight more.

More interesting was why this tow was so important to Leroy. Who the hell was in that ditch on the reservation?

CHAPTER EIGHTEEN

The winter sun stood directly overhead by the time Fox arrived with Geneva at the scene of her crash. A Navajo police car sat with lights flashing on the narrow shoulder overlooking the arroyo and her car. The big Navajo who had helped her and Tucker the night before leaned against his car. He gave a nod as they approached.

Fox extended his hand. "Good to see you again, Sergeant Tsosie. Thanks for being so prompt."

Tsosie shook hands, then ducked his head toward Geneva. "Got a call while ago. Tow truck is on its way." He started toward what passed for the path downward. Fox followed for a few paces, then turned.

"Wait, if you will, Sergeant." Fox pointed far down to the left where the arroyo flattened out some. "I wonder if we might find a way to come around from the opposite direction. Would one of those little ranch roads we passed lead around to that point, you think? It might do less damage to the car if it can be pulled out in that direction."

The policeman fetched a pair of binoculars from his car and walked along the edge of the pavement past Geneva and Fox a good distance, stopping several times to focus on what looked to her like miles of a featureless plain rising toward a long mesa dimmed by faraway blue haze.

Tsosie returned. "Maybe so. Let me drive down that way and get a better look."

Geneva gazed down into the arroyo and studied her car, remembering how cold and cramped she had been the night before. She was surprised to see its rakish angle, still high even after Tucker had jumped down on it, he said, and lowered it a couple of feet so he could open her door. She didn't remember that, but smiled now imagining hefty Tucker leaping off the bank above. That racket must have scattered the wildlife. And dented her hood, too, although she couldn't see any dent from here. Only then did it occur to her to wonder who had sent the tow truck. Her girls, without a doubt. She was going to have to put a stop to this Managing Mom.

Fox squatted at the edge of the pavement, examined the ground, then surveyed the shoulder to the weedy, crumbled edge of the bank. "Only one set of tire tracks going this direction, and the footprints right here might be those of you and your friend Bayless. Stay here, please, Mrs. Granger. I'm going down a bit farther."

Fox side-stepped his way down into the arroyo, well away from the path her car had taken yesterday. He stopped often and looked back and forth, sometimes snapping a photo. Not a single vehicle passed in the next ten minutes. She welcomed the heat of the sun on her sore shoulders, marveling how only the merest scraps of snow from Monday night's storm dotted the shadows in the sandy bank below. She thought again of poor Bessie, her snow-covered body hidden in an even deeper arroyo behind the Chinle chapter house. Uncovered by a pack of marauding dogs. Geneva shuddered and turned to watch Fox, who was now climbing back up to the road.

He touched her arm and pointed. "I can see Officer Tsosie coming around to a road down there. Can you see his car out to the left?" He leaned close so she could follow his pointing arm. "Let's drive down and join him, shall we?"

At that moment, a small silver car coming from the direction of Ganado made a sharp U-turn and braked to a stop in front of them. Fox drew Geneva back.

Mason Drake stepped out of the car, his face full of concern. "Geneva! Are you all right?"

Fox moved forward, still holding Geneva's arm. "A bit of a dangerous move there, sir. What's your hurry?"

Geneva shook off Fox's hand, her gaze fastened on the car. "Mason! What are you doing here? Whose car is this?" She moved to the car, looking from it to Mason and back again.

Drake ignored Fox and reached for Geneva's hand. "My dear, Julianna called me. She said you'd been in an accident. Are you all right?"

Fox stepped closer. "Sir, I assure you that Mrs. Granger was not seriously hurt. I'm Justin Fox, FBI, here to investigate the accident, so there's no need for you to —"

"Tell me, Mason. Why are you driving this car?" Geneva took a step toward him.

"What possible importance is that, Geneva? I've come to take you home, to take care of you, to —"

Geneva spun around to Fox. "This is the car! This is the car that ran me off the road!" She faced Drake again. "Mason, did you do it? Were you driving this car yesterday?"

Fox took Geneva's arm again and tried to draw her toward his car. "Please, Mrs. Granger. Let me take care of this. Will you wait in my car?"

"No, I won't! I know this is the car that followed me yesterday, then sped in front of me and put on the brakes. I saw it plainly. And that bright yellow decal there on the windshield — I remember it!"

Fox pulled her around to face him and held up his hand. "Stop. Please. Wait in my car." He guided her to it and held open the door. She continued to stare at Drake, but got in. She rolled the window down so she could hear.

Fox returned to Drake, who stood rubbing the back of his neck, still gazing after Geneva. "Now, Senator, if you'll just show me your license and registration, I'm sure all this can be cleared up."

A red tow truck had crawled to a stop on the other side of the road a few minutes before. The driver, the brim of his cap pulled low, waved what looked like a map, but said nothing. Fox nodded and signaled him to wait. "Be with you in a moment." He turned back to Drake. "That registration, please?"

From Fox's car, Geneva could see Drake bend over, open the glove compartment, and hand over a small folder. Fox examined the registration and insurance card. "Albert Goldtooth? The councilman?"

"Yes, he's my friend, Agent Fox. I've borrowed his car this morning. I just flew in to Window Rock at the request of Mrs. Granger's daughters to assist her. They want me to bring her back home to Flagstaff, and I mean to do just that. You may certainly verify that I was in Phoenix all day yesterday and that Mr. Goldtooth was in Window Rock, and nowhere near here. I'm afraid Mrs. Granger is confused about the car."

Fox didn't reply as he finished making his notes. "I'm sure she will decide for herself how she'll get home, Mr. Drake. In the meantime, please let us finish with this business. Do you have a number in case she wants to call you when she and I get back to Window Rock?"

"She knows my number," Drake growled.

Fox motioned for the tow-truck driver to turn his truck around. "Driver, you'll want to follow me. The car is in this wash down here. But it has to be taken out from the other side."

Fifteen minutes later, Geneva still sat in Fox's vehicle, now on a dirt track below the highway, and watched her car wobble and lurch upward on the chains of the tow truck. Fox and the policeman stood at a distance talking. She couldn't hear what they said and didn't care. The scene with Mason troubled her. She glanced at the sky, now clouding over. Her head and limbs ached. All her earlier determination to deal with her car, get to Gallup for a rental, and do whatever else this business required seemed to dissipate in the wind that now thrashed the scrubby bushes a yard from where she sat.

What was she doing out here anyway? She hadn't learned anything solid about Edward's death. And what could she do about any of it if she did? Maybe her girls were right. She needed to go home, finish her new book, stop playing the sleuth. Next time she could end in a bloody snowbank in some even deeper ravine. The chill in her bones seemed to gather around her heart. Face it, she told herself. You're not up to this.

Fox came to Geneva's side of the car and leaned on the lowered window. "Mrs. Granger, your car can't be driven after all. The tow-truck driver wants to know where to take it. Do you want to speak to him? He's got it loaded on now. Oh, here he comes."

Geneva sighed. "I was afraid of that." She buttoned her jacket and stepped out to meet the thin, stubble-whiskered man walking toward them.

"You got at least a bent axle, ma'am. She can't be driven a-tall. You want to give me the address to deliver to?"

Geneva found her business card and that of the dealership in Flagstaff. "Just deliver it to Mountain Motors, Mr. uh . . ."

"Smith, ma'am. R. J. Smith with Holbrook Trucking & Tow, at your service." He bobbed his head and presented his own card. He turned hers over in his hand. "This your address in Flagstaff?"

"Yes. I suppose one of my daughters called you, but this is where your bill should be sent."

"No, ma'am. Wasn't a woman."

She looked at him full in the face for the first time. He cocked his head and raised his eyebrows as if waiting for her to say more. She knew then it must have been Mason but refrained from engaging this man any further. She pointed to her business card, which he still held. "Have your office send the bill to my address."

"Yes, ma'am."

Geneva heard the weeds and gravel crunch underfoot as he went back to his truck. She turned away, wondering how Mason knew where to send the tow truck. Well, of course he'd know how to get that information from the Navajo police. So would Julianna, she supposed.

Fox met her and fell into step. "I've had a call to go to Chinle, Mrs. Granger. Sergeant Tsosie will take you back to your friends' home at Window Rock." He nodded at the policeman, who opened his car door for her.

Fox smiled at her and reached to shake her hand. "I know you must be tired, and the temperature is going down again." He closed the car door behind her and leaned down. "Was there anything besides the glove compartment contents you wanted us to get for you?"

She shook her head. "No. But thank you. I'll call my friends to let them know I'm coming back." She pulled out her cell phone and looked at it, but didn't dial.

"Mrs. Granger, are you really all right?" Fox bent closer. "You've had quite a hard couple of days here, what with your friend Mrs. Jim, and then this accident. Maybe you should let Senator Drake fly you back home. He said you have his cell phone number. The officer here can have you at the Window Rock airport in less than an hour. You could be in your own house and bed tonight."

"I'll be fine, thank you. Agent Fox, you haven't said a word about finding anything on the bank above my car, the place I showed you where that man, that . . . person danced last night."

Fox straightened. "I'm going to take another look before I go." He gave the car door a smart pat and stepped back. "We'll be in touch."

Two hours later, Mason Drake, his suit jacket folded on the seat beside him, sat in a back booth of the almost deserted dining room of Window Rock's Quality Inn. He tried Albert Goldtooth's number again. No answer. Lunchtime traffic had cleared out, and the wait staff stood around the front desk chatting, finally tired, Drake guessed, of asking him if he wanted anything else. He hoped he'd convinced them he was busy by bending over some papers he'd spread on his table and avoiding eye contact. He tried Goldtooth one more time.

"Yeah. Goldtooth."

"Albert, I need to talk to you. I'm at the Inn. Can you get over here?"

Twenty minutes later, Goldtooth, resplendent in a tan Western-style suit, ostrich-hide boots, and massive turquoise bracelets, stood in the dining room doorway and signaled with his chin for Drake to follow. Without a word, they went up to a second-floor conference room. Goldtooth lowered his bulk into a chair and waited for Drake to speak.

Drake remained standing, letting a moment pass. "It's about Brandon," he said. "Where was he yesterday afternoon?"

Albert Goldtooth didn't answer his partner for a long moment, but regarded the agitated Drake, now pacing the conference room. "What do you mean? How the hell do I know where Brandon was yesterday? He picked you up at the airport like you wanted this morning, didn't he?"

"Yes. This is Wednesday. I'm talking about yesterday, Tuesday afternoon. Did he have the Viper Tuesday afternoon?"

"Why?"

"Damn it, Albert. He ran Geneva Granger off the road

north of Ganado! Her car landed in a hell of a deep ditch. She was hurt and would have frozen to death if Bayless hadn't found her. That's why, damn it! That's why!"

Now Goldtooth got to his feet but stood still, eyes narrowed. "Who told you that? Who said it was my grandson?"

Drake took a step forward and stood just as still as the other man. "She recognized the car when I got there this morning. That's how. How many silver Vipers do you think there are on this reservation? And there's only one in the whole damned country with that tacky yellow decal on the windshield! She recognized the car!"

Goldtooth gave a dismissive wave of the hand and sat again, crossing his legs. He calmly adjusted the bolo tie around his neck, touching its palm-sized turquoise bear. He picked up his Stetson and flicked a bit of lint from it. Finally, he lifted his eyes again to Drake.

"No, she didn't. Brandon was with me Tuesday, I remember now. I picked him up at his girlfriend's place over near Fort about eleven. We had lunch with his mother and dad right here in Window Rock and I left him there at home." Goldtooth stood and put on his hat. "Then I drove the car back to my office. You can ask at least three people who saw it. That car stayed right in front of the council chambers all afternoon. Your would-be sweetheart is wrong."

Mason Drake stared at his partner and struggled to control his expression.

Goldtooth stared back. "You forgot, didn't you, *Sen*-a-tor?"

Goldtooth's accent on the first syllable spoke contempt to Drake. He drew in a vast breath. "No, Albert. I didn't forget. I asked you to keep an eye on Geneva Granger while she was on the reservation." His voice grew hard. "What I did not ask was that young Brandon run her off the goddamn road and risk killing her!"

Goldtooth got to his feet again. "Maybe you should pay

attention to what we told you then. She's been snooping around, asking a hell of a lot of questions. And not just about *Sen*-a-tor Edward Granger, either."

Drake knew his face had gone red, but he maintained his frown.

"One more little thing," Goldtooth said. "My man in the police department said old Harrison Billy is not likely to be charged in that ASU professor's death."

Drake folded his arms across his chest. "Not with Layton's murder, I know that. But conspiracy is just as good. And his grandson's little toy is going to do it for both of them."

"I'm glad you think so, Drake. But unless we can put him or his pup grandson at the Chinle chapter house the night of that education meeting, your bright idea about stopping that damned Bessie Jim is going to blow up in our face."

CHAPTER NINETEEN

R ollie Smith fingered Geneva's business card for a
moment before tucking it into his shirt pocket and
easing the tow truck, her car attached, back onto the dirt track.

So this here's your little lady, Leroy, he thought. She's got
some sass to her, boy. Wonder do you like 'em sassy. If I heard
right, you come a ways just to fetch her, and her not wanting to
be fetched. Leastways not by you. Now that other feller, him a
FBI man, he said, he's a-gonna move in on your territory,
don't-cha-know. I seen it clear as day. Maybe you'll be wanting
to go after her worse, what with a FBI man sniffing around.
Wonder just how much she's worth to you now, boy?

Smith pulled his truck onto the highway and looked for the
silver Viper, but it was out of sight. He headed back toward I-
40 behind the Navajo police car that carried Geneva Granger.
He followed for a time, but it soon turned off, headed for
Window Rock, while he stayed on 191 bound for I-40 and
Flagstaff.

Darkness had fallen when he off-loaded the damaged car at
the Flagstaff dealership's service yard, got the necessary papers
signed, and stopped for some supper. As he waited for his

order, he pulled the business card from his shirt pocket. On one side was her address and phone number. On the other:

G ENEVA BOND GRANGER, PhD
Education is the ladder for the spirit

W hen the waitress set his plate before him, he read Geneva's address to her. "Do you know whereabouts this street is, honey?"

He left the restaurant with a Flagstaff street map, directions clearly marked, and found a motel. Dropping his duffle bag on the bed, he pulled out his cell phone and called the foreman in Holbrook. "Milburn? Made the Granger delivery to Mountain Motors. I'm overnight in Flag. Call me if there's anything on the way back tomorrow. But not too early, hear?"

Prison had taught Smith many things. One was how to sleep for exactly the time he wanted and to wake instantly alert. Midnight, it would be.

And midnight it was. He woke, pulled on a dark jacket and cap, and called a taxi. Twenty minutes later, he stepped out, a block from Geneva's house. When the cab disappeared, he walked around the corner and down her street. Few houses and almost all of them dark. Lots of trees and shrubs. Nobody would notice the high-shouldered old man striding along in the night.

At her house, the porch light and a small interior light burned, but no one answered the bell. Smith moved quickly around to the back. Patience wasn't the only thing he'd learned in prison. Tyko, a big Swede and Smith's cellmate for the last fourteen years, proclaimed himself the best burglar in five southern states. And he never got caught for burglary. Tyko was in prison for cracking the skull of a bouncer who tried to throw him out of a bar. Prison was boring, Tyko said, and so he proceeded to teach Smith about the "pure finesse" of breaking and entering.

And Smith had been practicing here and there. Two, three places in Natchez. Two more in Tyko's hometown of Baton Rouge, just to honor his old teacher. Enough to buy that jalopy that made it to Arizona so he could look up his big important senator son. And now Mister Big Shit's little lady. He smiled and stuck out his grizzled chin.

I'm ready for that big exam now, Tyko, he thought.

Once inside, he took out a small flashlight, stopped to look and listen at each doorway, and finally climbed the stairs. Assured, he stepped into a room with a desk and bookshelves and closed the heavy drapes over the French doors.

Here was a whole wall full of photographs. He took his time, shining his light on each one. Lots of a man together with this Granger woman—husband probably. Twin girls, pictures of them at different ages. Now those girls as brides, then with babies. Lots more pictures of this woman and man, one in front of a castle. A little picture of her at a table full of books. Looked to be writing in one of them and smiling up at some people.

Whoa, here's Leroy right in the middle of somebody's birthday party. Him in a party hat. Here again with the husband and one of the twins with ski gear on. Grinning like some ape. Well, well, Leroy, ain't you the bosom buddy? Now I wonder how come you went out there on the Indian reservation today to get this woman, instead of her husband. Why wasn't he out there to fetch her or, more like it, why wasn't he with her to begin with?

Smith turned his attention to the desk. Within a quarter of an hour, he had what he thought was a good notion of Geneva Granger's life. Newspaper clippings. The husband, him a senator, too, by damn, dead in a plane crash three years ago. Letters and cards about her winning some award for writing a book about Indians. Indians. Huh.

Mindful of Tyko's instruction, Smith carefully replaced every item as he'd found it and made his way out without leaving a trace, he was certain.

So, Leroy, you ready to move in on this famous book-writing widow-woman, are you? Her price is going up. What'll you give for her, boy?

He was down the stairs and out the back door before it occurred to him to wonder what this Geneva Granger was doing out in that godforsaken Indian land in the middle of last night anyways.

Sergeant Tsosie parked and followed Geneva up to the Bayless' doorway late that afternoon. Tucker stepped out to meet them. "Thank you, Officer Tsosie," he said, reaching to shake hands with him and taking Geneva's arm with the other. "You've sure put in a day, haven't you, man?"

Geneva added her thanks and smiled at both of them.

Tsosie gave a nod and turned back to his car. "That's all right."

Tucker held the door open wide. "We're sure glad you came back, Geneva. Come on in. I've got a pot of green chile stew and some good old Arkansas cornbread just waiting for you."

Shándiíne's wan face lit with a wide smile. "I'm sorry about your car, Geneva, but glad for some more time with you."

Geneva dropped into a chair next to Shándiíne's bed and took her hand in both of hers. "Oh, my dear friend, thank you. Plans keep changing, don't they?"

"They do, they do," Tucker boomed from the kitchen doorway. "And Mom Yazzie and Millie are spending another night in Church Rock, just to prove the point. Aunt Nedra's new grandchild just can't do without her." Out of Shándiíne's view, he made a great face of surprise and delight, waggling thumbs-up at Geneva.

"It's a good break for Millie—and my mom, too," Shándííne said, winking to let Geneva know she'd guessed Tucker's silly gestures. They both smiled.

Geneva couldn't bear to mar this rare hour of pleasure and peace in the Bayless household with what she'd learned that morning. Shándííne seemed almost her old self, and Tucker's relief and happiness about it was nearly palpable. Geneva felt humble and blessed to be a part of it.

How wonderful to see the old spark in Shándííne and remember how endlessly playful she and Tucker used to be. Edward would always say those two were like imps—the best kind of imps, so much in love.

She managed to deflect every dart of memory of Mason behind the wheel of the little silver car with the dancing kachina on the windshield.

After a relaxed dinner that Tucker made into a picnic around her bed, and an hour's conversation, Shándííne was ready for sleep.

So was Geneva. She stood and stretched. Her shoulder and neck weren't her only sore spots. Seemed new ones had made themselves known all day. "I've arranged for Angie to rent a car in Flag and pick me up tomorrow. She'll probably be here before noon. And my girls, bless them, know every detail. Good night, dear hearts—and thank you again."

Tucker walked with her out to the studio. They talked and laughed on the way, and she thought again of the many wonderful times she and Edward had spent with these old friends.

Tucker was in the midst of recalling a particular visit long ago, laughing hard.

Geneva saw a flash of yellow light strike the photograph of Edward and herself in Europe on their anniversary trip. Then her desk. A hand opened the file drawer of her desk at home.

"Oh!" She stumbled forward.

Tucker caught her before she hit the ground. "Whoa, there! Geneva—what happened? Are you all right?"

He helped her along the last few steps to the studio door and flipped on the light. "Sit down here, girl. What's the matter?"

It was gone, of course, the flash of images, but the shock remained. "Someone's in my house."

"What's that? Here, let me get you some water, or maybe whiskey. You're white as a sheet, hon." Tucker steadied her, seeming afraid to let her arm go long enough to get to the sink.

"I'm all right, Tuck." She looked up at him, her gaze clear. "But somebody is in my house in Flagstaff. I've got to call the girls. Julianna lives closer—no, the police. I've got to tell Julianna to call the police." She bent to pull her cell phone out of her purse.

"Geneva, is this one of those—those visions you get? Is that what it is?"

She stood then and clasped his arm. "Yes. But you must go back to the house and be with Shándíine. I can do what needs to be done. I'm calling Julianna this minute. Sorry if I startled you, Tucker. Go on, you mustn't leave Shándíine alone any longer." She managed a smile and what she hoped was a normal expression. "It's all right, really. Go. Don't worry. Please."

He finally did go, but not before seeing her into the bedroom and finding a bottle of sherry and a glass. "Here you are, Geneva. I'm putting this right here on the table. It'll help you relax and get some sleep. But buzz me on my cell and let me know what's going on in Flag. It won't bother Shándíine. You hear me?"

Just as the studio door closed behind him, her daughter answered the phone.

"Julianna, honey, I'm at Blue Wind and I'm just fine. So

are Shándiíne and Tucker, before you ask. But something's wrong at home."

"What? Mom—what? How do you know? Oh, of course, never mind. What did you see?"

"An intruder, Julianna. Someone, a man, in the house, upstairs. I want you to call the police, but don't go there before they do. He might be dangerous."

"Did you see a face? Can you identify him?"

"No, honey, but you're wasting time. Please call the police now. And call me back and let me know if they catch him."

In the years since Geneva had sought and received not only grief counseling but repeated professional assurances that her psychic ability was not the curse she believed, she'd tried hard to agree. After all, what choice did she have? Again, she wished she could call it up with a purpose in mind. All she'd seen was a light striking her photographs. And a hand reaching into her desk files. As she waited for Julianna's return call, she leaned back against the pillows on her bed and put herself through the relaxation exercises she'd learned to rely on.

She closed her eyes. All right. Try to see it again. It was a man's bony hand, yes. What else? A small beam of yellow light. Flashlight, no doubt. Light on a photograph. No, photographs. Light on one after another of her photographs. What was he doing? Sometimes the light moved quickly. Then it paused. She and Edward at the Edinburgh Castle. Edward and the twins. Edward and Karen on the ski slope. With Mason. Mason at the twins' tenth birthday party. Mason. Edward. Mason again.

Her cell phone rang at half past ten. "Mom, it's Julianna. I think you're mistaken this time. Since you called at nine fifteen, the police and I have been through every inch of the house. No one's been there. Everything is tight. They said they'd cruised through your neighborhood as usual around nine—nothing amiss, not even any barking dogs. Honest."

"Oh." Geneva sank back into her pillows. "Oh. Well, then,

if you're certain. I'm so sorry to make you go to all that trouble."

"Mom? Are you sure you're all right? Thom's back from his business trip a day early—I can come instead of Angie to get you tomorrow, you know. Let me do that."

"Nonsense, darling. I know you have court on Friday and need time to prepare. Angie's all excited for the trip—you know her. I'll be home well before dark, unless we stop at Alfredo's for dinner. Anyway, I'll call you. Thank you, sweetheart."

After calling Tucker as promised, Geneva undressed and went to bed. So she was mistaken. But she knew she was not mistaken.

Never mind, go to sleep. She called up the calming litany so long practiced since Edward's death: *Sleep, sleep. Feel yourself floating downward into a billowing cloud of relaxation. Ten . . . nine . . . eight . . .*

Two hours later she woke. In her dream, the word *Jefferson* in elegant Spenserian script, had dropped, one letter at a time, to hang shining above a flat surface of water. But what it meant, why she saw it, was unclear. No feeling of terror or foreboding accompanied it. But a deep sadness, her sense-code for illness or inevitable wrong. It had to do with Edward, certainly, but in a distant, slightly removed way. Odd.

She went back to sleep.

In the shower early Thursday morning, Geneva stood with her eyes closed, willing her sore shoulder muscles to relax under the steaming water.

The clock on her desk at home caught a flash of yellow light—*12:52 a.m.* The man's hand pulled out a newspaper clipping. SENATOR EDWARD GRANGER KILLED IN PLANE CRASH. Back to the wall of pictures. Mason with his arm around Edward's shoulders. Another flash of light—*12:53 a.m.*

CHAPTER TWENTY

Angie arrived mid-morning Thursday, earlier than expected, for which Geneva was grateful. After a quick snack, they bade the Baylesses good-bye and set out.

The minute they were on the highway, Angie frowned at Geneva and shook her head. "Eeeee, that black eye is something, Geneva. This Navajo reservation is a bad place for you, no? Lucky thing you have good friends here to save you, I think."

Geneva sighed and settled back in the passenger seat. "Good friends, yes, Angie. Better friends to me than I have been to them, I'm afraid. Dear friends I've neglected while wallowing in my sorrow these past three years. And poor Bessie, too."

When she finished telling Angie about what had happened, Angie shuddered. "*Dios mio*! Buried in the snow in that arroyo? A pack of dogs — Ee-e-eee."

"Yes," Geneva said. "It's hard to accept. My old friend and teaching partner murdered. Her daughter is only eighteen and now has no parent at all. A multitude of other relatives, of course, but . . ."

Angie knew nothing of Geneva's vision of the blood-stained

snow days before it happened, and she decided to keep it that way for now. She'd heard Angie's wide-eyed stories her Mexican grandparents and many aunts had told her of magical *curanderas* and witches. Better she not know of Geneva's own private spookiness.

"And what about you?" Angie's hand flew off the wheel, gesturing toward the windshield. "Does anybody know who ran you off the road? What are the police doing about that?"

Geneva didn't mention seeing Mason with the silver car.

"I don't know, Angie. I don't know. But maybe I will rest a bit if you don't mind. If I fall asleep, please wake me when we get to Holbrook."

Mason. Of course he was telling the truth. Somebody else had to have been driving that car on Tuesday. He'd tell her later how he came to be driving it yesterday. She'd been too hasty. Shouldn't have gotten so upset. He'll explain later . . . Mason was their old friend . . . Edward's best friend . . .

Angie touched her arm. "Geneva, wake up. There's a sign to Holbrook up ahead. You want to stop?"

Geneva retrieved the business card the tow truck driver had given her. "Yes. I want to find this Holbrook Trucking & Tow. Let's see if we can spot a city police car or mail carrier and find out where it is."

I can do this much, she thought. Finding out who sent the tow truck can't send me into an arroyo. Certainly not a snowy one to be dug up by dogs. Then I'll stop digging for answers.

An elderly Holbrook policeman gave them directions to the edge of town. They soon came upon a high fence with a small sign at the gate. Geneva gestured, palm up, at the sign. "Here we are. It all looks big and new, but it's rather—um, modest, almost hidden, wouldn't you say?"

"Well, they sure don't know how to advertise, if that little sign is all they've got," Angie said.

The wide gate was open, however, and they drove up to a

long metal building with a small segment at the end marked OFFICE.

Geneva got out of the car. "I'll just be a minute, Angie. I want to know who called this company to send a tow truck all the way to the reservation for me when there are two or three much closer in Gallup."

"Take your time, Geneva. I'm going to walk around a little, stretch my legs."

In the sparse office, a Navajo man of about forty stood behind the counter and greeted her with a nod.

A door that led into a large, high-ceilinged garage behind him stood slightly ajar, the odor of gasoline and grease floating through it. Geneva smiled at him and glanced at the maps and truck ads on the walls. In the corner to her right stood a full-length cardboard cut-out photo of a fancy-dancer, the high fan of his feather headdress and huge yellow bustle bent and furled with the force of his leap. Despite the painted face, she recognized Brandon Goldtooth, the young man who confronted Harrison's grandson at the gas station in Navajo last month. The same fellow she saw briefly at the panel discussion.

The same dancer, the same photo as the decal on the windshield of the silver car.

"Help you?" said the man behind the counter. "You want to hire a truck?"

She pulled her gaze away from the cardboard figure. "Actually, I'm already a customer. My name is Geneva Granger. Your driver, a Mr. Smith, picked up my car near Ganado yesterday." She paused, waiting for a response.

None came.

"I want to know who sent that tow truck," she said.

"Sent it? The dispatcher."

"Yes, of course. I mean the person who called for a tow truck to pick up my car."

The man's expression didn't change. "I wasn't here. Milburn works nights."

"But surely you have a record of that call. Please find out who requested your truck to go out there."

"You got I.D.?"

Geneva produced her identification and composed her expression into polite expectation. She waited, remembering that most Navajos, unlike most Anglos, were perfectly comfortable with long silences during a conversation. But she was the customer here after all, and her question was not improper. Her gaze went back to the tall dancer cut-out.

The man flipped through what she assumed was some sort of log. "Boss called it in. Seven thirty a.m."

"And who is that, please? The owner. What is his name?"

The man opened a drawer and produced a glossy red fold-over business card, quite different from the plain one the driver had given her. "Here," he said. "It's on the bottom."

She looked where he pointed. *A. Goldtooth & Associates.*

"Is that Albert Goldtooth, the tribal councilman?"

He nodded.

"Thank you." She slipped the card into her purse and turned to go. "By the way, who is the dancer pictured there, the fancy-dancer? Is that Mr. Goldtooth's grandson Brandon?"

He nodded again.

Not until she was back in the car did she wonder who Albert Goldtooth's associates might be.

Angie pulled the car back onto the street, smiling in her impish way. "Guess what I found out, walking around stretching my legs," she said.

"That this outfit is owned by Councilman Goldtooth?"

"What? Who's that? No, it belongs to Senator Drake!"

For a moment Geneva could only stare at her.

"It's true," Angie said. "I got into a conversation out back there with a Mexican guy. He was bragging about knowing the senator personally. Said Drake is *el jefe. Muy importante.*"

Geneva sat back and thought about that for several miles.

Back in Flagstaff after she and Angie had ordered their

meal at Alfredo's, Geneva called Karen. "I'm in Flagstaff, honey. Angie and I are going to enjoy our dinner and then she'll drop me at home. All's well. How are you, dear? Ray and the kids all right?"

"We're fine, Mom. But I'm worried about that intruder — Julianna said you were mistaken. But I know you're never wrong. What time will you be home? I'll meet you there."

Geneva started to protest but changed her mind. "That would be sweet, darling. I'm eager to see you both. Shall we say seven?"

"Great — I'll let Julianna know. We'll meet you."

Promptly at seven, Angie pulled into the driveway behind the twins' two vehicles. "I guess they missed you, Geneva. A nice welcome home." She lowered her window and waved to Karen and Julianna stepping from their cars.

Twenty minutes later Geneva was brewing tea for her daughters in the kitchen.

Julianna stirred honey into her tea and passed the cream to her sister. "Karen says your visions are never wrong, that somebody really was in the house last night. But, Mom, I was here with the police. Nothing was taken or even out of place — I checked."

"Well, dears, you are both right." To their looks of surprise, she lifted her hands, palms out. "I know that someone — a man, I'm sure — was upstairs in my study flashing a light on the photographs and then pulling files out of my desk drawer. But it didn't happen at the time it first came to me."

Karen leaned closer. "What does that mean?"

Julianna put her hand to her chest. "You saw it again? After nine or so last night when you called me?"

"Yes. It happened later, almost one o'clock. I saw the clock, his light on my desk clock, when I was in the shower at Blue Wind this morning."

Her daughters exchanged a look.

Karen frowned and flipped her hair back. "This is something new, isn't it? Having a second — what? Second look? I've never known you to do that."

"Does that mean you're able to do what that counselor in Phoenix tried to teach you — to control and call back your visions in detail?" Julianna said.

Geneva's eyebrows lifted. "Well, yes. I guess so. But the important thing is who was that man? And what did he want?"

"That does it," Julianna slapped the table. "You've got to go ahead with that alarm system we talked about. It will notify the police immediately if someone opens a door and then fails to punch in the right code."

Karen stood up. "Absolutely. You're out of town too often with the speeches and such, Mom. This can't happen again."

Geneva remembered the powerful waking vision at Blue Wind last night and again this morning. "All right," she said. "All right, I will." She also remembered the shining word *Jefferson* and the reflecting water. Puzzling, but that one hardly needed an alarm system.

CHAPTER TWENTY-ONE

The next morning, Geneva sat at the dining table sorting through her mail and enjoying the play of light on the San Francisco Peaks through her window. The bare upper slopes glowed with light snow. Below the timber line, the tips of the evergreens caught fraying scraps of cloud, now lighted with refracted pink light, now shadowed in dark blue. She felt at peace for the moment, so glad to be home.

The telephone rang. Her mellow mood came through her voice. "Good morning, this is Geneva."

"Mrs. Granger, this is Agent Fox. I have a bit of news for you." He told her the details of Bessie's upcoming funeral and more about the autopsy than she wanted to know, concluding with, "That means the killer was a good deal taller than Mrs. Jim and probably left-handed. Unfortunately, we've found no knife yet."

Geneva's mind flashed to the night of the panel discussion and seeing Brandon Goldtooth coming from behind chapter house, tucking something under his right arm.

"Agent Fox, I must tell you something—it may be nothing important, of course, but . . ."

When she'd finished, Fox said, "I have a police artist's

sketch here done during our second interview with Mrs. Jim's daughter. And I'd like to see the pictures you took of the Peshlakai hogahn. I can be in Flagstaff in about two hours. May I come to your home?"

Geneva agreed. Maybe he would also have some information about the dancer on the ridge above her wrecked car.

She stifled her worry about the silver automobile and Mason Drake. No doubt he would call and explain it all. She would just wait.

Gathering up yesterday's mail, Geneva went up to her office, but stopped short at the doorway. Fingerprints. She should have thought of that before. The man's hand she saw in her vision wore no glove—there must be fingerprints. She turned from the doorway and ran downstairs.

Back at the kitchen table, she dropped the mail and sank into a chair to think. Flagstaff police had satisfied themselves that no intruder had been in her house. Unlikely they'd want to return and dust for fingerprints. Agent Fox? Oh, no. She couldn't imagine how she would explain why there should be fingerprints of an intruder to either the police or Fox. She leaned back and squeezed her eyes shut. But there would be fingerprints. She knew it.

She bustled about the kitchen inventing little chores for a long time, but was no closer to an idea of how to get fingerprints from her desk or anyplace else when the doorbell rang.

"Agent Fox. Come in, please."

"Thank you, Mrs. Granger." He let her take his overcoat and gray Stetson.

"I've made coffee, Mr. Fox. Will you sit here in the dining room?"

Settled at the table, Fox accepted coffee with fervent thanks, remarked on the difference in the weather from Phoenix's low elevation to the nearly 7,000 feet where Flagstaff sat. "Two different life zones, altogether," he said. "I've always liked it. Born and raised here. My father lives here, still in the same old house."

"Really? Oh, is the big law firm, Fox and Grayson, connected to your family?"

"Yes. My father's firm. Jedediah Fox and the late Arnold Grayson." He raised his coffee cup in a kind of salute and smiled.

His smile surprised Geneva. He'd been pleasant enough when they'd met before, of course, but she didn't recall a real smile. It transformed his rather plain angular face into a—a handsome one. The thought unsettled her.

Smile gone, Fox bent over the large envelope he'd brought. "Charlene Jim agreed to talk with us again," he said. "She remembered several incidents on the night of her mother's murder." He glanced at Geneva. "One was something of a confrontation with Albert Goldtooth during the panel discussion at the Chinle chapter house. Do you recall that?"

Geneva described Bessie's accusation of both Goldtooth and Drake about the quarry.

"The quarry, or proposed quarry, in Black Canyon," Fox said. "The one she and Professor Layton were warning residents of Black Canyon about."

"Yes." Geneva expected more questions about that, or about how Drake figured into it, but none came.

"We know about the connection between Senator Drake and Albert Goldtooth," he said, surprising her again. "They worked together to get the permits to build the quarry. They mean to sell that hard, volcanic rock of Black Canyon to the state highway department. Mrs. Jim was right about that."

Geneva could only nod.

"And they're partners in the trucking company they expect to use to haul the rock away to the state depositories for road work. Holbrook Trucking and Tow, it's called."

Instantly she heard in her mind the old driver's words: *R. J.*

Smith, Holbrook Trucking and Tow—at your service, ma'am. An icy explosion seemed to strike her eyes.

"Oh!" she cried, holding her temples and bending low, knocking her empty cup away.

Fox jumped to his feet and clasped her shoulder. "Mrs. Granger, what is it? What's wrong?"

A moment later Geneva lifted her head and met Fox's gaze. "I'm sorry. I—I just had a . . . a thought. I mean, please excuse me for a moment."

She started toward the little bathroom off the kitchen, but Fox was right behind her. "Are you ill, Mrs. Granger? Can I help you somehow?"

Geneva paused, her hand on the back of a kitchen chair. "No, I'm not ill, Mr. Fox." To her complete amazement, she heard herself say what only her immediate family and close friends knew. "I . . . I know things. I mean, I see things sometimes. I just saw the man who was in my house last night."

Fox took her elbow and led her back to her chair at the dining table. He righted her coffee cup, and sat beside her without speaking. He poured more coffee for both of them and sat looking at her for a long moment. "Perhaps you should explain."

The momentary urge that impelled her to tell Fox of her visions had evaporated, but she went on. "I know you'll think this is ridiculous. Or worse. But I sometimes have pictures, images in my head, or feelings of—of certainty about . . . things." She trailed off without looking at him.

"And just now," he said, "you had a . . . feeling or picture? Of what, exactly?"

She had to tell him; no way around it. And she did, feeling his cool doubt rise as she spoke.

When he said nothing more, she drew a deep breath. "I want you to see about fingerprints, Mr. Fox. There must be fingerprints this intruder left behind. Because he didn't wear gloves. I saw his bare hand."

After a short silence, Fox said, "Maybe we can talk about that later. Right now, can you examine this sketch and see if you recognize the man Charlene Jim thinks might have harmed her mother?"

He pulled a sketch from the envelope.

There was no doubt. "That's Albert Goldtooth's grandson. Brandon Goldtooth is his name," she said. "He's the one I told you about on the phone. The young man I saw coming from the back of the Chinle chapter house that night."

Fox nodded and slid the sketch back into the envelope.

"Do you have more evidence?" Geneva asked. "What are you going to do next about Bessie's murder?"

"That, Mrs. Granger, I'm not at liberty to discuss. Are these the photos you took in September?"

"Yes, and you may take them, of course. I have another set."

He slid the packet of photos into the large envelope with the sketch, murmuring his thanks. He looked distracted, distant.

She wanted to ask him a dozen questions—what else Charlene had said about young Goldtooth, what Fox might have learned about the dancer on the ridge—and tell him she thought it might be Brandon instead of Mason who'd been driving the little silver car. But now she remained silent, too. Fox must think she was crazy.

He rose and held her gaze. "Thank you for your assistance in identifying the person in the sketch, Mrs. Granger." He stayed where he was, apparently considering something.

She stood as well, hoping her desperation didn't show. But she had to ask. "Please, Mr. Fox. Can you possibly check for fingerprints? Upstairs, I mean."

"Have you or anyone else handled things since this alleged intruder entered your office?"

"I don't think so. As I said, I had my daughter Julianna and the Flagstaff police search the house before I returned.

But I myself haven't touched anything. I didn't go in there this morning. Still, my own and my family's prints must be everywhere."

"Yes," he said. "They would be. But I will do what you ask." He went out to his car and returned with a boxy satchel. "Show me, please," he said.

Together they went up to Geneva's study. She indicated the wall of family photographs before them. "I don't think he touched any of these," she said. "He shined his flashlight on them."

Fox's gaze swept over the pictures and back to her. He said nothing, and she felt her face flush.

"But he went to my desk. Over here," she said, turning toward it. "He opened this file drawer. And pulled out some—" She was nearly choking with the certainty that Fox thought her a fool. He must be humoring her, seeing how far she would go with this craziness. She couldn't look at him.

"Some files, you said earlier." Fox bent and inserted a pen at the edge of the lower drawer to pull it open. "Particular files?"

"Well, several. Some in particular."

"All right. We'll get to those. I'll start with the outside, the drawer handle and such." He set his kit down and opened it. "You can show me which particular files you . . . saw . . . the man pull out in a moment."

Geneva retreated several feet behind Fox as he began his procedure. She could feel her face and throat still flaming.

"Mrs. Granger, I understand you have taught classes both at Diné College on the reservation and here at NAU. Would your own fingerprints be on file in your credentials somewhere?"

"Yes, of course."

"Any other members of your family?"

"My daughter Julianna Wade is an officer of the court in this district. I suppose hers are. I don't know how Karen's—

Karen Medina, that is—would be on record. But, really, now that I think about it, while both are often in this room, neither of them would be likely to open this drawer. Certainly not recently anyway."

"You didn't have your daughter and the Flagstaff police examine your desk, check your files?"

"No. I didn't mention any of this. They searched for an intruder."

"And found none," he said.

"No." Her voice had gone small. "No, they didn't." She dreaded telling him of her second vision, the flash of light on her desk clock that showed the time the man was really here. Or of her certainty that it was the tow-truck driver, Smith. But she would have to. She remained quiet as he worked.

A few minutes later, he stood and turned to her, his face showing nothing. "Which files now, Mrs. Granger?"

With a long, tweezer-like instrument, he drew out the ones she indicated and dusted the plastic file jackets with the dark powder. "These old newspaper clippings won't yield good prints," he said. "But the firmer material of the folders might."

Geneva decided that she had nothing to lose in this man's estimation of her sanity and drew a deep breath. "Mr. Fox, I believe I know who the intruder was."

He straightened and looked at her, frowning. "Really. How's that? Are you telling me everything you know about this incident, Mrs. Granger?" He pointed to the nearby rocking chair. "Why don't you sit down and explain?"

He drew her desk chair around and sat to face her as she took the rocker.

Geneva closed her eyes for a moment. When she opened them, she saw Fox's unsmiling green eyes and slight frown. "Mr. Fox, I am not crazy, as you must think. All my life I've had these episodes, flashes, visions—whatever you may call them. They don't always make sense, even to me. At least not at first. They're like snapshots sometimes, or pieces of a puzzle. Or strong feelings with only bits of images or scenes."

"Go on."

"The moment you mentioned Holbrook Trucking and Towing, I knew it was the tow-truck driver, Smith."

"Smith. You saw him in your . . . vision?"

"No. Only his hand. But now I know. Please, Mr. Fox, there must be a way to find his prints and compare. But nothing is missing. Who is this man really and what reason would he have to come here and go through my files?"

He didn't answer, but clicked his kit closed and gestured for her to precede him through the doorway.

A few minutes later they stood in her entryway downstairs. She handed Fox the business card Smith had given her. "When will you know? Something about the fingerprints, I mean," she said, wondering when this flush she felt from her sternum to the roots of her hair would go away.

"I'll have the Flagstaff office start processing these prints this afternoon. And as I mentioned, my father lives here in Flagstaff. He's not in good health and I'll be staying with him for several days. I can monitor whatever progress might be made with these—" He indicated the fingerprint kit he held. "I'll know something by the middle of the week, I should think. As for Smith, we'll see."

When Fox had gone, Geneva felt both relief and the old familiar shame. She paced the length of the dining room. Then she went to the kitchen and put on the teakettle just as the phone rang.

"Geneva." Mason's voice sounded both cold and somehow choked. "I'm in Flagstaff. I must talk with you. I'll be there in fifteen minutes."

"No, Mason. Don't come. I'll meet you at Romero's Coffee Shop." She hung up. *All right. Maybe now he's ready to talk about his employee, the one who ran me into that arroyo with his fancy little car.*

CHAPTER TWENTY-TWO

They met at the door of the coffee shop and she led the way to a booth, a step ahead of his hand reaching for her elbow.

When the waiter left with their coffee order, Mason drew a long breath. Geneva looked at him without smiling.

"Geneva, you can't possibly believe I had anything to do with your accident."

"I think now that you were probably not driving the car that day. But it was no accident, Mason. And what you might have had to do with it is precisely what I'd like to know."

He couldn't have looked more shocked if she had slapped him. "What?"

Several people at other tables turned at the sound of his cry and looked in their direction. He lowered his head, took out a handkerchief, and patted his beard and mouth. "What in the world do you mean? I had nothing whatever to do with—what happened."

"Who owns the silver car, Mason? The one you told Agent Fox belonged to Albert Goldtooth."

"Why, Goldtooth does, of course. Just as I said." He leaned back to let the waiter put down their cups and coffee carafe.

Geneva lifted her chin. "Do you want to tell me more? Do you want to tell me about Holbrook Trucking and Towing?"

Drake now seemed to have recovered his usual poise. He smiled and tucked his handkerchief away. "I'll be happy to, my dear. Albert and I are partners in that enterprise. I'm a silent partner, of course. I have little to do with operations. He oversees the day-to-day business. Naturally, there are employees."

Geneva kept her voice low and steady. "Was it one of his—and your—employees, Mason, who ran me off the road with that car?" She raised a hand to stop his reply. "What I want to know is why someone connected with Holbrook Trucking and Towing would run me off the road and another employee—your employee—would then appear to recover my wrecked car." She let a beat go by. "Sent by none other than the boss. *El jefe.*"

"Geneva, I was trying to save you—to take care of you! What are you implying? You must know how I feel about you—" He reached for her hand, but she withdrew it.

"Who was driving that car, Mason? And who sent him?"

Mason glanced around and picked up his coffee cup but said nothing. Before he lowered his gaze to the cup, Geneva caught a flinty spark in his eyes that struck somewhere near her solar plexus. Another long moment went by without his saying anything or looking at her again.

A flash of memory rose in her mind of a sulky childhood playmate named Philippe, whose lower lip often looked like Mason's did at this moment. She stood up. "When you're ready to tell me the whole story, Mason, give me a call." She drew out her car keys and walked out the door.

The next morning Geneva watched the alarm-system installer go down her front walk to his truck. He turned and gave a jaunty wave as he drove away. She sighed and closed the door, eyeing the plastic box with its glowing little slits now mounted at the edge of the door facing.

"You'll do," she said to it, wondering for the first time how this break-in hadn't become another bullet point on Julianna's list of reasons why Mom should move into a snazzy condo and be done with this big house. Or maybe it had. Probably a big bullet point. Karen agreed, she knew that. And maybe they were right. In any case, she'd hear about it later, she guessed. For now, she shrugged and went to file the alarm system instruction booklet in the kitchen desk.

The middle of the week came and went, but Agent Fox did not call. At one point, Geneva had her finger on the two entries for J. Fox in the Flagstaff telephone directory, guessing that one of them would be his father, Jedediah. But she could not pick up the phone.

A third listing, Fox and Grayson, Attorneys, jolted her memory. The law firm was well known for its size and importance, not only in Flagstaff, but in all of Arizona and much of New Mexico. And Justin Fox's mention of his father living in "that big old house" clicked into place now. It stood in the foothills, a grand mansion that had in the past been the scene of many charity balls and other civic and art events. She guessed the artist and children's advocate Xenia Taylor Fox, whose funeral a couple of years ago overflowed the biggest church in town, was Justin's mother.

CHAPTER TWENTY-THREE

On the Navajo reservation several days later, Geneva and Desbah stood with a mixed crowd of Navajos and Anglos waiting for the graveside service for Bessie Jim to begin.

"This delay and the autopsy have caused some serious problems among the family," Desbah said, glancing toward the knot of Bessie's siblings and mother, who stood apart from the others a few yards from the head of the grave. "Let's go and pay our respects to Mrs. Ashi."

Geneva peered toward them, hoping to catch sight of Bessie's daughter, Charlene. "Problems? Is that because of the old rule of same-day burial?"

"That, yes, but I believe the mother is even more upset by the autopsy. And a couple of the less traditional—non-traditional, really—of Bessie's brothers are not helping the situation."

Charlene stood silent, apparently composed, a little distance away with some of her female relatives. Geneva turned her attention back to Desbah. "Who are these brothers?"

"One of them is a lawyer for the tribe over in Tuba City,

and the other is a political science instructor at the University of New Mexico in Albuquerque. They aren't interested in the traditional beliefs—or even the feelings of the others, so far as I could tell while I was at the mother's place."

"So, what are they doing?"

Desbah frowned. "They are really pressing the investigators, including your friend Fox. 'Going to build a fire under him,' as one of them put it. And it's making the poor mother and the others feel even worse."

Geneva wanted to challenge "your friend Fox," but let it go. She'd seen him earlier standing alone near the far edge of the crowd. Maybe he was watching to see if anybody looked guilty. She'd heard killers sometimes attended the funerals of their victims.

"How could they do that, Desbah? What power could her brothers even bring to bear on the investigation?"

"I'll tell you later. Come on, let's speak to Mrs. Ashi."

Bessie's mother, a tiny, bent woman in a plain navy dress and stout shoes, stood holding the handles of her youngest daughter's wheelchair, the special motorized chair Bessie had so recently reminded Geneva that Edward helped them get. The seated woman had to be in her forties, but looked much younger, as if the multiple sclerosis she developed at twenty had somehow stopped her thin limbs and unlined face from aging.

As Geneva and Desbah approached, two of the men moved away from the group.

"Mrs. Ashi and Sylvia, this is my friend Geneva Granger," Desbah said.

"I remember you," Bessie's mother said. "Thank you for coming here."

Geneva extended her hand to Mrs. Ashi. "I'm so sorry."

"I remember, too," the daughter in the wheelchair said. "Your husband was a good man."

Geneva, struck with surprise, said, "Thank you, Sylvia. It's been a long time since we met. Your sister Bessie was a wonderful woman. Her students all thought a great deal of her, as did my own family."

She would have said more, but Harold, Bessie's usually taciturn brother, stepped forward and introduced Geneva to several more of Bessie's sisters. "Mrs. Granger was Bessie's good friend," he said. "You remember her telling us how much she admired Senator Edward and how Geneva here made her teaching days really happy and good."

"Wait," Sylvia said, holding out her hand. "Do you remember that picture when Senator Edward brought my wheelchair?" Her voice dropped then, and she looked a little embarrassed at having called out. But Mrs. Ashi came close, looking eager and nodding.

"I do remember it, Sylvia," Geneva said. "I think I still have a copy. Would you like to have it?"

The happy glow that suffused the woman's face brought a lump to Geneva's throat. Together, Sylvia and Mrs. Ashi nodded, the mother even offering a timid smile.

"Then you'll have it," Geneva said. "I'll have a copy made for you." She remembered it clearly now. There was Bessie in the foreground, smiling a huge smile. That's why they want the photo, of course, she thought.

Charlene and her pimply boyfriend, whom Geneva remembered from the panel discussion in October, came forward and quietly greeted her and Desbah. Soon another group of people came to speak to the family, and Geneva and Desbah moved back down the hill toward the main crowd.

Harrison approached and greeted them. "Lot of people here."

Desbah glanced around. "How many would you say, Harrison?"

"Two hundred, two-fifty, maybe."

It was the first time Geneva had seen Harrison since that

194

day at the Navajo police station. She wondered again why he had been there, apparently with—or was it in custody of?—Officer Nez. Again there was no opportunity to find out.

She caught sight of Ooljee Blackgoat making her way toward them. Harrison stepped forward to help her over a rough patch of ground, then turned away to answer the greeting of a young couple moving towards him.

A sudden conviction seized Geneva. She must talk with the old medicine woman. Not here and now, of course, but soon.

"I'll be at my granddaughter's hogahn tomorrow," Ooljee said, looking directly at Geneva. "You come then."

Geneva could only blink. She opened her mouth, but no sound came out.

Without another word, Ooljee followed Harrison toward the small rise where Bessie's family stood.

When they'd gone, Desbah stepped close to Geneva. "What's all that with you and Blackgoat?"

Geneva shook her head slowly. "I'm not sure. I just have this strong feeling that I must talk with her. But I don't even know where her granddaughter's place is."

"Oh, I can tell you that. It's near Canyon de Chelly off Indian Route Seven, not far from my house, maybe twenty-five minutes. Come on, I think it's about to begin."

Geneva and Desbah moved with the crowd toward the grave, where an elderly Navajo man had taken a position at the head and seemed ready to speak. Nearby stood an uncomfortable-looking younger man Geneva understood to be the Episcopal minister from Bessie's church in Chinle. His face shone with sweat despite the chilly November breeze.

The old man prayed in Navajo. The Episcopalian followed with his eulogy and prayer. Two or three others stood and either offered prayers or chanted briefly, and soon the ceremony ended. The family turned and led the way down the hill away from the grave. Rather hurriedly, it seemed to Geneva.

Then she remembered the custom that only two men should see to the burial. Those two men would afterwards have a cleansing ceremony to guard against the possibility that the *chindíí*, the spirit of any evil lingering with the body, might attach itself to them. Corpse sickness must not be risked.

Safely down the hill, the crowd slowed. The immediate family got into their cars and left, while others gathered in small groups and talked.

In the moving crowd, Geneva again caught sight of Justin Fox. He saw her as well, nodded, and gravely touched the brim of his hat. Then he turned and melted into the ragged string of departing mourners.

Desbah, looking back in the opposite direction, touched her arm. "Geneva, do you see that girl over there trying to get your attention? I think she's one of Mrs. Ashi's granddaughters."

A girl in her late teens or early twenties, whom Geneva had noticed earlier with Charlene Jim, now beckoned shyly.

Leaving Desbah talking with an Anglo couple, Geneva joined the girl standing alone under a tall oak still clinging to its brown leaves.

"Hello there," Geneva said, smiling.

The girl didn't smile but gave a quick nod and glanced about. "Are you Senator Granger's wife?"

Taken aback, Geneva said, "Yes. Yes, I am. Did you know him?"

"No. But my cousin Daniel was flying the airplane that day. Then he crashed in that big lake."

"Oh." Geneva curbed her urge to pat the girl's hunched shoulders. "I'm so sorry about your cousin. My name is Geneva. What's your name?"

"Louella Ashi. Daniel called me on my cell phone that day. That day when he was going to fly back to Phoenix."

"He did?" She wanted to ask more but stopped herself. Clearly the girl was struggling with her words.

Luella twisted the ends of her flimsy scarf. "Just before, yes. Daniel said he was worried and a little scared because of the bad clouds. He said his boss Mr. Drake told him Senator Granger wasn't going to fly back to Phoenix that day after all."

"What? I don't understand. Are you sure, Luella?"

"Yes. Daniel said two men came and made him help put a big heavy trunk on the airplane. He said Mr. Drake told him on the radio that the weather would clear up right away, and he should just take off and it would be all right." Luella's eyes filled with tears. "But it wasn't all right."

"No. It wasn't all right, was it? Not at all." Geneva put her arm around the girl's shoulders, swallowing a frisson of bitter certainty and trying to ignore the looming picture of a battered green trunk tumbling, sinking in dark water. "Did Daniel say who the two men were? Did he recognize either of them?"

"No. I mean, he said he didn't know who they were, but the young one called the old one Jefferson. You know, like that president in the history book?"

The dream. *Jefferson* in fancy script, shimmering above water. Geneva suppressed her reaction and forced herself to wait in silence. She moved her hand on Luella's shoulder in what she hoped was a comforting pat.

"One of the men was tall and pretty young, with slicked-back hair, Daniel said. And he wore a gold necklace with a kind of strange pendant. Odd-shaped, my cousin said, green with something like gold lace covering it. Not Indian, he said."

A small gasp escaped Geneva.

"He was my best cousin." Luella touched her chest. "He always brought me presents. He always said when I finished high school, he would teach me how to fly." She turned and ran away down the hill.

Geneva knew the girl was crying. She, too, wanted to cry. But that need was crowded out by an odd buzzing in her ears. And the deafening certainty that the big trunk had held Edward's body. But not his half of their exquisite heart.

The early November day hadn't been particularly cold, but as evening approached, navy-blue, flat-bottomed clouds gathered and the wind rose. While Geneva made tea, Desbah started a small fire with piñon logs. They changed into jeans and sweaters and now sat relaxed before the welcome blaze, warm mugs in hand.

"That girl on the hill looked upset," said Desbah. "You both did. Is that what's bothering you?"

"That's one thing—a very big thing," Geneva said, pulling her little notebook and Edward's last letter out of her briefcase. She told Desbah what Luella Ashi had said.

When Geneva finished, Desbah let out a long breath. "Drake again. And you said Edward mentioned in his letter he thought he'd seen him earlier right there in Window Rock. When Drake was supposed to be in Phoenix."

"That's right." Geneva opened the notebook on her lap. "I want to make some notes. Tell me the name of that council-woman you know who lives here in Chinle, will you? Maybe she saw Mason in Window Rock the same day Edward did."

"I can do better than that," Desbah said. "My old boyfriend Dash Kingman is the manager of the Window Rock airport. He can find out if Drake flew in there that day. I'll call him tomorrow."

After a surprisingly good night's sleep, Geneva woke to a decided nip in the air and a surge of gratitude for Desbah's steadfast friendship. For all those drowning months after Edward's death, it was Desbah who would not let her sink into complete despair. The twins were grieving as well, of course, and they all tried to support each other. Both girls had wonderful husbands, their lifelines, each daughter said, who kept them emotionally afloat. And neither Karen's small son nor Julianna's pressing court cases allowed time to give in to their grief.

But Geneva was alone. Would have been alone. Desbah came and spent more than a week, helped her through those agonizing hours of waiting for news of the search, the state police dives in the wide reservoir. The bitter, endless days. And when it was time for the memorial service, Desbah returned to Flagstaff and steered them all through decisions and details. Strong, gentle, empathetic Desbah, so long alone herself, anticipated and met Geneva's every need, even when Geneva wasn't sure what they were. Desbah guided her into activities when Geneva thought she couldn't face other people or even the light of day. Sometimes let her cry, sometimes made her laugh.

Desbah, Tucker and Shándíne, Bessie Jim. All friends from her years on the reservation.

She and Edward had other friends, of course, and many in Flagstaff. But it was Desbah whose constancy seemed to glow and flare like northern lights in Geneva's waking mind this morning. With a burst of clarity, Geneva came to two realizations at once. First was how she had failed to adequately express her appreciation of Desbah; second was the sense of her own coming back to health. She felt the urge to rush from her room, find her friend, and tell her how much she loved and appreciated her. She rose on one elbow and listened but heard nothing to tell that Desbah was awake and about.

Showered and dressed half an hour later, Geneva tiptoed into the kitchen to find the coffee maker puffing out its final fragrant breaths before the "ready" light would go on. Two mugs and a pitcher of cream stood on the counter. The side door opened, and Desbah, carrying a huge armload of firewood, blew in with a great gust of cold air.

"November's about to get serious," she said, pushing the door closed with her hip. "I'm glad it's Saturday and I don't have to go in to work—let's stir up the fire, want to?"

Last night's embers caught readily enough, and soon the two had a sumptuous breakfast under way, laughing and talking as always. As they sat down, Geneva touched Desbah's arm.

Desbah looked up. "What? You need something?"

"Well, yes, I do. I need to tell you how much I appreciate you, old friend. I think I've failed to realize—and certainly failed to tell you—how dear you are to me. Your friendship means, and has meant, more than I can say. Especially these last three years . . ." Her words failed and she felt tears rising.

"You're not going to get soupy on me, are you?" Desbah made a wry face, then smiled. "Hey. I know. I'm just so glad you're coming back to—to life, I guess." She rose and went to the coffee pot on the counter. "Enough said, all right? More coffee?"

Geneva grinned and wiped her eyes. "Right. More coffee."

The next morning, she said good-bye, clutching the map Desbah had drawn to the Blackgoat granddaughter. Sure enough, it led to a new-looking hogahn with a bee-hive-shaped *horno* several yards off to the side, from which came a thin stream of light smoke. When Geneva stepped out of her car, she could smell the bread baking inside. She stood for a moment looking at it. A young woman wearing a thick sweatshirt and jeans came around the side of the house carrying a long wooden paddle made for handling the loaf. She stopped in surprise and looked at Geneva.

"Good morning. I've come to see Mrs. Blackgoat," Geneva said. "Are you her granddaughter?"

The woman nodded and pointed with her lips to the front door of the hogahn.

Ooljee Blackgoat opened the door. "Come on in."

Ooljee led Geneva into the center of the circular room, where a great rectangular woodstove gave off welcome heat. A teakettle steamed on the back of the cooking surface.

The old woman settled into a rocking chair and tipped her head toward an orange overstuffed armchair for Geneva.

"Thank you," Geneva said. As her eyes adjusted to the

dimness of the room, she noticed a child's bed near the wall and a curtained-off area toward the back. Sleeping quarters for the adults, she guessed. Unlike many other hogahns she had been in, this one had a wood floor instead of dirt and several curtained windows. She brought her gaze back to Ooljee, who bent to a basket at her feet and pulled out a small wool rug, which she spread on her lap. Another dip into the basket yielded two fist-sized stones of some kind, one a pink crystal, the other almost clear.

"Harrison doesn't need to lie to that police for the boy," Ooljee said, placing the stones side by side on the patterned gray rug. "But it will be all right."

"What? What do you mean?"

Ooljee waved a hand toward her. "Give me your necklace."

Geneva blinked but drew it from beneath her sweater and over her head. Uncertain, she held it out.

Ooljee took the jade pendant and held it over the crystals on her lap, letting the chain twirl slowly before settling it all between the two stones. She closed her eyes and leaned back in her chair for a moment, then cupped her hands above the outside edges of the stones and bent over them, her head tilted as if listening.

Geneva could barely breathe.

After another moment's silence, Ooljee said, "You should not be afraid of your sight. You should learn how to make it stronger."

Geneva knew what she meant. Her psychic sight. "But I don't know how."

"For you, water has the most power," the old woman said. "Get one of those little electric fountains with white pebbles. Learn to listen. And trust. You will understand the codes."

For some time, neither of them spoke. Ooljee's eyes remained closed, her ear and cupped hands just above the crystals.

"The other heart will catch that witch that killed your man. Don't worry about that."

Other heart. Geneva thought Ooljee meant the other part of the jade pendant. Edward's half of her heart. That seemed impossible. And witch? Some Navajos saw witches everywhere, the agents of evil. Maybe Ooljee meant "killer."

"The other one makes danger. He's the senator's dad. He hates him. You got to be careful."

"Who?" For a wild moment, Geneva thought of Edward's father, dead for nearly twenty years. "Oh, you mean Mason's father. But he died many, many years ago. Both his parents in a fire, when he was just a boy."

"No. He's alive. His chin's like a cactus. You must hide from them. You will try to make the one with hair looks like straw hide with you. But he must kill the biggest one."

A rising wave went through Geneva, carrying not a visual image, but certainty like a great channel of water. Smith. The truck driver with the grizzled chin. The intruder with his hand drawing the newspaper headlines out of her files. Ooljee was saying Smith was Mason's father. Her statement fell like a stone into that water. At this moment Geneva had no reaction, neither doubt nor acceptance. It seemed to slip into some medium she couldn't follow right now. But she felt the answers coming, like fish moving through deep water toward her.

Abruptly, Ooljee opened her eyes and straightened. She returned Geneva's necklace, shaking her head.

Geneva took the pendant and slipped it into her pocket. She remembered Desbah's advice, drew out some bills, and laid them on the chair seat as she rose. "Thank you. Thank you very much, Ooljee."

A toddler rocketed into the room from a side door and ran to his great-grandmother, squealing in delight. His mother followed, flushed and trailing delicious smells of bread, wood smoke, and mountain air. Ooljee put away her rug and crystals and picked up the boy. She nodded in response to Geneva's good-byes and stood up.

Back in her car, Geneva took a deep breath, feeling the pulsing current continuing to move around and through her. "One with hair looks like straw," Ooljee had said. Now a picture did come. Geneva saw clearly the thatch of straight, sandy hair slanting above Justin Fox's green eyes.

CHAPTER TWENTY-FOUR

Back home in Flagstaff, Geneva could think of little else than last Sunday's visit with Ooljee Blackgoat. The old woman's words still stirred in Geneva's mind. *You must hide from them.*

If Mason Drake had, as Daniel Ashi told his cousin, ordered the young pilot to take off with the trunk carrying Edward's body, then Mason was somehow responsible for Edward's death. But she saw again the agony in Mason's face three years ago as he sagged against her doorway in the rain, telling her of the crash. She could not reconcile the two ideas.

Well, she wasn't going to hide from anybody. She would go and find Mason and make him tell her the truth. What R. J. Smith — or some other employee — might have to do with any of this was a puzzle for another day. "Damn it!" she said and started for the phone.

Senator Drake, his secretary said primly, was not in. Would Mrs. Granger care to leave a message? No, Mrs. Granger would not, thank you.

She tried Mason's home in Tempe. Rodriguez, "his man" as Mason called him, said he didn't know when Mason would return. She thought it unlikely that he would be at his condo here in Flagstaff on a weekday but tried it anyway. No answer. She sat with the receiver still in her hand when the phone rang.

"It's Justin Fox, Mrs. Granger. I have those fingerprint results."

Geneva had been heatedly rehearsing in her mind what she would say to Mason. It took her a couple of seconds to respond. "Oh."

"Mrs. Granger? Did you hear? I said—"

"Yes, I did hear you, Mr. Fox. Of course. Please tell me."

"Actually, Mrs. Granger, I have some photos I'd like to show you. I'm here in Flag, may I come over in a few minutes?"

Geneva spent the few minutes unnecessarily tidying up both the kitchen and herself. She made coffee, set out a plate of cookies, replaced the napkins with some prettier ones, and waited. When he rang the bell, she checked her reflection in the hall mirror on the way to the door.

"Good afternoon, Mrs. Granger. You know, I believe the temperature has dropped fifteen degrees since noon. My, that coffee smells wonderful." His smile again unsettled her, but again it quickly disappeared. He let her take his overcoat and hat.

"Yes, I heard there might be snow showers this evening. Please come into the dining room, Mr. Fox."

Once seated with their coffee in front of them, Fox laid a folder between them on the table. "I have three pictures to show you. But first I'll tell you that the fingerprints I collected belong to Rollie J. Smith, the tow-truck driver." He glanced up at her. "As you guessed." After a beat, he went on. "Many years ago, Smith was convicted of killing his wife, one Anna Jasperson Smith. He served thirty-six years of a forty-five-year sentence and was released early for good behavior seven months ago."

She watched him slide a black-and-white photo, yellowed and curled at the edges, out of the folder. A younger, clean-shaven Smith stared out, holding a card with a long number on it.

"Murder—my God! And his fingerprints prove he was the intruder I saw going through my files."

Fox gave her a serious look. "It proves he touched your file drawer."

Geneva felt a slow wave of uneasiness roll along her back.

"Here is a more recent photo, taken last summer when he was hired by the Holbrook Trucking and Towing Company." He turned the picture around to face her. She looked down at Smith's grizzled chin and peculiar squint. "I see. What is the third one?"

Now Fox paused, fingers resting on the folder. He looked pensive, almost uncertain, she thought. He took a breath. "This is a copy of a family portrait, almost forty years old, of the Smiths with their only child, a son. Please look at it carefully."

She saw it immediately. Mason. The tall, unsmiling teenager standing between his parents could be no one else. The mother, also tall but leaning slightly to one side, looked unhappy, her large dark eyes identical to the boy's. Geneva gasped. "Where in the world did you get this?"

"It came to us in an odd way. Smith's former parole officer, whom I called for the prison shot here, found the portrait in Mrs. Smith's belongings in an old evidence box he inherited from the original detective. For some reason, the officer copied and faxed it along with the others. And I just wondered . . ."

"The boy looks like Mason Drake. You saw it, too," she said.

"I did." Fox stood up, walked to the window, and stood quiet for a time. "The date on the back of the picture showed it was taken only a few months before Smith killed his wife. I read in the old files that Smith was also charged initially with the death of the boy, Leroy Smith—his name is there on the back, too. But those charges were dropped for lack of evidence. A body was never found, and two witnesses came forward to say they'd seen him running for a train about a month before the murder of Mrs. Smith."

Images in Geneva's head swirled. "Mason has always said his parents died in a fire when he was just a boy—ten or so. That he was injured, wandered for a long time, suffering from amnesia—and—" She stopped. Certainty, like an arctic wind, swept against her eyes. His story, all of it, had been a lie.

Fox returned to the table and stood watching her. "So apparently Leroy Smith ran away, grew up, and changed his name to Mason Drake. But recently gave his father a job in the company he owns with Councilman Goldtooth." He let a beat go by, his gaze still on her. "Drake gave no sign of recognition that day the old man picked up your car. Strange, wouldn't you say?"

Geneva couldn't shake off the chill of Mason's lies, the fact that he was this murderer's son. A green trunk tumbled downward through dark water somewhere at a great distance. She could barely nod.

Fox bent and leaned on his hands on the table in front of her. "Senator Drake is your good friend, you say. A long-time friend of your husband's, you said. So, what would this old friend want to know about you that he would send his father—whom you say you never met before two weeks ago—to learn by breaking into your house?" He turned his head as if to listen for her answer, then went on. "Leaving almost no trace, by the way, and stealing nothing. But searching through your files. For what?"

"I don't know!" Geneva jumped to her feet. "But Mr. Fox, if you are implying that Smith came here in my absence with my knowledge or permission, or at some other time with Mason, you are mistaken." She leaned across the table toward him. "You may not want to believe in my psychic sight—God knows I never asked for it, cannot control it or get rid of it, much as I'd love to—but you may not imply that I'm a liar."

"No, I don't think you are. Not at all. But I need to learn

more about this psychic ability of yours." He paused, then seemed to come to a decision. Sighing, he resumed his seat and poured himself another cup of coffee. "Mrs. Granger, let me tell you about my experience with people who claimed to have psychic or other-worldly . . . ah . . . knowledge. I hadn't been on the job six months when I was assigned to a case in Tennessee. A couple in their thirties had killed all three of their children, one in each of the states of Georgia, Alabama, and Tennessee." He stirred his coffee, seeming lost in memory.

Geneva sat down and waited.

"The kids were not just stabbed to death—horrible enough, certainly, but it might have been quicker. No, they were cut in such ways that each little girl bled slowly to death." He looked away from her to the window. Then into her eyes. "The couple was baffled, the mother even indignant that they should be arrested for the deeds, since God had spoken to them plainly. 'As plainly as you, sir,' she said to me. God was the one telling her and her husband just how and when they should open each blood vessel so as to drain away the incipient evil festering there."

"Dear heaven," Geneva whispered.

"And there've been others. A kid in the barrios in Albuquerque that people said was a saint. Looked like Jesus, they said. Praying night and day." Fox squeezed his eyes shut. "Except when he was sexually molesting his two little cousins, that is. Claimed his dear old grandfather in heaven told him just how to do it." Here he rubbed his jaw and leaned back in his chair. "So, you see, I don't have what you'd call an open mind about psychic abilities."

"Few people do," Geneva said. "Believe me, I know."

"All right. I've said my piece. Please tell me about your —visions."

So she began. And this time she felt that he truly listened. She told him how images or sensations—or conviction—would come to her. There were even times the images turned out to be symbolic, their meanings not clear until later. "Like a code of some kind," she said, glancing up at him and finding his gaze neutral, attentive. Not scornful or condescending. She knew those looks well.

"Sometimes they come when I'm not even worried or anxious," she said. "Once—I was just washing dishes—but I knew we had to take back permission at the last minute to let the twins go on a skiing trip. Oh, they were so upset." She closed her eyes, remembering. "But that afternoon, something happened to the tow line and four others of their group were hurt. Badly hurt."

She told him then of the worst time—the night before Edward's death. "I was almost asleep, I think, but then I was running, running, trying to find Edward, to tell him something. Warn him. But I couldn't find him, even when I felt sure where he was. Not far at all. I knew I had failed him, was failing him with every step."

His voice was gentle now. "What did you see that night? Did you see your husband?"

Her hands went to her throat and chest. She closed her eyes. "No. I felt great pain. And choking. Choking." She opened her eyes. "But I couldn't see him." She paused for a long moment, looking away.

She could feel Fox's gaze on her, but he said nothing.

"I saw the most peculiar rock formation, a part of a line of mesas, I think. It looked like the wings of a great bird. Even more unusual was the middle, what you could call the breast of the bird—it was shiny green, mossy, as if it had a source of water. I had the sensation of being airborne, as if seeing it from a helicopter or hot air balloon . . . drifting above it. Then there was only blackness. Then cold, cold water."

They were quiet for several minutes. She watched him moving the picture of the Smith family idly back and forth on the table with his fingers but gazing toward the window. And she wondered about herself. She'd never told anyone else this much detail of that vision. She couldn't have said why she wanted him to understand.

"There's more I should tell you," she said. "A week or so ago, at Bessie Jim's funeral, I met Louella Ashi, a cousin of Edward's pilot, Daniel Ashi. She told me that Daniel telephoned her just before he took off. He said that Drake, whose plane it was, had radioed him saying that Edward wasn't coming that day. Instead, two men were bringing a large trunk aboard, and Daniel should then take off for Phoenix immediately."

Fox's head snapped around. He looked at her hard.

"I know my husband's body was in that trunk, Mr. Fox."

"You know? You know this—in the same way? When did you come to know? How? I mean—" He seemed unable to go on.

"I knew it the minute the girl spoke the word *trunk*. I don't know how." She passed a hand across her eyes.

"All right. I'll accept that. For the moment. Did Louella Ashi say her cousin knew the men with the trunk? Did he describe them to her?"

Geneva drew a long breath, aware of the jade pendant resting between her breasts. "Only that both were Navajo, one older, one a young man, tall. His hair was short, slicked back. And he wore an odd-shaped necklace. A green stone, with gold, her cousin said." She drew her necklace out of her blouse, up past her chin. "Like this." She held the pendant out for him to see. Then she reached to the back of her neck, unfastened the gold chain, and laid it in his hand.

"Half a heart." He turned the warm stone slowly. "I assume your husband wore the other half."

"Yes. Edward designed it and had it made for us." She pointed to the inner edge of the filigree fan that covered the jade heart. "These tiny clasps close when the two halves are put together, making them one."

"And you believe the young Navajo took Edward's necklace from him. Perhaps from his body."

She didn't want to say *I know it* again, so merely nodded.

Yes, I do know. This to whatever part of herself it was that delivered these things to her more conscious self. *Perfect picture, thank you.*

She couldn't turn her face and look at Fox, to see what his reaction must be to this crazy woman burning scarlet to her hairline.

She'd said enough. No reason to mention that dream with the ornate word *Jefferson* glittering above water.

Once more Fox went to the window and gazed out. His cell phone rang. Geneva went to the kitchen to give him some privacy, glad herself of a respite from this harrowing interview.

A few minutes later Fox came into the kitchen, snapping his briefcase shut. "That was my daughter-in-law calling. I think I told you my father, here in Flagstaff, is not well. I have to go now, but we'll talk again. I'll call you."

Geneva stood at the window and watched him drive away. She gathered up the cups and cookies and returned to the kitchen. She couldn't imagine why he said he'd call her. After all, he'd completed this little detour from his investigation of the murders on the reservation. Taking the fingerprints on her desk and bringing her the photos and other information about Smith were not germane to either Bessie's or the professor's murder. The Roosevelt Reservoir, where Edward's plane crashed, lay far to the south of Navajoland.

She'd identified the sketch of Brandon Goldtooth the first day he'd come. Her being run off the road was hardly an FBI matter. In short, Geneva Granger's burning need to learn the truth about her husband's death did not constitute a case for FBI Agent Justin Fox.

Her hand carrying a saucer to the dishwasher rack halted above it. *Unless he saw a connection between Edward's death and the two reservation murders.* She clicked the saucer into place, closed the dishwasher and leaned against the counter.

The answer came full force. If Edward was already dead when Daniel Ashi took off from the Window Rock airport — and she knew he was — then his, too, was a reservation murder. A case for the FBI. Fox believed her.

And the connection had to be the two Navajo men and Mason Drake.

CHAPTER TWENTY-FIVE

Harrison gave his daughter some money for delivering him and his groceries home from Window Rock and sat down at the table, frowning at his grandson. Margaret, her hand on the coffee maker, frowned at Terry as well.

"So, you sold your firecracker machine to Brandon Gold-tooth. What else?" Harrison said.

Terry had already answered this question on the way to Granddad's place. At least twice. Now Granddad was making him say it again. He prepared his voice as best he could. Sometimes it would break, making him sound like a little kid. A scared little kid.

"That white mask I made. I told you before."

"And you did some jobs for him, is that right?"

Terry's mother had kept silent through these and other questions, but the worry in her face, illumined only by the dashboard lights of her truck on the way here an hour earlier and again now, had not escaped her son's notice.

"Different stuff," Terry said, picking at the rubber edge of his sneaker.

Harrison waited.

"Well, sometimes I'd find certain kinds of rocks or shells he wanted. And paint. A couple of times I brought him some paint."

"From here in my hogahn, I think," his grandfather said.

Terry gave a one-shoulder shrug. "I didn't think you'd care."

Margaret set the coffee pot down with a sharp clack. "Son, the police think you set that fire at the Peshlakai place. They think you killed that professor." She clapped her hand to her chest. "I told you not to go around that Goldtooth." She then launched into rapid Navajo to her father.

Even though Terry's facility with Navajo was pretty poor, he caught the meaning well enough. "But I didn't do nothing. I just sold that firecracker machine to Brandon. I didn't know what he was going to do with it."

"I told Lieutenant Nez all that," Harrison said. "But Brandon's grandfather will have a story ready to say Brandon was somewhere else that day we brought Mrs. Granger and her friend up here to Wheatfields. You said nobody saw you early that morning before you got back to your mother's house. But maybe somebody did. And you didn't notice. Maybe you want to think some more about it. You might remember somebody."

"Terry, where were you really?" His mother bent her frown on him again. "I don't think you just fell asleep in your van out by the lake . . . all by yourself."

Terry knew he should just give it up, but telling his mom about being with Francine most of that night was just too hard. She didn't like his girlfriend anyway, and since he'd gone last spring and joined his mom's Jesus church, promising to obey all its rules, this was more than he could admit. Better to break one of those rules and tell a little lie than . . .

"I told you. Me and a couple of the guys from the boarding school were over here at Wheatfields fishing. I got tired and went to sleep in my van. When I woke up, it was morning and those guys were gone. I had to hurry to get back home."

A volley of barks from Sarge told them a stranger was coming up the drive.

Margaret stood up. "Maybe that's the police now." Without a glance toward her father, she signaled with a quick lift of her chin to Terry. He jerked his jacket off the chair and slipped to the back of the hogahn, through the little store room and out into the night. His mother picked up Terry's cup and pushed his chair in. She moved to the sink, washed the cup, and hung it on a rack with the others.

Harrison went to the door and waited. Sarge and the visitor arrived together.

Albert Goldtooth sat in the silver Viper, headlights still on.

Harrison spoke a single word, and the dog moved to his side but remained standing, staring at the man in the car.

Signaling to Goldtooth to wait, Harrison turned to Margaret. "Albert Goldtooth."

She nodded and gathered up her things. She and Goldtooth met at the door. He moved aside, murmuring the barest of greetings. Margaret said nothing, got into her truck, and started down the hill.

The two old men nodded to each other, but did not shake hands. In Navajo, Goldtooth said, "That's the same old dog you've had for years."

"It is."

Margaret stopped her truck at the bottom of the hill and waited. The fear and worry that had been growing for two months felt like a green pine knot in her stomach. Goldtooth. She knew, had known for years, that Goldtooth men were bad medicine, bad trouble. Not witches, her father said. He'd told her many times that Navajo witches were not real. And she had gone to the Mormon school where they said

Navajo witches were not real. So, she did not know what name to call the Goldtooth men.

It was old Albert's son, Rueben Goldtooth, who had lured Archie, her husband, first into drugs and then petty crime, and finally into virtual abandonment of his family. Rueben owned and trained horses for rodeos, and horses were Archie's love, his one shining skill. An accident in his youth had left Archie with a crippled foot and leg, and he'd never learned to drive a car, but he was graceful and powerful on a horse. People often sought him out to train their horses, and even before the drugs, he would be absent for weeks at a time.

Even though Archie didn't drive, twice her truck had disappeared, only to be found on some back street in Gallup, filthy and littered with drug paraphernalia. On the infrequent occasions of his return, he seemed a different man, silent and garrulous by turns, always red-eyed and disheveled.

Then, on the first morning of the fair in September, Margaret saw the young Goldtooth, that slick-looking Brandon, surreptitiously handing her son a small envelope. And she had not been able to keep her son away from him since.

The knot in her stomach gave her a new surge of pain. She left her headlights on and waited. A few minutes later, Terry opened the door and swung into the seat beside her. She could see how his face was drawn, his eyes big. But he shook his head. "No problem," he said. "Let's go home."

For several hours after Fox left, Geneva tried to write, spent time reorganizing first her desk upstairs, then a hall closet, then the little kitchen desk. She tried to eat some supper, and finally went back upstairs, changed into her pajamas, and sank into Edward's big recliner in the bedroom. She turned on the electric fountain with its white stones that Ooljee said would help make her power stronger. Pulling the old angora afghan that Edward's mother made for her so long ago up to her chin, Geneva sighed a long, deep sigh.

It didn't happen the moment she closed her eyes, of course. It came later.

Harrison Billy grasped the steel bars of a cell and lowered his head. He spoke in Navajo, but sleeping Geneva understood his words: *I have to lie. The boy is weak, confused. Albert said he'd break him, make him say anything, and he will. They know I carve all the time. They know I could've made the firecracker machine in half a morning. I could have put it in the old hogahn when Jerome took me up there, any time in the last two months. They will believe me. The boy can't hold up. Not strong like his mother and grandmother. They will believe me.*

Geneva did not startle. She wasn't thrown to the floor by the power of her vision. She merely opened her eyes and knew. The tiny electric waterfall on the bureau bubbled and murmured. She looked at the glowing green numbers on her clock. There was time. She was glad she had some new hiking boots. Sleep again, she told herself. Sleep.

CHAPTER TWENTY-SIX

Monday morning Justin Fox arrived at his office feeling very good indeed. His father's favorite cousin — a retired RN, no less — and her husband had arrived Saturday night in their grand motor home for an extended stay. Both of them were as wild about bridge, chess, and bird watching as his dad.

He found himself smiling as he tossed his jacket onto a chair.

LaKeesha, his secretary, rang his private line. Fox knew that meant he'd need to frame his questions so that LaKeesha could answer without anyone in the outer office knowing what it was about.

"A Mrs. Littleben here to see you, sir," she said.

"She doesn't have an appointment, of course, but I should see her?"

"Yes, sir."

"And your uncanny radar has, in the two minutes our doors have been open, found this woman's concerns to merit my immediate attention." He refrained from chuckling and said it only to give himself time to sweep the clutter of papers on his desk into stacks and fetch his suit jacket from the chair. He and LaKeesha understood each other perfectly.

"Of course, sir."

Fox grinned. LaKeesha never called him *sir* except in this silly code she'd made up.

The door opened and Margaret Littleben, clutching a worn leather purse across her middle with both hands, stepped in.

Fox stood. "Please come in." He smiled and drew out a chair. "Will you sit down?"

She remained standing.

"How do you do, Mrs. Littleben?" He smiled again. The woman looked both terrified and determined. "What can I do for you?"

She took another step into the room, paused, then took a deep breath and came to sit, straight as a steel pipe, in the waiting chair.

Fox resumed his seat and waited, not looking directly at her but maintaining, as he had learned, an open and respectful countenance.

"My son is gone. My son is Terry Littleben. Those police have my father. My father is Harrison Billy."

Fox had heard, the night before, of Harrison Billy's confession in Window Rock to the murder of Dr. Allen Jerome Layton.

He leaned forward. "Please tell me when you last saw your son."

"Two nights ago. He was asleep in his room. Next morning, he was gone. Out the window. His van, too." She opened her purse and pulled out a large photo of the boy in cap and gown. "From last year. Window Rock High School."

He took the picture and studied it, then laid it down. "Any idea where he might have gone? A friend's house, maybe?"

She shook her head. "He's gone off."

"But have you looked for him, contacted his friends or

other relatives, the local police?" Her look stopped him. This woman was no fool and far from hysterical.

"Does . . . his father know Terry is missing?"

"His dad doesn't come around much."

"But might Terry have gone to his dad—does he visit him?"

She looked uncomfortable, but remained quiet.

Fox waited for a time, but decided not to press. "You've driven here to Tempe this morning, Mrs. Littleben?"

She nodded.

"From . . . where, exactly?"

"Fort Defiance. By Black Canyon."

She must have left hours before dawn, he thought. "How old is Terry?"

"Eighteen last summer."

Fox might have recited the usual explanation about an adult's not being considered a missing person until after more time than this. He could tell her, too, that none of it was an FBI case. But he didn't.

"Mrs. Littleben, I understand your son was at the scene of a fire in September when an abandoned hogahn burned, in which the body of Dr. Jerome Layton was later found."

"Yes. He told that sheriff and then that police, too. He only drove up there just before it happened. He didn't do anything wrong."

"But you know that your father has now confessed to Layton's murder."

"He didn't kill anybody. Can you find my son?"

"Why have you not gone to the Navajo police at Window Rock to report this?"

"Those police think my father killed that man. They already took my son to the criminal investigation office and asked him a lot of questions four days ago. They will think my son ran away because he made that firecracker machine. They think he is bad. My father, too. They will hurt my son if they find him."

Such a long speech seemed to drain the woman. The skin around her nose and mouth looked tight and pale.

He dropped his gaze to the photo, considering what to say. Geneva and her secretary, the Sanchez woman, could easily confirm that they, the boy, and the old man came upon the scene of the fire together. But what was a firecracker machine? He hadn't heard about that.

"Mrs. Littleben, I'll look into your son's disappearance. My secretary will make a copy of this photo and take your contact numbers and the information about your son's van. You'll hear from us as soon as we know anything."

Fox spoke briefly to LaKeesha, who motioned the woman to a chair next to her desk and closed the door between the offices.

He then called his investigator in Gallup. "Carter, what do you know about a kid named Terry Littleben and anything the Navajo Police might know about something called a fire-cracker machine?"

"Firecracker machine? I don't know what that is, boss, but we got a tip last night from the Navajo police. Some guy called in from a pay phone. Said to look in that burned hogahn for something with a long bead chain and a couple of steel balls. Said Littleben started the fire with it after he stabbed that professor."

"A long chain. Maybe I do know what a firecracker machine is after all."

"Huh. Okay, I'll see about the Littleben kid."

"Good. His mother is here right now. I'll fax you his picture and the details about his van."

Nothing like a two-for-one trip to the rez, Fox thought a few minutes later. He stood looking down to the street below where Margaret Littleben was climbing into her pickup. *The taxpayers will get their money's worth on this one.* He reached for his calendar.

Not ten minutes later, his private line rang again.

LaKeesha said, "Do you know a Geneva Granger?"

"Yes."

"Uh-huh. Nice voice. A friend, maybe?"

"None of your business, my dear. Put her through."

Without preamble, Geneva said, "Agent Fox, I want to tell you about something odd that I saw. I should have told you before, but let it go. Now I have a strong feeling to describe it to you."

Oh, no, he thought. Not another of those visions.

"And good morning to you, Mrs. Granger."

"Oh. Yes, I'm sorry. Good morning. Are you terribly busy?"

"I'm happy to talk with you, of course. What odd thing did you see?"

"The name *Jefferson*, being spelled out, a letter at a time, like something in a movie. In fancy script, Spenserian script. Dropping down one letter at a time. And all of it shining, glittering, reflecting on the surface of dark water."

He let a beat go by. "I see. Is that all?"

She seemed to hesitate. "Well, yes."

"Jefferson and water. And shining."

Her voice changed. "Maybe I shouldn't have called. Never mind."

"No, no, it's all right. Anything else?"

"No. Nothing else. Good-bye."

After the call, Fox sat for a long time doodling on a pad. He wrote *Jefferson* above a body of water. Was it a river? A lake? What had Geneva Granger seen? If she couldn't make out meaning in that, he certainly couldn't. But the thing wouldn't leave him alone, even as he blocked out time, called the Navajo police lieutenant, and made his appointment to discuss the missing Littleben boy.

Carter was good at puzzles. Fox looked at his watch and

called him. "I'm going to fax you a sketch, a kind of puzzle. Don't read too much into it, Carter—just give me your first impression."

"Okay."

"I think I told you that I'm considering opening a case regarding Senator Edward Granger."

"Yeah. Plane crash might not be an accident. Something new come up?"

"Probably not, but this little thing, uh, might be something worth unraveling."

Fox hung up, thinking his statement to Carter about investigating, making a case of what had been ruled an accident could be worse than premature. All he had to go on was Geneva's visions. Hearsay, a judge would call it. Worse than hearsay, in fact. But he believed . . . what? Believed in her. And since he was going to the reservation anyway . . .

LaKeesha's voice on the intercom ended his reach for justification. "Carter on line one."

"That was quick, Carter. What did you see?"

"Easy one. 'Toli' means 'of water' or 'watery.' The guy's name is Jefferson Toli. And I already know about him."

"The hell you do!"

"Yeah. He's something of a character around Window Rock and Gallup. Got in on the tail end of Viet Nam and was wounded. I guess he got hooked on pain pills while recovering. Became a serious drunk after that. He had some small parts in four or five westerns shot up at Monument Valley in the sixties or seventies. He was raised in a Los Angeles slum, but he says Hollywood. People say he tells some tall tales that grew out of his movie parts. Likes to talk about knowing important people —Clint Eastwood, Fonda—brags about being a personal friend of Senator Drake."

"But you can locate him now, right?"

"Oh, yeah. He stays at a cabin up near Buffalo Pass on his

great-niece's land—when he's not drinking in Gallup or Winslow. But I think he's probably up there now. It's getting cold, you know. You want me to bring him in?"

"No, Carter. I'll be at your office tomorrow morning. We'll go visit him."

CHAPTER TWENTY-SEVEN

Geneva wasn't sure she'd heard it at first. She paused partway down the stairs, half-distracted by what the kids always called Mom's ski-knee, and the follow-up thoughts that had become more frequent lately of moving to a smaller place without stairs. Then she listened again and continued down. There it was, a muffled thump against the side door, she was sure. The neighbor's cat again, she thought.

She unlocked the door and started to open it when a crouching Terry Littleben, his bloodied head down, arms wrapped around his middle, tumbled inside.

"Terry!" Geneva cried.

Geneva helped him to a kitchen chair, pushed the hair back from his face, and wiped away dirt and dried blood with a damp towel. One of his eyes was swollen shut and his face bruised and scraped.

"What happened to you, Terry?"

"Brandon Goldtooth caught me over by Lupton. Ran me off in a ditch."

Geneva thought of the infamous Lupton road, the "liquor run" from Window Rock to Interstate 40 and off-reservation bars and bootleggers. She hoped Terry hadn't been on a liquor run.

"Did you get these bruises in the accident?" she said, doubting it.

"No. Except my elbow. Brandon beat me up."

"Where did that happen? How in the world did you get here, Terry?"

"Hitched. I had that card you gave me with your address on it. I was coming to tell you, warn you."

"Warn me? About what?"

"Brandon was the one that ran you off the road that time over by Ganado. He's been bragging about it. Says he'll teach you not to snoop around, teach you for good if you ever come back where you don't belong."

Geneva's fingers holding the peroxide-soaked cotton ball halted for a second in mid-air. "I see. Well, thank you for telling me. That's very kind of you."

A few minutes of silence passed as she finished her first aid. "Pretty chilly out there, isn't it, Terry? How about some breakfast? But first we'll call your mom, let her know where you are."

By the time he'd warmed up and had some food, Terry looked both better and worse. Cleaner, less anxious looking, but the bruises were turning deeper blue and magenta.

Margaret Littleben was neither at home nor work. Archie Littleben, Terry said, didn't have a telephone and he thought his father was up in Cortez training some horses anyway. Harrison did not have a phone, either, of course.

Maybe Geneva would let Justin Fox know and drive Terry to Gallup herself. He could meet them and see that Terry gets home.

Good excuse, that snappy little voice of truth sang inside her head. *There are law officers by the dozen within a mile who can and should take on this responsibility.*

But then she remembered the box of Johnson O'Malley

supplemental materials and lesson plans she'd developed for the Window Rock School District, the box she'd been promising a teacher friend in Gallup for a month. "Perfect," she said to herself, feeling quite virtuous. She poured more coffee into Terry's cup and went into the dining room to call Justin Fox.

LaKeesha found her boss in the Gallup office. "Miz Very-Nice-Voice Granger called for you…. second time in two days, lover boy."

"Egad. Remind me tomorrow to fire you," Fox said. "Put her through."

They made a plan that Geneva would drive Terry down to Gallup that afternoon and meet Justin at the old El Rancho Hotel on Route 66. For his part, Fox located Margaret Littleben, who elected to have him not send Terry home by patrol car but would drive to Gallup and pick him up herself.

Some three hours later, Geneva swung into the hotel parking lot next to Margaret's pickup. And Margaret herself, who stood stalwart and frowning next to it in spite of the raw wind pushing fans of dust and debris about and plastering her clothes against her body.

As Geneva and Terry got out of the car, Margaret gave her son a silent appraisal and a quick sideways nod. He got into the truck. Then, with tears starting to flow down her cheeks, she turned to Geneva. "You brought my son," she said, holding out her hand. "Thank you."

"Glad to do it." Geneva took Margaret's hand, expecting the customary quick touch and release.

Margaret held on. "I thank you."

Geneva smiled. "I'm a mother, too," she said, returning the squeeze. "You are most welcome."

Margaret got into her truck. Geneva turned toward the

hotel entrance at the same time Fox and another man got out of a nearby car. They waved to Margaret as she and Terry pulled onto Route 66 and disappeared into the late afternoon traffic.

Both men joined Geneva and all three, buffeted by the wind, hurried into the hotel.

"Thanks for doing this," Fox said to Geneva. "Puts a nicer face on the law than they generally see."

"Amen to that," said the other, a strikingly handsome man with an athletic build and Athabascan features. His tawny skin set off the most remarkable amber-colored eyes, Geneva thought, eyes that surprised only a little less than the dark auburn mop of curly hair above them.

They stepped into the ornate lobby out of the rattling wind, all three smoothing hats, hair, and clothing.

"Geneva Granger, please meet Agent Moses Carter, whose unenviable job it is to range over western New Mexico and this whole side of the reservation day and night, just like this relentless, scouring wind."

Carter gave a dismissive little snort, and took Geneva's hand. "He's really bad at poetry," he said, smiling. "Pleased to meet you, Mrs. Granger. I knew your husband, if only briefly. Fine man. And I've read *The Longer Walk*." He held her gaze. "I was, am, impressed. So was, is, he." Carter gave a sideways nod toward Fox, just like the one she'd seen Margaret give Terry.

"Thank you," Geneva said, thoroughly surprised. "Both."

They sat together in the dining room, almost empty despite the approaching dinner hour, and chatted over coffee for a while before Carter looked at his watch.

"I'm due home in a few minutes. And my queen is not to be kept waiting. Ever," he said, rising and twitching his eyebrows in a comical way. "A pleasure to meet you, Mrs. Granger."

"What a delightful fellow," Geneva said when Carter had gone.

"With a genius IQ and a big heart," Fox said. "Moses sets up sports and tutoring 'sandwiches,' he calls them, in little school districts here and there, mostly on the reservation."

"I know something about those," Geneva said. "But not the originator."

"Right. And he really is married to a queen." Fox gave a little laugh. "A Navajo rodeo queen and champion barrel racer as a teenager, now a trainer and mentor for girls. Not just in rodeo—Haseya finds them scholarships and other help. She's going to be another Annie Dodge Wauneka or Annie Kahn. Together the Carters are a real force, practically an institute."

"Haseya Carter, of course! She and I serve on a committee to write grants for those scholarships. But we've met only once—when the bookmobile was launched last spring in Tuba City."

"And Moses's father is that red-headed Irishman, the horse breeder Shaunessy Carter up near Tuba City that everybody in four states knows. Moses's mom was another Navajo rodeo queen in her day and later an excellent potter."

He turned and gestured to an approaching waiter, a Navajo boy of maybe seventeen, looking uncomfortable in a tight white shirt and black vest and trousers.

Well?" Fox looked back to her. "Will you stay and have dinner with me, Geneva Granger?"

When she agreed, he turned that transforming smile on her, startling her once more.

And so, the rest of the evening passed swiftly. Justin told of his divorce sixteen years ago and raising Taylor, not entirely on his own, since his parents took such a strong part in the boy's upbringing. Only in the last year had his father's health begun to fail. Justin spoke of his worries on that score, and his efforts to find a helper for his dad in Flagstaff.

"But happy news last spring," he said, flashing that smile again. "Taylor and his sweet Connie were married at Kartchner Caverns State Park. Do you know the place?"

"Oh, yes, both my girls have always loved it. Karen is the astronomer, and Julianna the spelunker. In fact, that's where Julianna met her husband, Thomas—on a caving expedition. It's a beautiful park."

He put down his fork and gestured one hand up, the other down. "So, one searches the skies above the earth and the other explores its depths—that's cool."

"Julianna's sense of adventure is like Edward's in that way and many others, too. People say Karen resembles me and her voice is like mine. They're fraternal twins and as alike or different as any other pair of siblings. Edward often called them Pro and Con—sometimes it made them, or one of them, laugh. Other times definitely not."

"You know, I met Edward several times over the years," Justin said. "Our jobs brought us together from time to time. Once we were both speakers at a luncheon—in Mesa, I think it was. We got a little better acquainted there—especially when we found out we had Flagstaff in common. He had a great sense of humor."

The meal, the dessert, coffee, all went smoothly and pleasantly. The dining room emptied around them without their notice. A different Navajo waiter leaned against the wall near the kitchen archway, equally unnoticed.

"Were your parents able to attend Taylor's wedding?"

"Only my dad. Mom died two years ago." To Geneva's murmur of sympathy, he waved his hand. "She told me she would, two weeks before," he said. "And delivered a scolding at the same time—in case I should mope, she said. Threatened to come back and haunt us all if any of us did." He shook his head, a wry grin on face. "Xenia Taylor Fox was an extraordinary woman. In every way you could name."

Geneva smiled and brought her hands together under her chin. "Xenia T. Fox—I've admired her sculptures in all the city parks for years. And I remember what a huge event her funeral was."

"She taught me something about death," he said, giving Geneva a level look. "She said it was a doorway, one that leads to a greater plane of existence, another field of service. And if I should begrudge her a moment of it, she'd 'jerk a knot in my tail,' as she often threatened Czar Nicky."

Geneva laughed. "Czar who?"

"Czar Nicky, the elegant—psychic, mind you—cat that ruled the house, my parents, and Taylor since he was about eight. A Maltese with the most sumptuous fur. Gray fur—deep, gorgeous gray." He smiled. "Like your eyes. A beautiful color."

Those eyes widened now. She couldn't think what to say.

"What about Taylor's mother? Did she go to the wedding?" Where those words came from, Geneva couldn't have said. She was a little shocked at herself.

"Ah, yes. Annabelle Wilder Fox," he said, shaking his head a little and leaning back in his chair. "I'll try to make it brief. You may even have heard of her—another writer, in fact. She never dropped *Fox*—even after a couple of subsequent marriages. And now writes those flaming romances under A. Wilder Fox." He crossed his eyes and threw up his hands.

"Oh." Geneva wanted to giggle, but tried to suppress it.

"Go on and laugh," he said. "That's what I have to do. But she does love Taylor in her own way, despite being mostly somewhere else while he was growing up."

"We're closing, sir," the waiter stood at their table, bill in hand.

An hour later, Justin lay awake and alone, knowing Geneva was in bed three rooms along this upstairs corridor adorned on one wall with a Chester Kahn mural depicting lively Navajo life. Justin pushed his mind away from her to the other wall's photos of movie stars from the forties, fifties, and sixties — the celebrated dead.

In the empty dark above his bed, Fox saw Geneva's lovely, animated face, those deep gray eyes and that funny wayward lock of hair that kept bouncing out of place. Their conversation floated through his mind. He thought of Edward, larger-than-life Edward. Handsome as any of the movie stars on El Rancho's walls. Shoulders like a fullback. Justin knew his own homely face and bony frame couldn't compare. Granger's thick hair glowed silver, not like the colorless flat mat that covered Justin's skull. And the senator's voice compelled listeners the entire length a room. Well, Fox could make himself heard, but . . .

It didn't matter, he told himself, punching his pillow for the umpteenth time. If Geneva's rising suspicions and his own unanswered questions should start coalescing the way they seemed to be doing now, the FBI would have to initiate an investigation into Edward Granger's death. Agent Fox could not have anything but a professional, and properly distant, relationship with the widow Granger.

But a barrage of arguments against investigating sprang up in his mind. No viable evidence likely to exist out there after all this time, the body never found. No recoverable DNA in water after this long, certainly.

But he knew he'd have to search. He punched his pillow again.

Three doors down, Geneva finally gave up and turned on her bedside lamp. She swung her legs over the side of the bed, picked up her robe, and then dropped it. They've got it too hot in here, she thought. No wonder I can't get to sleep.

The overnight bag she always kept in her car for just such unexpected stops as this lay open on the chair under the old-fashioned crank-out window. She moved the bag, opened the window, and sat listening to the city sounds below. In the rumble of yet another train passing through Gallup, Geneva seemed to hear Justin's astonishing, warm, all-out laugh. What was there about it that made her feel—all right, she admitted it to herself—hot. Desirous. And she had seen it in his eyes, too, when he said goodnight in the hallway, holding both her hands for a long moment. Then he'd just brushed her cheek with his lips and turned away to find his room. Even in the dim light of the corridor, she could see the deep flush on the back of his neck.

She cranked the window open as far as it would go and stood fanning herself with a magazine.

The next morning, the desk clerk said that Agent Fox had left early. Urgent business, he said. Gone since before six, but had left this note for Mrs. Granger.

She walked away from the desk opening the small envelope. In it was another of his business cards. On the back, a scrawled line: "Have a good day—JTF."

CHAPTER TWENTY-EIGHT

The sun-warmed planks of the convenience store/café's east wall felt good against Jefferson Toli's back as he slid slowly into a squat. If only the throbbing behind his eyes would quit, he might enjoy the last fumes of a pretty good drunk. Instead, the red blot behind his lids darkened as a tall form blocked the sun.

"Mr. Toli? Jefferson Toli? I'm Agent Justin Fox, FBI. This is Agent Carter. Will you stand up, please?"

Toli opened his eyes to a squint. Too bright. "What?"

"Can you stand, sir?"

The old man struggled to his feet and slid along the wall a yard or so into the shadow of the sign on a high pole across the way. "What?"

"Let's go inside, Mr. Toli. I'll buy you some coffee. Have you had breakfast?"

Half an hour later, Toli could see better. He mopped up the last of his fried eggs with a crust of toast and nodded to the offered refill of coffee. "All right. Say your piece, FBI man."

"People say you've sometimes done some work for Senator Mason Drake. Is that right?"

"You bet." Toli drew in a big breath through his nose. "Per-

234

sonal friend. I rode in his airplanes plenty of times. Personal friend the senator."

"Yes. My question is about the work you've done in the past for Mr. Drake. I understand you used to work for him three or four years ago."

Toli scratched his ear and said nothing.

Fox waited.

"You want to know did I help kill that other senator."

Fox's expression didn't change. "That's right. Did you?"

"I don't remember. I was pretty drunk."

"Where were you when that other senator got killed?"

"At the sheep camp with some other guys. Over there by Sawmill."

"Who else was there at the sheep camp?"

Toli's eyes started to close again.

Carter bumped Toli's elbow. "Who was up there with you that day?"

No answer.

"Let's take a ride, Mr. Toli," Fox said, "so you can show us that sheep camp."

Fox guided Toli to his patrol car, where Carter waited to put him in. "We'll go on up toward Sawmill and you can tell me where to turn."

Moses Carter, son of an Irish father and a Navajo mother, spoke Navajo, English, Gaelic, and Welsh. Carter had shared with Fox the valiant efforts of both his grandmothers to instill a special love for her language and how it had sharpened the youngster's linguistic prowess and led him to graduate work in that field. Until he discovered a new love: law enforcement. That, and a beautiful young Navajo rodeo performer, whose culture dictated that the husband join the wife's clan, not the other way around.

Now Carter took over the winning of Jefferson Toli. He sat in the back next to the old man, and the topic of movie stars broke the ice.

"Me and Clint, now, we was like that," Toli said, putting his two index fingers together.

"He wouldn't talk to the other Indians, or those fat Mexicans pretending to be Indians. Cowboys, neither. But we'd sit together on one of those petrified log stumps they have up there by Winslow and just talk and drink between takes. Drink and talk." He raised his eyebrows and rolled his head about. "Did you know that?"

"What all would you talk about, you and Clint?" Carter asked, his face perfectly serious, Fox noticed in the rearview mirror. Carter was damned good.

"Why, acting, of course. He'd ask me for tips sometimes. And I'd give him one or two."

But Carter was especially skillful in bringing the conversation around to the recent past and the topic he was after.

Soon came a description of a young man in a fancy car with the fine whiskey, then the name Goldtooth, and, "Him and me worked for our friend Mason the year that big ice storm tore up southern Arizona. We're all still good buddies. Both of them know what a good actor I was, still am. Still am." Again, the raised eyebrows and the wide grin.

"The storm that destroyed all those trees in the Tonto National Forest?" Carter asked. "Three years ago, wasn't it?"

Toli paused in another movie story to point out the old lumber company road where "the boys" had their sheep camp that year.

Fox pulled the car onto the dirt road that passed the burned ruin of a house, and climbed through thickening stands of trees. "How far now, Mr. Toli?"

When Toli pointed and grunted, Fox stopped the car in a clearing that ended at a curving sandstone mesa with an overhang. Not until they got out did Fox see a hut near some car-sized boulders.

"Looks like a good place for a camp," he said. "Do you

remember what happened that time? Did Senator Granger come up here?"

Toli seemed entirely sober now. He put his hands in his pockets and strolled toward the shack.

"Brandon brought him up here," Toli said. "Told him Harrison's grandson was hurt, said he fell down off that ledge up there." He pointed with his lips to a part of the mesa where a jumble of block-shaped boulders had separated and tumbled down from the main formation. "He found him down in Window Rock, told him the boy had been drinking. Brandon knew the senator wouldn't want Harrison's grandson to be drinking."

Toli kept walking toward the hut. Fox and Carter followed.

When the old man reached the shack, he looked at Fox, then back at Carter, just joining them. "Wait a minute," he said, squinting hard as he drew open the weathered door and stepped inside.

Fox turned and motioned for Carter to come forward, then caught the edge of the door before Toli could close it. Inside, the old man squatted beside a low plank structure, dark with dirt and age. Likely used as a cot by sheepherders, Fox guessed.

Mumbling in Navajo, Toli reached underneath.

Carter bent to hear. "You got yourself a stash down there, man?" he asked in Navajo. "What you looking for?"

Toli pulled out a small, ragged knapsack and sat back on the dirt floor. He untied the several strings that held it shut and shook it out between his feet. Nothing fell out.

"Where's that knife?" he said in English. "Cost fifty dollars, Brandon said." He shook the bag again.

"You want to tell us about this knife, Mr. Toli?"

"Pretty near nine, ten inches. Cost fifty dollars, Brandon said. Was in this bag."

Carter squatted next to Toli. "You had a sing a while back.

Some people say you have a ceremony every year for your bad dreams."

Toli nodded. "My spirit don't ever heal." With that, he bent forward and started to sob. "The boys had liquor up here. Too much liquor."

Fox waited until Toli quieted, then helped him up to sit on the wooden bench. "Who were those boys? Who was up here with you?"

"Brandon and his brother, Clarence. Some others, too, but they left when Brandon and Clarence went down to Window Rock. They brought the senator in here and made him drink all that booze. Tied him up. Laid him down right here and put the bottle in his mouth, made him drink. I did that, too. The skin-walker made me do it."

Toli lowered his head and hunched his shoulders dramatically, his eyes sliding back and forth in the best evil-doer pose of any sixties B-movie.

Fox and Carter exchanged a look. All the old guy needed, Fox thought, was a long, greasy moustache to twirl.

"What else did you do?"

"The skin-walker had Brandon's knife. He cut open the man's throat and stabbed him in his heart. Then he told me to stab him in his heart. I said that wasn't in my contract. But the skin-walker made me do it anyway."

"What happened then?" Carter asked.

"The skin-walker flew away."

"What happened to the man, the senator?"

"Brandon's brother Clarence had brought a big green trunk, big as a bank vault, looked like, in the back of his pickup. Brandon and Clarence put the senator in the bank vault. I threw up over there," he said, pointing vaguely toward the road. "Clarence threw up, too. Then he walked home. Wouldn't ride."

Fox and Carter stood quiet as Toli bent, head between his knees, and sobbed again. Finally, he stood and wiped his face on his sleeve. "You can take me to jail now. Tuba City jail. Tuba City's got good chow. Not Window Rock."

"Not just yet," Fox said. "Tell me what all this had to do with Mason Drake."

Toli looked surprised. "Why, it was his green bank-vault trunk," he said, as if that explained everything. "He gave Brandon five brand-new, hundred-dollar bills. One was for me."

Fox thought he saw a glint in Toli's eyes with that memory, the same eyes still wet with tears of remorse, supposedly.

He let another beat of silence pass, watching the old man.

"Well. Then me and him, Brandon, took the trunk down to Window Rock and put it in Mason's airplane. He said he'd get me another bottle of that fine whiskey afterwards. And he did. The same brand that my friend Clint likes, you know. Not the kind Fonda drinks. No sir."

It was only as Fox turned back toward the car that he took notice of his surroundings. The flat ridge they stood on dropped away to the northwest. He could see that it curved to the right and downward.

"Put Mr. Toli in the car, please, Carter," he said. "I'll be along." He strode toward the mesa. Beyond the hut, slightly behind and below a bend in the mesa, stood a formation that looked like a great headless bird with a pair of partly folded wings.

There, between the wings, at the top of what looked like the breast of the bird, a spring caught the afternoon light. At the edges of its downward track, a wealth of ferns, moss, and other plants flourished, even in this November cold. Several of the plants had vivid red and orange leaves. Fox stood for a long time looking. "This is what she saw," he said under his breath.

CHAPTER TWENTY-NINE

The enthusiastic weather reporter Edward always called "cute beyond all redemption" waxed rhapsodic over her map full of white. The predicted snow showers had bloomed overnight into a serious storm. Geneva yawned, glanced at her half-packed overnight bag, and padded down to the kitchen for coffee.

On her last try the night before, she still hadn't located Mason. Probably out of town. Just as well. She still needed to cool down and plan what she would say to him.

She'd barely finished breakfast when Karen called. "Mom, remember I'm hosting Thanksgiving dinner this year. Besides Uncle Mason and Ray's folks, can you think of anybody else we should have?"

Well, here it was. In the weeks since the spiral of suspicion about Mason had begun to rise, Geneva hadn't voiced any of it to her daughters. Even now a tiny feeling of disloyalty darted through her cloud of doubt and anger thickening around Mason. Where to begin? No. Not now. Better to confront him and get everything clear before telling the girls anything.

"Hmm, have you spoken with Mason lately, honey?"

"Oh, not for a couple of weeks. But he told me he'd be here for Thanksgiving. He's bringing that wine you like, and avocadoes, like always. Probably mangoes for the kids, too."

"Yes. Getting fruit from the Phoenix area in the winter is always a treat. But no, I don't have any other suggestions for guests." She wondered what Justin Fox's family would be doing for Thanksgiving. Wondered, too, how she could have so misread his . . . warmth, that evening in Gallup. Clearly, she had been dismissed with that "Have a good day" message and no word since.

"I called for another reason, too, Mom. Did that FBI agent get back the fingerprint results? Do you know who broke into the house?"

"Yes. I do know. A man named Smith, but I haven't decided what to do about it yet, since nothing was taken. And before you ask, I did have the alarm system installed. So you mustn't worry anymore, Karen."

"Smith, huh? Probably a phony name. I'm just glad he didn't steal anything. Was it some transient, you think? Oh! Emily is climbing out of her high chair! Talk to you later."

Saved by the baby, she thought. For the moment, at least. Julianna the lawyer won't be so easily distracted. She'll want every detail and guess immediately that the man might have a record, which she'll uncover. And she already knew about Agent Fox. Next, she'll be on the phone to him. But not just yet. They were visiting Thom's folks in California.

Geneva sighed and straightened up the kitchen. This time she called Mason's cell phone.

"Geneva! I was about to call you. I just got back from D.C. My dear, we parted unhappily that day at the coffee shop. Please tell me you're no longer angry with me. I brought you a present from the Library of Congress gift shop, that book we talked about with Julianna, and—"

"Where are you now, Mason?"

"I'm at home in Tempe, at last. And glad to be here. It was cold and rainy in D.C. and I want to—"

"I'm coming down to see you. We need to talk."

"Of course! Wonderful! What time will you be here?"

"It's snowing a little, and I have a few things to do in Flag, so I'll not leave for a couple of hours. Say I'll arrive around four-thirty or five."

"I'll have dinner waiting for you!"

Geneva protested about dinner, and soon said good-bye, feeling jangled by his glee. She wondered what he'd say if she could show him the copy of his family portrait. Pouring herself the last of the coffee, she sat down at the kitchen table and opened the phone book. This time, she did dial one of the listings for J. Fox.

Justin Fox answered. "Mrs. Granger! Are you all right? Is anything wrong?"

Well, she thought. We're back to formal appellations.

"No, of course not, Mr. Fox. I hope your father's health has improved."

"It has, thank you. So I'll be returning to the Tempe office later this morning."

"I'm going down to talk to Mason Drake," she said. "And I wonder if I might have a copy of that Smith family portrait you showed me."

He protested, but finally agreed to fax it to her. He didn't say anything more for a moment, then cleared his throat. "Mrs. Granger—Geneva—do you think it's safe to confront Drake? What exactly do you expect to learn by talking with him?"

Now Geneva went quiet for a few beats. "I'm going to make him explain about his connection with this man Smith breaking in here, and what he knows about Goldtooth's grandson running me off the road, and—"

"I can't prevent you, of course," Fox said. "But I'd advise against going there alone. If Drake did have something to do with any of those things, he might not be the good friend you think he is."

"I appreciate your advice. But I'm not afraid of him."

"But maybe you should be. Or do you think he can explain all that away? Are you hoping he can?"

That brought Geneva up short. She had to consider whether the years of friendship, Edward's close ties with Mason, the girls' affection for him . . . might be clouding her judgment.

"I'm not afraid of him, Mr. Fox," she said again.

He verified her fax number and then said, "Do you still have my card? My cell phone is on it, remember. If you need me, please call."

She thanked him but dismissed the thought. Both thoughts.

While waiting for the fax, she e-mailed her daughters and told them she'd be in Tempe for a couple of days at her usual little motel and reminded them of the number. Then she opened Desbah's e-mail message:

"Old boyfriend Dash Kingman looked it up and said Drake did fly in to Window Rock the day Edward thought he'd seen him. Dash said he remembered Councilman Goldtooth hustling in right after noon, swearing, biting heads off right and left about being late for a meeting at ASU, as if it was their fault. He and Drake took off, despite the storm warnings. Two hours later, weather no better, little Danny Ashi took off, too."

Geneva bit her lip and swore some herself.

In her bedroom, while she dressed in jeans and boots, she turned on the too-cute weather girl again. The snow—the "bee-yoo-ti-ful snow!"—would end by early afternoon. Geneva ran a brush through her hair and checked her overnight bag. The snow would disappear anyway as she left Flagstaff and dropped over the Mogollon Rim. Southern Arizona, barely over 1100 feet, was already in the upper sixties, headed for eighty-one. Sweaters here, shorts there. If she didn't feel so grim about what she was about to do, she'd throw in a bathing suit and enjoy the little pool at Fiddler's Inn.

And what was she going to do? she asked herself, standing in front of the fax machine. She studied the portrait of the Smith family sliding into her hand. Leroy Smith. The son of a murderer.

CHAPTER THIRTY

The snow was already waning to lazy dances. Only a few flakes landed on Geneva's hair and lashes as she left the supermarket. She unlocked her car and tossed in the bag that held such miscellany as dried apricots, a new toothbrush, and a package of flashlight batteries. Soon weak sunlight broke through the flying blue clouds. Finishing up her few errands had a settling effect on her mind as well. She stopped at a little Greek café on the NAU campus for her favorite snack and carried it back to her car to enjoy on the way to Mason's house.

Finally entering the Interstate, she heaved a satisfied sigh and gained highway speed, clearer in her mind about what to say to Mason than she had been all morning. An hour later, only a few high, mare's-tail clouds marked the vivid blue above. In another hour, she knew, she'd turn off the heater and descend into what the twins used to hail as "Summertime!" with the first sight of a saguaro cactus.

Geneva nibbled on her dried apricots and thought about Justin Fox's—and her own—question: What would Rollie Smith, Mason's—no, Leroy Smith's—father be looking for in her files?

It was late afternoon when she parked near a bank of oleander at little Fiddler's Inn, which she'd discovered last year when teaching a week's seminar at ASU, then staying on to do research on her new book. She felt lucky to get the suite in the far corner again, the one with a window that looked out on a slender globe willow, and beyond that to distant Spanish mission-style homes with red tile roofs. She thought of the place almost as her own, having lived in it Mondays through Thursdays for many weeks last year. After chatting with the proprietors for a few minutes and putting her things away, she checked her watch and got back in the car.

Justin Fox pulled into the FBI offices in Tempe just before noon and sat, still in thought, tapping his fingers on the steering wheel. Two men came out of the building, saw him, and, both with big grins, banged on the hood of his car.

"Hey, man—you asleep in there? Come to lunch with us. Tell us what you've been doing for the last week. Brady here is buying!"

Thus roused, Fox got out and greeted his men, dragged his briefcase and laptop out, and stood talking for a few minutes. "Sorry, guys, can't do it right now. Too backed up." He transferred his overcoat and suitcase to his SUV, and went into the building.

In the elevator, he rubbed the back of his neck and frowned. Well, it was none of his business, after all. If Geneva Granger wanted to go to Drake—or Smith or whoever he was —and give him hell, the FBI couldn't say a word. It was none of his business. *She* was none of his business. Besides, if he did have to mount an inquiry into Senator Granger's death, he couldn't be thinking of the widow like this. He'd have to squelch these feelings.

And Dad may not make it through the next bout of heart

trouble. Taylor and his Connie, just beginning their life together, shouldn't be burdened with looking out for Grand-dad. Maybe Fox should transfer back to the Flagstaff office, demote himself, as it were. Life would be easier.

He stepped off the elevator, went to his office, greeted LaKeesha, and took the handful of messages she held out to him. He tossed them onto his desk and closed the door. Putting down his briefcase and laptop, he pulled off his jacket and settled behind his desk to thumb through the pink message slips. He made notes on three of them and set them aside for LaKeesha, pulled two others in front of his phone, and sighed, hand on the receiver.

She shouldn't go there alone. He pictured Geneva Granger's intelligent face, framed with a short, curly mop of more-pepper-than-salt hair, a lock of which often fell in what she seemed to consider the wrong way, since she was always pushing it back or sideways with an air of absent-minded exasperation. But he saw the whole exercise as unaccountably charming. And those gray eyes could pin a man at ten paces. He'd hate to make her really mad, and he'd almost done it on Friday. He remembered the fire in those eyes.

He riffled through the messages again. Pushing aside those he'd set before the phone, he dialed and waited. "Carter? Fox here. What have you learned?"

He listened, frowning.

"And those two cowry shells I found out there by the Ganado turn-off—any useable prints? Sure, I'll wait." He pulled out a pad and pencil and drew looping designs, a reclining figure eight, a pyramid. Then in block letters, GENEVA. He blinked and snapped the pencil down on the desk.

"Yes, Carter, I'm here. No matches? But did you get the authorization to dust the Viper?" After another minute, Fox grinned. "Pretty smart, Carter. His soda can, too, eh? And they matched—good. Yes, go ahead and fax them."

He swung his chair around to face the window and gazed out at the Camelback Mountains.

Dove gray. Yes, that must be the color of Geneva's eyes. And he was certain the irises were ringed with what looked, for all the world, like the most perfect tiny black flowers. Extraordinary.

He spun his chair back around to his desk. If she was right in her suspicions of Brandon Goldtooth, he might be the younger Navajo who'd made Daniel Ashi help load the trunk holding Edward's body onto the airplane. The one who wore Edward's necklace. The other half of Geneva's heart.

The one Mason Drake might have paid to kill Edward.

Fox got to his feet, yanked a notebook out of his briefcase, consulted it briefly, then grabbed his jacket. On the way through the outer office, he said, "I'll call you later, LaKeesha. Will you deal with those messages on my desk?"

"Hold it, Fox." LaKeesha waved another pink message slip at him. "This one sounds urgent. Came in while you were on the line with Carter."

He slung his jacket over his shoulder and executed a U-turn. "Okay, let's have it." Back in his office, he tossed the jacket at a chair, where it slid unnoticed to the floor as he read the message and reached for the phone.

"Hello, this is Agent Justin Fox, FBI. Is this Julianna Wade?"

"Thank you for calling back so quickly, Mr. Fox. Geneva Granger is my mother, and I'm worried about her. I just got her e-mail message that she's going to see Senator Drake in Tempe. She shouldn't go there, Agent Fox. Not alone, anyway."

"I agree with you, Mrs. Wade. But what reason do you have for saying so?"

"I've been doing some checking on this Smith, who broke into my mother's house in Flagstaff. I found out that Senator Drake is half-owner of the tow truck company that pulled my mother's car out of that arroyo on the reservation. Smith works for that company. For Drake."

"I know all that, too. Do you think Drake sent Smith to break into your mother's house?

"I don't have any idea about that, Mr. Fox."

"Do you think Drake may pose a danger to your mother?"

"I do, sir. And for more than one reason. But my husband and I are presently in California, and I haven't been able to reach my mother. I've tried that little inn where she always stays in Tempe and Drake's house. That worries me even more. I wonder if you could send someone, or—"

"What about her cell phone?"

"I've left messages, but half the time she doesn't bother to turn it on."

"Give me your number, Mrs. Wade. And the name of the place she stays—the number, too, if you can. I've got the sena-tor's numbers and his address."

He jotted down the information Julianna gave him. "I have reason as well to believe your mother may be in danger. I'm going to find her. I'll be in touch."

"Wait, Mr. Fox. One more thing. You should know that my mom—well, she can be stubborn. And sometimes she's not afraid when she should be."

After the call, Fox tapped his pencil on the memo pad for a moment. Yep. I got that one already figured out, he thought. He punched the line for his secretary. "LaKeesha, I'm off the clock. See you Wednesday." He retrieved his jacket from the floor, went to the small closet off his bathroom, and changed into a black turtleneck sweater, jeans, and hiking boots. Then he took the back stairs and headed for his SUV. Yes, Geneva Granger should be afraid, he mused, pulling an old hooded sweatshirt out of the back seat and his Glock 23 and shoulder holster from their case under the dash. So why doesn't that psychic ability of hers kick in and warn her?

CHAPTER THIRTY-ONE

Geneva had called Mason from Fiddler's Inn, but that was more than half an hour ago, so she was surprised to arrive at his ornate gates and find them already open without her calling from the phone at the entrance. She'd seen no one coming out on the narrow, twisting road into this secluded neighborhood, if that word could be applied, since the grand homes out here sat about a mile apart, not one in view of another.

Well, maybe someone visiting Mason had gone out the other direction. Dismissing the matter, Geneva was merely glad to be done with that tunnel-like passage to his property, made even darker now with the early twilight of November. She parked in the long, semi-circle drive, mentally scolding herself for imagining eyes upon her.

Mason came to the door, throwing it wide before she could reach for the bell. "Welcome, Geneva! I gauged your arrival from town exactly. You found the gates open for you already, didn't you? Dinner is almost ready—how do you like my new chef's outfit?" He bowed and gave his tall white toque a smart pat.

"Mason, I told you I wouldn't have dinner."

"Ah, but you must—it's your favorite, *pieczenie baranine*. Roast lamb with cream. And, as you've taught me, the perfect wine to go with it and—"

"Please, Mason, can we just talk?"

His eyebrows went up and the smile disappeared. "Of course, my dear. Something serious? I see you're carrying a folder there. But surely, we can have a drink while we talk. Come into the kitchen with me, then."

She followed him to the breakfast nook tucked into a bow window, its many panes of leaded glass catching splinters of the peach after-glow of sunset. He whisked off his apron and chef's hat and brought glasses and a chilled bottle of wine to the table.

"What is it that makes you look so somber, Geneva? Are the girls all right? I spoke with Karen only this afternoon. I—"

"Mason, never mind the wine. Sit down."

Now that the moment had come, Geneva's emotions clashed and tumbled together. Anger—no, fury!—combined with the pain of his deceptions, his betrayal of Edward over SB500. Maybe even worse. Tears rose in her eyes, which made her even more furious. She didn't know where to start.

"Who are you, really, Mason? I want you to tell me the truth."

Mason's whole scalp seemed to jump backward. His eyes widened; his face went white. "What in God's name do you mean? You've known me for more than twenty years."

Her voice wasn't going to work, she could feel it. She opened the folder and slid out the Smith family portrait of forty years ago.

He clambered to his feet, bumping the table so hard the wine bottle toppled and fell to the floor. Neither of them seemed to notice. His gaze never left the picture.

"That's you," she whispered. "You are Leroy Smith. And your father," she tapped the page, "who murdered your mother

—is out of prison and working for you. He broke into my house and went through my files. Why?"

For an instant she thought he might fall. He grasped the edge of the table, then sat down hard, making his chair screech against the tile. He passed a hand over his face and took a ragged breath.

"It is not me," he said after a moment. "It's my cousin, Leroy Smith. We were often mistaken for each other as boys. That's my aunt, my mother's sister. She and my cousin drowned in a ferry boat accident not long after that portrait was made." He looked at Geneva for several beats without speaking. His effort at control showed in the working of his jaw. "Where did you get this? You've given me quite a shock, seeing my aunt and cousin Leroy there. Where in the world did you get it?"

"And the man?" Geneva's voice had returned, but it was still painful to speak. "Who is he?"

"Why, my uncle, of course. Uncle by marriage, then. J. R. Smith."

Geneva closed her eyes. She knew he was lying. His story about his parents' death and his wandering for days, being taken in by migrant workers, schooled by an old grandmother of the clan—supposedly happened when he was ten or eleven. The so-called cousin was a teenager. A teenager doesn't often look so much like a ten-year-old as to be taken for one or vice-versa. She drew a long breath. "Tell me about Daniel Ashi."

"Who? What are you talking about, Geneva? Why are you asking me all these questions?"

"Daniel Ashi, the young pilot who replaced Mickey the afternoon Edward was to fly to Phoenix from Window Rock." She leaned forward. "You remember Daniel—you told him Edward wouldn't be leaving Window Rock after all that day. The pilot you ordered to help two men put a heavy trunk on board your airplane—and take off in a storm." She stood up. "With Edward's body in that trunk! Surely you remember

Daniel Ashi!" Tears streamed down her face. She struggled to catch her breath between sobs.

Mason got to his feet and seized her shoulders. "Geneva! I did no such thing—who told you that?" He pushed her back down in her chair and stood over her, breathing heavily. "Who told you that?"

She pulled out of his grasp. "It doesn't matter who." With a great effort, she forced her breathing to slow and the tears to stop. "I'll have some of that wine, now, Mason. The bottle didn't break—it just rolled over there."

Mason's efforts to calm himself weren't working as well. He continued to stare at her, his pallor replaced now by a dull red flush. Finally, he bent and retrieved the wine bottle. Almost in slow motion, he opened it and filled both glasses, and then sat still, holding onto the bottle.

She took a long swallow of the wine. They held each other's gaze for another moment. "Who put the trunk on board your airplane, Mason? Two Navajo men, I know that much—but what were their names?"

He made no answer.

"I think they were Albert Goldtooth and his grandson, Brandon." Her tears and shaky voice were gone now. Both her gaze and her words held steady.

Mason still sat silent. But his eyes held something new. Her momentum carried her past analyzing what she saw there. She stood up.

"I think you had them kill Edward and put his body in that trunk. And I believe that Brandon, also on your orders, killed Bessie Jim in Chinle and tried to kill me by running me off the road."

"Geneva, you must stop this. You must—" He slapped the table hard.

"And, also on your orders, didn't your father, Rollie Smith, break into my house looking for something in my files the same week?" Her voice took on a gravelly, mimicking sound. "'R. J.

Smith with Holbrook Trucking and Towing, at your service, ma'am.' Didn't he, *Leroy*?"

Mason leaped up, knocking wine bottle and glasses to the floor. He seized her shoulders and shook her. "Stop! You don't know what you're saying!"

Something metallic clicked.

"Oh, yes she does, Leroy boy. I believe your little lady has done found you out." Rollie Smith stood in the kitchen doorway pointing a small, shiny revolver at them. "Oughtn't to leave your gate open like that, Leroy. Never know what might wander in. Or who. Like your old daddy here, come to say howdy."

Both Geneva and Mason stood motionless, staring at the withered old man with the gun.

Mason then let out a stream of curses, pushed Geneva aside, and started for the man.

Smith raised the gun. "Get back, damn you. We got business to discuss, but I don't mind a bit taking off a ear or two if you get sassy."

Smith stepped forward and grabbed Geneva's arm, pulling her in front of him. "Or making Miz Doctor Granger here, what loves Indians, a little less pretty." He pushed the barrel of the gun against the side of her neck, still pointing it at his son.

Geneva, too stunned to think until this moment, started to pull away. Smith tightened his grip. "Or a whole lot less pretty. Be still, Missy. I'm going to get what I come for, whether I have to shoot you first or not."

She stood still.

"What the hell do you want?" Mason's voice became a low snarl.

"What do I want? Why, I expect you can figure that out, smart as you always was, Leroy. I want what *Sen-a-tor May-son Drake* has got. I want some pay-back for ever' damned stinking day I spent in prison. Ever' bit of it your fault, you lying, smarter-than-anybody shit."

Geneva could feel his quivering fury in his grasp of her arm.

"Get in there and set," he said to Mason, pointing with the gun to the dining room.

"Go to hell," Mason said, his glance measuring the distance between himself and the opposite doorway that led, Geneva knew, first into a small area with a desk, then into a laundry room and a side door. His body tensed, ready to run.

Smith fired, hitting the circle of heavy cookware hanging from the ceiling. Geneva cried out. Mason ducked and swore.

"You don't think your pappy can put the next one right through your balls? You forget how I could take the eye out of a tree frog at twenty yards. You know I never miss. Now get in there and set down."

He herded them into the dining room and pulled a pair of handcuffs from what looked like an old-fashioned school satchel sitting next to the living room doorway. "Now put your right hand out behind you, boy. You're still left-handed, I reckon. You're going to need that writing hand in a few minutes." Both of them grunted. "Come on, nice and straight or I shoot your little lady's right ear off. Unless I forget this thing tends to shoot left a tad."

Mason hesitated, but stuck out his right hand, which Smith cuffed to a slat in the back of his chair.

"Now, then, Miz Doctor Granger, you set down there a piece. I might let you bring me some of whatever that is that's cooking in the kitchen. In a minute or so." He fastened her hands together in front of her with an odd cable and lock device that made her think of the one she used to fasten her bicycle to the rack at the library. Her next thought was how crazy her last thought was under these circumstances.

"You won't wander off, now, will you, Missy? Cause if you should try to, I'll start with Leroy's ears and then his right-hand fingers. He won't be so pretty to look at, then." Smith cackled. "Or listen to, either, crying and all, don't-cha-know." He waggled his gun at her.

"Right now, you can bring me a bottle of whisky from that fancy cabinet yonder."

"What do you want?" Mason's voice came out as a snarl. "Why in hell are you here?"

"Want? What do I want?" Smith's voice rose in affected surprise. "Why, I want to share in my son's good fortune, that's what. But for right now, what I want is a drink. And for you to hush up. Don't say another word until I tell you to." He let out another raucous laugh. "Children should be seen but not heard. Ain't that the way it goes?"

For the next twenty minutes Geneva watched and listened as Smith ranted about his privations and hardships in prison: "Ever' day of it your fault, Leroy. Ever'—damned—day."

Mason roared a stream of obscenities and struggled to his feet, his chair wobbling and rearing up with him. Quick as a cat, Smith fired a shot past Mason's ear, shattering a glass case across the room. Mason let out a cry and fell back. Smith laughed and turned to Geneva. "You know where the stove is, I reckon. Step in there and bring me a plate of whatever that is Leroy's got cooked up for supper. And don't get prissy. I got a clear view of the whole path to the back door." He waved his gun. "And Leroy can tell you. I never miss."

The fragrant leg of lamb waited in the oven. She donned mitts and brought the steaming meat out. Nervous and trying to hurry, she carved several generous slices, added the tiny potatoes and creamed onions. Finally, snatching up silverware, she carried the plate into the dining room.

Smith stood behind Mason, moving the gun barrel playfully through his hair. Mason's face was a grayish yellow, his mouth a thin line.

"Set it down, little lady. Now get back over there."

"There's garlic bread. And a salad in the refrigerator," she said, moving toward the doorway.

"Mighty fine," Smith said. "Bring me some of that bread."

"I'll have to heat it," Geneva said, turning toward the kitchen.

"Heat it then," he said, as he dropped into a chair and dug into the food. "Just make it fast."

CHAPTER THIRTY-TWO

She stepped back into the long, elegant kitchen, clattered some pans together, then slipped into the pantry and pulled her cell phone out of her jeans pocket.

Can't call 911—can't risk talking, she thought. And if police sirens should sound, nothing would stop Smith from killing them both, she was certain of that. She went back to the oven, turned it on, and slid the buttered garlic loaf Mason had already prepared under the broiler. Text, then. Julianna had showed her how to text, but whether a person could text 911 . . . no. Fox. She thanked whatever power had given her an ability to remember phone numbers easily and punched in his cell number, then wrote *SOS quiet*, an instant before Smith roared, "Where's that damned bread?"

"Almost ready," she called, stuffing the phone into her pocket. Would Fox remember that she was going to Mason's house? She should have written that in her message. Would he know where it was? Yes. An FBI agent could easily find out. But she didn't know if he was in his office, or how many minutes away that might be from where she was. She pulled the browned loaf out and started to turn off the oven when she had an idea. Crumpling the paper wrapper from the bread, she thrust it, a dish towel, and a straw trivet she plucked from the wall into the oven. They would take a few minutes to start smoldering, she knew. She lurched toward the table, pretending the metal baking sheet was burning her fingers.

"Oh, oh, hot, hot," she cried, letting one pot holder fall. "Watch out." Stumbling as she came near, she thrust the hot pan into Smith's face, grabbed his gun from the table, and sprinted away several yards. Thank God her sons-in-law had taught her how to use a gun. To the surprise of all, Geneva included, she'd become a superior marksman. "Get down on the floor, Smith," she said. "Right over there."

"The hell I will," he cried, seizing a chair and lifting it to throw. She fired, hitting his right shoulder exactly where she aimed.

Smith yelled and spun sideways but regained his feet and started for her again.

She shot his other arm, barely nicking it, she knew. He fell to his knees, cursing.

Mason yelled, "Kill him! Kill him, damn it!"

"I said on the floor—put your face on the floor." This time Smith obeyed. Geneva saw a pool of blood forming around his right arm. Swallowing hard, she stepped forward and pulled the chair out of his reach. At that moment the smoke alarm in the kitchen went off. A minute later another, even louder, alarm sounded throughout the house.

"Mason, how long before that gets bad enough to summon the fire department?" She'd read her new alarm system booklet well.

"Three minutes," he said. "Unless you punch in the right code. Or they'll phone. Can you get me out of this manacle?"

"Good. Let them come. What about the gate? It closes and locks automatically, doesn't it? How can I open it for the firemen?"

"The panel is in the foyer," he said. "You have to press a series of buttons."

"No need," said a deep male voice from the entryway. "I've taken care of it for you. The gates are closed until I open them. No one is leaving for a while."

A huge black man stood in the doorway holding a large gun. "Put that little pistol there on the table, Doctor Granger. Mine is bigger and I am faster."

"Who the hell are you?" Mason's voice rose to a bellow. "What are you doing in my house?"

The black man swung around, leveling his weapon at Mason's chest. "I'm the gentleman who's going to keep your old man from shooting your balls off," he said in a cultured voice.

Geneva put the gun down. The man picked it up and slid it into his jacket pocket.

Smith groaned and swore. "You're late, you black bastard."

"Apparently not too late." The telephone rang. He turned to Mason. "Now, Senator, you must answer and say it was a false alarm. Just a little kitchen towel too near the burner." He held out the receiver and stepped over to Mason. "Do it now."

Mason spoke his password into the receiver, never taking his eyes off the man who held it to his ear. The louder alarm went silent.

The black man took the handset with him, leaned into the kitchen and shot the screeching smoke alarm. "Silence at last."

Geneva heard the oven control being clicked off. He returned and looked down at Smith on the floor, trying to sit up, still swearing. Mason, at the table, kept up his own curses.

"Shut up, Drake. Can you get up, Smith?"

"Shoot that bitch, damn you, Kramer!" Smith yelled.

"No, not quite yet." The big man pointed Geneva to a chair farther down the table and stood over Smith. "Messy. Shall I help you up?"

"I can get up. Get me a towel or something."

The man called Kramer pulled several of Mason's big linen napkins off a tray, shook them smartly, and dropped them into

Smith's bloody hand. He stood, weaving, until Kramer slid a chair toward him and he dropped into it.

"Doctor Granger, look in that buffet over there and find something to staunch the bleeding of this shoulder you so inconveniently made a mess of."

He glanced at Smith, laid his gun on a side table and tied a napkin around Smith's forearm. "The left one's just a scratch. Lean forward. That bullet seems to have gone straight through the fleshy part of your right shoulder. You'll live. Hand me those towels, Granger. Can you write, Smith?"

"Good enough for what we have to sign. Get on with it, damn it."

Geneva could see a little blood coming through the napkin on the left arm. But the shoulder wound bled down his right arm. Kramer waved her away and pushed the towels inside Smith's shirt sleeve. "Put some pressure on that. It'll stop in a few minutes," he said, wiping his fingers on the remaining clean napkin.

She glanced at Mason, whose eyes were squinted almost shut in a malevolent stare at both men. His breathing seemed rapid.

Kramer took a large envelope from his inside pocket and put it on the table at the far end. He motioned with his gun for Mason to pull closer, then dragged Smith in his chair next to himself at the end and directly across from Mason. Geneva sat where Kramer indicated, several places away from the men and nearer the other end, where Smith had eaten. Her shoe touched a piece of the scattered bread under the table.

Kramer peeled off the top page of the stack of papers. "Seventy-five thousand will cover the initial attorney fees." He gave Mason a pleasant look. "My fees. Then a million five to set your esteemed father up in Florida in a fashion he means to become accustomed to. We'll talk about the monthly payments in a minute."

Mason let out a choking sound. "Go to hell."

"Senator, you're failing to grasp the significance of this meeting. Your career, your hopes for the governorship, the profitable business you and the Navajo councilman expect to set up, not to mention the two TV stations in Tucson, the chain of print shops across Denver,"—he leaned forward and grinned broadly at Mason—"and even—ah—your continued excellent health depend upon your cooperation here. Otherwise . . ."

"Otherwise, I'll come calling again and shoot off little pieces of you, real slow," said Smith, showing his teeth. "I learned a whole lot in prison, boy. A whooole lot."

"And even dead, you'll provide your father with a handsome sum," Kramer said. "I have all the necessary papers right here. And Doctor Granger will serve as witness."

Suddenly Geneva saw the danger she was in. Even if Smith and Kramer let her live, Mason himself could not. How damned naïve I've been, she thought. Her daughters' faces floated in her mind. The little grandchildren . . .

"Better to buy our silence," Kramer said. "You have terrific earning potential, Drake—'scuse me, Leee-roy. Let's all work together here to protect it. And you."

The cell phone in her jeans pocket vibrated. She coughed violently and wiped her eyes.

Kramer glanced her way.

She bowed her head, trying for a look of terrified defeat. It wasn't hard to do. She sniffled and pointedly shifted her body to take a tissue out of her jeans pocket, sniffled again, and dabbed her eyes. With her other hand, she opened the phone on her lap. *Patio. Fox.* She could hardly believe it. He must have been nearby already.

Geneva's mind skittered from the scene before her to the doorway into the living room, slightly behind her and to the right. If the front gates were closed, her car was useless. She was trapped. But there was a service gate on the north side of the property. She'd have to go through the living room, cross the hall to the game room, which opened to the atrium, and finally through the French doors, to the east. A massive oak china cabinet stood against the dining room wall next to the living room doorway. She didn't dare look in that direction.

"As I was saying, seventy-five thousand for legal fees, and a million five for your father's pain and suffering, and his care and rehabilitation the first year in Florida, which comes to—"

A window exploded in another part of the house and the lights, indoors and out, went out. Someone screamed. Geneva was sure it was Smith.

She scooted off her chair, bent low, and rushed past the china cabinet and through the living room. Another explosion of glass and splintering wood, followed by Smith's curses and what sounded like overturning chairs and grunts. She managed to dodge most of the furniture in her path to the French doors. Once there, she opened one door and paused, looking out. The light-colored patio flagstones outside barely showed in the faint light of the quarter moon.

"Geneva—this way."

She closed the door behind her. The patio seemed empty. She crouched, looking back and forth, when a pair of arms pulled her behind the big oleander bush next to the house. She let out a squeak of surprise.

"Shhh," Fox said in her ear. "Come on." He pushed her past the bush and took her arm. They ran toward a redwood gazebo atop a terrace a dozen yards away, the back of which opened, she remembered, into a long arbor covered with vines. Once inside, he knelt and pulled her down beside him. "Give me your hands." Glancing back toward the house, he pulled out a tiny flashlight. In less than a minute, he'd opened the little lock and tossed the cable contraption to the floor.

"Thank you. How in the world did you get my message and come so fast?"

"Never mind that. My vehicle is parked back there. I found a people gate next to the main service gates."

"Yes. The delivery entrance. But can't we just call the local police, have Smith arrested? I guess it's not an FBI case, but . . ." Her voice trailed off.

"For what? I'm sure both men—maybe even Drake—would say you'd come in and shot Smith. They might even enlist police help to hunt you down." He bent and took her arm to pull her up. "Let's keep moving."

"I think not," said Kramer, barely three feet away. A blinding light shone into their faces. "Put your hands up and kneel down. Now." His big gun gleamed.

Fox shoved Geneva, sending her reeling behind him. She heard a loud grunt followed by sounds of blows and scraping feet. When she came up on hands and knees, she saw the bright flashlight lying at the bottom of the terrace, its light now angled upward, illuminating one of the two tall Chinese porcelain dogs next to the gazebo. The two men struggled in and out of the flashlight's beam, lunging and falling.

"Run, Geneva!" Fox yelled. His voice cut off with a grunt.

She got to her feet, trying to see him, trying to think what to do. Below, at the far edge of the patio, Smith, visible because of his white hair and light-colored shirt, clung to a lamp post. She remembered that Kramer had picked up Smith's little gun and put it in his jacket pocket. Maybe it was the only one in Smith's possession, although she doubted he could shoot Fox without hitting Kramer. But he could hit her. If he saw her. If he had another weapon. And if he didn't pass out from blood loss.

These thoughts flashed through her mind only peripherally as Geneva ducked back inside the gazebo and felt around on the floor for the bicycle cable. She found it and moved toward the fighting pair, who'd now tumbled several yards away from the flashlight. She didn't look at the light, hoping to preserve her night vision. Kramer wore a white shirt under a light tan jacket. Fox wore black, but his pale hair caught what little light there was. At the moment, the big man was on top of the lean agent, both of them growling, pounding each other and grunting. She held the cable ends in her hands until she saw her chance, then darted up behind Kramer and brought it down over his head. She lunged backwards with all her might. Fox sprang up, adding to her momentum, seized Kramer's arm and shoved it hard up between his shoulder blades. "Get his gun," he gasped. "Down there to your right."

"He has another one, too," she cried.

Geneva saw the glint of the gun on the ground and Smith scrambling for it at the same instant. She threw herself against him, pushed him aside, and picked up the heavy revolver. But before she could turn, he kicked her legs from under her and she went down hard on the flagstone. The gun flew into the darkness. Smith crawled forward and grabbed both her ankles.

"Federal agent!" Fox yelled. "Put your hands on your head, Smith. Get on your knees!" He'd been able to extricate his own weapon and now pressed the barrel against Kramer's back.

Despite being old, thin, and wounded, Smith still outweighed Geneva considerably and stood nearly a foot taller. Or in this case, knelt taller. He seized the back of her jacket and pulled her in front of him. In an instant, he had his left arm around her neck, tight as a vice. The more she struggled, the tighter his hold. He managed to get to his feet, pull her backwards into the house, and slam and lock the door. The next moment, Geneva felt him turn and thought he was about to release her. Then something hard crashed against her head.

CHAPTER THIRTY-THREE

After what she thought was only a minute, Geneva sat up. Smith was no longer in the room. She got to her feet and stumbled to the French doors. Outside she saw Kramer, partly lit by his fallen flashlight, pull away from Fox, bring the little pistol from his pocket, and fire.

Before she could catch her breath, she saw another flash and heard the shot. Kramer fell straight across the tilted beam. In it, she saw Fox bend and check for the huge man's pulse.

She slipped out the door and met him at the edge of the patio.

He pulled her behind the oleander bush. "Are you all right, Geneva?" Fox asked, taking hold of her shoulders.

"Yes, I'm okay. Smith must be inside somewhere. With Mason."

He dropped his hands. "Please go back up there into the gazebo and stay out of sight," he said in a hoarse whisper.

She didn't answer. Or turn to go.

"Mrs. Granger, I insist. Smith could have another weapon. Return to the gazebo now and call 911. Get the local police out here. Hurry!"

"Oh, the police. Of course."

She struggled up the terrace on rubbery legs, realizing only then how the back of her head and her whole right side, including her ankle, throbbed. Once inside, she dropped onto the bench and started to pull her cell phone from her jeans pocket. But it was stuck somehow. She worked it back and forth and finally freed it. She touched the dark, broken face of the phone, remembering how she had fallen on her side when Smith kicked her feet from under her.

"Oh, no," she whispered.

Gunshots split the air. They came from the house. One was a shotgun. Geneva knew that sound. The other a handgun, she thought.

She went to the gazebo doorway. The night had cooled considerably and she took in a deep breath. But she couldn't detect any sound to tell her where Justin might be. She stood still, straining to hear. Only some night birds called, back in the direction of the wooded lane that led to Mason's house. Now she thought she heard a far-off coyote yipping. Yes, an answering four-note cry came a moment later.

Ten minutes or more passed with no sight or sound of Justin. But her senses were full of him, despite the dangerous events of the last two hours.

Questions tumbled through her mind. Where was Smith? Who had fired the shots? She thought of Mason's gun cabinet and his several hunting rifles and shotguns. But he kept it locked, she was sure. He'd showed off his collection once when she and the twins and their husbands had visited, and she remembered Mason pulling the key to the cabinet out of his pocket. Smith wouldn't have been able to open it, certainly not in the dark. But maybe he had another gun in that satchel he'd left in the dining room.

Geneva's mouth felt utterly dry and her throat threatened to close altogether.

If Mason had somehow freed himself and been able to get

to his cabinet, then he must have fired those shots. If he'd shot Smith, what would his next step be?

A chill ran through her. Justin had called out as Smith dragged her into the house. So Mason had to know the FBI agent was there and would surely mean to kill him.

She started running toward the patio before she knew it, but then remembered Kramer's body lay close by. Dear God, she wouldn't want to step on or stumble over it. She halted, scanning the ground in the faint moonlight.

At the same moment, the two Goldtooth men—old Albert and his grandson Brandon—came around the corner of the house toward the patio.

"You sure you want in there, Granddad? Whoever's doing the shooting might be right behind those glass doors. Didn't you hear those shots?"

"I heard. If this one is locked, too, we're going to bust in. Kramer's deal means too much money to both of us. Something's damn wrong here for sure."

Geneva dropped and flattened herself behind a big agave plant, seeing at the same moment how the decorative swath of white gravel around it would make her dark clothes all the more visible.

"It's locked, too. Damn. All right, let's find a rock or something to break out some of those panes next to the latch. Shine your light out across the yard there, son."

When the beam of light touched Kramer's body, only a couple of yards from where Geneva lay, she thought her heart would stop. Her breath did.

"What the hell? That's Kramer! See if he's breathing, Brandon."

Geneva heard the crunch of gravel as Brandon stepped around Kramer's body.

"No pulse, Granddad. You think the FBI man, that guy Fox, killed Kramer? Where's Smith and Drake? Maybe he killed them, too."

"Don't know. Or maybe one of them killed the fed. But we've got to get those legal papers Kramer brought, signed or not. Reach in there in his pockets. See if you can find a packet or envelope with those papers."

"Me?"

"Yes, you. Don't tell me after all that rantin' and ravin' you're always doing about old superstitions and such, you're now afraid to touch a dead body."

"Well, you aren't traditional anymore, either, Granddad. You know what the papers look like. You get them."

"It's black dark out here, you fool. Nobody can see anything. Use your flashlight, reach into his pockets, feel around. Start with the inside jacket pocket."

She was close enough to hear the rustling of clothing and Brandon's disgusted snort.

"Nothing here. The papers must be in the house. Maybe they started without you."

If Albert answered, Geneva didn't hear it. The second the two men bent over Kramer's body, she rose as quietly as she could and struggled back up the terrace.

"Hey, did you hear something, Granddad?" Brandon's voice was no longer a whisper. "Back up there by that shade house." He paused. "Granddad?"

"I heard it. Be quiet."

Geneva hesitated, then slipped behind one of the two enormous porcelain dogs flanking the gazebo doorway. After a moment, she crawled far back inside the gazebo and crouched down again. For several seconds, she heard nothing.

A flashlight beam moved to one side of the terrace, paused, then moved back along the front of the gazebo. And twice more.

Geneva hoped she was timing the flashlight passes correctly, rose from her crouch, then leaped out of the door-way, pushing one of the great dogs over. It tumbled down the terrace toward the kneeling pair. It stopped with a sickening thud.

"What the hell?" Brandon cried. "Naali! Are you hurt? Naali! Naali!"

Geneva rushed down the far end of the terrace to a small stand of bushes. She almost yielded to an impulse to hide there, but she was still too close. The long path across the yard to the service gate—and escape to call the police—lay before her, completely exposed. She ran.

Fox heard someone moving in the living room. And someone else rustling papers, he thought, in the dining room. He moved to the end of the game room in time to make out Mason in his light-colored clothes creeping along the edge of the living room toward the dining room, keeping to the walls.

The skylight between kitchen and dining room admitted only the faintest light, but enough that Fox—and probably Drake as well, Fox thought—could see Rollie Smith bend over his satchel near the kitchen doorway.

"What are you doing, packing up that legal malarkey for another try someday?" Drake yelled. "Stay right there, you bastard."

"Hold your fire, both of you—FBI!"

"To hell with that!" Smith yelled.

Drake stepped forward and fired a single shotgun blast across the room.

"That ain't a friendly way to treat your long-lost pappy, now is it, boy?"

Fox bounded forward to push the barrel of Drake's shotgun down with his left hand and jam his handgun into Drake's side with the other.

But Drake lunged away and fired again toward Smith's voice in the dark.

"Bad shot, pissant."

A strong light hit Drake's eyes.

"Federal agent! Cease firing. Come forward to the dining table, both of you. Put your shotgun on the table, Senator. Now."

Drake could do nothing else, now seeing Fox's steady weapon leveled at his chest.

"Step away from it, Drake. Sit there, at the end of the table."

When Drake obeyed, Fox picked up the shotgun, stood the big light on its end in the middle of the table and moved back into the shadows.

"Rollie Smith!" Fox called out. "Put your weapon down and come out here."

"Ain't happening, you fucking fed."

A single shot blew the flashlight into a shower of spinning bits.

Drake scrambled to his feet and headed back toward the living room.

Fox stepped out of the shadows and pinned him with a smaller beam. "Get back here, Drake."

"And wait for that maniac to shoot me? Like hell I will." He spun away around the corner.

They both heard another shot, splintering glass, then a door banged back against something.

"Laundry room door—he's getting away," Drake yelled. "I'll get him."

"Stay here, Drake," Fox said. "Sit down!"

But Drake had already reached his gun cabinet and had a rifle in one hand and a box of shells in the other.

Fox stepped in front of him, flashlight trained at Drake's face, and gun pointed at his chest. "Drop it."

Drake started to charge past the agent, who put out a foot

and tripped the larger man. Drake fell face down. Fox kicked the rifle away.

More clattering came from the direction of the kitchen or laundry room.

Fox jerked Drake to his feet and shoved him back around the living room wall. He pushed him down and hastily clamped one wrist to the leg of the big gun cabinet.

"He's getting away," Drake screamed, his voice muffled against his luxuriant carpet. "Uncuff me! He's a murderer! I'll kill him!"

Fox moved fast into the dining room and the shadow of the china cabinet.

"Ain't so, boy. I didn't run off. Your pappy is right here getting you out of your fix. You going to be happy as a pig in mud signing them papers now."

Brandon Goldtooth and Rollie Smith stepped forward together from the kitchen doorway, both aiming flashlights — and weapons — at Justin Fox.

"Hands up, mister Fuckin' B-I agent. Me and Brandon-Boy here both got guns and plenty ammunition. Throw down that pistol of yours and come here. Right now."

"Do it!" Brandon barked. His smooth face gleamed in the reflected glow of their flashlights, its expression of malice almost a caricature.

Fox dropped his weapon and raised his hands.

"Looky there, ain't that a sight!" Smith said. "Keep that right hand up, you stupid fed, reach around there in your pocket with your left hand, and bring up that handcuff key. We got to have the high-and-mighty sen-a-tor loose, so he can sign over his money to us. Give it to Brandon real nice and slow."

"First, get up against the wall," Brandon said, waving his gun and flashlight in the direction of the kitchen. "Hurry up! Move your ass!"

Fox moved to the only clear space of dining room wall, a

yard from the kitchen doorway.

"That'll do," Smith snapped. "The key. Real easy now."

With his left hand, Fox reached slowly across his chest and down toward his right-hand pants pocket.

"I said hurry up! Hurry up!" Brandon yelled, and then stepped too close.

Before the fancy-dancer could take a breath, Fox had his arm bent up hard between his shoulder blades and Brandon's own gun barrel tight under his jaw.

"Shit! Ain't you got no sense, you damned Indian?" Smith yelled.

Geneva ran for the service gate. She was still yards and yards away when the sound of gunshots stopped her. A shotgun blast. Then two more quick reports. Handguns, she thought. She dropped to her knees, then flattened herself against the manicured lawn. The crescent moon was higher in the sky now, stars bright above. Again, she imagined her dark denim jacket and jeans making her form perfectly visible against the silvery winter grass.

More gunshots. What if Brandon and his grandfather had gotten into the house? Smith was in there, too. The Goldtooths for their reasons, and Mason for his — reasons that she herself had handed him — made a force of four against Justin. The next second, she rose and started running back toward the house.

In the shadow of the oleander bush next to the patio door, she stopped and tried to think what to do. The gun — Kramer's big revolver she and Smith had struggled over. Did Smith find it — come back after dragging her into the house and bashing her head — and find that gun?

She closed her eyes and pictured the scene when she'd had the gun in her hands, the second before Smith kicked her to the flagstones. *Come on, whatever power you are—now's the time. Show me where that gun went.*

She saw. In her mind the revolver spun upwards out of her hands, tumbled in a slow, arc—down, down, then landed and slid along the grass to stop against an Arabian jasmine. *Thank you*, she said in her mind, took four steps, bent, and plucked the heavy gun out of the fragrant plant in the dark.

"You think I give a good goddam about this fool Indian, you fool fed?" Smith snarled. "Go ahead and shoot his head off, for all I care. You ain't going to stop what I come for this night."

"Is that right, Smith?" Fox said. "So, where's your buddy Albert? And your lawyer? What about a witness? Why do you imagine the senator will sign those papers now? Or that they could be legally binding at this point?"

Smith fired, shattering plaster from the wall above the heads of Fox and Brandon.

"I'll make that swaggering, snot-nosed shit sign, don't you worry about that. As for your grand-pappy, Brandon, where the hell *is* he? And where's that black ape Kramer?"

"Kramer's dead, Smith," Brandon said. "That damned woman, Granger—I know it was her—she hurt my grandpa, knocked him down with one of those statues and then ran off. He's in the backyard out there, getting his wind back. I want to go back and see about him."

Damn, Fox thought. Why is she still here and not down at the gate waiting for the police? They should be here by now. He felt exasperation and worry rise together in his gut. Something was wrong.

That instant of his distraction must have telegraphed itself to Brandon, who seized the gun held against his jaw, elbowed Fox in the chest, then bucked and twisted away in a single motion. He dived behind the big overstuffed chair near the kitchen doorway, then scrambled through the kitchen and out the laundry room door to the outside.

Smith let out a shrill laugh, "Oooo-eee!" and kept his flashlight steady in Fox's eyes. "Hands up, pig," he said. "That kid's a hot-damn ath-a-lete, don't-cha-know." He cackled and let out another "Oooo-eee!"

Holding Kramer's revolver at her side, Geneva eased herself as quietly as she could through the patio door, through the game room, and into the living room just in time to hear Smith say, "a hot-damn ath-a-lete, don't-cha-know." And his cackling "Oooo-eee!"

The next thing she heard was Mason's growling curses nearby, inside the living room to her right. She stood still then, trying to understand what was happening, both with Mason and the two men at the other end of the long dining room. Only two. Brandon Goldtooth had to be the athlete Smith meant, but where was he now?

With her next step, the scene at the end of the dining room came clear. Smith's flashlight beam lit the gun he pointed at Justin's somber face. And his hands, raised in surrender.

Geneva ignored Mason, tethered to something, apparently, and making so much noise he never noticed her.

She moved forward, but out of Smith's view and hearing. For the moment, anyway. He faced the kitchen doorway, still holding his flashlight—and gun—on Fox, who faced the dining room.

She wondered how to get Justin's attention—and avoid Smith's. And especially how to do it before the Goldtooth men came in. They and Smith might think getting those papers signed was still the thing to do, even without Kramer. In any case, she and Fox were expendable.

CHAPTER THIRTY-FOUR

Staring at the small tunnel of Smith's flashlight focused on Justin, Geneva wished for some equally narrow beam, just to pinpoint the big revolver now growing heavier by the second in her hand. She thought of her smashed cellphone and felt a wave of near nausea squeeze her dry, dry throat.

If she stayed where she was, pressed between the wall and the china cabinet, Mason, on the other side of the wall, probably wouldn't see any light she might have. But the only thing Smith, maybe even Mason, had to do was move just a bit and her chance would be lost. Lost, anyway, she thought. I have no light. She squeezed her eyes shut hard.

Eyes still shut, and almost without knowing, she lifted her hand. And plucked a long butane lighter from the open shelf of the cabinet, just behind a pair of squat candles exuding a cinnamon scent. She raised it and the gun in front of her face. And made the flame flare.

She saw Justin react, the merest movement of his eyes.

"All right, Smith," he said, "let's say you can somehow make your plan—whatever the hell that is—work. If all three of you mean to benefit from those legal documents and need to sign—and can somehow make Drake sign, you'll need a witness who is not a beneficiary. Have you thought of that?"

"That's the only reason you're still drawing breath, pig. You think you're the only one with brains? I know how it all works. Kramer gave me some tips. Him dead just means more for me. Now shut up and get moving. The mighty senator's business partner and the kid will be coming through that back door in a minute. Enough time for you to unhitch Leroy and haul him back in here to the supper table. Move!"

Geneva still stood against the side of the china cabinet, the darkest corner in the dark room. Smith came in fast, his revolver at Justin's back, his flashlight jabbing him every few steps.

"All right, stop right there, fed. Now step to your right one pace, then make a nice little two-step left around the end of the wall. Shut up that caterwauling, damn you, Leroy! This here FBI man's about to cut you loose, pretty as you please."

As they came even with the china cabinet, Justin stumbled, seemed to fall against it, and reached out. Geneva slapped the big gun into his hand and dived under the table.

The next second's actions were all noise to Geneva. Gunshots—several—boomed at once.

And one empty click.

"Geneva," Justin's rasp of a whisper, "call the police again! And run!"

"I didn't call! My phone broke when I fell."

"Hooked to my belt, my right side—hurry!"

Somehow, she got his phone and ran for the front door.

She was barely out when she heard Brandon's voice at the east side of the house.

"I'm not going back in there, Granddad. Your head's still bleeding and I don't like the way you're breathing. Here, lean on me. We're going back to the truck and I'm getting you to a hospital."

Good, Geneva thought. Those two will be out of the way.

And Mason seems to be tied up in the living room. There's poetic justice in that somewhere. Better yet, Smith was out of bullets. She'd heard that loud, tell-tale click.

But the gates were still locked. Kramer had made certain of that. Maybe the police could force them open.

Before her next breath, the thought landed in the hollow of her throat like an arrow. Justin's whispered command was made close to her ear. She'd been on the floor huddled under the dining table. That meant he was on the floor as well. And all those shots the minute after she gave Justin the big gun . . . Whose gun had made that empty click?

Her ever-drier throat wouldn't allow her hard attempts to swallow. An icy dread flowed across her shoulders and down her breasts. She could barely lift his phone to her lips.

Smith still seemed stunned from the blow Fox had managed with the empty revolver, but as soon as Geneva was outside, Fox planted a knee on his back anyway and felt about the floor, trying to find the old man's gun.

A bright beam hit them both. So did the strong smell of oil, gun oil. Fox knew it immediately. Drake stood in the doorway to the living room holding a wide flashlight. And a pistol.

"Did you kill him, Fox? Is the bastard dead?" Mason's yelling had gone on so long, his voice now came out a two-level screech. "Stand up, get him to his feet so I can see him. Now!"

Fox could hardly believe his eyes. How had Drake gotten out of the handcuff?

"Not dead. He's just unconscious."

"Surprised to see me, Agent? I'll explain later. Maybe. Get that bag of shit up, slap him, whatever it takes. I want him wide awake so he sees me, so he knows exactly what I'm about to do. I want him to see—me—kill—him."

"Put down your weapon, Drake. Do it!"

"You're not the one giving orders now, Fox. There's a chair there to your left." Drake flipped his beam to it and back. "Get him up, put him in it. Wake the bastard up so he can see me! Now!"

His back to Drake, Fox took his time bending over Smith, reaching to grasp the limp man under the arms. As he stepped, his foot touched Smith's gun. He went down on one knee, hoping to appear to be getting a better hold, grabbed the gun, and hid it behind Smith's back. Without turning around, he struggled with Smith. For a second, he thought the wiry old man tensed. But no. Fox staggered with him the few steps to the chair and set him into it. He then made to step away but Smith, head lolling, started to fall sideways.

"Hold onto him! Wake him the hell up!" Drake yelled.

Fox turned back, pocketing the pistol in the same move, and took hold of Smith's shoulders. "He's really out," he said to Drake. "His head should be on the same level as his heart. Equalizes blood flow."

"Heart—that's a laugh. All right, get him up there on the table. Hurry up."

"Are you kidding? This guy may be old, but he's solid as oak. And right now, dead weight. You get his shoulders. I'll get his legs."

"Oh, no, I'm not falling for that."

"You're afraid of him, even now, Senator?"

"I'm not afraid of him—I was never afraid of him!" Drake's raw voice split. "Just get him up—wake the bastard up! I want him to see me!"

Fox felt the gun leave his pocket and Smith's knee in his groin at the same instant. He lunged against Smith, tried to hold him, but Smith half-rose. And fired.

The two shots, almost simultaneous, deafened Fox. Smith fell against him, and didn't move again.

Drake screamed. And screamed.

CHAPTER THIRTY-FIVE

Geneva stumbled back to the front door and listened. All she could hear was Mason, cursing and yelling. But something was different. His voice came from farther away than the gun cabinet in the living room. She moved toward the dining room window below the one Justin had shot out.

On the far side of the dining table, Mason lay on the floor, lit by a hunched figure playing a flashlight along Mason's side. Nearby, only now-and-again illuminated by the flashlight, she saw a chair overturned on a mound of something—a person? Smith? Or was it Justin? She rushed back to the door and let herself in, staying close to the living room wall. Near the gun cabinet, she smelled gun oil. She paused at the doorway to see the figures in the wavering light.

"Well, you managed it, Drake. You killed your father."

Justin's alive, she thought. Thank God.

"He shot me! He shot me!" Mason's cracked, high-pitched voice.

"You're damned lucky, I'd say, Senator. Can you sit up? I'll take a look."

"No! Damn you! Get me an ambulance. Geneva, there you are—Help me!" Drake cried.

Justin's head whipped toward the living room doorway. "Are they on their way?"

"Yes."

"Then go down to the gates and let them know the situation. Please."

The next hour passed in a black-and-white, red-and-blue blur for Geneva.

But someone gave her a bottle of water, pressed her folder and purse into her hands, and led her to her rental car.

She drank every drop, closed her eyes, and reclined in her seat, still holding the bottle to her middle. For thirty seconds, maybe. Three Tempe police cars pulled beside and behind her small rental. And now two Phoenix police vehicles came leading an ambulance. Behind them, what looked like a caravan of media vans rose one after another into the wide oval driveway.

A helmeted head popped into the driver-side window. "You all right in there, ma'am?"

Geneva pulled the lever on the side of the seat, which threw her upright with a loud clunk, almost into the officer's face. Her chest struck the steering wheel.

"Yes!" she gasped.

They were both wordless for a beat, then she began to laugh. "I mean yes, I am. Are you?"

The officer, now a foot away, bent toward her and chuckled a little. "Yes, ma'am. Sorry I scared you. Or whatever that was."

"Don't worry, I'm fine." She looked around at the gathering crowd of vehicles, medical and police personnel. "I should move this car, so the ambulance can get closer to the door."

"I came to do that for you, ma'am."

She gave him the keys and moved out of the way, but close

to the open door. As she did, four white-clothed men carrying two gurneys followed a man with several brilliant halogen lanterns into the house. She stepped in directly behind them.

Justin Fox stood in the kitchen doorway and watched Mason Drake being loaded onto the gurney. When Justin saw Geneva, he gestured sharply for her to leave, go toward the game room. His severe expression startled her into motion. She turned and hurried past the departing gurney whose attendants seemed not to notice her at all. And she kept going, past the glaring lanterns, across the end of the living room, and then through the dark to the far end of the game room, where she sank onto the love seat in the corner. She kicked off her shoes and swung her feet up, pulled a soft throw over her legs, and worked to slow her breathing. Why did he send her out? And why did he look so fierce?

Sometime later, Geneva came awake as a bright light entered the room. Or maybe it was the weight that settled beside her legs that woke her.

"They've cleared out. All of them," he said. "I didn't want you to have to go through that tonight. You can give a statement later."

"Oh, I didn't know. Thank you."

"Let me drive you back to your motel," he said. "The patrolman gave me your keys. How about something hot to eat?"

There was that startling smile again.

CHAPTER THIRTY-SIX

Justin ordered dinner from his cell phone, and it was delivered a few minutes after they arrived at Fiddler's Inn.

He told her of Julianna's call earlier, so Geneva called to assure her she was in no danger. "Let your sister know, too. I'm back at Fiddler's Inn and will be home tomorrow."

Justin produced a cup of tea from the tiny kitchenette and brought it to Geneva as she opened the several containers of Chinese food on the small table.

"A miracle," she said, taking the steaming cup. "How did you do that?"

"Ah, just one of my agent tricks. They teach you those at FBI school, you know."

"Did they teach you how to use these short chopsticks, too?" she said, unwrapping them.

"No, but I did learn searching skills, and that's how I found these genuine plastic forks and plates on that top shelf up there. Let's eat."

Geneva felt herself relax. Questions circled the edges of her mind about what had happened in the previous three hours, but she let them wait. It felt good to share a meal, to know she was safe. To know they were both safe. Her little corner suite seemed charmed tonight, so different from her many nights here in the past doing research, grading papers, writing. Alone then. Always alone.

Justin set their plates on the table, flourished a fan of paper napkins, offering them like a bouquet. "All right, Miz Geneva Granger, tell me—I'm dying to know. Where did you learn to shoot so well?"

Her hand stopped midway to the waving napkins. "You saw that? When did you arrive?"

"In time to see you and Drake being marched to the dining table, I guess." He rose and poured more tea. "I thought you were doing very well indeed. Pretty soon, though, the odds changed." He leaned forward. "But you know—um, I'd rather talk about other things. Let's just unwind a bit, shall we?"

Geneva glanced up to see his look of warmth, an unguarded flash of fondness. Of . . . desire?

She felt a barrage of surprising sensations. All at once, as if he knew she'd seen his expression, he looked downright shy. His ruddy face and neck deepened by several shades of red. She felt a flush of pleasure. They both laughed.

A beat passed. Then, still smiling, he said, "I really do want to know how you learned to shoot like that."

Her own smile widened. "My sons-in-law. The twins, too, but mostly Ray and Thomas. They decided after Edward died that I must be able to defend myself should anyone break into what Ray calls 'the Big Adobe.' So they bought me a revolver and taught me how not only to fire and mostly hit a target, but also made me take it apart, clean it, and put it back together—a hundred times, I think!"

"Good for them," Justin said, a serious look in his eyes. "I've made sure Taylor knows how to handle a gun. And he's teaching his bride of five months. It just makes sense in the world we live in."

"And what I really want to know from you is about your mother's psychic cat," she said.

"Czar Nicky! The tales I could tell about his highness. Most of 'em you would never believe." He threw back his head and laughed.

Again, his wonderful laugh filled her with an unaccountable stirring.

He got to his feet. "But that's a story for another time. The police chief wants to see me first thing in the morning."

"Thank you for bringing me home to my little nook, Justin."

"I'm glad to see you relaxed—and safe. For now. But Geneva, you must realize the danger you're in. Smith and Kramer are dead. But Drake is not. And you know his real identity. Neither his injuries nor any legal entanglements from this night's violence in his house will stop him from seeing that you never reveal it."

"But if he had something to do with Edward's death—"

"That's still to be proved. It was ruled an accident, remember." Justin went quiet for a moment. "Do you have any idea why the two Goldtooth men were there?"

"Not exactly, but they knew Kramer, even looked for the papers on his body. Maybe they know who Smith was, too."

"Geneva, I don't think you realize how dangerous your situation may be—no, definitely is."

Car lights outside flashed twice. "That's my ride," he said. "Please tell me you'll accept your college friend's invitation for that visit to Nantucket you mentioned."

She made a vague gesture. "Perhaps," she murmured.

"Do it." He bent and kissed her forehead, a quick brush of a kiss.

And then he was gone, his kiss still warm on her brow but a new dread cold upon her spirit.

Geneva went to bed soon after Justin left, but woke a few hours later. Unable to go back to sleep, she packed her things and opened the door of her motel suite, rolling her suitcase behind her as quietly as she could.

A car door opened right next to her vehicle.

She started, ready to dart back in.

"Where are you going, Mrs. Granger?" said a slender man, stepping out of the car.

"What? Who are you?" she stumbled back into the room, making her wheeled case bump and wobble.

The man stepped into the dim light of the overhang. "It's all right, Mrs. Granger. FBI." He held out a badge for her to see. "Agent Fox assigned me here. Ma'am, it's only three thirty a.m. Where are you going?"

"Agent Fox assigned you. I see. Well, I'm going home. And I'll be perfectly fine." She forced her breath under control. "You can tell Agent Fox that I have dismissed you. But thank you all the same."

"I'll have to notify him, ma'am. He told me to stay here all night."

Geneva took a closer look at the man. He seemed so young. And thoroughly rattled.

"Ah. You know, that's a good idea. If anyone suspicious approaches this door, please let Mr. Fox know. But otherwise, don't bother him. He had a busy day yesterday."

With that, she left him standing there. She waved, got into her car, and pulled onto the quiet street.

CHAPTER THIRTY-SEVEN

Geneva stopped only for a cup of coffee and a warm muffin before swinging onto I-17. By the time she passed the turnoff for Prescott, she had determined not to tell her daughters about Mason's real identity. If they knew, they might be in danger, too. She would not, in fact, imply any kind of danger.

And she would call Justin when she got home, once a decent hour arrived, to find out just what a police report might say about her presence in the Drake home last night. Julianna, bless her, would surely check.

Hours later, but well before that decent hour, her kitchen phone rang. She reached past her steaming coffee maker to answer.

"Mom, it's Julianna. I heard about Mason! It's on the news. What happened? Are you all right?"

"Oh, Julianna, darling. I thought I'd wait to call you until I was sure you and Thom were up. I'm perfectly fine. Everything's okay. Did you enjoy your trip to California?"

The worry that had plagued Geneva all the way back from Tempe was about to be realized this minute, she knew.

"My trip! That's completely irrelevant—what happened

down there? Did Agent Fox reach you? What about those two men who were killed? Have you spoken with Karen? Tell me what happened!"

"Goodness, honey. I'm just fine. No need for all this fuss." At the same moment, Geneva plucked the TV control out of its basket and clicked it on, muted. All three network news programs had footage of Mason Drake, looking aggrieved, one shoulder and arm swathed in bandages, a big patch on one cheek.

"Mom! Tell me. No, never mind. I'll be there in ten minutes." She hung up.

As for calling Justin, she didn't have the chance. As soon as she sat down at her computer, her phone rang again.

"You got an early start on the day," he said.

She thought she could hear a smile under his words and decided not to make a mountain out of his protective move. "I did. You might have told me you'd assigned someone to watch over me."

"I might have. But I knew you would object."

"I would have. But I suppose I should thank you."

"No need."

"And no harm done — except the poor boy was troubled by my leaving. I'm glad he didn't feel compelled to follow me."

"Mmm."

She wondered then if the agent had followed her, but let it go. "What have you learned about the police report and my being at Mason's house last night?"

"Nothing so far. I'm just going in to the police chief's office now. But I wanted to know that you're home safe."

After the call, she swiveled around to face her beautiful mountains and tried to sort out the mix of feelings flowing through her. Sweet to have a man care about her safety. But of course, it was his job.

The San Francisco Peaks began to glow with the rising sun. Funny, she thought now, just how hard she'd worked in this last year to suppress the wish that someone would — could — love her as Edward had. Someone she could love that much, too.

All that work, she knew now, was based on the underlying conviction that such a man didn't exist. It couldn't happen twice in her lifetime. And the old saying was true: all the good ones were married. Or dead.

But now a layer of backlit cloud drifted just below the shining sacred peaks. And Justin Fox's startling smile flashed again in her mind.

Geneva sighed and poured herself another cup of coffee. It hadn't reached her lips before the doorbell rang.

Her other daughter stood there — or rather, bounced about — nervously flipping her hair back.

"Karen, dear. It's not even seven o'clock. But I guess you've seen the news, too."

Karen had her arms around her in a flash. "Yes! Mom, are you all right?"

"Of course I am. Please come in and have some breakfast, honey. Your sister will be here shortly."

Geneva had rehearsed what she would tell her girls . . . for miles and miles. And she did tell them. Most of it. Not Mason's real identity. Nothing of her shooting Smith or being threatened by him and the lawyer Kramer. Nor about the Goldtooth men. Goldtooth men — Lord, had they known or even guessed she would be there last night? And what if they did? What would that mean?

Nor did she tell the entire story of Justin's rescuing her. She let the twins think she had left soon after arriving, and stated honestly that she hadn't witnessed the two deaths reported in the news. Or Mason's injuries.

And nothing of Justin's warning about the danger she was in.

That one was racing around in her head now with a new

urgency She did tell them the truth about how little sleep she'd had. And how glad she was to see them.

The twins left an hour later. Mollified, she thought. She hoped.

But by mid-afternoon, Geneva could not live another hour with her own duplicity.

She sat now in Karen's living room, holding the baby and watching her daughter pace in front of her, trying to accept the news about Mason.

"You mean you already knew something was wrong, Mom —you suspected something weeks ago? Months, even?" Karen said.

Geneva started to answer, but Karen swung around to her sister, sitting uneasily on the arm of the sofa. "And you, Julianna. Why didn't you tell me what you found out about that man Smith when you were in California? Why have you both kept everything from me?"

Geneva and Julianna both spoke at once. Julianna stopped and gestured for her mother to go on.

"Karen, I didn't want to accept what I was learning at first," Geneva said. "About SB500, about the pilot's name and his connection to Bessie Jim. I couldn't be sure, and so what could I say to you? Mason has been our friend for most of your life."

Julianna leaned forward. "I wanted to wait until I got home to tell you, Karen," she said. "And here I am." She waited a beat before continuing. "Dear *Uncle* Mason—Hah! But the worst part is that he betrayed Dad. Lied about working for SB500."

"Let me put Emily in her crib," Geneva said, rising. "There's more I must tell you."

An hour later, all three sat quietly, drained. Both daughters had cried and raged and scolded and cried some more. From time to time Julianna would mutter, "Leroy Smith. Unbelievable."

And Karen hadn't lost her stricken expression from learning some and imagining more about the violence her mother had endured and witnessed in Tempe. And taken part in. Tears came again to her eyes.

Geneva stood up and embraced them both. "So now you know everything. Everything I know, anyway. Yes, I will have to testify, Agent Fox said. But exactly when and how is still not clear."

Geneva might have corrected "everything I know" to "almost everything." Or "certain parts of everything." But she didn't. She could not shock her daughters further with her suspicions that Mason Drake—Leroy Smith—might have arranged the murder of their father.

Back in her own kitchen that evening, Geneva glanced occasionally at the muted TV and sighed. Six o'clock news was showing Mason being interviewed, looking brave in his bandages. She couldn't listen, but she couldn't turn it off, either.

She sat down and called Desbah.

The minute she answered, Desbah said, "Tell me you did not go down to see Mason Drake after all yesterday."

"I wish I could," Geneva said, letting out a deep breath.

"He's in both Phoenix papers, and even the *Gallup Independent*. And at five o'clock, Channel 4 had a picture of him in a hospital bed all bandaged up. The center of attention, of course. Telling about the attackers who invaded his home."

"Yes. It's on again right now," Geneva said. She clicked off the set and walked to the living room, where she sank onto the sofa.

Desbah said, "Tell me. Everything."

So Geneva told her friend. Everything.

Desbah listened with her usual quiet, only letting out a

little squawk when she heard the part where Smith appeared with a gun in Mason's kitchen.

"Did you get out of there with that portrait?"

"I did, yes. A policeman picked up the folder it was in and returned it along with my handbag. I'm sure it was Justin who saw to that."

"Geneva, your name can't be kept out of it if you were identified to the police. No matter what Justin Fox might try to do to protect you."

"Yes, I know that's true."

Desbah made telephone wires sing with her string of Navajo curses. "Do you believe the Goldtooth men don't know Drake's real identity? And if they do, wouldn't they know you do, too?"

Geneva thought a moment. "They did recognize the lawyer —his body, I mean. And I heard them mention Smith."

"It doesn't matter. Mason will kill you or have you killed before either of the Goldtooths will have the chance. You've got to get away from Arizona. I think you should start planning a good long vacation—a good long distance away, like Nantucket. You said you hadn't yet given your old college roommate an answer."

Justin's warning came back to Geneva. The one she could not bear to tell her daughters about.

CHAPTER THIRTY-EIGHT

The next morning, Geneva's phone rang at same instant the coffee maker gave its beep.

"Geneva, sorry to call so early, but I have to drive to Phoenix and catch a plane," Desbah said. "I really want you to skip Nantucket and get out of the country. Maybe you can just make a deposition about what you saw and heard at Drake's house. See if Fox will agree. And then you and I go to Switzerland. We could help Chee research doctors for Shándííne."

For the first time in what seemed like days, Geneva gave a hearty laugh. "Even at the serious risk of making the infamous crowd of three, I'd love to go with you to see Chee Hamilton, and Switzerland, of course, but—"

"I know you'll come up with a hundred objections. Just say you'll consider it."

"I will consider it, Desbah. I promise. And I'm glad you called. I had the weirdest dream—vision a few days ago." She told her friend about seeing the word *Jefferson* written in fancy script over water.

"I know it had to do with Edward. Something bad, Desbah. But it's vague. Does *Jefferson* ring a bell with you?"

"Hmm. Over water, you say. Maybe this is one picture

puzzle I might help with. *Toli* means water or watery in Navajo. And I know about a Jefferson Toli.

"You do?"

"Yes, he's an old guy who claims to have been in some movies shot around the reservation in the early seventies, I think. Only reason I know is that he was in a little theater production in Window Rock with my nephew Bidzi last fall. Finally got thrown out for showing up at rehearsals drunk. Was that all you saw?"

"Actually, I had another vision earlier that night." Geneva told about her vision of Harrison Billy planning to confess to Jerome Layton's murder. "He's taking the blame to save Terry."

"That's crazy!" Desbah said.

"I think so, too. But I haven't heard anything about what's going on out there. Justin hasn't told me, and I haven't read the *Navajo Times* online since, well, since last week, and then—"

"Then the horrible business in Tempe," Desbah finished for her. "So. It's 'Justin,' now, is it? And he calls you?"

"He wants me to leave the area for a while."

"See? Forget Nantucket. Let's go to Zurich. My office can get us tickets right after Thanksgiving."

"Oh, Desbah, I want to know what really happened to Edward! I've been chasing here and there ever since September when I first heard from Harrison. But now I have a strong feeling to, to—"

"To what? You said yourself that the Goldtooths knew that lawyer. And Rollie Smith. And they might have known you would be at Mason's place that night. Probably did. What can that mean? Don't you see the danger in coming here to the reservation—right here, where they live?"

Geneva drew a long breath. "But I still want to go, right after Thanksgiving."

Desbah let a few beats of silence pass. "Well, if you're that determined, you know you can stay with me. I'm driving back to Phoenix the day before Thanksgiving and having the holiday there with my nephew Klah and his wife. Then I'm bringing his German shepherd back home with me for a week while they go see her folks. So I guess we'll have some protection. The beast weighs about eighty pounds."

"Thanks, Desbah!"

Plan made, Geneva started packing a suitcase, including her new hiking boots, wondering why she had such an urge to do it.

CHAPTER THIRTY-NINE

Thanksgiving dinner at Karen's house passed with fewer comments about Drake than Geneva had feared. She played dinosaurs with Josh and cuddled the babies. Then went home in the late afternoon, anticipating a call from Justin.

And call he did. "I've just finished the second dinner of the day here with my dad," he said. "Right now, he's settling in for his favorite TV recap of the big game and a nap—not necessarily in that order. Taylor and Connie just left, obeying the rule that nobody interrupts the recap. Want some company?"

She did. When he arrived, he kissed her cheek. Again, he looked almost shy afterwards. Somehow that tickled her. She smiled as she settled them at the kitchen table and poured coffee. And told him of her plan to go to the reservation on Monday.

He set his coffee cup down. "Geneva, that's not a good idea. What about the Goldtooth men? If they are willing to threaten young Terry Littleben—and Brandon beat him up, remember—what might they do to you? You said yourself that it was Brandon who ran you off the road."

"Justin, I'll be perfectly safe. I'll be staying with Desbah in Chinle. And she even has a big German shepherd now." She smiled at him across the table and slid the pumpkin pie his way. "Whipped cream?"

He frowned and didn't speak for a moment. "But what exactly do you plan to do once you get there?"

She took a breath. "I want to visit some people I know — Harrison Billy, for one," she said. "Maybe Bessie's family and some others. Somebody might know who this Jefferson Toli is and what he could've had to do with Edward."

"No, Geneva! It's too dangerous to go back to the reservation." He stood then, looking frustrated, and walked the length of the kitchen and back.

He continued to stand, saying nothing.

"All right," she said, in a softer voice. "I'll tell you all of it. But please sit down."

He turned his chair and sat.

"I . . . think Harrison has or will confess to Dr. Layton 's murder to save Terry." She looked at him and waited for his questions.

"You think. Do you mean you had a . . . a vision that made you think so?"

"Yes, and I hope to find that formation, the headless bird in the sandstone mesa near Sawmill. You said you saw it yourself. It exists. It's real."

He breathed out. "Ah. I see. And once you do, what then?"

"Will you tell me where it is?"

He looked at her for a long moment. "Just wait 'til Wednesday, please. I have to finish with Drake and the Tempe police. And . . . and other things. But I can meet you in Window Rock on Wednesday and take you up there. So you'll be safe."

She gave him an uncertain smile but didn't speak.

Finally, he said, "All right. It's just northwest of Sawmill. About a mile or so, there's an old chimney where a hogahn or a house, I guess, once stood. No road number — it's just a lumber company track. You turn west there." Again he went quiet, looking troubled.

Geneva took the scratch pad and pen from the kitchen desk and wrote quickly.

"Please let me go with you," he said. "Tomorrow is Friday and I'm hoping his doctors let me interview Drake—Smith—whatever the devil his name is."

Then he smiled that smile. And she hesitated. But she couldn't quite tell him why she wanted to be alone there. It was important that she find and experience the place where Edward died. She must see what he saw. Feel it. Know it.

And, perhaps, say good-bye at last.

CHAPTER FORTY

O n Monday morning, Geneva glanced again at her to-do
list and sighed. Everything done except to finish packing, and it was only seven o'clock. But her gaze went back to
the drawer of her nightstand. She sat down on the edge of her
bed and tried to think. Why she felt she should take her
revolver with her, she couldn't say. She'd had no vision of
danger, no clear urge exactly. The little electric waterfall on her
bureau hummed its monotonous hum. She went to Edward's
recliner, sat, leaned back, and closed her eyes. She was learning, she might say to Ooljee Blackgoat. She was learning.

Half an hour passed, but the only clear image that came to
Geneva was that of her small revolver in its tan case. The
picture lifted and moved closer and larger. No other picture
came, no jigsaw scenes turning and fluttering. But certainty
settled into her mind.

She rose, opened the drawer, and lifted out the loaded gun
and the extra magazine that lay beside it. She passed the open
suitcase and carried the gun and clip downstairs, where she
laid them next to her handbag and camera.

Geneva found a padded envelope for the promised photo
for Bessie's sister Sylvia and looked at it for a moment. She had

299

taken this picture herself four years ago and remembered now how embarrassed Edward looked at the effusive thanks from the family as he rolled Sylvia's new wheelchair into their house. And there was Bessie at one side, facing the camera, her long braid gleaming in the sun, her wide smile telling it all.

Geneva had let her girls know last night that she would leave in time to meet Desbah in Window Rock, where she would be working today, and follow her home to Chinle. Hours from now. But if she left Flagstaff this morning, she might meet Desbah for lunch and then go find out about Harrison for herself. She could recall her vision and the old Code Talker's worried words clearly.

Finishing the packing took only a few minutes. She decided to call the girls from her first pit stop down the road in an hour or so. Great things, cell phones.

Geneva swung out onto I-40, remembering some of the back roads she and Edward used to take on weekends going home to Flag from Diné College at Tsaile. The short twenty-five miles over to Chinle, then south, picking up Navajo Route 15, sometimes visiting former students on the way or just soaking up the beautiful scenery. But not today. She felt a quiet but growing urgency to get to Window Rock.

A hundred miles later, she stopped at the edge of Holbrook and called to let her daughters know her changed plans. She hoped to have lunch with Desbah in Window Rock, she told them, and then "shop a bit" until time to follow her friend home to Chinle after work.

Soon she stood before Desbah's secretary in Window Rock. But Doctor Chischilly had been called away early, the secretary said, to help conduct a workshop for prospective college students at the high school. Wouldn't be back here for lunch and probably not until five this afternoon. Should she call Doctor Chischilly for Doctor Granger?

"Oh, no, please don't bother her. I'll be back this afternoon."

Five minutes later Geneva pulled into the police complex parking area. Lieutenant Nez was out, the officer at the desk told her. And no, Harrison Billy was no longer here.

"FBI let him go," the officer said. "His daughter picked him up last night. Took him home with her and the boy, I believe."

Geneva thanked him and left.

She turned her car north toward Fort Defiance, hoping Harrison would be at his daughter's place and further hoping she could find it after being there only once and then as Tucker's passenger.

But she did. Of course, Margaret would be at work, but there sat Terry's old van. Geneva hadn't heard from Terry since he climbed into his mother's truck at El Rancho Hotel in Gallup.

Of course, she hadn't expected to hear from Terry or Margaret Littleben. Or even Harrison. Only through her vision did she know—know?—about his confession to Dr. Layton 's murder.

She parked her car in front of the long mobile home and waited. Music blared from inside. She got out and knocked on the door. It opened and a surprised Terry stood looking at her.

"Hi, Mrs. Granger," he said. He reached back and turned off the music, then scooped up a kitten about to dash outside. "Come in."

Harrison Billy emerged from the hallway, wiping his hands and trailing the scent of turpentine. "Mrs. Granger—what a surprise. Please come in and have some hot tea with us."

They'd been working on a new kachina doll and showed it to her, Harrison pointing out Terry's part of the work, and Terry glowing under his grandfather's praise. Nothing was said about Harrison's confession or spending hours in jail.

Geneva was stumped. She wondered how to bring up the subject. Or whether to do it at all. Only when Harrison sent Terry to the shed in back to find a certain can of blue paint, did he sit down with his tea across from Geneva.

"I think you might have heard about me going to jail," he said. "They told me not to leave the reservation, but they didn't charge me with anything. Or Terry."

"That's good news," Geneva said. But she noticed Harrison's frown. "Isn't it?"

"Well, it is for now. But Albert Goldtooth came to see me. Let me know he's after Terry. He's gathering up somebody to say they saw Terry up at the Peshlakai place the night before Jerome Layton's body was burned up in that hogahn. Albert's not done."

Terry returned at that moment, and Harrison rose to inspect the paint and respond to Terry's questions.

Geneva knew the topic was finished. Soon she rose to leave.

At the door, Harrison said, "I hear Tucker has taken his wife to a doctor in Switzerland that Chee Hamilton found for her."

Unexpected tears came to her eyes. "Yes. I pray this treatment will work."

"Everybody wants Shándííne to get well," Harrison said.

He walked with her to her car. She felt that he had closed the subject of his confession. And she couldn't guess what Albert Goldtooth might do to make Terry look guilty. But she did have another question.

"Harrison, do you know an old man named Jefferson Toli?"

Harrison's gaze went to the streak of thin, navy-blue clouds to the west. "I don't know that man. But I heard he got arrested and taken down to Phoenix a week or so ago."

"Arrested? Do you know the charge?"

"No. That's all I heard. Are you here to find out about Toli?"

"Partly," she said, getting into her car. "I'm to meet Desbah Chischilly this afternoon in Window Rock. Then we'll go on to her house in Chinle. And I want to see Bessie Jim's mother and sister."

No need to tell Harrison about looking for the bird formation.

He nodded and closed her door. As she turned her car around, she saw him lift his hand in farewell.

Toli arrested. If he was taken off the reservation, then it must have been the FBI. Justin Fox and his agent Carter. That meant the charge must be murder. Whose murder?

Geneva remembered the clarity of her dream, how the fancy letters of *Jefferson* hung shining above the dark water. And her sense that it had to do with Edward. Connection, but not the horror she'd have expected if Toli had killed Edward. Still . . .

She resolved to put it away for now and think of something else.

Harrison's mention of Chee Hamilton trying to help Shándiíne made Geneva remember how, that summer fourteen years ago, Chee found tiny Millie Bayless, who'd wandered away from the picnic hours earlier. And carried her back to Shándiíne's arms. It also made her think of Desbah, who, Geneva knew, was in love with Chee. She also knew, but Desbah didn't often mention it, that Desbah had a large box of Chee's letters, mailed from the many countries he traveled for the Bahá'í Faith. Maybe he would return to the reservation with the Baylesses from Zurich. Desbah hadn't mentioned such a possibility. But Desbah Chischilly's Navajo heart was never worn on her sleeve.

Geneva looked at her watch. There was plenty of time to see Bessie's mother and sister and deliver the photograph she had for them.

The road through Black Canyon turned to a rocky track as she climbed. Pleased with herself that she remembered the way, she finally stopped her car in the Ashi family's yard and waited for recognition. A pair of dusty, tired-looking dogs of uncertain parentage, woofed, then sat down and watched. A little boy, probably no more than four years old, shot out of the door and down the ramp, where he halted and looked at her with more curiosity than the dogs had.

Mrs. Ashi stepped out onto the porch, shading her eyes. Geneva picked up the envelope, got out of the car, and waved.

"Yah-teh-ay. Come in," the old woman said, smiling broadly.

Sylvia's MS was giving her a bad day, her mother explained, and she was "sleeping with the medicine" now. Mrs. Ashi accepted the photograph with dignified thanks and insisted on making a fresh pot of coffee for Geneva.

"Thank you," Geneva said, then asked about the child, who had climbed on a chair and watched them with big solemn eyes for a few minutes, then sped outside again.

Daughter Dolores and her husband would be along after work to fetch him, Mrs. Ashi said. "He likes to run. And dance," she added.

Presently a little silence fell between them, and Geneva couldn't resist the opportunity.

"Mrs. Ashi, do you know a man, or a family, named Toli?"

Bessie's mother smoothed back the strands of hair that had slipped out of its tight hourglass bun and passed a hand over her eyes. "I don't think so," she said. "Only a long time ago in the boarding school, there was a brother and sister. They called them Toli. He was older than his sister. He got whipped a lot."

Geneva's eyes widened. "Whipped. Oh. Do you remember what for?" She fought down the urge to take out a recorder or notebook, as she had always done when researching her book.

"What for?" the old woman said. "For everything. Just like all of us. Probably talking Navajo or complaining about something. Wearing those hard shoes, maybe. I don't remember. He ran away."

"Hmm. Do you remember where this brother and sister were from?"

Mrs. Ashi rose to pour the coffee and bring sugar to the table. She shook her head. "No. But maybe Buffalo Pass or somewhere like that."

Geneva drank her coffee and, fearing that she had somehow imposed, didn't ask more questions.

Saying good-bye, Geneva restrained herself from giving the old woman a hug, but did shake hands and pat her briefly on the shoulder, trying to remember just what the Navajo custom was among the elderly. She was pretty sure it wasn't a hug. Once outside, she lingered another few minutes to hold a solemn conversation with the little boy about—the best she could tell, "Dozers. Big dozers going up our hill."

Making her way back on the sandy road, she admired again the tall black columns of dark basalt alternating with red and gray sandstone cliffs. At one particularly grand vista, she stopped and got out. Closing her eyes, she drew in a pine- and sage-scented breath and felt again the magic of mountains. They called from her an involuntary, wordless prayer of praise and gratitude to their Creator. This time, every time. She once told Edward she could easily have been a pagan. She'd expected a chuckle, but he had simply nodded. He knew.

Geneva and Bessie used to take their daughters down in the canyon bottom for picnics in the summers when they taught together at the high school. She remembered Bessie showing them a grassy little cove at the edge of the winding creek. They would spread their blankets and lunch in the shadow of the canyon wall and watch the girls play in the cold stream.

Good stories. Good times, those were.

CHAPTER FORTY-ONE

Geneva still had hours before Desbah would return to her office. As she gained the paved street near the old church, she was surprised to see Terry's old brown van at a gas station ahead. He replaced the gas hose, saw her, and waved. She pulled in beside him.

Justin's directions had been from the main highway in Window Rock. But Sawmill was north, she was sure. Maybe there was a connecting road and she wouldn't have to go back to Window Rock to pick it up.

"Terry, do you know how to get to Sawmill from here? Would I have to return to Window Rock first to pick up that little road?"

"No, there's another way," he said. "I'll show you. You can follow me."

Geneva looked back as they passed the dark Catholic church and noticed the collection of tumbleweeds and dirt against the door. She and Edward had attended a wedding there once. How dismal and abandoned it looked now under the winter sky.

Ahead, Terry was signaling a turn, and she pulled her attention back to keeping him in sight.

He made a series of turns, sometimes running on dirt lanes, but finally emerged at a paved crossroads, where he stopped next to a lone metal building with a huge sign in front: BEST NAVAJO TACOS. He got out, smiling, and waved her into a space next to his van.

She glanced at her watch—almost two o'clock. And she was hungry. She got out and spread her hands, as if beholding the big sign. "Are they really the best?"

Terry grinned. "Oh, yeah. They are."

"So, let's make them prove it," she said. "It's cold up here—I hope they have some 'best coffee,' too."

Terry was still in a light-hearted, talkative mood, and they enjoyed their meal. Geneva didn't want to spoil it by asking questions. Whatever had come of Harrison's confession to Layton's murder, it didn't seem to be important, at least not to Terry.

He led her north on Indian Route 7 for several miles before stopping and walking back to her car. "That lumber company road is your next right," he said, "just about a mile that way." He tilted his chin toward the north. "You'll see it."

Geneva was glad Terry hadn't asked her for an explanation for wanting to go there, and bade him good-bye with a smile. She watched him turn his van and drive away, and then pulled out her note with what Justin had told her about the ruined chimney and the shack farther on. That shack, he'd said, was a haven for deer mice and thus, the hanta virus. She should stay clear of it.

Sure enough, the lumber company road opened wide and smooth, flanked by several fluttering signs tacked to trees, advertising firewood by the pickup load, a round dance that had taken place in June, and a rodeo in Rough Rock last August.

But the forest soon closed behind her and the track became narrow and rutted. Strands of snow streaked the damp ground under the Ponderosa pines and cedars around her. She guessed the elevation was a good deal higher than Fort Defiance. Even higher mountains rose to the north, and successive mesas to the west, the direction she was headed. She would see the headless bird formation soon, she was sure.

She glanced at her odometer and frowned, but finally the woods gave way to a clearing and she saw a black chimney jutting skyward. Burned rubble lay around its crumbled fireplace and scattered broken glass nearby reflected the blank sky. Geneva slowed, feeling a sadness that seemed to emanate from the ruin.

The trees still loomed plentiful on her right, but the lumber company had clear-cut the forest on her left. The open land yielded a view of a few scattered hogahns, mobile homes, and sheep corrals, all several miles away down the mountain. Soon she saw the shack in the distance. She backed her car into a relatively flat place and got out. Justin had mentioned the hut she would pass on her way to the mesa with the bird formation. Deer mice, he'd said. Hanta virus, give it a wide berth.

The structure looked empty. It had been a sheepherder's shelter, she guessed. No need to stop. But the path toward the mesa she sought veered closer to the shack, avoiding some sharp-looking boulders.

As she neared the place, the palms of her chilled hands began to sweat. An upwelling of electric dread vibrated in her lower abdomen and tailbone. Ridiculous. Stop it, she chided herself. Nothing here. Nobody. Nothing to dread.

But her legs took her back to the car and, without reasoning why, she pulled her gun from the glove compartment and slipped it into her pocket. No sound came except the breeze in the pines and dead grass at her feet. Still feeling unsteady, she regained the path leading past the shack, trying to put down her fear. No reason, she told herself, to go closer. But she kept walking, hot tears falling with every step.

Edward had been here. This was the place.

A foot away, she stopped. The weathered planks of the hut

stood crooked and wide apart. The door hung on bent hinges, swaying open several inches. Pain tore through her chest and throat. She staggered, clutched at the door for support, then sank to the dirt floor, sobbing and coughing. When she could catch her breath and see through her tears, she focused on a rough bench attached to one wall. The sight of it brought a scream she couldn't stop.

Here. Edward had been killed at this spot. She knelt beside the bench, reaching her arms across it. Pain threatened to extinguish her breath. It went on and on.

She saw the knife point come down toward him.

Felt first only the strike, the push into his throat just above the bone. Red pain came a beat later, but it was the hit, the odd sound of the tearing, that loomed in his mind before, before the choking, the wet . . . can . . . not . . . breathe . . . Can't . . .

She could not scream another breath. Only the tears and strangling pain went on and on.

Geneva

Her breath stopped. She looked all about the empty space, back and forth, again and again.

Don't cry anymore, darling.

"Edward! I hear you!"

No more crying, sweetheart. And no guilt. You were never, never guilty of failing me. Never.

Geneva felt something sweep away, like a heavy shawl pulled off her bowed shoulders and head.

Good-bye, my sweet girl. Go now to the love waiting for you.

She saw in her mind Edward's signature caricature of himself, grinning and clasping his heart, from which rose swarms of butterflies imprinted with "I love you!" The way he always signed his letters to her.

When she lifted her face, she saw only sky through the wide crack in the door. "Good-bye, my darling," she whispered. "Good-bye."

How long she knelt beside the rough wooden bench, she

would never be sure. But when she stood and walked outside, she was calm, smiling. The wind, however, now whistled, not murmured, through the pines, and the scattered navy clouds had gathered into a solid bank in the northwest sky.

"All right," she said aloud to herself. "But I still want to see that bird with the shiny green breast."

She turned and noticed for the first time that the high mesa ahead extended farther to her right than she could see from the car.

A few minutes' walk brought her to a line of jumbled boulders and a stop. She scanned the vertical sides of the sandstone mesa slightly below where she stood. There it was. Exactly as she had seen in her vision. A fold in the rock almost concealed it, but now it was plain. One slanted wing nearly closed against a high, rounded breast that shone wet and smooth, lined on both sides with bent grasses and remnants of wildflowers. The opposite wing stood slightly away from the breast, curving downward, sheltering more plants that resembled ruffled feathers. The hidden spring at the top must form a pool at the bottom where sheep would drink, she was sure. In the waning light, the scene gave Geneva a sense of peace. The pain and horror of her vision were gone. She did not hear Edward's voice and did not again feel his presence. A new sense of warmth seemed to surround her. And an upwelling of certainty in her heart.

Justin Fox's surprising smile filled her mind's eye.

She stood a while longer, watching the low rays of sunlight touch the gleaming breast and bent wings, then turned and started for her car.

As she came even again with the sheepherders' hut, Brandon Goldtooth stepped out into her path.

CHAPTER FORTY-TWO

"Well. Miz Doctor Granger. We meet again."

Geneva's breath stopped. Her tongue and throat felt solid, foreign to her body, unmovable. The sensation of freezing started down her chest and spread across her breasts. Only her eyes seemed to function, but her mind refused their message.

Brandon Goldtooth stepped toward her. "Want to see where he died?" His voice was low, almost pleasant. He sounded like a curator about to draw back a curtain to show an interesting painting.

She could not move.

"It's an appropriate place you came to," he said, reaching with his right hand for the slack wooden door. "Come on in. I'll show you how it happened." With his left hand, he lifted a long, shiny knife, and gestured with it for her to enter.

"No," she said, surprising herself. "I won't." She backed away, thinking how she might outrun him the twenty yards or so to her car.

He spun around and caught her arm. "Yes, you will. You've been a pest from the start." He shoved her inside and flung her down on the bench.

"You don't even know what a mess you've been making," he said, leaning now against the warped doorframe. "Or what your big dumb senator husband was poking into, checking all the quarry paperwork. But I stopped him. And that stupid Bessie Jim and her *biligaana* professor. I stopped them all." He paused and looked around as if waiting for applause. "And now I'll stop you." Again he lifted the knife, turning it this way and that to catch the failing light, playing with it, watching her terror.

She managed to sit up. "How did you find me?" she said, her voice barely audible.

"Oh, that was easy. I was coming back down the canyon when I spotted you in Fort Defiance. Saw you follow that kid's van. He never even noticed me in my brother's old truck. Then I guessed, no, I *knew* where you were heading. Didn't even have to follow. I had plenty of time to take my brother home and even eat lunch before starting up here."

He was pacing now, back and forth in the small space in front of her. "It was easy, you know. I figured it out, figured you would eventually come to see where it was, where the senator got his due. That weak son of a bitch Toli showed the FBI guys. So, I knew some day you would come."

Geneva said nothing and tried not to look at the moving knife.

"Now, Miz Doctor, kneel down right there," he said, pointing with the knife to the dirt floor at the end of the bench. Put your hands out behind you. Since you're not drunk, like we made your husband, and nobody else is here to hold you down, I got to tie your hands. But all the rest will be the same. Starting with your throat. All the way to your belly button, just like him."

Geneva blinked. She remembered the choking, drowning pain of her vision.

"Now get that coat away and take off the sweater. I mean to draw a lightning eagle with this knife, just like I did for the senator. Slow. Gave him, and now you, the chance to remember how you interfered, got in my way. I'm going to own that quarry, build up my business. The Lightning Eagle, that's my dancer name—and that will be the name of my company. I'm going to run those trucks all over the reservation and half of Arizona. Now get down there!"

She stood, felt the weight of the pistol in her coat pocket. Shrugging out of the left side, she moved her hand to the opposite side as if to peel the coat away, and closed her right hand over her gun.

"Hurry up!" he shouted, catching the bottom edge of her sweater with the knife point.

She pulled back with enough force to entangle the knife, struck his wrist, and spun away. But he held tight, and the blade scored her side before her belt and waistband of her jeans deflected it. She cried out, pretended to double over with pain, freed her gun from her coat pocket, and pointed it at him.

"Get away from me!" she said, with more force than she felt capable of.

Brandon grinned and raised his arms above his head, twitching the knife playfully in his left hand. "Well, look at that —a little bitty woman with a little bitty gun. You think you can look me in the eye and shoot me? I can throw this knife and hit your throat faster than you can get up your nerve, and we both know it. Look how your hand is shaking . . . shaking, shaking."

She clutched her gun with both hands but did not take her gaze from his face. "Turn around and go back to your car. Truck. Whatever. Get out!"

He grinned even more broadly. "You want me to carve you outside? Pretty cold out there." Again he toyed with the knife. "Don't you want to see just how I made your dear Edward bleed?"

"Turn around and go!"

He cocked his head and looked at her, his sardonic smile never wavering. "No."

He was only three feet away from her, and she knew she could not back up without falling to the bench. Grinning, he drew back the knife over his shoulder. "Ready?"

There was a blur of motion and a thump as the knife struck the wall and fell to the bench behind her.

At the same moment, she bent and fired, hitting his ankle.

Brandon screamed and crumpled.

She jumped over his nearly prone figure and ran.

A minute later, the flying knife hit her right sleeve, slicing the back of her arm just above the elbow and then skittering across the hard ground. But she didn't stop running. She looked back only as she started the car. Brandon sat, one leg drawn up, just outside the shack. She turned on her lights and headed back down the mountain.

CHAPTER FORTY-THREE

The clock on her dashboard read 4:38 as she reached pavement in Fort Defiance. At the same moment her new cell phone rang.

"Geneva! Thank God!" Justin's words ended in what sounded like a sob. "Are you all right? I've been calling you for hours!"

"Oh, Justin! Yes. I am. I—" Unable to go on, she pulled her car to the side of the street and stopped. The terror of the last hour, which she'd managed to suppress while escaping, flooded out of her in hiccupping sobs.

"My God, Geneva! Where are you? Is anyone there with you? Are you hurt?"

When she could speak, she said, "No. No one. I'm in Fort Defiance. Across from a café, um, B-Benally's Diner. I—"

"Geneva, go inside the restaurant. Make sure people there see you but sit as far as you can from the door. I'll send a policeman to get you. Do you understand?"

"A policeman? Why? Where are you?"

"I'm in a helicopter almost to Black Canyon. You're in some danger, Geneva. Brandon Goldtooth is after you. He's—"

Her laugh was just short of hysteria. "Too late. He already

found me. But I'm all right now. He's the one needing rescue."
She stopped speaking. Her breath wasn't working right.

"He got to you? Geneva—what happened?"

"I sh-shot him—his leg, ankle, I think. Justin, I'm freezing.
Let me go—I need to meet Desbah. At . . . f-five." She got her
breath under control. "No, wait—why are you going to Black
Canyon?"

"Brandon tried to kill my investigator. Carter's alive, but he
was trapped in some rocks at the bottom of a chasm. A couple
of kids found him. I've got a crew here and we're about to load
him on and get him to a hospital. I'll call Desbah and send her
to you. Can you give me her number?"

How mundane a little question, she thought. Or rather how
mundane her automatic answer. "Phone number. Of course.
Got a pen?"

"Please go into the restaurant and get warm, darling."

She was glad to do that, but it took more than one cup of
hot tea before she could stop shaking. On the third cup, her
mind's continual replay bumped to a stop. *Darling!* Did he say
darling? No. She was hysterical, her insides jumping around
like frying frog legs. She had cried, blubbered into the phone.
But not now. Not here. She glanced around the café. Nobody
was paying any attention to her.

Just then, the door flew open and Desbah rushed in, her
red and black cape flaring out behind her. She spotted Geneva,
darted to her, swept her up in a trembling hug, then held her
out at arm's length. "Is that blood on your sleeve?"

The waitress, who had stopped cold when Desbah dashed
across her path, stood and stared. Half a dozen customers
turned to look.

Geneva glanced down at her arm. "I guess it is. Come sit
down. I'll tell you all about it."

CHAPTER FORTY-FOUR

Fox felt relieved to learn from Desbah that she and Geneva would stay at the Inn in Window Rock rather than driving to Chinle. Still his heart was thumping as he turned to recheck the straps on Carter's rescue basket.

"Okay!" He signaled to the pilot. "Let's get him to Gallup. His wife will meet us at the hospital."

An hour later, Carter's injuries were judged no worse than a broken ankle, banged-up ribs, some other bruises, and a ripped jacket. Brandon had missed, Carter said. "I took the canyon instead of the bullet."

Fox gave his friend's shoulder a last pat as the nurse settled him into the wheelchair and started down the hall. Carter's wife walked at his other side, never letting go of his hand.

Fox watched them for another moment, then turned and made for the door. Full dark now, the wind picking up instead of dying down as predicted. He turned up his collar and looked around for the rental car, which was supposed to have been delivered an hour ago. It arrived ten minutes later.

Once in the car, Fox clutched the top of the steering wheel and leaned his head against his knuckles. God, what a day. First half a day listening to that bastard Mason Drake—Smith, whatever—trying to lie his way out of killing his own father. Then Carter, hurt in the bottom of the canyon, but relaying a warning to Fox through a kid with a cell phone on the ridge: "Goldtooth said he'd take care of that senator's wife next."

Then another three hours not knowing where she was. Not knowing if Brandon Goldtooth had already found her.

He let go of the steering wheel and drew in a long, ragged breath. *Thank God . . . Thank you, thank you, God.* He wiped away the tears sliding down his cheeks. Aloud, he said, "I love her." A second later a wide smile lit Justin Fox's long face. He started the car and turned it northwest toward Window Rock.

B enally's Diner in Fort Defiance wasn't up to Desbah Chischilly's standards, hot tea notwithstanding. "All right," she said, holding Geneva's jacket out and easing it over her injured arm. "Let's go on to the motel. We'll get room service if you want. Can you drive your car to Window Rock Inn?"

"Yes," Geneva said. "I can drive."

In their room half an hour later, Desbah cleaned and bandaged Geneva's wounded arm.

"More blood than hurt," Geneva said. "No doubt he was aiming for my lung or heart but hit the back of my arm instead."

She was about to mention the other slice Brandon's knife had made, just above her beltline, but was prevented by a great fountain of Desbah's colorful Navajo-cum-English invective.

"Never mind, I'll live," Geneva said, taking the bandage from Desbah's waving hand. "Unless I die of hunger in the next five minutes, that is. Hand me a clean shirt from my suitcase over there, will you? And let's go down. I don't want to wait for room service and cold food."

At the end of the next half hour, they sat enjoying a hot

meal and watching the snow swirl against the tall windows of the dining room. Only a few other diners remained.

"Well," Desbah said, reaching for another sopapilla, "are you going to tell me the rest of what happened to you today? The secretary at the admin building said you showed up before noon. How did you come across Brandon Goldtooth . . . and his knife?"

Geneva gave brief accounts of her visits with Bessie's mother and sister and then Harrison and Terry. She didn't mention the report of Jefferson Toli's arrest. That would need confirmation and more detail. Besides, she knew now who the murderer was and didn't want to think more about it at this moment.

"All right," Desbah said. "But Brandon?"

"I wanted to see that formation. The headless bird."

Desbah nodded and frowned. "Yes, I remember. Your vision the night before Edward died. But how—?"

"Justin told me where it was."

Desbah halted her coffee cup halfway to her lips. "Justin. Justin? How did he know?"

"He saw it himself. Up there near Sawmill."

Desbah put the cup down with a clatter and leaned forward. "You went to Sawmill? Brandon Goldtooth caught you way up there at Sawmill?"

Geneva smiled. "You ask a lot of questions." Some day she would tell Desbah about approaching the shack the first time, feeling and knowing that Edward had died there. Then hearing him speak to her with such love. And finally coming to know that he was safe now. She could, and did at last, say good-bye. Some day she would tell her friend, the sister of her heart, all about it. But not now.

Instead Geneva told about finding the spectacular bird formation. And how, as she was returning to her car, the man bent on her destruction had stepped from the sheepherders' hut.

When Geneva described his threatening her with the knife and her shooting him, Desbah smacked the table with both hands and laughed aloud. "My God, Geneva! That's the second man you've shot in less than a month!"

"Yep, she's one hell of a shooter, I'd say."

The women looked up to see Justin Fox striding toward their table.

Geneva couldn't speak.

"Yah-ta-hey, Fox," Desbah said as he came near. "You look like you've been dragged through a knothole. Better sit down."

"Something like that," he said, dropping into the chair next to Geneva.

Another beat of silence. And another.

Desbah looked first at Geneva, then Fox. They simply gazed at each other.

"Please excuse me," Desbah said. She picked up her purse and left, glancing back only when she reached the dining room door. Geneva heard her tell the hovering waiter, "He'll get the ticket," indicating Fox with a quick pucker of the lips and tilt of the head. Smiling, Desbah waved and made her way to the stairs.

CHAPTER FORTY-FIVE

"Are you really all right?" Fox asked. His hand covered hers on the table.

She smiled and covered his hand with her other one. "Yes, I am. Truly. Your hands are freezing—where have you been? I thought you took Carter to the hospital in Gallup."

"I did. He'll be all right." He leaned back and laughed. "Rental car heater doesn't work. Desbah told me you were coming here. I had to see you."

She couldn't seem to stop smiling. "I'm glad. How about something hot to eat?"

He ordered coffee and a bowl of green chile stew. Only when it came did he release her hand.

Even before he finished, the wait staff were making it clear they wanted to close.

"I called ahead and registered," he said as they stood. "Let me get my key and duffle at the desk. Will you go up with me? I—I need to tell you something."

"I need to tell you something, too," she said.

If the sleepy old Navajo clerk thought anything about Geneva going up to a room with another woman two hours earlier, and now with a man, he gave no hint of it.

It took Fox three tries to make the key card work, but when the door opened and he flipped on the lamp, they stepped into a pleasant room decorated in warm earth tones. "Almost as nice as Fiddler's Inn, wouldn't you agree?" He dropped his overcoat on a chair and turned to her.

She smiled. "I do agree."

Justin stood with his hands hanging at his sides and looked at her. "Something happened to me today," he said. "I want to tell you about it."

A sweet sense of peace flowed over Geneva. "And I want to hear."

They sat down on the sofa and turned to face each other. For a long moment, neither spoke.

Fox reached for her hand again. "Brandon Goldtooth caught Carter early this afternoon in Black Canyon and threatened to kill him. Tried to kill him. Brandon was in a bragging mood, ticking off his accomplishments—like murdering Bessie Jim and Jerome Layton." He leaned toward her. "And Edward, Geneva. He killed Edward."

She drew a breath. "I know."

Justin's eyes widened a fraction.

"Go on, Justin. What happened to Carter? You said he fell into a canyon or crevasse, but he was able to get a message to you?"

"Yes. But Geneva, that's not what I'm trying to tell you. Brandon told Carter he was going to . . . *to take care* of you. I knew you were coming to the reservation, and that you wanted to see that formation. And then, when I couldn't reach you anywhere, for hours, I knew."

"Knew? You knew what?"

"I knew then that . . . I love you."

They sat there, both smiling broadly, both with tears rising in their eyes.

"And I love you, Justin."

EPILOGUE

On New Year's Day, Geneva Granger stood with Justin Fox as they said their marriage vows before his beaming father; his son and daughter-in-law; Geneva's happy, tearful daughters and their families; and the newly appointed interim senator, Dr. Desbah Chischilly.

In late March, Mason Drake, Brandon Goldtooth, and Jefferson Toli were convicted of the murder of Edward Granger. In mid-April, Leroy Rollie Smith, aka Mason Drake, was convicted in the death of his father, Rollie J. Smith. At the end of May, Brandon was convicted of the murders of Bessie Jim and Dr. Allen Jerome Layton.

On the first day of June, Desbah Chischilly made up her mind, stepped out of the upcoming senate race, picked up the phone, and accepted Chee Hamilton's proposal of marriage. The traditional Navajo wedding and the Baha'í marriage vows would take place near Canyon de Chelly in their homeland before family and friends on the last day of June.

On the seventeenth of July, Geneva, Justin, Desbah, and Chee sat at a round table lighted with gold candles and yellow roses in a ballroom in Zurich, Switzerland. They all applauded as Tucker and Shándiíne, she in a glittering evening dress, strode to their table. At Justin's signal, the band struck up a great fanfare of happy music. They all toasted Shándiíne's physicians, seated at the next table, and Chee Hamilton, whom Shándiíne pulled to his feet and whirled into several fast dance steps, to everyone's wild applause and cheers.

Then they all rose and danced the rest of the dark night away.

ABOUT THE AUTHOR

Born in Arkansas, Kathleen Park has lived, and listened to people talk, from California to Cape Cod, resulting in a love of language and lifelong fascination with its depth and variety. She lived and taught school on the Navajo Reservation for eleven years and learned to admire the people's humor and endurance, despite their many hardships. She also learned that a good Navajo woman is among the strongest women in the world. Kathleen holds an MA in English, belongs to numerous writing groups. and has contributed columns and articles to newspapers and blogs. *The Code Talkers*, her debut novel, is heavily influenced by the people, especially the women, she met during her years on the reservation.

Made in the USA
Monee, IL
07 June 2023

35423414R00194